'Grab a hot drink an[...] this – you won't want t[...] [...]ping story with vivid charac[...] [...] real wisdom to make you think. I loved this book. [...] [...]ker.'
Penelope Wilcock, author of The Hawk and the Dove *series*

'*The Gardener's Daughter* is a poignant story of loss, searching, exile and return. Get on the ride to damnation or salvation and you will not be able to step off until the very last page.'
Dr Anne Richards, National Advisor for Mission Theology for the Church of England

'K A Hitchins has done it again! This beautifully crafted story was all absorbing, and I thought about it long after I had put it down. I thoroughly recommend it to everyone who loves a good read.
Hazel Paine, author of Soulsight *and* Soulvision

'An all round fabulous read you do not want to miss.'
christianbookaholic.com

The
Gardener's
Daughter

K A Hitchins

K A Hitchins

**instant
apostle**

First published in Great Britain in 2018

Instant Apostle

The Barn
1 Watford House Lane
Watford
Herts
WD17 1BJ

The saying, 'The only thing necessary for the triumph of evil is for good men to do nothing,' is attributed to Edmund Burke.

British Library Cataloguing-in-Publication Data

A catalogue record for this book is available from the British Library

This book and all other Instant Apostle books are available from
Instant Apostle:

Website: www.instantapostle.com
E-mail: info@instantapostle.com

ISBN 978-1-909728-82-0

Printed in Great Britain

Also by K A Hitchins

The Girl at the End of the Road

The Key of All Unknown

Dedicated to the memory of
Alec Stanley Hitchins, my father.
He loved his garden.

Prologue

A man sits in a car. He's parked on a muddy track with a view of the South Downs. Grassy undulations roll towards cliffs as sheer and deadly as a fall from grace. From this angle, it looks as if a giant bite has been taken out of England, leaving teeth marks in her soft green skin, exposing the bone.

He squints at the horizon, dazzled by the brilliance of the low winter light. The sky is as blue as his enemy's eyes; the sea as grey as his own. The car radio croons unobtrusively as he considers his next move.

He's been diagnosed with 'a terminal condition of the heart', a quaint phrase from his Harley Street specialist. If anyone knew of his recent medical appointments, they might conclude that the cliffs are the reason for his visit. Faced with slow deterioration and increasing disability and pain, who wouldn't consider a jump from a precipice as a viable alternative? The sea would be as cold and cruel as his hatred, sudden, remorseless. But he's not ready to admit defeat yet. In any case, no one else knows the diagnosis.

He tries to imagine the thing that's beating in his chest. Something black and decaying. Something that needs to be dug out and replaced, if only a suitable substitute can be found. He bites into an apple, relishing the squirt and the crunch and the wincing sharpness. He wipes his mouth with the back of his hand.

He must crush his rival now. He'd wanted to do it slowly, savouring each moment, using those his adversary loved the most to inflict the deepest wounds. He'd been playing the long game, but the rules have changed and he can no longer wait to possess the things he wants.

He turns his head inland, chewing the apple slowly. His eyes rest on the glittering panes of a vast dome built on the crest of the Downs. He's sat in his car on this track many times, watching the glass biosphere flash like a diamond in the sunlight, glow like a beacon in the night. The world-renowned dome, garden centre and horticultural institute should be his, together with the secret patents that could change the future of the planet. He covets Greenacres as an estranged prince covets the crown of the king.

A dual carriageway slithers past the enormous glasshouse down to Westhatch-on-Sea, its grey skin crawling with cars. From this angle, he can see a splatter of houses on the outskirts of town. Most of the buildings are hidden in a crease in the landscape, but he catches a glimpse of the Promenade. A Ferris wheel, helter-skelter and big dipper poke their heads above the grey line of the shingle beach like toys spilling from a box.

At the far end of town a cluster of pale caravans peppers the lower slopes of the Downs. Fun World Holiday Camp. Second largest employer in the area, second only to the Institute. He used to feel like a god or an angel, looking down upon his empire. But one domain is no longer enough. He wants control of both.

He presses the button that opens the driver's window and throws the apple core onto the grass. First he must find a suitable heart transplant donor. He knows the ideal candidate. The window closes with a soft thud. He turns the key to the ignition. What if she *is* his only daughter? If you want to make an omelette, you have to break an egg!

Chapter 1

My father is a gardener. He digs. He prunes. He waters. His heart is in the soil. I've seen him crumble it through his fingers, sniffing out the personalities of loam and clay. He knows when to fertilise and irrigate and when to stay his hand.

'Plants watered too regularly have shallow roots, Ava-Claire. A short dry spell will force them to push deeper.'

'Boring, Dad. Boring, boring, dull, dull, dull!'

'A little adversity brings resilience.'

Perhaps that's my problem. He cleared the troubles from my path and watered me so much with his love that I never needed to push down hard in search of my own resources.

If I close my eyes I can still hear his spade cutting the soil with the rhythmic ticking of a clock, smell the damp peatiness of the earth. Then the quick rasping stabs of his fork as he turns the clods, worms recoiling at the invasion, until the soft, crumbling earth is ready for planting. The sound reminds me that some things have to be turned over and broken down before they are of any use.

I remember my last hours of ignorance as though they were yesterday. Not a blissful ignorance, because I thought I knew it all back then and was easily irritated by others. But at least I knew who I was and understood my place in the world. The thing with ignorance is you don't know what you don't know. I didn't understand that knowledge can instantly change a life for good or evil. If I had, I might have reined in my impetuous nature. I know now that discovering the truth can open doors that slam shut behind you, doors through which you can never return. For me, the truth brought immediate, irredeemable pain. Discovering a bleeding hole where your heart should be will do that to you.

It was Monday, 2 February 2003 and I'd stumbled up the hill to work that day, my skirt flapping against my legs like a sail in the wind. I was cold in my tights and tailored jacket. The clear skies had tricked me with a promise of warmth, but a bitter breeze from the English Channel raced me up the drive, whipping my hair forward and tossing the curls around my head like florists' ribbon tied to a balloon.

Gone were the ugly trousers and khaki Greenacres sweatshirt. Gone were the dirty fingernails and aching back. It was Apprentice Rotation Day and I was moving out of the hothouse and into the Greenacres gift shop. At last I would begin to put some of my business skills to good use and prove to everyone I would be a worthy successor to Dad one day.

I checked my watch. There was no time to go back for a coat. I would just have to totter up the muddy track in my heels as quickly as I could. I wanted to catch Dad before the first customers arrived, to tell him my new idea. Why not offer a free gift-wrapping service in return for a small donation to the Golden Acres project? I could buy some tissue paper, cellophane and ribbons. With a little practice I was sure I'd get the knack of it.

I shivered with cold and anticipation. The path from our house led directly to the staff entrance to the dome. It wouldn't be long before I was cocooned in the stifling heat of the glasshouse. At least no one was going to tell me off for being late. I might be an apprentice, but I was still the boss' daughter.

The dome at the Greenacres Garden Centre and Institute reminded me of a bluebottle's eye. Dad had shown me one under a microscope once, a compound structure with thousands of individual lenses: alien, watchful, ominously intricate. Dad liked to imitate nature's more impressive blueprints in his designs. Other biospheres had been built since. Plant conservation projects, opera houses, parliament buildings, museums. Ours was not the largest, but it was the first. Built at the highest point of the South Downs, it was an eye with a 360 degree view, a bubble stretching thirty metres into the sky, supporting thousands of glittering panes which winked conspiratorially at me as I approached.

I unlocked the back door with my key, one of only three copies. Dad, Marcus and I were the only ones who approached the dome from the lane that led from our farmhouse and Marcus' cottage. Muddy footprints were already evident on the mat, an annoying reminder that once again Marcus Becker, Dad's laboratory assistant, had beaten me in to work.

The air within was as warm and fecund as a womb. The first customers of the day were already drifting into the glasshouse, amazed as always at the profusion of flowers. Velvet-eyed pansies. Red tulips standing to attention. White narcissi shining like stars.

I circumnavigated the tubs of winter annuals and cut through the house plant department, lush with ferns and waxy orchids. Fully grown trees arched overhead, their leaves dappling the paths, their branches heavy with lemons, oranges and figs. By the time I reached the far side of the dome, a feverish warmth had seeped through the cold folds of my clothes. My face was damp and I hoped I didn't look as childishly excited as I felt.

I swiped my employee card by a door marked 'Staff Only' and ran down a flight of stairs. The door to my father's underground study was slightly ajar. I burst through without knocking. I hadn't had a chance to speak to him the night before. He'd worked late, returning home long after I'd gone to bed. As usual he'd left our old farmhouse before my alarm clock went off. Did the man never sleep?

I halted, surprised. Sitting at my father's desk, painstakingly jabbing at the keys of a laptop, was Marcus.

'Where's Dad?'

He didn't raise his eyes but held his hand up as a signal for me to wait until he'd finished. He looked incongruous behind

Dad's large mahogany desk, its fading leather surface piled high with dog-eared scientific journals, back copies of horticulture magazines, volumes of poetry and rare first editions. Dad's brass desk lamp crouched like a giant grasshopper, eyeing the sleek laptop suspiciously.

Marcus was well known among the staff for his vast collection of naff slogan T-shirts, usually paired with scruffy cargo pants. That day he'd carried his laptop up from the lab, but was still wearing his white coat, unbuttoned as usual, and revealing a fluorescent orange T-shirt which read, 'Beard Season Never Ends'. It was a far cry from Dad's tweedy jackets and gold-plated fountain pen.

He rolled his index finger across the touchpad and right-clicked.

'Done!' He sat back in the chair and breathed a smile. 'Ava. How's things?' His eyes burned bright under dark brows.

'What are you doing here? Where's Dad?'

'I'm amending the apprentice rota... Theo's on his way to Africa.'

'Africa!'

'His plane took off,' he checked his watch, 'about half an hour ago.'

'Is this a wind-up?'

'He decided to visit Golden Acres to see how the ionised water trials are going.'

'Don't muck about, Marcus. It's my first day in the gift shop. I'm not in the mood. I need to talk to Dad about my ideas for a gift-wrapping service.'

'I'm not teasing you.'

'But he would have told me.'

'He said he'd sent you a text.'

I rummaged through my tote bag, fingers clumsy with annoyance. I dragged my phone out from underneath a muddle of make-up, tissues and sweet wrappers. I'd switched it off before bed the previous night and had been too restless with excitement to check my messages at breakfast. It blinked to life and I found a text from Dad.

'Ava. It's short notice I know, but I'm needed at the Golden Acres Farm Project. The architect wants me to approve the greenhouse designs, and I want to see the results of the ionised water trials. I've left Marcus in charge. He has permission to act on my behalf while I'm away. Paloma said she would stay with you if you don't want to be alone up at the house, but I'm sure you'd rather be by yourself. Marcus is just down the lane if you have any problems. I've left you some money in the top kitchen drawer to tide you over. Be good. All my love, Dad.'

'How long's he going to be gone?'

'He didn't say. I'm sorry if this is a shock.'

My hand was shaking with anger as I began to type a reply.

'I don't think your father's going to be able to get any messages for a while,' Marcus said quietly. 'He'll have his phone switched off on the plane, and there'll be no signal where he's going.'

I threw my mobile back in my bag, promising myself I'd try to ring Dad later when I was alone. I had plenty to say.

'You shouldn't be in here. You know Dad's study is strictly private. No one's allowed in here without him.'

'Then why did he leave me his keys?'

He took an enormous bunch from a pocket halfway down his cargo pants. I recognised the fob. My stomach lurched as though I'd plunged over the edge of a roller coaster. I'd never seen my father without them. Many members of staff had the front door keys or the keys to the stock room. But no one had *all* the keys, including the back door key, the key to Dad's study, the laboratory and our house. Now there was nowhere Marcus couldn't go. I swallowed down the sharp sting of betrayal. Why hadn't Dad trusted *me* with the keys? After all, Greenacres was *my* home and *my* inheritance. Marcus was just another member of staff. It all seemed so out of character.

'Your father's given me full executive powers in his absence. I'm looking forward to getting stuck in – '

'This is a commercial business. It needs someone who understands the concept of maximising profits, marketing, sales. In the last year I've worked in every area of this place, apart from the gift shop – '

'And the laboratory.'

I snorted.

'Whatever! I know this business inside out. I set up the new staff rota system. I can cash up and bank the day's proceeds. I understand the stock control system, the accounts, the plant-watering regime... You're stuck in your laboratory all day and half the night playing around with formulas and chemicals, dirt and seeds. How on earth did you persuade Dad to leave you in charge?'

'He trusts me.'

'He trusts me too.'

'He never pushes people further than they're able to go.'

'What does that mean?'

'It means you're only eighteen – '

'Nineteen!' I interrupted.

'... and leadership comes with experience. There aren't many nineteen-year-olds who could run a business with an annual turnover of a couple of million pounds. Theo needed someone who understands his vision and values.'

I took a breath and made an effort to control my voice.

'I'm his *daughter*. I think I know what makes my own father tick. There's nothing you can tell me about his values.'

'Let's not argue. I'm looking forward to us working together as a team. We have different skill sets. No one doubts your competence. You're one of the most hard-working and determined people I know. Proactive, strong-minded, efficient...'

'But?'

'You can be a little impetuous.'

'Greenacres needs someone with practical business skills. Someone who can make decisions and get things done. You won't find the profit and loss accounts in a Petri dish, or the stock inventory under a microscope.'

'And some people might call you hot-headed. Not me, of course,' he smiled.

'At least my head's not up in the clouds, dreaming up unrealistic vision statements and weird experiments, too idealistic to be of any earthly use. We're not saving the planet here. I'm running a garden centre!'

'Careful, Ava. I think I'm running it now.'

A horrible sense of doubt began to scratch its way to the surface. I tilted my chin and stared hard. Marcus didn't look away or respond to the challenge in my eyes, but waited for the tension to break. My mind turned furiously, imagining possible alternative explanations for my father's absence. Had Dad sent that text message or had someone got hold of his phone and faked it? Was he really on his way to Africa, or had something else happened? Something unspeakable. A sudden heat warmed my cheeks. I hoped Marcus couldn't guess what was going through my mind. Things were certainly not as they should be. I looked away first.

'I better get to the gift shop. I've got things to do.'

He stood up and walked round to my side of the desk, touching my arm lightly.

'About that… There's been a change to the rotation. I've put you in the laboratory for the next three months and moved Harmony into the shop.'

I pulled my arm away and stepped back.

'You can't do that!' All thoughts of Dad momentarily flew from my mind.

'It's already done. I was sending out the email to the admin team when you came in. It should be up on the staff noticeboard by now.'

'But I've been looking forward to this. You know I have. I've got loads of ideas. I've looked at the figures for last month. I think there are ways we can increase profits in the shop. Stocking some cheaper items and displaying them with the other merchandise will ensure we have gifts at every price point.' I reddened again under his gaze. 'I know people love the hand-crafted articles, but mass-produced items – if carefully selected – can offer great value for money and a good mark-up for us. Veronica said I could source a small range to see how they sell… if Dad agreed.'

Marcus stroked his beard. There was dirt under his fingernails. He looked at me intently.

'Why don't you hold on to these ideas for a few weeks? We can discuss them once Theo returns.'

'I'm not going to blow the stock budget, if that's what you're worried about.'

'It's not about how you spend the money… It's about how you spend your heart.'

'And what does *that* mean?'

'Stop thinking about how much things cost and how much they'll sell for, and start thinking how much they're worth and what value they bring to the world.'

A scorching wind blew through my head. *Don't think I don't know you've been sucking up to Dad. And maybe something worse!* I bit my lip, not wanting to give anything away until I'd had a chance to dig deeper. I needed to talk to some of the other staff to find out whether they knew what was going on.

Marcus must have read my silence as acceptance.

'I thought it would be good if, while Theo's away, you could learn a bit more about his scientific work. The big picture of what he's trying to achieve here. Everything boils down to the basis of organic life. The building blocks and the fluids that sustain those blocks.'

'I hate science. You know I'm no good at it. Why are you doing this? Harmony would be great in the lab.'

'Spend some time with me, Ava. See this wonderful thing your father and I are doing. The gift shop will still be there in three months' time. By then, you'll see it's peripheral. There are more important things going on here at the Institute than selling birthday cards and potpourri.'

Hot tears swelled behind my eyes. I blinked them back, determined not to show any weakness.

'Does Paloma know about this?'

'Yes. You can talk it over with her if you like. Go and get yourself a cup of coffee. There's no rush. Harmony's already in the shop. I caught her on the way in this morning and told her about the change. Meet me in the laboratory after lunch. We can talk further then. I'm off to check the irrigation system before I walk round the dome to chat to the customers. I'm planning to spend more time on the shop floor while Theo's away. After that I'm going to go through some of this paperwork.' He gestured to my father's heavy wooden in-tray.

An image of the metal steps that ran up the side of the dome like a giant zip flashed to mind. The steps grew thinner and steeper the higher they went, until the last few feet became a ladder to the elevated walkway servicing the dome's overhead irrigation system. A metal water pipe ran the entire circumference of the biosphere's roof, with sprinkler nozzles spaced a metre apart. When switched on, fine jets of sparkling water would cascade onto the plants below, misting petals with dew and polishing the leaves so that they shone like green mirrors. The sprinklers were automatically activated for a couple of hours each evening after the garden centre was closed, allowing the stone pathways to dry thoroughly before the next day's business.

'Staff aren't allowed up there.' Even to my own ears my voice sounded entitled, patronising, but I couldn't seem to dial it down.

'I wasn't aware I was staff. I'm a partner now, remember?'

How could I forget!

'Nobody's allowed up there apart from Dad.' I rephrased my objection. 'It's dangerous. It might… invalidate the insurance,' I improvised. 'Anyway, what's wrong with the irrigation system?'

'Nothing, as far as I'm aware. I just want to double-check.'

'Your funeral!' I snapped, turning on my heel and marching out.

I stomped up the stairs and walked towards the sound of clinking cups and the hiss of the coffee machine, and picked up a tray at the entrance to the cafeteria, sliding it along the counter to the till.

'Morning, Babyboss,' Paloma exclaimed. 'What I get you?'

'My usual, thanks.'

I glanced at the chairs and tables. The only customers were an elderly couple enjoying a full English breakfast. It would be crowded soon enough. Our dome, warm even on the coldest of days, attracted customers like butterflies to buddleia.

'Wholemeal muffin?'

'Just coffee.'

'What's the matter? You sick?'

'No.'

'Your nose is the pink colour.'

'I've just blown it… and, no, I don't have a cold. Have you got time for a little chat?'

'Eunice!' she yelled towards the kitchen. 'Can you take over the till for five? Babyboss need to talk.'

'Don't call me that.'

'You've been Babyboss since you first speaking. So like Papa-Boss.'

'I'm not a baby any more… or the boss.'

'Ahhh. Now I sees the *problema*. I bring cappuccino over. You sit down. I come when Eunice budge her bottom.'

Abandoning the tray, I walked to the table at the far end of the café and sat with my back to the wall. I gazed out of the window to my left.

The sky was fresh out of the packet, unused and radiant, blue as spring, despite the February chill. Pots of herbaceous plants on raised pallets encircled the garden centre, rippling outwards to meet the smooth expanse of the Downs, which in turn gave way to the distant grey of the sea. Past the shoreline, blue touched blue. White flecks on the water smiled up at cumulus clouds that sailed through the sky, plump and dazzling and stately as a fleet of liners. The horizon seemed to stretch forever.

To my right was the hexagonal-paned glass wall between the café and the garden centre. I scanned the dense foliage. I could only see a fraction of the dome's interior through the green profusion. Looking up at the enormous glass roof, I gazed at the walkway that ran round the circumference of the biosphere. It was out of bounds except for essential maintenance. A fall from that height would almost certainly be fatal. I wondered if Marcus was up there now, surveying his kingdom, feeling smug. An unexpected sensation of claustrophobia gripped my throat.

Paloma bustled to my table, carrying my coffee with a muffin perched on the saucer.

'In case you change your mind.'

'I won't.' I pulled out the chair next to me. 'Did Dad tell you he was flying to Africa?'

Paloma sat down heavily and grunted.

'Papa-Boss works too hard. I always tell him that.'

'When did he tell you he was going?'

'Marcus tell me this morning.'

'Don't you think it's strange we didn't know earlier?'

'Papa-Boss is always a big surprise. He likes to do the new thing.'

'But it's completely out of character for him to disappear like this without making sure everything's in order.'

'Marcus have everything under control, I thinks.'

'It's not his place to take control.'

'You listen to what Marcus is speaking. He knows how everything should be. You don't need to worry about anythings at all. He's a good man. Your papa knows.'

I tried a different tack.

'Dad sent me a text saying you'd be happy to stay with me until he gets back… in case I get nervous on my own. Which I won't, by the way. He must have spoken to you.'

'I say that to him a long time ago. I would always look after you if he went away. He knows. It will be like old times, yes?'

Paloma had been Dad's housekeeper before he married Mum. She'd carried on doing the heavy cleaning after their wedding, because Mum's health had been fragile. After Mum died, Paloma moved in to take care of me, only relocating to her own little cottage on the outskirts of Westhatch a couple of years ago. She was the only mother I'd ever known.

'I can look after myself. That's the whole point of being nineteen.'

She laughed and leaned over to kiss the side of my head.

'Don't be in such a hurry to be big. Why the frown? Eat my cake. It will make you happy, yes?'

I gave in and took a bite.

'I'm just worried about Dad… And Marcus has already mucked up the rotas.'

'Why you like him no more?'

'It's not a question of liking. It's a question of competence. I don't dislike Marcus. It's just that – '

'Everybody love Marcus.'

'Maybe that's the problem. Maybe it's time someone started to ask some difficult questions. How has a nobody from nowhere managed to ingratiate himself with Dad so completely? What's his agenda? He started out as an apprentice, learning everything from scratch. Now Dad's telling Marcus things before telling me.'

'Don't be the monster with the green eyes. Papa loves you. Nothing can change that. So Marcus find out about Africa first. No biggie, is that how you say it? Don't go looking for trouble.'

'You forget one thing… I *do* have green eyes.' I stirred a sachet of sugar into my coffee.

Paloma laughed and patted my hand.

'It will all be good, you see.'

'Not if I have to work in the laboratory for the next three months, making Marcus cups of that disgusting herbal tea he drinks and washing up his test tubes. It's not fair. I've stuck it out in the greenhouse, potting up and taking cuttings, and before that I was down in the stockroom for what seemed an eternity, not to forget the months I spent in your kitchen prepping veg and clearing tables. Marcus knows I want to go into retail one day. He knows I've earned a placement in the shop. Veronica said I can help choose next season's range of gifts. I've been going through the catalogues. And we were going to rejig the displays this week. I've got lots of ideas. But now Harmony gets to do it all.'

'But no other apprentices has been in the lab before, I think. Only Papa-Boss and Marcus works there. Maybe there is silver linings coming. You get to know how comes Greenacres is growing plants so good.'

I hadn't thought of it like that. Was the placement in the lab actually a compliment? Although Dad had shown no favouritism, maybe this was an indication that I *was* different to the other apprentices. Conceivably I was being prepared for a bigger role. My mood began to lighten.

'I smell the burnings of bacon,' Paloma said, pushing back her chair. 'I must go see what Eunice is doing. Chins up, Babyboss. It will all work out OK.'

I drank my coffee. Marcus had probably finished his inspection of the irrigation system and was now checking everything was working smoothly in the dome. More customers drifted in, carrying trays and collecting cutlery and sachets of sauce for their sausages. I had nothing to do until after lunch. I could go back home and watch daytime telly until it was time to meet Marcus in the lab, or I could find a sympathetic ear to complain to and do a little detective work at the same time. I pulled my mobile out of my bag and scrolled through my contacts.

'Hi, Uncle Colin. It's Ava.'

Colin Hildreth and Dad had been friends since their university days. He was another brilliant scientist and engineer, first working for the Ministry of Agriculture, then moving to the private sector to become head of research at a large biochemical establishment.

'Hello, poppet. How's my favourite goddaughter?'

'I'm your *only* goddaughter.'

He laughed.

'OK. How's my worst goddaughter?'

'She's fed up, actually. When you saw Dad a couple of days ago, did he tell you he was going out to Africa?'

'Not that I remember. Obviously at some point he needs to check on things out there. We talked a bit about our research, but mostly about you. It seems you're growing up to be quite the business whiz.'

'Did he say that?'

'Maybe not in those words. But he's very proud of you. So am I. You seem to have skipped the obnoxious teenage stage completely.'

'Then why doesn't he tell me what's going on? I had no idea he was flying out this morning. He's disappeared for goodness knows how long, without saying goodbye, and leaving Marcus Becker in charge. He's changed all the rotas and is meddling with the irrigation system. It's only ten o'clock on Monday morning and it's already chaos!'

There was a pause at the end of the line. At first I wondered whether we'd lost connection. When Colin replied, his godfatherly tone had morphed into professional mode.

'I think perhaps I should ring him.'

'Marcus?'

'No. Your dad.'

'He's flying over continental Europe as we speak. His phone is switched off.'

'I must be honest with you, Ava. I'm shocked at the timing of this trip. When I came to Greenacres on Friday, it was specifically to discuss the progress he's been making. We've been collaborating on some ideas relating to his ionised irrigation system. I advised him to patent his methods immediately and increase the security on his laboratory.'

'Why all the fuss? It's just a fertiliser, isn't it?'

'It's much more than that. Seedlings have been growing at twice the usual rate. There's been a significant reduction in pests and mould. Ionising the water supply not only sanitises it for human consumption but also seems to make the same amount of water go even further as far as crop yields are concerned. Theo might have solved the problem of the food deficit in the developing world. I agreed to help him present his findings to the government. We were supposed to be having a meeting at the Overseas Development Ministry next Thursday.'

'Thursday! That's only ten days away.'

'He's cutting it fine.'

'Should I call the police?'

'The police?'

'Don't you think his sudden disappearance is suspicious?'

'I think your imagination is getting the better of you, Ava. He's kicking back in business class with a large latte and a copy of *The Times* as we speak. However, I'm very concerned about the way he's left things. I was hoping to have another meeting with him this week to go through our presentation.'

'I'm worried something bad has happened.'

'I'm sure Theo's fine. He always manages to land on his feet. Unfortunately, however, I left some of my papers with him on Friday. I wanted him to cast an eye over my plans for improving the delivery system. I'm developing a prototype lightweight ionising pump for use out in the field. There are several big companies who'd love to get their hands on those specifications. If Theo's not going to look at my work before our meeting with the Ministry, then I need it back ASAP. I'll have to get one of my own engineers to peer-review it for me. Can you go down to the laboratory and find my file? It might be in his study, of course. You can't miss it. It's bright green and contains all the data relating to our research and the designs for the water pump. I'll drive down and collect it tomorrow afternoon. I'll take you out to dinner while I'm at it.'

I hesitated. 'Dad's study is out of bounds. And I've always been told not to go into the lab on my own. Strong chemicals and stuff.' I sounded like a child. I lifted my chin. 'Having said that, Marcus was at Dad's desk this morning, smug as a slug. Even *I've* never sat there. You know how fussy Dad is about the arrangement of his papers. And apparently I'm starting work in the lab this afternoon. Maybe the rules don't apply any more. The problem is, Dad's left his keys with Marcus.' The heat of that encounter burned once more on my cheeks.

'Marcus is a nice enough man and a half-decent phytologist, but I don't like to think the only thing standing between our project and several ruthless and well-funded organisations is a left-wing idealist who's naïve enough to think the world would be a happier place if we all start growing organic potatoes and talking to trees. Perhaps I'd better come now… I'll have to rearrange several important meetings – '

'There's no need for that. Leave it with me. I'll ring you later to let you know if I've found the file.'

'Clever girl. I know you can salvage the situation. It's taken several months for Theo to arrange this meeting with the government ministers. We get one shot at showing them the technology. If they back the research into ionised water, it not only gives your father the credibility he so obviously deserves, but it opens the doors to all sorts of possibilities. Just imagine if we can bring back fertility to the Horn of Africa… Ethiopia, Somalia, Eritrea. We could control the pests that are taking food from the children's mouths without contaminating the soil with chemical fertilisers and pesticides. I don't want our presentation to be anything less than perfect. It's too important to mess up now.'

We said our goodbyes. I sat and folded the empty paper case from my muffin in half and in half again, until it was too fat to fold any more. I'd heard Dad and Marcus talking about the ionised water that irrigated the plants at Greenacres, but I'd had no idea my father's discovery was so important. Perhaps if I'd shown more interest, Dad would have told me all about it and trusted me to hold the fort and keep his research safe in his absence.

I remembered the bunch of keys in Marcus' baggy pocket. If Dad had left them with me rather than with that dozy twerp it would have been easy to locate the file. This was what happened when people were given responsibilities above their pay grade. If I could solve Uncle Colin's predicament and save their presentation, perhaps I could prove to Dad that he needed to keep me in the loop in future.

I briefly considered explaining the situation to Marcus to see whether he would give me the keys, but I knew what his answer would be. We both knew I was not allowed in the laboratory or Dad's study on my own. It was the one area where Dad expected absolute obedience. His second-in-command would be too worried about losing his job to defy him openly. A daughter, however, could get away with it, particularly if her motives were good and she was acting in her father's best interests.

That was how I justified my actions to myself that day. Looking back, a subtle resentment had been growing in my heart. I wanted to be indispensable and appreciated; instead, I'd been snubbed. I'd seen my father turn the soil often enough to know that small weeds should never be ignored.

'Every root has to be removed,' Dad would say as he stripped the bindweed from the borders, picking out the fleshy strings that slithered through the soil like anaemic worms. 'Each one will grow back in the spring, stronger than ever. Don't let them get too comfortable. It pays to be ruthless.'

If only I'd taken his advice and pulled the worm from my heart before it poisoned everything I had ever known.

Chapter 2

I wonder now why I'd never examined the foundation upon which my world was built. At the time, I imagined myself to be in the antechamber of life, waiting like a babe in the womb to be launched triumphantly upon the world. I'd been impatient for the exciting stuff to start, not content with the comfort and happiness that existed within the dome. I was a spoilt child, irritated by trivialities, unaware of the darkness ahead. I never questioned the riches that were mine, or asked why I deserved such indulgence when so many in the world lived in poverty and fear. Now I know it's the darkest suffering that asks the best questions. Who am I? Why am I here? What's the point? Only pain would pop my bubble and open my eyes to the truth. But I'm getting ahead of myself.

Hoisting my tote bag onto my shoulder, I plunged back into the warmth of the dome in search of Marcus.

The plants were arranged in concentric circles, the aisles radiating from the central pond like spokes on a wheel. I passed Ruby the nursery cat, stretched out in a puddle of buttery sunlight. Tired from hunting the field mice that crept under the wooden pallets, she lay gazing at the vaulted ceiling, watching for any bird that might fly through an open fanlight. I shooed her off the carved wooden bench retailing for £399, and she padded away, sulking.

As I circled the dome, moving ever closer to the middle, my eyes automatically scanned the petals for any sign of deterioration. Deadheading the flowers was no longer my job, but a constant quest for visual perfection was a hard habit to break. Plus, with Dad away, standards were bound to slip among the other apprentices, mostly difficult boys with no qualifications or social skills who Dad would take under his wing and train to prick out seedlings and sweep up fallen compost. My father would turn them into proper gardeners if he could, digging, pruning and watering until they grew into men who would get out of bed in the morning and speak whole sentences without swearing.

'We are changing the face of the earth, one pebble at a time,' he would chuckle. 'What better way to use our strength?'

The boys laughed at him behind his back, but over time their faces would soften and open like flowers towards the sun.

I stood for a moment watching the koi tumbling in the central pond, scales shining silver, white and gold. Ruby had sat herself on the wall to paw at the fish. A couple of women stood on the other side of the water, pointing out the rainbows that danced in the fountain and gawping at the overarching glass above, awestruck. The fish swam towards my shadow, their mouths opening wide like baby birds.

'Sorry, guys. No pellets with me,' I murmured before turning away and walking down the houseplants aisle.

Fresh slices of orange, lemon and mango were scattered on a stone bird bath halfway along the mosaic pathway. I recognised Dad's fingerprints. Several species of butterfly had adapted to life under the glass and he liked to put out wedges of fruit to tempt their long tongues. Even though he'd left before dawn, he'd remembered the daily ritual.

I spotted Marcus helping Ted to unload a trolley of orchids and cyclamen in the canopied area of the dome reserved for shade-loving plants. He stood under the gazebo, up to his ankles in a sea of stiff petals – crimson, magenta, cerise, cream. A hairy satyr in paradise. I was surprised to see him getting stuck in. Obviously his elevation to senior management hadn't gone to his head. I hovered behind an enormous banana plant, chewing my bottom lip and wondering how to extract the bunch of keys from Marcus' pocket. I could see the outline of the metal cluster in the cargo pocket on his outer thigh, low down near his knee.

A young mother turned into the aisle, the baby in her buggy sobbing inconsolably. She slowed down and rocked the pushchair back and forth, shushing the infant. An idea began to form in my mind. I hurried from my hiding place and came face-to-face with the pair just as they were passing Marcus.

'Someone doesn't sound very happy,' I commented.

'She's teething,' the woman grimaced.

'Oh dear!' I peered into the stroller. A red-faced baby in a pink sleep suit arched her back, two small fists punching the air with uncoordinated fury.

'Let's see what we can do to cheer her up, shall we?' Before he knew what I was doing, I reached across and dipped my hand into Marcus' pocket. I pulled out the bunch of jangling metal. 'What's this?' I cooed, shaking the keys in the baby's face.

The crying stopped. After a couple of stuttering hiccups, the tiny fingers reached towards the silver cluster.

'That's better,' I smiled. 'We don't want anyone to be unhappy at Greenacres.'

'Thanks,' her mother said. 'She's been doing my head in all night. I brought her here to see if I could walk her to sleep somewhere warm. She's so overtired.'

'So are you by the looks of it,' I continued, shaking the keys.

Marcus watched me, legs apart, arms folded.

'That's done the trick, Ava.'

I caught his eye and was surprised at the warmth of his smile. He wiped the sweat from his forehead with the back of his hand. Taking a gamble, I pulled the bunch away from the baby and held it out to Marcus. Immediately the small face crumpled and a thin wail rose from the pushchair.

'I seem to have started something here,' I said, taking back the keys and dangling them before the baby's tear-stained cheeks. She quietened, eyes wide, fixed on the treasure in my hand.

'She looks as though she might drop off if she calms down,' I remarked, sounding more knowledgeable than I was. 'Why don't I walk you to the café? Hopefully she'll have fallen asleep by then. You can have a coffee on the house. Is it OK if I borrow your keys for five minutes, Marcus? I'll bring them straight back.'

He nodded. 'Anything to keep our young customers happy.'

'Let's get you that drink,' I said firmly.

'Are you sure?' the woman asked. 'Won't you get into trouble?'

'She's the boss' daughter,' Marcus declared. 'She can do anything she wants.'

Yes, I can, I thought in triumph. And you'll be none the wiser.

By the time we reached the café, the child's eyes were drooping. I stood in the queue with the mother and explained to Paloma that the pot of tea for one was on the house.

'Here, I have rusk for the little one,' she said when she heard our story. But the baby was already asleep. I carried the tray to the far wall and settled the pair in the corner where Paloma and I had sat an hour earlier.

Smiling my goodbyes, I walked to the door marked 'Staff Only' and swiped my card. The laboratory was below ground level, down the stairs and next to Dad's study. With neither Dad nor Marcus inside, I knew it would be locked. Fumbling hurriedly through the bunch, I found the small Yale which opened the door.

I turned the key and pushed. The door swung shut behind me and I was plunged into darkness. Groping to my left, I located the switch for the fluorescent light. It flickered and buzzed before stabilising into a continuous, uncompromising glare.

'Let there be light,' I murmured, dazzled by the unrelenting brightness of the blue-tone lamps specially installed to mimic the impression of daylight. Before me lay the world Dad had created from the proceeds of his university research. Those patented formulas had also financed the building of the dome. By the time the money ran out, the garden centre was operational and had begun to bankroll an altogether different type of experiment.

Brilliant white with high-gloss cupboards and stainless-steel tops, the lab looked like a futuristic kitchen. A couple of metal sinks were set in the counter to my left, next to a dishwasher for cleaning flasks and test tubes. An enormous American-style fridge-freezer for preserving samples loomed next to a small coffee station. A long white island stood in the centre of the lab with a computer, microscope and a couple of Bunsen burners on the top. Stacks of clean Petri dishes were balanced at one end of the island next to a rack of test tubes, each of the glass cylinders containing a dribble of liquid – clear, yellow, or greenish-brown.

Dad's tall stool was adrift in the middle of the floor as though he'd just pushed it back and stood up to leave. Everywhere I looked there were signs of his presence. A used coffee mug on the pottery coaster I'd made him as a child, his lab coat hanging from a hook.

In stark contrast to the white fittings, multicoloured sticky notes fluttered like luminous leaves. They attached themselves to cupboards and shelves, stuck out of books and garnished the walls with my father's jottings and hastily scrawled diagrams. Like many brilliant men, he'd developed the habit of leaving prompts and clues to remind himself of anniversaries or items needed from the shops. It looked as though he used the same system for his work. There was no sign of the green file.

My heels clicked on the white-tiled floor. I passed a bench covered with rows of seedlings at various stages of growth and approached the grey, four-drawer filing cabinet on the far wall. I sifted through the bunch in my hand and found the key.

I opened the top drawer. It contained thick printouts showing the results of Dad's experiments, rows and rows of figures reporting the height of batches of seedlings compared with the number of drops of ionised water they were fed each day.

The second drawer contained personnel files. I resisted the temptation to flick through the pages. It would be highly unethical to take advantage of the situation. My motivation was to help Colin and my father, not to play nosy parker on my colleagues.

The third drawer was stuffed with financial papers relating to the work of the laboratory: accounts and invoices, bank statements and correspondence with suppliers and auditors. The bottom drawer held nothing more exciting than back copies of scientific journals and horticultural magazines.

I quickly opened every cupboard door and drawer, including the fridge, before concluding that the file wasn't in the laboratory. Switching off the light and locking the door, I crept along the corridor.

A fluttery feeling agitated at the back of my throat. I'd never been alone in Dad's study before, and now I was breaking in with stolen keys. My breathing quickened, my heart jumped against my ribs. The same mixture of guilt and daring had coursed through my veins when I'd stood outside the head teacher's office in my last year of primary school, knowing I would be suspended for shaving my head in the girl's toilets with one of Dad's razors. Once again I savoured the tang of transgression on my tongue.

I switched on the light, a soft yellow glow here instead of the clinical intensity of the lab. I could smell the soap my father used, musky like a forest at night-time but with a hint of freshness – pine needles or cut grass. Unexpectedly, I blinked back tears. Perhaps a premonition.

I crept quietly across the Chinese rug that covered the floor and approached the desk. A quick survey of the piles of paper on the top was enough to tell me that the green file was not among them. I hurried round the other side to find several books under his desk, facedown and open at the page my father was reading, together with an unsteady pile of files. Dad's organisational skills were like quantum mechanics – complex, contradictory, apparently random and in many ways inexplicable, but functional nevertheless. I crouched down and flicked through the files carefully, anxious not to disturb the order, but my search was in vain.

I stood and stretched my back. A large Victorian sampler hung on the wall over the bookcase. Faded flowers stitched in red, blue and gold, bordered the words, 'For where your treasure is, there will your heart be also (Matthew 6:21).' Feeling along the edge of the frame, I located a small button. I pressed hard and pulled the side of the picture. The hinged frame swung away from the wall, opening like the cover of a book. Hiding behind was a large safe with a keypad for the security code.

I'd seen my father open the safe many times, but had never known the combination. His long fingers had punched the keys too quickly for me to remember the sequence, but I knew it was an eight-digit number. Disappointingly, there were no sticky notes on the safe door giving me a clue to the code.

He wouldn't have chosen anything as obvious as a telephone number or a birthday. Neither would he have chosen a completely random series. I knew him well enough to know that everything he did had reason and purpose. The number for the lock would hold some personal meaning. Otherwise, how would he remember?

I swung the sampler back over the safe door and gazed at the words. 'For where your treasure is, there will your heart be also.' Was there a clue in the words? Maybe he'd used the embroidery as a giant memo to signpost his treasure and remind him how to access it?

An eight-digit number with a personal meaning. I fidgeted with the bunch of keys as I scoured my mind for inspiration. Dad's heart had never been set on money. It was something he needed, of course, but he wasn't particularly materialistic. In fact, he could be overgenerous, something I scolded him about when he was taken advantage of by an undeserving cause. No, his treasure could never be confined to a two-foot square metal box. He loved the sun and the sky and the wind. He cherished his plants and the wildlife they attracted. He adored making things with his hands. He prized physics and mathematics, conundrums and ciphers. And he loved me. He often called me 'Treasure' the way others said 'Darling' or 'Dear'. I chewed my lower lip in frustration. Marcus would be expecting my return at any moment.

Then it came to me. Our secret code! The game Dad and I played together when I was a child. Dad would leave me private notes around the house. Paloma, our housekeeper at the time, would huff and clatter around the kitchen in pretend exasperation that she couldn't understand the jokes and memos stuck to the washing machine or left under my pillow. Yet, it was such a simple puzzle to crack. Every letter in the alphabet was assigned a number, with A being number one and Z being twenty-six. And an eight-digit number was always on the outside of the envelopes he left. My name, Ava Gage, in numeric form: One, twenty-two, one, seven, one, seven, five. His treasure! I held my breath and tapped in the numbers. I heard a clunk, and the, door swung open.

Looking back, I wonder why I didn't question the ease with which I accessed the safe. Perhaps the combination had been chosen because Dad knew the way my mind worked. The puzzle was difficult enough not to arouse my suspicions then, but now I wonder how much choice I had in the matter. Knowing my ambition and restlessness, he must have guessed I'd one day open the door without his permission. That day, I congratulated myself on my intelligence. Now I realise I'd failed the test.

The safe was stuffed with papers and files. I removed the pile and placed it on the wide seat of Dad's desk chair. At the back of the safe was an envelope stuffed with cash. Dad hated taking time away from his work to drive down to the nearest bank – a twelve-mile round trip to Westhatch – and often made large withdrawals. Our personal money was kept rigidly separate from the garden centre takings. Since Marcus had become a partner, Dad received a salary like the rest of the staff. His company credit card, used to order scientific and horticultural supplies online, was also in the safe. No doubt he'd left it behind thinking travellers cheques would be the safer option on his visit to Africa.

I knelt on the floor in front of the chair and examined the papers. It only took a moment to locate the bright green file halfway down. I lifted the papers off the top and placed them to one side. 'Water of Life Project' was typed on the front. I glanced inside and saw the words 'irrigation', 'ionisation' and 'crop yields'.

I was just about to replace the other papers back on top of the pile, when my eye was caught by a large brown manila envelope which had been immediately beneath Colin's file. Typed on the address label on the front was my name, Ava-Claire Gage.

Perhaps it was my father's will, prepared well in advance and waiting for when the inevitable would happen. Maybe he was worried about his trip to Africa and had left his affairs in order. I knew I would inherit the farmhouse. I would always have a home, he had assured me a couple of years ago when a virulent strain of flu swept through the Greenacres staff and I became needlessly anxious for his health and my future. But what of the dome? I glanced at my watch. I'd been gone about ten minutes. Hopefully Marcus would think I was still soothing the baby in the café. The envelope wasn't sealed. I lifted the flap and slipped out the contents.

Unexpectedly, several photographs spilled onto my lap. A girl standing on a beach, red hair whipping in front of her face, the thin material of her summer dress stretched across an extended stomach. My mother. Pregnant with me. Laughing. The next photograph showed my mother again, obviously taken on the same day because she was still wearing the white sundress. This time she was sitting on a towel. The beach was stony and she looked uncomfortable, pulling her skirt around her knees. A green bead necklace circled her neck like a snake.

The third photograph was taken by a funfair. I could see the silhouette of a Ferris wheel in the background, the struts dark against the blue sky. My mother was eating an ice cream. Standing next to her was a clean-shaven man in an open-necked shirt and shorts, his arm casually draped across her shoulder. He was not my father. He was shorter, more heavily set though certainly not fat. His hair was dark and wiry, growing up and away from his head in a heavy clump. He was wearing sunglasses so I couldn't see his eyes.

There were several old letters still in their envelopes, stamped and addressed to my mother, Sandra Hewitt. There were some legal documents. I flicked through them quickly, but none of them looked like a will. Lastly, my birth certificate, pink and neatly folded concertina style. I pulled it open. Ava-Claire Gage, born 20th January 1984. Mother's name: Sandra Hewitt. Father's name: Unknown.

Chapter 3

My memory of what happened next is hazy. I see shaking hands thrusting a file and an envelope into a patchwork tote bag. I see the stitches clearly even now, the silky sheen of the thread, a loose cotton hanging from a corner. I tugged at it in irritation, snapping it off and discarding it on the floor. I put the papers back in the safe and stumbled from Dad's study, locking up behind me and staggering into the small toilet cubicle opposite. I see a dark stream of coffee and lumps of muffin being vomited into the sink. An ashen reflection in the mirror, my face damp where I'd splashed it with cold water.

The young mother was still sitting in the café. She waved as I passed, gesturing to the baby who was fast asleep. I smiled as best I could and hurried on, praying Paloma wouldn't catch sight of my white face.

An overwhelming desire to hide myself away prevented further tears from falling. Now was not the time to give in to the emotions clawing at my heart. I needed to bury my misery until I could escape the scrutiny of my colleagues and return to the empty farmhouse. Then I would process the information I'd stumbled across. Before that, I had to return the keys to Marcus.

Heavy-footed, I navigated my way round the spiralling aisles, groping for a possible excuse for my delay. Fleshy leaves and spiky grasses brushed my legs as I pushed blindly past the customers. Despite the tropical heat, my skin was chill and shivery as a fever on a summer's day. The familiar colours and scents, intense as a dream, now belonged to a magical realm beyond my reach. I was not the biological daughter of Theo

Gage. My life was a lie. Bright petals blurred as I blinked back tears. I turned a corner and bumped into a trolley. Apologising hurriedly to the man pushing it, I tottered along one of the central spokes leading towards the koi pond.

'Are you all right?'

I rubbed my eyes. Marcus stepped from behind a trellis draped with purple bougainvillea.

'I think I'm going to have a migraine.' I could barely speak. My cheeks were stiff with shock.

'She did have quite a pair of lungs on her.' He paused. 'The baby. She had a pair of lungs.'

'Oh… yes. But it was probably the sunshine this morning. That low bright sun in my eyes… and the stress of Dad leaving without telling me.' Even though I was having difficulty squeezing the words past my rigid lips, I couldn't resist a dig.

'You do look pale. Paler than usual, if that's possible. Perhaps you'd better go home and get some sleep. You might be coming down with something. Would you like me to tell Paloma?'

'No! I just need some peace and quiet.' A little spurt of fear loosened my tongue. 'You know what she's like. All that fussing. A couple of painkillers and a nap and I'm sure it'll pass. Please don't tell her.'

He must have heard the desperation in my voice, because for once he let me have my way.

'OK. Give me a ring later to let me know how you are. I can pop round tonight after work.'

'There's no need.' I dropped the keys into his hand. Our fingers touched briefly. I flinched as though I'd been burned.

'Your father asked me to keep an eye on you.'

'I'm all grown up, remember. Stop fussing. I can manage on my own.' I turned and walked away.

'You don't need to manage on your own, Ava,' he called, but I didn't look back.

I slammed the back door and pushed back the bolt before running through the kitchen to put the chain on the front door. Marcus had all the Greenacres keys now and Paloma had our spare house keys for emergencies, and I didn't want to be disturbed. A physical pain squeezed my heart so tight I wondered briefly whether I was having a coronary. I sat on the bottom of the stairs and curled over, resting my head in my lap.

The farmhouse had never felt so empty. Dad was gone in every sense. Theo Gage wasn't my father. Never had been. It was as though I'd fallen into a parallel universe where everything was the same except the most important element... me. I was no longer the person I thought I was. Gasping sobs echoed around the high-ceilinged hallway. Tears splashed on the black-and-white Victorian floor tiles at my feet, as loud as the tick of the grandfather clock. So this was the sound of a breaking heart.

I rocked back and forth, head in my hands, trying to alleviate the pressure behind my eyes. My brain felt like porridge – a grey mush bubbling with pain, grains of hurt splitting and expanding against the restricting bowl of my skull. The events of the morning swirled through my mind. A sense of loss washed over me like a tidal wave. I couldn't breathe. I was sinking below the surface, down into the gloom where underwater demons swam, eager to tear me apart.

Then a sudden rush of release as I pushed the pain upwards and outwards into an explosion of anger. This was not my fault! Grief for the father I'd lost turned to boiling rage at Theo's betrayal. I staggered to the kitchen, grabbed a glass from the draining board and filled it from the tap. I drank it in one go and refilled the glass. I would need fluids for later, when I regained enough energy to cry again. My tote bag was by the back door where I'd flung it on my return home. I picked it up and pulled out the brown envelope, emptying the contents onto the kitchen table.

A heap of cash and the Greenacres credit card – taken from the safe in a moment of madness – also spilled onto the oak surface. I don't know why I'd taken the money. I certainly wasn't thinking logically at the time. A deep-seated instinct for self-preservation must have whispered that I needed a haven. In the absence of emotional security, money and a credit card would do. Everything of value had been taken from me. Surely I was entitled to a little compensation. Somebody owed me something and I was going to take what was mine.

I placed the bundle of £20 notes, the credit card and the photographs to one side and sorted through the papers. A letter from a lawyer blurred before my eyes, the words dancing and registering separately, as though from a great distance: 'post-natal depression', 'no living relatives', 'adoption'...

Among the typed documents, there was a handwritten letter to my father signed 'Delia Ozzles'. The handwriting was small. She had pressed hard with her green biro; I could feel the words indented through the back of the paper like braille.

Dear Mr Gage

I was very sorry to hear of the sad demise of Sandra. She was a valued member of the housekeeping team here at Fun World Holiday Camp for nearly two years, until she unexpectedly resigned a year ago. Thank you for letting us know the details of the funeral. Unfortunately, because it is the high season, I cannot release any members of the team that day. I myself will be representing the Fun World Holiday Camp 'family' at the church service and cremation.

I am sure you feel the loss as keenly as we all do here.

Yours sincerely

Delia Ozzles

Housekeeper

I read a letter from a private investigator called Walt Marshall, dated eight days after Mum died. Apparently, my father – or perhaps I should say, Theo – had been trying to trace my mother's family with details of the funeral. Sandra Hewitt, Mr Marshall reported, was an orphan with no siblings. He had spoken to some of her friends – chalet maids at the caravan park in Westhatch – but they all swore they never knew she was pregnant and had no idea who the father could be. They'd lost contact with her when she left the caravan park suddenly in August 1983, five months before I was born. Although tactful, the private investigator suggested my mother might not have known the father's identity herself.

I flicked through a bundle of official-looking documents. A wedding certificate revealed my mother had married Theo on 19th May 1984, four months after my birth. Her last will and testament had been drawn up by a solicitor in Westhatch-on-Sea when I was six months old. She'd left everything to me, naming Theo as my guardian in the event of her death. Routine correspondence from the solicitor's office indicated she didn't have anything to leave me, apart from some debts which Theo had paid, and a jade necklace. There was a copy of the official guardianship papers signed by Dad… Theo… and witnessed by Paloma Bianco and Colin Hildreth. I would have been about ten months old.

Paloma! Uncle Colin! They both knew! The conspiracy of lies and silence spread like a dark stain, seeping across memories from my happy childhood, blotting out the pleasure they held. My mother, figment of fond imaginings in the absence of any memories, was not the saint I believed her to be. I was the illegitimate sprog of a promiscuous chalet maid. My beloved father, teacher and guide was a biological stranger. Those closest to me had failed to point out the most important fact of my existence. I was a cuckoo in the nest with no one to turn to for comfort or advice. An abyss opened before me.

The blast of despair turned my rage to ash. They were all in on it. Everyone was implicated in the conspiracy. None of the people in my life could be trusted. Everything in the past had been based on a lie. If my parents had both died in a car crash, at least I would have known who to grieve for. Now I had a depressed ghost for a mother, and an impostor for a father. Everything in my past life had to be re-evaluated. This morning I'd been the offspring of a loving mother, prematurely taken from me, and a brilliant and respected man. The boss' daughter. Someone important. I thought I belonged to Greenacres through birth, not charity. Now I was no different from Marcus or Harmony or any of the other apprentices. Just another experiment to demonstrate how a nurturing environment could overcome a genetic predisposition.

'If you feed a soul with love and quench its thirst with acceptance, anyone can change for the better,' my father had told me when he confessed to taking on one more unnecessary apprentice. I was merely another example of Theo's need to father the fatherless.

It was lunchtime, but I had no appetite. After reading the contents of the envelope several times, I took a cup of tea into the lounge and lit the wood-burning stove. Dad had left kindling, newspaper and logs in the cast-iron range ready for me to light. I took a large photograph album from the bookshelf and huddled on the sofa in front of the flickering fire.

I opened the book. The first page displayed several photographs taken of my mother in hospital. She was looking down at what could have been a bundle of dirty laundry in her arms, except that the very top of my head was poking out, thin strands of dark hair plastered over a whitish scalp. In the next picture she lay propped up on pillows, her skin grey with exhaustion, eyes dark and anxious despite her smile. Who had taken the photograph? My real father? Theo? A passing nurse? Next, a picture of me in a transparent plastic cot, red-faced and screaming, battling to get loose from the cotton blanket that ensnared me.

I turned the page. I'd never thought it strange before, but there must have been a gap of several months. I looked at the baby pulling herself up to stand by the sofa with different eyes. There was a missing chapter in her life. I blinked back tears at the irreparable tragedy my younger self had experienced in the intervening months between the photographs. My hair was already turning red, one thing my mother *had* left me. A woman's lap and legs could be seen nearby. I'd always thought they belonged to my mother, but a close inspection of the plump calves confirmed they probably belonged to Paloma. She'd been a major player in my life, even then.

Next, a toddler in a greenhouse, Paloma holding my hand. Snaps of me sitting on a small push-along plastic trike. Digging in the garden with a red trowel. School photographs of a fiery-haired child, gap-toothed and Kirby-gripped. Dad dressed up as Father Christmas, sitting under a huge decorated tree in the dome.

Pictures of an unprepossessing teenager started to appear when I was about ten. Marcus, missing the beard but still with the same intense brown eyes, could be glimpsed in the background or with his face half out of the picture. In one photograph he held up a banner with the message 'Happy Birthday, Alfie'. 'Alfie' had been his nickname for me after I'd shaved my head, my cutting-my-hair-off-to-spite-my-face gesture as he liked to call it. I hadn't minded. Anything was better than the 'Ginger Fleabag' and 'Ginger Biscuit' taunts from school.

Next, a photograph of me on his shoulders, both of us laughing. I must have been about twelve, just before that self-conscious age when I decided I no longer wanted to be treated as a child or chased up and down the greenhouse aisles by a teenager with a watering can in his hand.

I turned another page. A photograph of Dad with his arm round Marcus' shoulders. Another stab to my heart. Perhaps it was Marcus who was being groomed to take over Greenacres. At sixty-one, Theo was approaching retirement, although he had the energy and enthusiasm of a man half his age. Ostensibly Marcus had been made a junior partner the previous year to release Theo to travel more and concentrate on his experiments. Now I wondered if there was a plan to ease me out of the picture. Did I have any rights at all? Was I even considered next of kin?

I closed the album with a snap. Not much to show for a life. Only now did I realise why there were no wedding photographs on prominent display. My parents had married in haste. No big white wedding for Mum with a baby in tow. I always assumed my parents' history together was too painful for Dad to discuss, losing her as he did so soon after they married. But it wasn't just his suffering he was hiding. A dark secret had been locked away in his safe waiting for the day when I would break his command and enter his study alone.

The distress of the last few hours had pumped through my body, seeping into muscle and bone. My limbs and shoulders ached with the shame of my discovery. A protective wave of exhaustion kicked in. A switch flicked. One moment I was awake and the next I sank into an oblivion so total and so dark that, when I woke with a start several hours later, I didn't know who I was, or why I was lying on the sofa in the dark.

My mobile phone was ringing in my jacket pocket. The fire had burned to a blue glow. I turned the handset towards the dim light and found the answer button.

'Hello,' I mumbled, pulling my cramped legs from beneath me.

'Poppet! It's Colin. Just wondered how you're getting along with my file retrieval.'

A crashing punch. I remembered everything.

'Are you there, Ava?'

'Yes… It's a bad connection. I can hear you now.'

'You sound a bit muffled.'

'I'm coming down with a cold.'

'You do sound bunged up. I hardly recognised your voice. That's come on quickly. I won't keep you long. Any joy with the file?'

'I don't think I'll be able to help after all. Marcus has the keys to the laboratory, and you know how he likes to stick to the rules.'

'Right… of course. Don't worry. It's my problem. I might give Marcus a call, just in case I can work my magic on him. You get yourself better. Is there anything I can do?'

'All I need is hot lemon and a good night's sleep.'

'Are Paloma and Marcus keeping an eye on you?'

'They're being very attentive.'

'I'm sure they are,' he laughed. 'Speak to you soon, sweetie-pie.'

Not if I can help it. I tossed the phone onto the sofa in disgust. I certainly didn't want him driving down to collect the file tomorrow. I would either have to pretend nothing had happened or start the sort of conversation I wasn't ready to handle yet. My wounds were too fresh and deep.

In any case, I was in no mood to help him with his problem. He had colluded in the lie. As my godfather, surely he should have insisted I be told the truth once I was old enough to understand. He could waste his time trying to persuade Marcus to open up the lab if he wanted. There was nothing to find. Neither of them would be able to figure out the combination to the safe. The whole point of the game Dad and I played was that our secret code was known only to the two of us. Dad – currently out of reach by mobile or the internet – wouldn't be home for who knew how long. It would be some time before my theft would be discovered.

What then? I'd broken into the safe with the best of motives. I had a right to know the contents of the brown envelope, I told myself. Even so, I was ashamed of my actions. At some point I would have to face the music. What were the chances I could return both the green file and the brown envelope to the safe without arousing Marcus' suspicion? If by some miracle I could borrow the keys again, how would I carry on as before, knowing what I'd done and who I was, or rather wasn't?

I couldn't hide in the farmhouse for ever. If I didn't turn up for work tomorrow, Paloma, Marcus or both would make it their business to winkle me out. I needed more time to think. It was half-past six. The dome would be closed. Paloma would have left an hour ago, bustling home to cook linguine in the small terraced house she'd bought once she realised I no longer needed a full-time babysitter. Marcus would be locking up and activating the overnight irrigation system in the dome. Soon he'd be walking down the path to his cottage, a converted cowshed a few hundred yards from our farmhouse.

I hurried to the kitchen and found a piece of paper and magic marker. In large letters I wrote, 'DO NOT DISTURB. SLEEPING OFF MIGRAINE', and stuck the notice to the front door. I could probably keep them at bay for another twenty-four hours at most. I turned out the lights downstairs and made my way to my bedroom. Pulling the curtains tight, I switched on the small bedside lamp. I dragged an old rucksack from the bottom of the wardrobe and began stuffing it with essentials. Underwear, jeans, unremarkable tops in black and grey rather than some of my more distinctive fashion combinations. A collection of make-up I didn't usually wear, lipsticks and nail varnishes that could have belonged to a different kind of girl. I carefully wrapped my mother's jade necklace in a woollen scarf and pressed it into a side pocket. Packing my toiletries, I caught sight of myself in the bathroom mirror.

The pallor of my face had intensified the startling red of my hair. I would be easy to spot in a crowd. Opening the bathroom cabinet, I located a pair of nail scissors and held a long strand between my finger and thumb. A perfect corkscrew. I pulled gently and watched as the curl unkinked, doubling in length. One snip and a bright coil fell into the sink, the remaining strand retracting like a spring to hang by my jaw. Another and another. Snip, snip, snip. The sink was filled with curling red serpents.

I fetched an old newspaper from the recycling box in the utility room and wrapped up the glowing pile, swilling the sink clean. I carried the bundle to the living room, opened the wood-burning stove and shoved the scrunched-up newspaper inside with a poker. It blazed immediately, the curls hissing and spitting in the range.

Returning to the bathroom, I removed a battered box of black hair dye from the cabinet. I'd purchased it in a fit of teenage rebellion but never had the courage to go through with my threats. It was a weapon for a big battle, not a minor hormonal skirmish. It had been my nuclear deterrent, reminding Theo and Paloma of the lengths I would go to if pushed. I started to read the instructions.

An hour later, a different girl stared out from the mirror. Shoulder-length hair, black as a raven's wing, fanning out like a crown of wriggling serpents. A pinched, white face. Eyes glittering green, rimmed in red. The face of an orphan.

I was about to underline my lashes with a defiant slash of kohl when the doorbell rang. Grabbing a towel, I ran to my bedroom window and pulled my dressing gown close across my chest. Marcus was standing by the front door, ignoring the notice. Blast him! I wound the towel round my head and opened the window. A gust of freezing air slapped my face.

'Marcus!' I called. He looked up.

'Are you OK?'

'I've just got out the bath.'

'How's your head?'

'No better. I'm going back to bed.'

'Have you eaten? Can I get you anything?'

'I've been sick.' Not a lie. I *had* been sick in the laboratory after scanning through the contents of the envelope. 'I'm probably infectious. Best keep away.'

'You know where I am if you need me. Don't hesitate to ring day or night. I'll check on you before work tomorrow.'

'No! I mean, I want to sleep until I wake naturally. That's the best way to fight a bug.'

'OK. I'll talk to you tomorrow night, if not before. Veronica and Harmony took up your suggestions for changing the shop displays this afternoon. It looks great. You have a gift for seeing what's needed, Alfie.'

'Thanks.' I turned away from the window and mumbled, 'Patronising jerk,' to make myself feel better.

'You've got my mobile number.'

'Yes. Goodnight, Marcus.' I watched him walk down the moonlit track. He turned one last time. I waved and pulled the curtains tight.

My mind was unnaturally alert. The deep sleep that afternoon, a recent injection of caffeine and another kick of adrenalin suggested a restless night ahead. I might as well make the best of it. If I left now, in the dark when I was unlikely to be spotted, I would have several hours' head start before anyone realised I was missing. Peeking from my bedroom window I saw a light burning from Marcus' cottage. I sat and watched for a few minutes before pulling on a pair of skinny jeans and a dark jumper.

I'd read my fair share of thrillers and watched enough detective dramas on television to know some of the steps I needed to take. I didn't want the police to become involved, or for people to think a crime might have been committed, or that a suicide was about to take place. I drafted a farewell letter.

Dear Theo

I have learned today that you are not my father. I wonder when you were going to tell me, or whether you were ever going to tell me at all. As I am not your daughter, you have no hold on me. I am of age. I have taken some money from the safe – call it my inheritance, if you like. I release you from any further responsibility you may feel for my care or well-being.

I see now that you have been grooming Marcus to take over Greenacres. I will get out of his way. He was the son you never had and I, as it turns out, am the daughter you never had. I'm going in search of my own identity now. Please do not try to find me.

Thanks for providing me with a home during my childhood, but I'm all grown-up now.

Ava-Claire

I left my house keys on the kitchen table together with the envelope, which I addressed to Dr Theodore Gage. I collected the money he'd left in the kitchen drawer for my use while he was away, together with a bottle of water, a cereal bar, a banana and a large torch from under the sink. I picked up the papers and photographs from the kitchen table and put them in the backpack, stuffing all the cash and the Greenacres credit card into a money belt. I slipped my own wallet and bank cards into the back pocket of my trousers. Rummaging in the cupboard under the stairs, I found a pair of gloves, a black beanie hat belonging to Theo and my oldest and most unflattering coat, one everybody was sure to have forgotten I owned. After a last-minute check of the house to make sure all evidence of my transformation had been cleared away, I let myself quietly out of the back door.

Chapter 4

Huddled against a windbreak, I ate the cereal bar and watched the moon streak the sea with silver. The cold stones ached against my buttocks; I pulled my rucksack closer, perching on its bulk, arms around my knees. The tide was coming in. Foamy fingers groped forward, luminous, grasping; each successive wave reaching higher up the beach then retreating with its horde of rattling pebbles. Further out, the waters flattened into one heaving surface – unbounded, dark and empty as my heart. I'd left the safe harbour behind. Now a shifting expanse of limitless freedom lay ahead. I was the captain of my own little ship now, and could steer in any direction I wanted and be anyone I wanted to be.

I would change my name. My birth certificate stated that Sandra Hewitt had given birth to a girl called Ava-Claire. Instead of Ava Gage, I would reinvent myself as Claire Hewitt. With my birth certificate, I would be able to open a new bank account. I would get a job, and somewhere to live. But there was only one thing I really wanted to do. Find my real father.

Midnight passed. My mind wandered over images from what was now the previous day. I let them go. Already there was distance, small but significant. I flicked through memories of my childhood. I let them go too. The cold seeped into my bones. I became a statue, my limbs stiff, my mind retreating to a safe place deep within. It seemed as though everyone in the world was asleep. If I could survive this pain and loneliness, I would be able to survive anything. A strange exhilaration pricked my heart. Nobody would be able to hurt me this much again.

The beach darkened towards morning. Even the white crests were difficult to discern, though the rhythmic shushing told me of their relentless approach. The moon had disappeared behind a bank of cloud; the sun had yet to rise. They say the night is darkest just before the dawn. I hoped this was true and that my despair would soon be replaced by the challenge of a new beginning.

Although insured to drive Theo's car, I'd left it in the garage. I knew from watching television dramas that nothing happened for a couple of days after an adult was reported missing. If Marcus and Paloma ignored my letter and wanted to find me quickly, the best way to do it would be to claim that the car I was driving had been stolen.

A bicycle would be almost impossible to trace, and I had liberated my old mountain bike from the back of the garden shed and coasted silently down the drive, past Marcus' cottage and along the winding country roads to Westhatch-on-Sea. The bike was now padlocked to a nearby lamppost while I waited for the town to awake.

I shook away a squall of tears and focused on the plan for the day. I knew the address of Walt Marshall, the detective Theo had hired to trace my dead mother's family. I would visit his office at nine o'clock, and either speak to him immediately or insist on an appointment. Although many years had passed, he was still my best lead.

The sky began to grey, then whiten. As the gloom lifted, I noticed the pebbles were strewn with rubbish. An empty drinks can, sweet wrappers, cigarette butts, a soiled nappy tightly wrapped and taped like a present. Strands of seaweed, oily black as the hair sticking out from beneath my beanie hat, were caught in the splintering windbreak. A jury of watchful gulls lined up along the wooden groyne as if to deliver their verdict. I took a swig of water and ate my banana, tossing the skin on the stones, watching as the birds squabbled over the evidence of my overnight visit.

Dog walkers arrived next, hurrying bleary-eyed along the Promenade as dawn streaked the sky. Newsagents and café owners unlocked their doors and placed racks of postcards and menu boards on the pavement. I bought a coffee and sat inside a snack bar as far away from the window as I could, hugging an antiquated radiator and nursing the warm cardboard long after the cup was empty. I sneaked into the customer toilets to splash my face with water and brush my teeth. The kohl had smudged beneath my eyes, ringing them with black stains which stubbornly resisted the attentions of a wet paper towel. There was no point brushing my hair. It would do its own thing anyway; the salty curls were tighter than ever without the extra weight which had pulled them into ringlets.

Half-past eight found me sitting on the basement steps of a tall, Edwardian terraced house hiding from the freshening wind. A motorbike was parked on a small area of crumbling concrete that would have once been the front garden, so it looked as though someone was home. A small plaque on the door at the bottom of the area steps advertised the office as belonging to 'Mr W P Marshall, Security Consultant and Private Investigator'. At least he was still in business.

An hour later, the office was still closed. I sat frozen to the stone, my gloved hands wedged under my armpits in an attempt to hug myself warm.

'Clear off. Find somewhere else to squat!' a voice shouted. I looked up. A scruffy boy carrying a motorbike helmet was locking the front door of the house to which the basement belonged. 'There's a hostel on Eastbeach Street.'

I stood up as he jogged down the steps from the front door and peered over the area railing.

'I'm here on business. I'm waiting for Mr Marshall,' I explained, squinting up.

'I'm Mr Marshall.'

'No, you're not.' Even silhouetted against the white sky, the boy looked about my age, a babe in arms at the time of Walt Marshall's correspondence with Theo.

'Yes, I am. What do you want?' He ran lightly down the steps, pushed past and pulled a key from the pocket of his jeans.

'I'm looking for my father.'

'There's a lost kids meeting point at the Tourist Information Office on the Promenade.'

'I'm not lost. And I'm not a kid.'

He looked at me more closely. 'How old are you?'

'Twenty. Nearly twenty-one,' I lied. He grunted and pushed open the door.

'Don't just stand there, then.' He stood aside to let me enter. For a split second I hesitated. I was being invited into an empty building by a stranger. No one knew I was here. He was quite a lot taller than me, of slim build, a wiry type with cheekbones like coat hangers. Probably stronger than he looked.

But I was cold and impatient. I swallowed my reservations and swaggered past. The door slammed shut. He switched on a light. A dingy hallway led almost directly onto an office on the right. Cluttered desk, chair, filing cabinet. He walked straight ahead to a tiny kitchen, dumped his motorbike helmet on top of the fridge, picked up a kettle and filled it from the tap.

'Tea?'

'Coffee, please.'

The kitchen walls were dirty white with mould in the corners. There were mice droppings on the faded lino. High above the sink, a small window with a flaking wooden frame looked out at an overgrown back garden. It was strange to look up to see the lawn, though 'lawn' was a rather grand name for the scruffy patch of grass above the steps from the back door.

'Did you say you were looking for your father or my father?' He dropped a teabag into a stained mug with 'Keep Calm and Crack the Case' written on the side. He spooned instant coffee into a china cup with a chipped saucer.

'My father. Though perhaps I'm looking for your father too. Is his name Walt?'

'Yes. But he's busy with another case.'

My heart leapt with relief.

'When can I see him?'

'You can see me instead.' The young man poured boiling water into two mugs, spilling a hot puddle onto the kitchen top and splashing his hand. He swore under his breath. 'It's fifty quid for an initial consultation. After that it's £100 a day plus expenses.'

'I need to talk to Walt Marshall,' I insisted.

'Not happening, dimples!'

'Are you even qualified to be an investigator?' I snapped.

'Qualified by years of practice.'

I pointedly looked him up and down. 'Are you bunking off school?'

'It's not about age. It's all about experience,' he winked. 'I've grown up in the business. Began helping Dad with surveillance when I was eight. Besides, much of our work involves computer records, and I know how to make my way around someone else's IT system, if you know what I mean.'

'One sugar for me,' I said as he poured milk into the cups.

'Don't have any. It's poison. More addictive than heroin, apparently.'

'And your name is?' My voice was as frosty as my feet.

'Zavier Marshall. You?'

'Av… ummm… Claire Hewitt.' He looked at me for a second longer than was necessary. He'd noticed my slip.

He carried the drinks through to the office, slopping my coffee into the saucer. I followed behind, lugging my backpack. He switched on an old-fashioned electric fire and we sat opposite each other, either side of the desk. He swept away some old newspapers and threw them in the corner.

'How did you get my father's name? Was he recommended?'

I pulled the brown envelope out of my rucksack and rifled through the papers, finding the letter from Walt to Theo. He glanced briefly at the letterhead.

'Looks like you've been digging up fossils,' he commented. 'Eighteen years ago.'

'More or less.'

He tossed the letter back without appearing to read the contents. 'Fifty quid, or drink your coffee and push off. I've got work to do.'

I glanced around the office. A television set and PlayStation in one corner. Fish and chip wrappers spilling from the waste-paper bin. Empty lager bottles lined up on the window sill, glowing green and brown in the morning light. A pile of unopened junk mail. Dead flies. A surfboard propped against the wall.

'You don't look overwhelmed with work,' I replied. '£20.'

'Forty.'

'Twenty-five and that's my final offer. I want to speak to the boss, not the teaboy.'

'Nice!' He leaned back in his chair and ran his eyes over my hair, my face, my clothes. A long, assessing gaze. 'OK. But I want the money upfront.'

I pulled my wallet from my back pocket, not wanting him to guess at the bulging money belt under my jumper and coat. I only had a £20 note.

'I don't take credit cards.'

I rummaged through my pockets, counting out loose change from my visit to the sea-front café earlier. £3 and ninety pence. My cheeks grew hot.

'That'll do.' He grabbed the notes and coins and stuffed them in the pocket of his leather jacket. He hunted around the desk, unearthed a biro and wrote the date on the back of an old envelope.

'What was your name again?'

'Claire Hewitt. I see you have a memory for detail!'

He ignored the jibe.

'What's your father's name?'

'I don't know.'

'You don't know.' He put down the pen. 'Have you asked your mother?'

'She died when I was a baby.'

'Right. I guess I won't be finding the answer at the Missing Persons Bureau.'

'No.'

'Any other relatives you can ask?' He tapped the biro on the desk.

'I don't think so.'

I passed him back the letter his father had written to Theo. He glanced at it again but didn't stop tapping.

'This is what your father found out,' I continued. 'I was wondering if there was anything more he wasn't saying. Perhaps he was trying to be sensitive. My mother had just died. Maybe he knew something else. There might be more in your files.'

'Who's this Mr T Gage?'

I hesitated. 'A friend of my mother's.' He must have picked up something from my tone because he stopped tapping his pen.

'But not of your father?'

'Obviously not. If you'd read the letter properly you'd know that Mr Gage employed *your* father to find out the name of *my* father and anyone who might be a relative of Mum.'

'Basically, you're asking me to find good-time Charlie.'

'Who?'

'A quick splitter… someone who doesn't hang around.'

I winced at his words.

'I have these photos.' I showed him the pictures of Mum on the beach and standing in front of the Ferris wheel with the mystery man.

'Is this him?'

'I don't know… but he was with my mum when she was pregnant. They look like friends at least, don't you think? If he's not my dad, he might know who is.'

He looked closely at the picture, his floppy blond fringe falling across his forehead.

'You don't look like him.'

'It's difficult to tell with his sunglasses on.'

'This was taken in Westhatch.'

'How can you tell?' Excitement fluttered in my breast.

'See that cliff in the background? That's Jumper's Mount. I recognise the shape against the skyline. I used to have rides on that big wheel as a child. It was demolished a few years back. The new funfair moved to the west end of town, near Fun World Holiday Camp.'

'My mother used to work there.'

'I saw that.' He handed back his father's letter to Theo.

'So what are you going to do?' I asked.

He stood up and walked to the end of the room and opened a door hiding behind a wilting yucca plant. I stood up and peered in. Another dingy room, this one lined with ancient metal filing cabinets, box files piled on their tops and heaped on the floor.

'Dad doesn't do computers. I can look through our files for a start. I'll probably check out Fun World, perhaps speak to someone in their human resources department. I warn you though, personnel records are confidential even if they still have them dating back that far. It'll take some nifty footwork to winkle anything out of them. I could try hacking into their systems. Then there might be something about your mother's death in the local rag, an inquest report perhaps. Somewhere there'll be an electronic trail.'

'How long will it take?'

'Give me a couple of days. But I need to know you can pay. You're looking at around £200 to start with.' He must have seen my expression. 'But because I like you I can do it for £175. Can you lay your hands on that kind of dosh?'

I looked at the dusty filing cabinets. I was itching to start looking through their contents.

'Can I use your toilet?'

'Sure. It's the door on your right before you get to the kitchen.' I made my way back into the hall, found the toilet and locked myself in. The seat was up. I tugged off a couple of sheets of loo roll. Holding the cheap paper between finger and thumb, I gingerly closed the lid and sat down. I lifted my jacket and jumper and unzipped my money belt. I counted out £175 and put another forty in my wallet. I didn't want to get caught out again without accessible cash. I pulled the chain and hurried back to the office, placing the notes on the desk in front of him. He raised an eyebrow.

'I'm not going to ask where you conjured that from!' He counted the money, rolled it up and put it in his pocket. 'OK. Give me your mobile number.' I reeled it off and he jotted it on the back of the envelope. 'Address?'

'I'm travelling at the moment. I'm on a gap year, backpacking around the country. I thought I'd take the opportunity to visit Westhatch while touring the south coast.'

'Where are you staying?'

'Bed and breakfast.'

'Yes, but where?'

'In Westhatch. I can't remember the address. It's near the Promenade. When can I speak to your father?'

'I'll pass this on.'

'I'd like to see him in person.'

'He's a very busy man.'

'He might remember something.' The hot, dusty smell of the electric fire was making my head ache.

'It's eighteen years ago. I'll ring you in a couple of days. Here's my card.'

'Do I get a receipt?'

'What do I look like? A supermarket? No refunds, no returns in this joint, curly!'

He stood up. Obviously I'd had my £23.90 worth of time. I picked up my rucksack and we walked into the hall.

'I know where you live.' I nodded to the ceiling, indicating the house above, and fortified my voice. 'So I'll be back if I don't hear anything.'

'Trembling already,' he retorted, slamming the door behind me.

I climbed the basement steps and wandered along the road. Could I trust him to look into the matter properly? I should have insisted I speak to his father, even if it was only on the telephone. I'd been fobbed off, possibly fleeced.

Gulls wheeled overhead, their cries grating against my nerves and shredding my thoughts to tatters. I began to shake uncontrollably. Exhaustion from my night awake on the beach was kicking in. I needed to find somewhere warm so I could dump my rucksack and crash for the rest of the day.

My bike was still chained to the lamppost on the Promenade. I calculated it would be safe there for now. A few doors down from Zavier Marshall's office and on the other side of the road, an identical Edwardian terraced house was advertising itself as a bed and breakfast establishment. Paint was peeling from the window frames and the garden was neglected, but a blue neon 'Vacancies' sign shone in the downstairs window. No one's first choice, but maybe that was a point in its favour. If Marcus or Paloma guessed I was in Westhatch, they would probably search the neat, sorbet-coloured hotels near the seafront first. This was more in keeping with my new identity – an orphaned drifter searching for a new life. Plus, it was likely to be cheap. I knocked on the door. An overweight woman in slippers answered.

'No hawkers, no traders,' she stated, pointed to a small sign in the window.

'I'm not selling anything.'

She eyed my rucksack suspiciously.

'I'm looking for a room.'

'It's £25 a night, including a cooked breakfast... Payment in advance.'

'Can I see the room first?'

'Follow me.' Her slippers slapped against the cheap laminate flooring as she led me to the stairs. Leaning heavily on the banister, she heaved herself up and pushed open a door on the landing. A double bedroom, overwhelmingly pink, with high-intensity roses on the bedspread. Ruffled curtains at the bay window. A grey veneer of dust had settled on the cheap, white chest of drawers and bedside cabinet. The landlady waddled to the radiator and turned the valve. The ancient metal banged and glugged as it filled with hot water.

'Bathroom's down the hall, but you have your own sink. Tea and coffee-making facilities provided.' She gestured to an ancient kettle and two cups placed upside down on their saucers.

I walked to the window, and pushed back the net curtains. Looking along the road I could just see the steps leading up to Zavier's front door.

'I'll take it,' I said and threw my bag on the bed.

'You can't stay now. Earliest check-in is four o'clock. Breakfast is from 7.30 to nine and you have to vacate each morning by ten at the latest. No food in the room.'

My heart sank. Despite the garish duvet, the bed looked clean and inviting.

'Can I leave my bag?'

'If you leave your money.'

We walked down the stairs. I took my wallet out of my back pocket and handed her the two £20 notes transferred from my money belt earlier.

'That'll be £15 change,' I said when she folded it into her apron pocket. She lumbered to the kitchen to retrieve her handbag and reluctantly counted out three £5 notes.

'I'll see you later,' I said.

'No food in your room, mind. And the door's bolted at eleven.'

I was desperate to catch up on a few hours of sleep. It was a quarter to eleven. There were over five hours to kill before my head could hit the pillow.

Back out on the street, I revisited the plans I'd made in the night. I might as well move the schedule forward by twenty-four hours, I told myself, and do now what I'd planned for the next day.

The weight of my money belt made me uneasy. Where could I hide a large amount of cash? I didn't want to carry £3,000 on my person and hadn't wanted to leave any money at the bed and breakfast. Dividing up the cash would halve the risk of losing everything if I ran into a mugger. I needed a safety deposit box, but I didn't want to open one in my old name, and I guessed a bank wouldn't let me open one in my new name without having a new account, which would take too long to open. Plus, a safety deposit box was likely to be prohibitively expensive.

I walked briskly towards the seafront and turned a corner onto the Promenade. Away from the shelter of the buildings I was suddenly exposed. A witch of a wind clawed at my clothes and sliced the skin on my cheeks. Long waves, edged with boiling froth, raced up the beach with a vicious hiss. Scudding clouds transformed the previous day's smiling sun into a ghostly face hidden behind a veil. The Promenade stretched away from me in both directions, embracing the grey of the sea and the grey of the sky in its unflinching concrete arms. I consulted a map of the resort on a salt-encrusted noticeboard and turned right.

Raised flower beds lined my route. The soil had been recently dug over and was sprouting chewing-gum wrappers and crushed tin cans while waiting for the spring planting. I passed a couple of elderly men on a bench staring out at the churning waters, smoke from their cigarettes whipping away with the wind. A skateboarder whizzed past, snaking between a lady with a shopping trolley and a workman in a fluorescent jacket.

As I neared the town centre, the number of pedestrians increased. Mothers, some younger than me, chatted on mobiles, ignoring the whining from their overloaded buggies. Distorted pop music blared from the amusement arcades facing the beach,

each battling to attract the unemployed hostel-dwellers who worshipped at the altars of luck and good fortune.

I asked directions from a woman at a bus stop. After another five-minute trudge, I crossed the road and took the slow incline into town. It didn't take long to reach the Leisure Centre, a vast warehouse of breeze-block and glass. The receptionist raised an eyebrow when I paid to swim.

'My friend's got my swimming bag,' I explained. 'I've been parking the car.'

I pushed open the door. The changing rooms belched hot air and chlorine. For an instant I was reminded of the dome with its damp heat and echoing ceiling. I swallowed back a bitter wave of grief and ducked into the ladies' toilets. I took £1,500 from my money belt and wrapped it in my beanie hat. I flushed the toilet and sidled back to the lockers. Two women were chatting in front of the mirrors, their backs to me. I carefully lifted my jumper and extracted the bundle from underneath. Throwing the money-filled hat into a locker, I inserted a pound coin in the slot and slammed the door. Pocketing the locker key with its rubber wristband, I ducked out of the changing rooms.

A coachload of children had arrived in the foyer as I sidled out. Trailing carrier bags and rolled-up towels, they chattered excitedly about the swimming lesson ahead. As a couple of harassed teachers guided them through the turnstiles, I slipped unseen past the receptionist five minutes after I'd arrived.

I continued walking inland, up the hill and past some rundown shops and a statue of Queen Victoria until I reached Westhatch-on-Sea railway station. Trains into London departed every hour. I had just over ten minutes to wait. I purchased a cheap day return and pushed my ticket through the automatic barrier. Several passengers were milling around the platform, looking at the departure and arrivals screens, texting, reading newspapers, drinking coffee. Nobody was interested in me.

I bought a cheese sandwich and can of cola at a kiosk, and sat and ate an early lunch on a cold metal bench. As I finished, the train pulled in with screech of brakes. The doors bleeped, decompressed with a hiss, and slid open. Finding a window seat, I slumped down in relief. At last I was somewhere warm and comparatively comfortable. My shoulders, stiff with exhaustion and fear, began to defrost. I felt rather than saw the slow pull of the train as it sped to a rhythmic clickity-clack, glimpsing back gardens and a flash of green fields before sinking into oblivion.

I awoke as the train pulled into London Victoria station. While I was sleeping, a businessman had sat opposite. He folded his newspaper and stood to retrieve his briefcase from the overhead luggage rack. Catching his eye, I became aware of a trickle of saliva on the side of my mouth. I coughed and wiped my chin with the back of my hand, suddenly frightened. I checked for my money belt. Still safe. Picking up my coat, I staggered off the carriage, light-headed and a little unsteady.

The concourse was filled with people rushing in every direction, balls in a pinball machine, particles wheeling through space. Briefcases, laptop bags, high heels: an overwhelming chaos of movement and noise. I made a beeline for a cash machine and while waiting in the queue racked my brain for a possible PIN number. When it was my turn I inserted the Greenacres credit card and punched in the code for Ava. One, two, two, one. It didn't work. I tried the code for Gage. Seven, one, seven, five. Nothing. Embarrassed, I snatched the card and moved away from those queuing behind me. I only had three chances to get the code right before the dispenser would confiscate the card. I had one guess left.

I ran over the other options. My birthday. Theo's birthday. Theo's name in code came to twenty, eight, five, fifteen – much too long. His initials, TCG for Theodore Christopher Gage, came out as twenty, three, seven. I re-joined the queue and after a few minutes reinserted the card and pressed two, zero, three, seven. It worked. I requested £750 pounds, the maximum amount I could withdraw for one transaction. Anxious not to advertise the presence of my money belt or the whereabouts of the wallet in my back pocket to onlookers, I stuffed the cash in my jacket, zipped up the pocket and sidled away before heading out of the station in search of a bank.

Although the lunchtime rush had passed, there was still a queue when I found the branch I wanted. I extracted my own bank card from my wallet and shuffled towards the counter.

'I'd like to withdraw all my money and close this account.'

'Pardon?' the cashier asked, leaning forward. 'Could you speak up, please?'

'I'd like to close this account.' I pushed the card towards her.

'Do you have any proof of identity?' I pulled my driver's licence from my wallet. The cashier looked at the photo on my driving licence and looked at me.

'My hair's a different colour... but still curly!' I said anxiously.

'Excuse me. I must just check with my supervisor.' She disappeared through a door and after a minute returned with a colleague. They both studied my features carefully.

'Have you a more recent photo ID?'

'Sorry. I only had my hair done a few days ago. Is it a problem?'

'I just need to ask a few security questions. I'm sure you'll understand. Can you tell me where you were born?'

'Westhatch-on-Sea General Hospital.'

'Your mother's maiden name?'

'Hewitt.'

'One last question...' The cashier fidgeted on her chair. 'This is one of the security questions you chose when you first opened the account,' she explained. 'What is the name of the first person you fell in love with?'

I swallowed hard.

'Marcus Becker.'

I scuttled along the busy London street as though a huge red target had been daubed on my forehead. The cashier had handed over an envelope containing nearly £1,800 and I'd zipped it into the inside pocket of my jacket. I was a pickpocket's paradise.

After a few minutes I became aware of a girl shadowing me. She was small, furtive, her shoulders hunched forward. I glanced sideways, not wanting her to know I'd become aware of her presence. It took a moment to realise the girl was my own reflection in a department store window. My appearance was a shock. Wild black hair, shapeless jacket, heavy walking boots which made my legs appear painfully thin. And I was walking differently too. Perhaps this was what body dysmorphia was like – incomprehension at the contrast between a mental image and reality. Somewhere I'd crossed a line. I was no longer one of life's winners. I looked like a loser: defiant, angry, vulnerable, scared.

Any missing person's investigation would discover fairly quickly that I'd withdrawn money in London. I'd chosen the capital because it was an easy place to disappear. From here, I could travel anywhere in the country. Who would believe I would be making my way back to Westhatch rather than running as far as I could? I would hide right under their noses until I decided it was time to reappear. But first I needed to sort out some loose ends.

I stopped off at a mobile phone shop and bought a cheap pay-as-you-go handset. I wasn't sure whether my old mobile could be traced if it was switched off, but I knew a network could trace the location where calls were made. I nursed an overpriced cappuccino at the café next door and checked the instruction booklet. Once familiarised with the basics, I plucked up my courage and switched on my old mobile. A voicemail from Paloma had been left for me that morning.

'Ava! Why you not tell me you is ill? Marcus has forbad me come visit. I worry about you all alone without Papa-Boss. You come stay with me tonight. I come by after work to see how you is getting on. In case you need doctor. Ring me back, Babyboss. When you wakes up.'

Marcus had sent a couple of texts, one at eight o'clock that morning. 'Hope you are feeling better. Don't think about coming in today. Take your time.'

Yes, he'd like me to take my time. His mock concern made me sick. Well, he's going to get what he wants. I'm going to take a very long time.

It was strange. They still thought I was at home in bed with a bug. So much had happened, yet for them life continued as normal. I'd made my grand exit but so far nobody had noticed. Should I be relieved or annoyed? I comforted myself by imagining the pain and regret they would feel for keeping me in the dark about my parentage.

A second text from Marcus had been sent at 9.47am. 'Just discovered there was a break-in last night. Your father's lab and study have been vandalised. Probably just kids. I've called the police. It doesn't look as though they got into the safe. Don't think they took anything. If you know the combination, you will be able to check. Let me know if you heard anything last night. I'm waiting for the police to arrive. Call me.'

My hands shook as I exited the message. A burglary? What were the chances that a few hours after I'd removed cash and documents from the safe someone else had broken in? Talk about bad luck. When they realised I was missing, there was every chance they would connect me with the crime, particularly as my fingerprints would be all over the safe door.

I finished my coffee and tried to digest the implications of the message. I'd probably lost my head start. The police would take my disappearance more seriously now there had been a crime at the Institute. Marcus might check the credit card statements and notice my withdrawals. In Theo's absence, there was every chance he would push for a full criminal investigation into my actions.

My mobile rang. Startled, I checked the number. Uncle Colin. Drat! Couldn't that man leave me alone? I switched the phone to silent and waited to see whether he would leave a message or send a text. Unable to restrain my curiosity, I checked my voicemail.

'Munchkin, I'm driving down to see you this evening. You didn't sound at all well yesterday. I take my godfather role seriously, you know! See you later.'

A spurt of anger surged through my chest. If he had taken his role seriously, he would have told me the truth. I couldn't resist texting back.

'Don't come. No need.' After a few moments my phone pinged.

'I'm worried. Can I come and stay at the farmhouse tonight?'

'Don't bother. I know everything!' I swung my foot impatiently against the table leg while waiting for his reply.

'It's not what you think,' my screen displayed after several minutes.

'You don't know what I'm thinking!'

'That I let you down.'

I sniffed and dabbed my eyes with a paper napkin.

'Exactly! It's unforgiveable!' I texted.

'Don't say that. I need to explain in person. Then you'll understand.'

'Don't want to talk. Still getting my head round everything.'

'Have you spoken to Paloma or Marcus?'

'No.'

'Don't talk to Marcus. I have concerns. You'll understand once we've chatted. Maybe we could meet privately?'

'Why?' I tapped.

'Marcus doesn't like me. His close relationship with your father is beginning to exclude everyone else.'

I thought back to Colin's visit the previous Friday. I'd been busy finishing off my last day as a greenhouse apprentice, tidying up the tools in the store cupboard, excited at the prospect of moving to the gift shop. My godfather had stopped to say hello and give me a hug on his way to the laboratory. He'd tried to help me with a pair of long-handled shears and ended up nicking my hand. It was nothing, but he'd made a fuss of dabbing it with his handkerchief. Marcus was passing and had spoken sharply to him for interfering with my work. He told me I had to write up an accident report and get some antiseptic and a plaster from the first-aid box. I'd watched as he escorted Uncle Colin downstairs. They didn't shake hands or anything. I'd been surprised at the coldness between them.

Colin texted: 'Let's meet at a pub somewhere tonight. I'll explain everything.'

'I'm ill!' I replied. And I did feel ill, drained and sick to the stomach. I shouldn't have started this conversation. I switched off my phone. It was a good thing he didn't know I was only a short tube ride away from his London office.

Obviously he hadn't heard about the burglary. If he had, he would have voiced some concern over the whereabouts of his precious file. The thought crossed my mind that perhaps that was what the robbers were after. Uncle Colin was pretty high up in the world of scientific research, a world where shady multinationals fought hard for the commercial rights to any new discovery.

A waitress came and cleared the half-eaten food I could no longer stomach. I ordered another coffee, not because I wanted one but because I needed to buy more time in the warm.

I scrolled through my saved numbers and began transferring them from my old phone onto my new pay-as-you-go handset. When finished, I deleted all text messages and contacts. I dropped the expensive device – a present for my eighteenth birthday – into the cold dregs of my coffee and crunched the top of the cardboard cup. I wanted a complete break from the past… for the moment. On my way out, I threw the cup into a large rubbish bin. *Track that!* I thought, and walked away.

I caught a bus to the West End and visited several other cash machines, withdrawing as much as I could on the company credit card until I reached the limit and the card was declined. By the time I arrived back at Victoria Station for my return journey to Westhatch, I was carrying nearly £4,000 stuffed into various pockets, down the back of my pants and shoved into my socks while visiting the ladies' toilets near Oxford Circus.

Back at Westhatch, I returned to the swimming pool. This time I carried a plastic bag with what could have been a swimming kit inside. In reality I'd purchased a couple of soft rolls, a packet of ham, a bunch of bananas and a bottle of water from a convenience store. Thankfully there was a different girl on reception. I opened the locker and retrieved the stashed cash and my beanie hat. It was five-thirty. At last I could check in at the bed and breakfast for a proper sleep.

Chapter 5

I awoke the next morning with a start of fear, disorientated by the unexpected direction of the morning light through the floral curtains of Mrs Bungay's bed and breakfast. In my previous life, the world had always been as I'd left it the night before, and the night before that, and the night before that. For a moment, I couldn't remember how I'd come to be sleeping somewhere other than the old farmhouse at Greenacres. I sat up, shocked by the reflection in the mirrored wardrobe opposite.

I ran my hand through the black tangle of hair that rose like a demonic halo around my face. What had I been thinking? Another grand gesture. Cutting my hair and severing myself from all that I'd ever known and loved, and all because of a childish sense of anger and spite. And the cut had been deep. My face was grey, my eyes sunken coals. How could this white-faced apparition in the mirror be the polished and pampered daughter of Theo Gage? She'd disappeared along with her fiery locks. Now a new self had emerged from the cinders, someone fractured and brittle whose memories of the past and motivations for the future were changed forever.

My stomach moaned. Something in me was alive after all and demanding to be fed. Not wanting to miss breakfast, I showered quickly in the bathroom down the corridor and pulled on jeans and a dark jumper. Mrs Bungay must have heard me moving about because she was banging pans in the kitchen as I crept down the stairs.

A place for one had been set at the dining room table. It appeared I was the only guest. Tinned grapefruit had been slopped into a bowl, a glacé cherry placed on the top. I sat down and ate the bitter fruit.

'Tea or coffee?' Mrs Bungay heaved herself through the doorway and removed the dirty bowl.

'Coffee, please.'

'It's instant.'

'That's OK.'

'Toast?'

'Yes, please.'

'There's only white.'

'I like white… Do you have any muesli?'

'No. Can't be doing with the stuff. Rabbit food. You can have cornflakes.'

'Thanks.'

She disappeared into the kitchen, her slippers flapping. By the time I finished the cereal, she returned with a mug of coffee and a plate of eggs, bacon and baked beans. The yolk had split. Watery juice from the beans spread like orange blood across the greasy plate. My appetite vanished, but as I'd paid for the food I forced it down. It was a relief when she returned with a rack of toast to soak up the fat.

After negotiating my way around the crumbs in the butter dish, I wrenched the dusty lid off the marmalade jar, and scraped out the last of the orange jam. The sticky jar must have been in the cupboard for months and I wondered how long it had been since her last paying guest. I remembered the dainty pats of butter and china pots of jam that Paloma served in the Greenacres café. My hostess must have seen my downcast expression.

'I can buy more for tomorrow!' she said. 'That's if you're staying.'

'I'll be staying.'

After breakfast, I washed my dirty underwear in the bedroom sink, leaving my socks and knickers draped over the radiator. My landlady knocked on my door at nine-fifty saying she needed to clean the room. I knew she was chucking me out.

Once again, she demanded payment for the next night's stay in advance. After counting the notes into her fleshy hand, I hurried out into the cold, carrying my money belt to the Leisure Centre and locking the majority of my cash away.

I mooched along the Promenade, shivering and bored. The call of the gulls was shrill on the February wind. Waves heaved onto the shingle like overweight aquatic mammals, inching up the stony incline only to be sucked back into the depths. It began to drizzle. I buried my hands in my pockets and ploughed on, my face and hair damp with the misty rain. Ten minutes later I was standing at the entrance to Fun World Holiday Camp at the west end of the Promenade.

Life moves in circles. We like to believe we're travelling forwards, but in reality we're fixed to the cycle of the seasons, the weeks, the hours that rotate around the clock face, the tyranny of our appetites, the tedious duties that endlessly return, the oppression of our genes. Chicken or egg? Free will or predestination? Trapped in the loops of time and the prison of our natures, we cling to a merry-go-round of learned behaviours and inherited predispositions, too scared or indolent to jump off and disrupt the pattern. And there I was standing where my mother must have stood all those years before, attracted by the mandatory jollity of the holiday camp, returning like a salmon to the beginning of my life's journey.

She'd been a couple of years younger than me when she started work at the holiday camp. An orphan too. I tried to imagine what she must have been like. A young girl, unsure and vulnerable, in need of a place in the world and a community of people to give her a sense of belonging. Instead, she'd met a man and been badly let down, left with a baby when she was no more than my age. Our situations were not so different. I'd been let down too and had to pick up the pieces. I wanted to know why.

There had been lies in my past, but perhaps there had also been tragedy. Maybe my mother's story had been one of young love torn apart by accident or illness. Maybe his family hadn't approved. Perhaps my biological father never knew of my existence. Maybe he'd been an irresponsible scoundrel, looking for a good time with no interest in the consequences of his actions. Worst of all, perhaps I'd been the result of a violent attack. Whatever had happened, I needed to know the answer. I wanted to stare the truth straight in the eye and know the story of my existence. Only by unravelling the past could I understand my genetic inheritance and step into the future. If possible, I wanted to meet the man who created me. Now I saw my restless, impetuous nature in a new light. Perhaps on some subterranean level I had always known I didn't belong at Greenacres.

I gazed up at two enormous plastic statues standing either side of the tarmac drive. They held in their shiny, three-fingered hands an overhead sign that read 'Fun World Holiday Camp. Where Magic Happens'. The characters were anthropomorphised junk food, a giant pizza and a hot dog. I didn't like the sly smile on the pizza's face. The red slash of her lips had been made from a slice of plastic pepper. She had a mushroom for a nose and sliced tomatoes for eyes. I knew it was a girl for she wore olives for earrings. A slice taken from her body resembled a slit in a skirt. Cartoon legs, shapely in pink heels, peeped through the oozing crust.

The hot dog's features were drawn with dollops of ketchup – a clownish nose and mouth, and a pair of sinister red eyes with dark pupils. His limbs were thin and jointed like an insect. He wore his bread roll like a cape, folded closely around his body against the sea breeze. His single accessory was a zigzag of yellow mustard from chin to groin.

I stepped under the arch and wandered up the wet drive, drawn by the desire to tread where my mother had walked. Printed banners flapped in the wind. 'Making Dreams Come True.' 'It's Your Time.' 'Relax, Refresh, Recharge.' Photographs of blond families smiled at me as I passed. Children running across sandy beaches. Toned parents lounging by the pool. Teenagers dancing under fluorescent lights. Banks of daffodils and tulips lined the drive, the blooms opening unseasonably early, as early as those nurtured under the warmth of the dome. As I drew closer, I saw the flowers were plastic facsimiles, crudely made and dusted with a fine layer of damp salt and dirt.

I passed a crazy golf course, the gates locked and the ticket booth shuttered. I rounded a bend. The first of the caravans appeared, cream and pale green, standing to attention in neat rows, each hedged off from its neighbour and with a gravel parking space to the front. Most of the caravans looked empty, but I passed an overweight couple huddling in their coats, hoods up, on the plastic decking attached to their static holiday home, drinking from steaming mugs. Faded washing flapped on the line that they'd rigged up between their caravan and a nearby tree. I wondered why they didn't bother to take it down. The drizzle was strengthening into rain.

I approached a barrier into the car park. A security guard looked up from his newspaper. He leaned from the kiosk and watched my approach. I hoped he wasn't going to ask for proof I was a resident.

'If you've come for the interviews, you need to check in at reception.'

'Thanks,' I shouted, ducking under the barrier.

Although it was nearly half-past ten, Fun World had a 'just waking up' feel. A man in brown overalls was litter-picking the walkways with a long-handled grabber. A woman walked away from a small supermarket swinging a plastic bottle of milk. A row of lager bottles balanced on a wall by the entrance to the amusement arcade waiting to be cleared away, the ground beneath strewn with cigarette butts. An open-mouthed bin in the shape of a penguin gaped hungrily at the rubbish.

A wrought-iron signpost directed me to the reception straight ahead. A flipchart had been placed outside the door. The top page fluttered with the words 'Interviewing Today' in red marker. Underneath someone had written, 'Join the Fun World Family. Great career opportunities. Entertainment,

Housekeeping, Maintenance, Catering.' I pushed open the door. Several heads turned as I entered.

'Pink Jacket or housekeeping?' a receptionist chanted.

'Sorry?'

'Are you interviewing for a Pink Jacket or chalet maid job?'

I didn't know what a Pink Jacket was so I answered, 'Chalet maid.'

'Name?'

'Claire Hewitt.' The receptionist consulted a clipboard.

'You're not on the list.'

'Oh!' I exclaimed, feigning annoyance.

'Did you ring?'

'Yes.'

'Dimwit Debby again! Fill out this form. You'll be called in to see Mrs Ozzles in about an hour. You'll have to go last.'

I took the form from the girl. Mrs Ozzles! The woman who'd written to Theo all those years ago was still working here. A spasm of excitement squeezed my chest. This was my chance to meet her. Perhaps I could ask if she remembered my mother and any boyfriends she might have had.

'Have you got a pen?' I asked.

The receptionist tutted and passed me a biro, unimpressed that I'd come so ill-prepared.

I sat next to a small woman wearing a headscarf. She glanced at me nervously and looked back down at her form. She'd written her name with an elegant flourish, but the rest of the boxes were blank. A couple of girls about my age sat opposite, their skin thickly oiled with foundation, lips shimmering, eyelashes as black as spiders' legs.

I was glad to be in the warm. I rubbed my cold hands on my trouser legs before writing my name and date of birth at the top of the form. The woman next to me was watching. My hand hesitated over the box asking for my National Insurance number.

'You have NI?' she whispered.

'What?'

'Sssshh. You have NI number? I don't have number. Friend said is OK… but…'

'No… I don't have a number,' I mumbled, beginning to realise some of the difficulties that lay ahead now that I was no longer Ava Gage. 'What did your friend say?'

'He say holiday camp gives work. I am good worker.' She gestured to her form. 'This paper is hard for me.'

'Me too,' I admitted, realising she was not much older than me despite her frumpy appearance.

'What is this?' she asked, pointing to a box headed 'Current Residence'.

'They're asking where you live.'

'OK.' She began scribbling. I wrote down 23 Seacombe Road, Zavier Marshall's address. I wasn't about to reveal where I was staying. In any case, I thought I'd paid Zavier enough money for him to hold on to my mail for me.

'And this?' She pointed to the next box headed 'Educational Achievements'.

'That's where you write your academic qualifications.' She still looked puzzled. 'Your school results.'

'School! But I am cleaner. School no matter.'

A door marked 'Private' opened to the side of the reception desk and a square woman emerged with a punch of perfume.

'Sonya Kreshnik!'

The girl stood up and picked up the plastic carrier bag at her feet. I smiled as she glanced back, her olive forehead creasing with anxiety.

I had a file of exam certificates back in my bedroom at Greenacres, but I didn't think my batch of A and A* results would be of use to a chalet maid. I left the question blank, planning to say I'd dropped out of full-time education. It was the truth. After A levels, I'd decided not to go to university. I'd had enough of studying and wanted to get out into the real world.

I completed the rest of the application as best I could. I didn't cite my work experience at the dome or provide any references. If news of my disappearance reached Westhatch, I didn't want Mrs Ozzles connecting the missing Ava Gage with her potential employee, Claire Hewitt.

I gazed around the reception area. A row of staff photographs lined one wall. The largest picture was of a middle-aged man with greying hair and unnaturally white teeth. I scrunched up my eyes to read the name underneath: 'Maxwell King, chief executive.' The only other middle-aged men in the row were Chucky Skittles, entertainer, and Sid Tulitt, maintenance manager. I searched for any resemblance they might have to the man in the photo with my mother, or to myself. I saw nothing.

The door opened. Sonya emerged, smiling. She hurried over and whispered, 'Is OK. No NI is OK. I get job.'

'Congratulations. What did she say?'

'They give me cash moneys at end of each week. I clean caravans. You can too.'

'I hope so,' I murmured, an idea forming in my mind.

What better way of hiding from my past than working incognito at Fun World, cash in hand, no questions asked and able to do a little investigating of my own?

The door opened. Mrs Ozzles walked back into reception. This time I looked at her more closely. Tailored suit, tombstone grey. A silky blouse revealing a slash of crumpled cleavage. A scaffolding of sticky lacquer lifting her hair into an airy chignon, a few girlish tendrils trying to disguise the absence of neck between a square jaw and a pair of massive shoulders. Lines of foundation collected in the cracks and creases of her sagging cheeks like new mortar between old bricks. An ancient monument with a new coat of paint. She called another name. A middle-aged woman followed the trail of perfume through the door.

Moments later a young man in a shocking pink coat and tie exploded into the reception area.

'Pink Jackets! Pink Jackets, come with me. Auditions now in the club bar.' He gestured to the two girls. 'I hope you're buzzing, my beauties.' They shrugged awkwardly. 'Cheer up! I'm fizzing my bonce off this morning. You've come to the best job in the world. Making people happy!'

A sturdy, fresh-faced youth also stood up. The material of his corduroy trousers whispered as he walked, his thighs rubbing together with an awkward shushing sound. His blond curls and flushed cheeks reminded me of cherubs and tractors – bully fodder if ever I saw it. He would have been the boy at school that nobody picked for their team. I smiled at him as he passed because I too had been the loser once, the girl with the comical hair. His mouth gave a startled twitch in reply. Head down, he hurried towards the door.

'Come on, Salty Spud! Into the pot with the sweet potatoes!' the Pink Jacket holding the door chirruped as the youth passed.

It had been twenty-four hours since I last spoke to Zavier Marshall, too early to nag him for a report, though I itched to know what progress he'd made. I pulled out the pay-as-you-go phone and texted him my new number, saying I'd be in touch the following day. The middle-aged woman stomped back through reception, her lips tight and thin with anger. I guessed her interview hadn't gone well.

I was now the last person sitting in reception. The telephone rang and the receptionist answered.

'Yes. There's one more. Debby didn't have her on the list.' She put down the receiver. 'She'll be with you in a jiffy.' The door opened almost immediately and Mrs Ozzles beckoned me through.

'This way please, Miss …?'

'Hewitt. Claire Hewitt.'

I followed Mrs Ozzles along a short corridor, her square hips and massive shoulders swinging to the click of her heels. If magazines categorised body shapes as apples or pears, Mrs Ozzles was a baked potato. Her tights revealed a relief map of veins, tan ridges curling like earthworms around her calves. We entered an office with 'Housekeeping' on the door. Easing herself behind a desk, she turned to face me.

'My name is Mrs Ozzles. Put your bottom on that chair.'

She held out a heavily ringed hand, which I shook. When our hands parted, she continued reaching across the table. She'd been holding her hand out for the application form, not to shake my own. I passed it over, suddenly aware this wasn't a meeting of equals.

'Claire Hewitt,' she emphasised, as though I hadn't already spoken my name. 'I see you haven't finished completing your form.' She clicked her tongue. 'You've been waiting quite a while.'

'I'm not very good with paperwork. But I'm a good worker. Very reliable.'

'Have you done this kind of work before?'

'Yes... no... but I will work hard.' I thought of the times I'd helped out in the café at Greenacres and potted out seedlings in the greenhouses for a little extra pocket money. 'I've done some waitressing... and worked in horticulture.'

'You haven't given any references.'

'It was all casual. Holiday work... cash in hand.'

'I see.'

'And your schooling?'

I shrugged. 'I dropped out. I didn't get on with my family. I'm on my own now. My stepfather was...' I left the sentence unfinished.

She nodded.

'I just want to make my own way. Forget the past.'

'All right, Claire. I see you've had some difficulties. Without references and a National Insurance number, however, we can only pay cash in hand. You understand?'

'Yes.'

'And you're willing to work hard?'

'Yes.'

'Because I'm something of a stickler.'

'Please. I need this job.'

Mrs Ozzles gave me a hard stare. I looked down at my hands, emulating the downtrodden expression Harmony had worn when she first came to work at the dome.

'Let me see them.' Her eyes had followed mine. She nodded to my hands. I held them across the desk and once again our flesh touched, though this time my fingers were deliberately limp. She inspected my palms with the intensity of a fortune teller.

'It looks like you've done some kind of manual work recently.'

The small cut on the back of my hand when Colin clumsily passed me the garden shears had scabbed over. I'd spent a few hours in the nursery greenhouses at the weekend helping Theo prick out seedlings. There were a couple of scratches and some rough skin from carrying wooden seed trays back and forth. One of my nails had broken and I'd impatiently cut the others short to match. I was grateful I hadn't had a professional manicure recently, although I'd painted my nails black the previous evening at the B&B in a spurt of rebellious boredom. Mrs Ozzles dropped my hands dismissively.

She had a small box of violet creams on her desk. She slipped out a dark chocolate disk and popped it in her mouth.

'Are you a Goth?'

'No.'

'Good. We don't want any of that morbid misery peddled around here.' She chewed and swallowed. 'This is a holiday camp. You need to look happy. Is that your natural hair colour?'

I shook my head.

'I thought not. Try and do something about it. Blonde is a nice summery shade. Of course, it will take a lot of bleach to turn that kind of bluish-black to blonde. Several sessions, in fact. What is your natural colour?'

'Light brown.' I wasn't going to let on I was a carrot-top.

'Pity you dyed it. Chantelle might be able to soften it down to a rich chocolate. The beauty salon here will give you the staff rates. Get yourself a spray tan, use some bronzer. Pink lipstick.

You could be quite pretty if you made an effort. And I don't want to see any more of that black eyeliner. Understood?'

'Yes, Mrs Ozzles.'

'You'll have to start at half-past six each morning cleaning the club bar and entertainment centre from the previous night. You'll need to help with the caravan changeovers. A deep clean of each van in your section. Check the inventory, strip the beds, put out new sheets and towels, sweep the verandas. You go off duty at 2.30. One hour for lunch. We'll get busier throughout the season. Those staying on site at the moment own their own caravans and can visit up to eleven months of the year. It's the half-term holidays the week after next, the launch of our 2003 holiday season. We need to get the whole site ready before then. It means there'll be no time off until the school holidays are over. Nine days on, then four days off. How does that sound?'

'Fine.'

'You can start on Monday. I'll be running an induction session for the new starters. You'll get your uniform and your rota then. You'll be paid at the end of each week. As casual staff, we retain the right to let you go straight away if your work's not up to scratch.'

'Thanks. I appreciate it.'

'I'll see you here on Monday. Nine o'clock sharp.'

'Is this is a good place to work?' I queried, wanting to prolong the interview and glean as much information as I could, perhaps steer the conversation round to my mother.

'For a person with no real work experience, education or references, I would say it's an exceptionally good place to work!'

I was in no doubt I'd spoken out of place.

'Are you the boss of everyone?' I asked, covering my blunder with a veneer of naivety.

'I will be your boss, though for the first few weeks you'll have another chambermaid telling you what to do and showing you the ropes. We all work for Maxwell King. He runs the holiday park, and several others around the country. He built Fun World up from scratch and is an inspiration to all of us of what hard work can achieve. You won't have anything to do with him, of course.'

I opened my mouth to ask if he lived on site, but she unexpectedly smiled. The picket fence of wrinkles around her mouth shifted.

'I see you are inquisitive. Fun World is a family. If you work hard and behave yourself, I'm sure you'll do well. I've got no time for slackers.' She stood up and escorted me to the door. Before opening it, she touched the jade necklace at my throat. 'Pretty. Did you know in China jade is used to attract love? It can also be used to bring money into your life and guard against misfortunes. Let's hope it brings you luck. Asking questions is good. You are interested in learning. Use that to your advantage, but I advise you not to poke your nose where it's not wanted. Like any family, you need to respect other people's privacy... or there'll be a falling out. Monday. First thing. Don't be late.'

Chapter 6

I spent a couple of hours wandering along the seafront and through the town, wasting coins in the amusement arcades to keep dry. The morning drizzle had evolved into icy spears which stung my cheeks and bounced on the pavement like ball bearings. I visited a charity shop and tried on some garments I would usually dodge like a bullet – animal-print stretchy nylon, a neon orange crop top, a jumper with a pink sequinned butterfly on the front – searching for a look that would please Mrs Ozzles but still distance me from my Greenacres past. I ended up buying everything that fitted. I ate lunch in a dingy pizzeria. I didn't have much of an appetite. The clichéd red-and-white checked tablecloths shimmered before my eyes; a sickening optical illusion, or perhaps the precursor to a real migraine.

On my way to the library in search of another temporary refuge from the weather, I passed a battered Ford Escort Estate. A sign on the back window read, 'For sale. £450. Six months tax and MOT' and listed a phone number to ring. From the registration number I guessed it was about seventeen years old. Almost as old as me.

A car! My homeless heart leapt at the possibility of an interior space to call my own. A place to sit out of the cold and the rain. Somewhere to store my food and my money. The dents and scratches to the bodywork suggested it'd had many careless owners. It could be the safety deposit box that nobody would think to steal because it was practically worthless. It wouldn't cost too much upfront, cash in hand, hopefully no questions asked, and it would offer more freedom than my bike, which was still padlocked to the lamppost on the Promenade.

I rang the number. After some negotiation and a short test drive, the Ford was mine for £400. We completed the vehicle licence registration form for the DVLA in the name of Claire Hewitt. Once again, I quoted Zavier's address as my own despite the beginnings of a nagging doubt that a private investigator was not the best person to embroil in a disappearing act or trust with my mail. He hadn't struck me as being overly intelligent or motivated. His saving grace was he obviously needed the cash. As long he didn't open my letters and discover where I would be working or the registration of my car, I could cover my tracks again when it became generally known I'd run away. Once Theo discovered I was missing, I wouldn't put it past him to arrange for my photograph to be plastered across the county – newspapers, flyers, local television – offering a substantial reward as if I were a missing cat or misplaced wallet. After all, I'd experienced first-hand the extraordinary efforts he made to rescue the lost. But I had little choice. I needed a postal address and didn't want to divulge my current whereabouts to anyone.

Forgetting my plan to spend the rest of the afternoon on a library computer, I collected my bike and heaved it into the estate boot, the front wheel resting on the top of the back seats. I shopped for a few essentials – washing powder, cans of cola, cereal bars, apples, a small loaf of bread, a tub of margarine, a pot of peanut butter and a block of cheese – and stored the food in a carrier bag in the footwell of the passenger seat. The car would be as cold as a fridge overnight.

I sat in the supermarket car park, glad to be out of the rain. I switched the car heater on high, sipped a cola and listened to the local radio, anxious to hear any news of my disappearance or the break-in at the dome. Such incidents would be big stories around here. Instead, the broadcaster wittered on about the new ring road planned for Westhatch, an increase in fly-tipping in the area year on year, a dog therapy project to help children learn to read, and the weather. I quashed my disappointment, telling myself that no news was good news as far as I was concerned.

I pushed the seat into the recline position and closed my eyes. At last I had somewhere to relax during the day. I'd been self-conscious hanging about in cafés and shops, looking like a shoplifter or homeless loser. Now I blended into the background. I'd be able to park in different streets and car parks, perhaps follow the comings and goings of Zavier Marshall to ensure he was earning his pay.

The last of my energy drained away like dirty bathwater, like blood spiralling from the brain just before the spangled darkness of unconsciousness descends. One moment I was excited at the purchase of my first car, pleased I'd found a job to help me in my quest, and the next I was plunged back to that dark, unfathomable place where I was lost and carried away by currents beyond my control. Fear at the enormity of what I'd done bubbled to the surface. Fear of being found. Fear of not being found. Fear of never finding an echo of myself in another person's eyes, a person who looked like me.

I thought again of my mother, running away from her past towards an unknown future, carrying me in her belly. Perhaps my impetuous nature was a gift from her, perhaps a curse. Theo had never spoken of her unless I pleaded, and even then the details had been sketchy. I always assumed it had been too painful for him to remember. But maybe it was because he had no stories to tell. The one photograph of their wedding, a snapshot outside the registry office, had been placed high on a bookshelf in the living room, gathering dust.

I rummaged in my pocket for my wallet and unfolded a photograph of me with Theo, Paloma and Marcus taken at Easter several years previously. My family, such as it was. Ironically, people said I looked like Theo. They must have been referring to our expressions and mannerisms, for frozen in time on photographic paper there was nothing to connect the group physically. Theo, thin and greying. Paloma, with her plump Italian arms folded across her bosom. Marcus standing in the shadows. And me at the centre, my hair flaming over my shoulders like the burning bush, holding a bunch of daffodils.

I remembered the conversation just before the photograph had been taken.

'Everyone's born with a seed inside them,' Theo had said. 'If it's fed and watered and gets enough light it will grow strong and bear fruit. That's the reason we're put on this planet. You have a seed inside you, Ava, a special gift. I know it.'

'But what is it, Dad? I'm fourteen and I don't know what I want to be yet, what I want to do with my life.'

'There's plenty of time. You haven't discovered yourself, that's all. The seed needs to grow a little bigger. When it begins to develop, you'll know.'

'How will I know?'

'Because it will always be bigger than the sum of your parts. What you do for yourself dies with you. But what you do for others is a legacy that lives for ever. Everyone's life has a ripple effect and the world is going to be a better place for having you in it, Treasure. Don't worry about what you're going to be when you grow up. Have a little faith that you'll know when the time comes.'

I'd felt special that day. Now I knew that everything I'd believed about myself had been carefully cultivated by Theo. I'd based my identity on my relationship with him. Any sense of self I had was held together by a chain of memories linking the past to the present. But if all my memories were a lie, and all my relationships were a fabrication, then the person in the photograph was no longer me. For how could the happy teenager in the picture be the desolate girl watching the rain track down a car windscreen five years later?

I screwed up the photograph and threw it out the window. Who was Theo kidding? My life was totally insignificant. My birth hadn't been planned. I wasn't even a happy accident. Mum had left her job and friends to hide her condition. She'd been ashamed of me. Theo was wrong. I didn't have a special seed inside or a gift to share with the world. There was no meaning or purpose to life. My existence hung on a random thread of poor judgement and bad luck.

There was a sharp knock on my window. I rubbed a hole in the condensation and looked up to see a man peering into the car. I wound down the window.

'You dropped this.' He was wearing a supermarket uniform and padded jacket. Raindrops streamed down his cheeks.

'Thanks.' I took back the photograph as though I'd dropped it accidentally. We both knew I'd been littering.

'You all right?'

'I'm fine.'

'Righty-ho! We're here to help. Have a nice day.' He shuffled towards a snake of trolleys and pushed the rattling line to the main entrance. It was growing dark. I started the engine and drove back to Seacombe Road.

I decided to park around the corner from the bed and breakfast. I didn't want Mrs Bungay or anyone else to connect me with the car. I made myself a cheese sandwich, using a plastic knife filched from a café to slice the cheddar and spread the margarine. I stuffed an apple and cereal bar into my coat pocket, collected my charity shop purchases and locked the car door behind me.

The rain had emptied the pavements. I scuttled round the corner. Head down, I approached number twenty-three cautiously, anxious that Zavier might spot me and discover I was hiding out at Mrs Bungay's B&B. His house lights were off but an electric glow rose from the basement office.

I imagined him sorting through piles of paperwork from his father's records, finding a file marked 'Sandra Hewitt' and discovering the genesis of my life. The urge to knock on the door was overwhelming. I was planning to visit him first thing in the morning for an update. I looked at my watch. Half-past five. He didn't look the type to burn the midnight oil. There was probably nothing he could tell me tomorrow morning that he didn't know tonight. Could I endure another evening stirring through my angry questions, imagining the worst but fearing most of all that I would never know the truth? I turned and walked down the area steps.

The door was ajar. I pushed it gently with my foot and peeped through the crack. The hall was in darkness but a light shone from the open office door. I heard a soft 'huff', something between a whisper and a groan. I unconsciously stepped forward. From this angle I could see Zavier's wiry forearm leaning on the desk, his sleeve rolled up, fist clenched. His other hand was pressing something into the skin of his upper arm. A syringe. I threw open the door.

'So this is what you're spending *my* money on!' I shouted.

He looked up, startled. When he recognised me he calmly finished pressing the plunger, removed the needle and rubbed his arm briskly.

'Come on in, why don't you,' he drawled.

'The door was open,' I replied defensively.

'Knocking was an option.'

'I was going to, but I heard something. Sorry… No! I'm not sorry! Why am I apologising? You're working for me! You shouldn't be feeding your disgusting habits on my time.' Anger surged up my throat like vomit.

'I'm on *my* time now,' he replied. 'It's after five o'clock. I've already knocked off. I just popped back because I forgot to get – '

'I see perfectly well what you forgot! What I want to know is whether you remembered to do what I asked. What I paid you for.'

He rolled down his sleeve, buttoned the cuff and stood up. His leather jacket was hanging on the back of his chair. He shrugged into it carelessly.

'Come back tomorrow in office hours. I think I have a slot free at around ten o'clock.'

'Are you sure you'll be in a fit condition?' I sneered.

'Always in a fit condition where the ladies are concerned.' His eyes ran over my body. 'Perhaps you should be worrying about yourself. You looked rough the last time I saw you but now…' He left the sentence dangling. 'What's that?' He nodded at my bag of old clothes. 'All your worldly possessions?'

'Of course not!' But he was closer to the truth than I cared to admit.

'As I said before, there's a hostel on Eastbeach Street.'

'Shut up! I'm not homeless. Just fuming that I'm being taken for a mug. I need you to get on with your job. I need you to find my father.'

'I'm on it,' he yawned. 'But taking your money doesn't mean you run my life.'

'Listen here –'

'I am listening. I'm listening very hard. I hear more than you think. I see things too.'

'What are you talking about?'

'I know the signs. This isn't about finding your father. I know a woman scorned when I see one. Been on enough adultery investigations in my time to know that someone's been done the dirty. Believe me, he wasn't worth it. Forget him. Go home where you belong. Running away in search of Father Christmas won't mend a broken heart.'

'You know nothing!' I spat.

'Tell me, then.'

'Just because I hired you, don't think you have the right to poke into my private business,' I hissed. 'I'm not paying for therapy. It's you who needs to talk to *me*. Have you found out anything, or are you just some loser smackhead who's stolen my money?'

'Whoa, stand back! No need to be so touchy. I was just saying.'

'You, you patronising…' I searched for an appropriate word, but my mind was blank with fury. Unexpectedly there were tears on my cheeks.

He stood before me, shifting his feet. I couldn't look up. I slapped the tears away, trying to control the ugly gasps which stuttered from my nose and throat. He stepped past and walked into the hall. Nerves of steel when mainlining illegal drugs, but a wuss when faced with a crying woman! A moment later he returned carrying a toilet roll.

'Here,' he said.

I took it grudgingly.

'Sit down.' He pushed me onto the chair facing his desk and patted me on the head as though I were a small dog.

'Sorry,' I murmured.

'No worries.'

I buried my face in a wad of toilet paper, my shoulders heaving. I heard Zavier's chair creak alarmingly as he threw himself back down in his seat. 'I've made some progress with your case,' he said, trying to distract me. 'It's a good thing Dad has a touch of OCD. He's kept everything, even shop receipts, going back more than thirty years.'

I lifted my head. His elbows were on his desk and he was leaning towards me, a pained expression on his face. I sniffed and tore a sheet of toilet paper into pieces in my lap. He straightened and cleared his throat as though removing a minor irritation and pulled a file out of a drawer.

'I can't talk this through with you now, Claire. I need to get going.'

I nodded. The effects of the drugs he'd taken should be kicking in any time now. I didn't want to be around when it started.

'I haven't read it myself yet. That was a job for tomorrow. If I lend it to you, can I trust you to return it? You can read it tonight, come back tomorrow morning at ten and we can go through the contents together. OK?'

I sniffed and stuffed the used tissue in my jacket pocket, putting the toilet roll on his desk.

'I'll let you get on, then.' I stood and picked up the file. 'Thanks for this.'

'See you tomorrow.'

I darted out of the half-open door without saying goodbye, hoping he hadn't noticed I *hadn't* agreed to the meeting.

Mrs Bungay grunted when she opened the door. I hurried up the stairs two at a time, carrying the file and my of bag clothes.

'No food allowed!' she cried.

I turned at the top of the flight and pulled out a couple of garments from the bag.

'No food,' I confirmed. 'I've been clothes shopping. I've got a job.'

'Does that mean you'll be staying longer?'

'Maybe. Do you reduce your rates for long-term bookings?'

'No. You're already on the low-season rate. It'll be school holidays soon. If you don't book in advance you might not have a room. I have my regulars – '

'I'll let you know.'

I didn't think people would be queuing to holiday with Mrs Bungay in February. There was no shortage of vacancy signs in the Westhatch windows. Once she'd had time to think about it, I might be able to negotiate a cheaper price by booking a week in advance rather than from day to day, but I wasn't ready to commit myself yet.

Back in my room I filled the small kettle with water. Mrs Bungay had washed up my cup and restocked the tray: one teabag, one sachet of coffee, one bag of sugar, two plastic pots of UHT milk. I would have to ration myself. I pulled the cereal bar and apple out of my jacket pocket and opened the file.

The first few pages were a collection of handwritten notes setting out the steps Walt Marshall had taken to trace my mother's family. They included a list of searches made through the registrar of births, deaths and marriages. My grandparents had died in a car crash when my mother was seventeen. She had no brothers or sisters. Walt had been unable to trace any aunts, uncles or cousins.

Conversations with neighbours in the street where she'd grown up in a rented two-bedroom house revealed she had no means of supporting herself after her parents died. Although intelligent, she was forced to leave school before taking her A levels and had taken a job at Fun World Holiday Camp. Walt had interviewed various staff members, but all were vague or evasive about her sudden departure. They painted a picture of a girl who enjoyed socialising with the holidaymakers and who had plenty of boyfriends. Frustratingly, they couldn't remember any of their names. Soon after leaving, she met Theo who employed her as a sales assistant at Greenacres.

There was an entry dated 3rd September with the heading 'Funeral'. Underneath Walt had written:

> *Private burial, poorly attended. Dr Theodore Gage with baby Gage, Miss Paloma Bianco, Dr Colin Hildreth, Mrs Delia Ozzles. Service conducted by the Rev Roger Broomfield.*

A pathetically small turnout to mark the passing of a life. Most importantly, there was no mention of a mystery man grieving a lost love. If my biological father knew of my mother's death, he hadn't come to pay his respects. I turned the paper on its side. Pencilled in the margin and at right angles to the rest of the notes was the cryptic query 'Serpent in paradise?' I wondered if this was a reference to me. Had Walt Marshall discovered there was an illegitimate child in the family, a bad seed, a weed in the herbaceous border?

Having seen my name in the report, I realised I hadn't properly thought through the implications of asking Zavier for help. It was a good thing he hadn't read the file and seen the reference to 'baby Gage'. Once my disappearance hit the local news, how long would it take him to connect Claire Hewitt, daughter of Sandra Hewitt, with Ava Gage, missing stepdaughter of Theo?

I turned the page and found a yellowed clipping from the *Westhatch-on-Sea Advertiser* dated 15th August 1984.

> *The body of a young woman was found in a car near Greenacres Horticultural Institute on Thursday. Police and ambulance crews were called to the scene by a member of the*

public, but were unable to revive her. The woman's identity and the cause of death have yet to be confirmed.

Paperclipped to the back of the story was a larger article dated several months later.

A twenty-year-old woman took her own life by overdosing on sleeping tables and insulin, an inquest heard. Sandra Gage of the Greenacres Horticultural Institute, near Westhatch-on-Sea, died on 11th August last year.

Coroner Thomas Murphy said Mrs Gage had been discovered by her husband on his return from work at Greenacres Garden Centre at 6.30 that evening. Theodore Gage, local philanthropist and owner of the famous 'Dome on the Downs', fought back tears as he described how he had found his wife in their car, parked on a lane leading to their home. He told the coroner that she had intended to spend the day in bed after several sleepless nights left her exhausted and depressed. Ambulance officers who were called to the scene noted empty insulin cartridges and sleeping tablets on the passenger seat.

During the inquest at the Coroner's Court on Wednesday, Mr Murphy reported that the recently married mother was suffering from post-natal depression and Type 1 diabetes. He said the cause of death was hypoglycaemia brought on by an insulin overdose combined with an overdose of antidepressants. However, it was unclear whether she had intended to take her own life. The coroner ruled that her death could have been an accident or a cry for help. He recorded a narrative verdict, arguing she might have been expecting someone to drive up the lane, find her unconscious and call for help. It was possible she had inadvertently miscalculated the amount of tablets and insulin which could be safely taken.

Mrs Gage, an orphan, leaves behind a husband and seven-month-old daughter who was being looked after by a family friend on the day of her death.

Accidental death! Suicide! There was no mention here of a lingering illness followed by a sudden decline, as described by Paloma. More lies. I strode around the room trying to grasp the enormity of the discovery I'd just made. Intentionally or not, my mother had a hand in her own death. It hadn't been destiny or fate or bad luck. She wasn't an innocent victim of a horrible disease. *I* was the victim. The victim of her stupidity and selfishness. The victim of Theo's inability to read the signs and stop her from taking her own life.

The file also contained copies of the toxicology and autopsy reports. They were difficult to understand, and the constant reference to tissue samples and body temperature made me feel faint. I tried to be dispassionate about the words in front of me, but my head buzzed and the lines blurred, coalescing into the vision of a young girl in a white sundress.

I drank my cooling coffee and forced myself to turn to the next paper in the file. It was a photocopy of a page from a small, lined notebook. The left-hand edge was ragged where it had been torn away from its spiral binder. The undated note wasn't addressed to anyone.

I didn't say goodbye because I knew you would try to stop me. This is better for everyone, especially for the baby, who will be able to grow up untainted by my mistakes.

I read it several times. It could have been a suicide note or equally a 'Dear John' letter to Theo. Had my mother been in the car because she was driving away from an unhappy marriage, or had she tried and failed to orchestrate a cry for help? My hand was shaking. Perhaps I was reading my mother's last words. If so, she hadn't even mentioned me by name or left a message that she loved me.

I walked over to the window and looked down the road. An upstairs light was on in Zavier's house. I hoped he was telling the truth when he said he hadn't read the file. If he managed to put two and two together and realised I was Ava Gage, not Claire Hewitt, he might ask Theo for a reward in return for information on my whereabouts. Now, more than ever, I wanted to keep my identity a secret. I wanted to punish those who had kept the truth from me for so many years. I wanted to find my biological father and discover what had really happened all those years ago. I wanted to start my life afresh.

Chapter 7

It had been a tumultuous week. I'd run away, found somewhere to live, been given a job and initiated the search for my real father. Monday should have started with a new rotation into the Greenacres gift shop. Instead, I'd been rotated away from the safety of my home and family and out into a hostile world that owed me nothing and cared even less. I was a satellite wrenched from its gravitational path around a blazing star, floating further and further away into the black emptiness of space. And it was only Thursday!

'I didn't know if you wanted cornflakes or grapefruit, so I've put both on the table,' Mrs Bungay shouted from the kitchen.

At first I couldn't see the grapefruit. It took a moment to register the marmalade jar in front of me. I opened the lid. The remains of yesterday's tinned grapefruit segments floated in juice like ghostly goldfish. A buttery film swirled on the surface of the juice. The neck of the jar was encrusted with hardened marmalade. She'd stored the remains of yesterday's fruit in the empty marmalade pot. Even worse, she hadn't washed it out first. I screwed the lid back on and poured myself a bowl of soft cornflakes.

There were four days to fill before I started work at the holiday camp. They stretched ahead, grim and empty. I had no intention of keeping my appointment with Zavier that morning. I'd got what I'd paid him for, and didn't think he possessed the wherewithal to take the investigation any further than rummaging through his father's filing cabinets. I'd got everything Walt Marshall discovered all those years ago and had no intention of returning the file. Why risk the possibility that Zavier was more intelligent than he looked? If he ever discovered my real identity, I was pretty sure he would make use of that information to extract a reward from Theo. I knew enough to know you could never trust a drug addict if they had the chance to make some easy money.

After being chucked out at ten o'clock, I stashed my money-filled beanie hat in the glove compartment for safe-keeping and drove to the library. I spent an hour on one of the public computers, first checking my email account. I didn't know much about technology, and hoped my location couldn't be traced back to the Westhatch library. I decided not to open any of my messages, and just skimmed down the list of names of those who wanted to contact me and the titles of their emails. That way, if anyone looked at my inbox, the messages would still be marked as unread. I was expecting a flurry of communications from the staff at the garden centre – Paloma, Marcus and Harmony in particular. But apart from junk mail, there was nothing.

I Googled 'Ava Gage' for local news reports about my disappearance. Again, nothing. What were Paloma and Marcus thinking? Had they even contacted Theo in Africa to tell him I'd disappeared?

It's hard now to imagine life before the all-seeing, all-knowing presence of social media, a world with unreliable dial-up internet connections and patchy mobile phone networks. But even back in 2003 I'd expected word of my disappearance to have filtered into the virtual consciousness of the worldwide web. How was it possible to fall off the edge of the world without anyone noticing? Something was dreadfully wrong.

I logged off and picked up a local newspaper. Scouring its pages, I found a small article on page eight headed, 'Vandals target Horticultural Institute'.

Police were called to Greenacres Garden Centre and Horticultural Institute on 3rd February after a break-in

during the night. Centre manager, Marcus Becker,
discovered a forced door on his arrival at work that morning.
Offices were trashed and files had been disturbed, but
nothing appears to have been taken.

Detective Constable Maitland stated that there had been
an increase in antisocial behaviour in the Westhatch-on-Sea
area recently. This kind of damage is particularly associated
with bored teenagers. I would urge all businesses and
homeowners in the area to increase their security, including
alarms, locks and lighting.'

The famous eco-Dome at the Greenacres Horticultural
Institute is open for business as usual.

Nothing had been taken. There was no mention of my
disappearance the same night. The theft of the credit card and
cash from the safe had gone unnoticed. Nothing was being
done. Nobody seemed to care. I'd run away, petulant and
immature, looking to punish those who'd hurt me. I'd expected
desperation and repentance. I wanted them on their knees
begging for my forgiveness and promising to spend the rest of
their lives making it up to me. My plan had backfired.

After lunch in town – lentil soup and a crusty roll – I bought
a swimsuit and beach towel in a small department store and
returned to the Leisure Centre for a real swim. The receptionist
greeted me as an old friend.

I stretched my body through the warm water, legs kicking
out behind, chlorine stinging my eyes instead of tears.
Facedown, I watched the silver bubbles rising as I crawled
towards the deep end. The passing water filled my ears with a
distant echo, a rumble of voices from the surface above. I
ploughed up and down the lanes, focusing on the bubbles and
the line of tiles that wavered beneath me until it was time for
another breath and a sharp burst of light and noise before I was
once again submerged in a world of muffled blue. If only I could
stay suspended in the turquoise fluid, counting strokes in a
bubble of detachment, all anxiety and fear sinking peacefully to

the bottom as my limbs grew tired, but a gangly youth jumped into the water in front of me and shattered my peace. Startled, I took a breath and inhaled a lungful of droplets. Coughing, spluttering and out of my depth, I doggy-paddled to the side of the pool. The youth was swimming away, not bothering to check whether I was OK. I had a strange feeling I recognised the shape of his head under his slicked-back hair. I climbed up the steps and hurried into the changing rooms.

On Friday, I drove around town, parking in the dingy street where my mother had lived as a child. It was inland, far from the tourist attractions, bundled away in a crease in the Downs, undusted, untidied, not fit to be seen by visitors. I wondered whether the bedroom at the front of the house had been hers. I tried to imagine my mother looking out at the world, a red-headed girl without a sea view, unaware of the misfortunes that were to strike.

I visited a tangled churchyard nearby trying to trace the final resting place of my maternal grandparents, but to no avail. I'd visited my mother's grave a couple of times with Paloma when I was a child. I knew there wasn't much to see: a small headstone in a row of similar stones. I was searching for ghosts from the past and I knew they didn't reside in Westhatch's well-ordered municipal cemetery.

Hungry and suddenly craving human company, I drove to the Promenade and parked near the bandstand. I mooched restlessly along the pavements, hopping between coffee shops to stay out of the cold. I was exhausted and anxious. The after-effects from the adrenalin of the previous few days were kicking in. But the deep fatigue in my body could not quiet my racing thoughts.

Westhatch was a large town, but I kept looking over my shoulder, anxious I might be recognised by someone I knew. And I was worried about Zavier. I'd used his address on my job application and to register my car with the DVLA. Letters for Claire Hewitt would start being delivered to his home. I began to imagine several complicated scenarios involving Post Office boxes, third parties and envelopes of money hidden in telephone kiosks or hollow trees, in return for my letters being dropped off without me having to come in direct contact with him.

In the end, I decided to leave it. I was living in the shadows now: no fixed address, no National Insurance number, no bank account, no mobile phone contract. Cash-in-hand anonymity. The freedom of invisibility. Why chance throwing that away for a vehicle registration document or an invitation to join the Fun World staff social club? It wasn't as though I'd be selling the car to anyone else. It was already on borrowed time. I could just abandon it in a car park once it had outrun its usefulness. And I was only going to work at Fun World long enough to see whether anyone remembered my mother. Then I'd be off.

There was no chance of a weekend lie in-with Mrs Bungay. She rapped smartly on my door at 8.30 on Saturday morning to say that breakfast would stop being served in half an hour. I went for another swim, but most of the adult lanes were being used for swimming lessons or families enjoying a splash-about with their children. I couldn't block out the happy shrieks and excited chatter. I couldn't escape into that warm blue bubble where the world floated away and the only thing I was conscious of was my body pushing through the water.

On Sunday I crept in the back of a nearby church and listened to the songs and prayers. A lady vicar spoke about the Father-heart of God. I might have cried, except that the previous night I'd wept for hours before falling into an uneasy, stuffed-up slumber. Not wanting to talk to anyone in the congregation, I slipped out during the final hymn and drove to Jumper's Mount.

Parking at the viewing point, I walked along a grassy path and gazed down at the town below. The roofs and streets were dreary under the grey sky, slick with the soft drizzle that had fallen at first light but had now been blown away by a biting wind. The holiday camp caravans stood to attention like pale tombstones. From this height it looked deserted, as did the

Promenade and beach. A weak shaft of light filtered through the banks of cloud, transforming the sky into a huge purple and yellow bruise. In the distance, I could just make out the misty silhouette of a tanker on the horizon.

I looked across the Downs, hugging my chest to ward off the spiteful gusts that buffeted my body. On the top of the rise, perched inland and on the other side of the bay, the Greenacres dome winked in the watery light. I'd been told our glasshouse could be seen by trawlers far out at sea. As I'd never been to sea, I didn't know if this was true.

My heart was filled with a yearning so strong that my legs buckled beneath me. I sat down suddenly on the damp grass. The sight of my former home was an unbearable reminder of everything I'd lost and the burden I'd gained: the curse of knowledge that could never be unknown.

At a quarter-past nine on Monday morning I found myself sitting at a round cocktail table in the Fun World entertainment centre. I hadn't changed my hair colour, despite Mrs Ozzles' instructions. My mop was unmanageable at the best of times. Since I'd cut it into a bob, the curls were growing outwards rather than down. Dowsing my hair with more chemicals so soon after I'd dyed it black might cause breakage and a gravity-defying upwards frizz, I reasoned. Instead, I'd avoided the black kohl, settling for a natural-looking brown mascara, a hint of green eyeshadow, a little blusher to soften the pallor of my skin and a soft peach lipstick. I'd been surprised by the effect when I'd stood back from Mrs Bungay's bathroom mirror. I was almost pretty.

Sonya was balanced next to me on a tall aluminium stool. The Pink Jacket girls I'd noticed at my interview were perched at an adjoining table. The blond boy with the curls had a table to himself. From his badge, I discovered his name was Jeremy. Other new recruits – half a dozen middle-aged women, a handy-looking man and a spotty youth in overalls – sat on pink squidgy sofas facing the bar.

Black carpets and low ceilings enclosed the new recruits as a cave might harbour a cluster of nervous bats. There were no windows in the bar. A glow of exhausted light filtered from the glass chandeliers above, as though hungover from the previous evening's revelries. Dark shadows hollowed out the eyes of those around me, and I hoped the gloom would disguise my own unease. The fire door had swung shut behind us with a soft thud and we were sealed in a vacuum smelling of polish and spilled beer. Feeling claustrophobic, I stared at the mirrored wall behind the bar, the nearest thing to a glimpse of freedom.

The male Pink Jacket I'd seen on the day of my interview pranced onto the stage, clipboard in hand. Someone behind the scenes switched on a spotlight.

'Good morning, campers!' he cried. When nobody replied, he took a step back, shook his head dramatically and swooped forward again with his arms outstretched. 'Good morning, campers!'

'Good morning,' we echoed.

'That's better. But not good enough! You are now on the Fun World Team and the Fun World Team is all about fun, fun, fun. GOOD MORNING!'

'GOOD MORNING!' we shouted back.

'Now you're all popping, I'm gonna introduce myself to yous good people. I'm Gavin Flynne, team leader for the Pink Jackets crew. Boom! I'm fizzing today.' He tap-danced a couple of steps, spun on the spot and yelled, 'Welcome to Fun World Holiday and Caravan Park. It's Holiday Season 2003! And we're going to make it the best one ever! So what d'ya think?'

There was a small ripple of applause. Someone whooped.

'Bing bang, thank you man! Back to my agenda.' He pouted at his clipboard. 'Julie Wellbeloved from *In*humane Resources,' he paused and grimaced at his joke, 'will be joining us in *uno momento* to give a rundown of her policies and procedures.' He pointed at the youth in overalls. 'Don't think I don't know what you're thinking, Don Juan!' Someone sniggered. 'Any questions about your terms and conditions of employment can be

105

addressed to her. Once the boring stuff is dusted, we'll break for an injection of caffeine – as if I could fly any higher than I am now – followed by a tour of the campsite organised by yours truly.' He gave a little bow. 'I'm going to walk you round blindfolded, run away, and the first one back here wins a stick of rock and a certificate to take home! Boom! Just kidding.

'Then we'll break into smaller groups. Pink Jackets will stay here in the club bar. I'll be running you through the party dances and camp songs,' he raised an eyebrow, 'and personally measuring you for your uniforms and costumes. You'll also have the misfortune of seeing Chucky Skittles, head of entertainment, as he prepares for the early evening children's show.

'Housekeeping staff will be going to the laundry with Mrs Ozzles for a wash and tumble-dry. Those in catering and waitressing will meet Mr Scarletti in the caféteria. Maintenance staff will be escorted to the shed at the bottom of the hill by Sid Tulitt for a complete strip-down and overhaul... But before all that, I have a massive surprise for you this morning. I'm buzzed to be able to introduce someone who started here as a Pink Jacket more than twenty-five years ago. He learned the business from the bottom up – don't look at me like that, missus – and brought Fun World back from the brink of collapse. Since then he's opened four more holiday camps along the south coast together with a string of nightclubs, gyms and restaurants.' His voice rose an octave, words spilling from his mouth in a sing-song rhythm. 'Business entrepreneur and multimillionaire... with all his own hair... current owner of Fun World Holiday Camp, our beloved leader,' he reached a crescendo, 'MR MAXWELL KING!'

A spontaneous clatter of applause erupted as a tanned man in a suit and crisp open-necked shirt sprang onto the stage and took the microphone from Gavin.

'Thank you. Thank you. My name's Maxwell King.' He walked once across the stage and back again, smiling at his audience. The glitter ball over his head scattered his face with oblongs of light. He waited dramatically until the hush in the room was so thick that no one dared move.

'Once upon a time I was sitting where you're sitting today. I left school at sixteen to start work at this holiday camp as a Pink Jacket. I didn't really know what I wanted to do or what I wanted to be. I just knew I loved people. That's been the secret of my success. Loving people and giving them what they want. Lots and lots of what they want.' He swept a thick lock of silver hair from his forehead.

'I've been privileged to work in this industry.' He looked slowly round the room. My skin prickled as he caught my eye. 'To give our customers one or two weeks a year of complete pleasure is a gift, an absolute gift. We allow them to escape their humdrum lives, spread their wings a little, learn to fly. And as with all gifts, the giver is as blessed as the receiver.' He nodded as though speaking as much to himself as to us.

'This is much more than a job. We're all about belonging. All about families. And you, the staff, are members of our family. You have the chance to be part of something truly amazing. Everything you do here contributes to another person's happiness. However menial or boring that task may be, I want you to imagine you're doing it for someone in your own family. Do it with love. Do it for the overworked dads and the harassed mums. Do it for the children. I guarantee it will show.

'This is the place where magic happens and dreams *can* come true. We're creating unforgettable experiences and memories. But most importantly, we're creating togetherness. I want people to say "Wow!" to our facilities, "Wow!" to our food, "Wow!" to the cleanliness of the park, "Wow!" to our activities and entertainment, and most of all "Wow!" to the attitude of our team. Let's share a little happiness. Let's share a little love.' He bowed his head as though he was going to pray, but Gavin sprang to his side to shake him by the hand.

'Let's hear it once again for our beloved boss, Mr Maxwell King. Thank you, sir.'

I looked around the room. Everyone was clapping. I was clapping. The atmosphere was electric. I turned to say something to Sonya and saw in the darkness the glint of a tear on her smiling cheek.

Chapter 8

I set my alarm for 5.45 the following morning. Mrs Bungay had rejected my suggestion that I could make myself a slice of toast and cup of coffee before leaving for work.

'Breakfast is served between half-past seven and nine o'clock. Not after and *never* before. If you choose to go out early, that's your business. Guests are not allowed in the kitchen. It's against health and safety. And don't even think about asking for a reduction in my rate. It's your choice not to be here for breakfast.'

I was too tired and bleary-eyed to point out that serving tinned grapefruit in a dirty marmalade jar was more a contravention of hygiene regulations than me putting a piece of bread in her crumb-encrusted toaster.

Munching a couple of chocolate digestives in the car, I drove to Fun World and swiped my new staff card in the slot by the entrance to the car park. The barrier opened automatically. As instructed, I parked away from the guests, round the back of the laundry room in a dingy courtyard lined with recycling skips and wheelie bins.

I'd been told to report to reception on arrival. Slipping a nylon housekeeping tunic over the blue polo shirt and jogging bottoms that Mrs Ozzles had issued the day before, I pushed open the glass doors. A night security guard was still on duty. A scar ran through the stubble on his jaw like a path through a dark forest.

'Hi. I'm Claire Hewitt. You might be expecting me. It's my first day.' His bloodshot eyes insolently scanned my body.

'Round back!'

He nodded his shaven head towards the door, jerking his arm to the right. I scuttled away. Around the corner, a girl in a cleaner's uniform was huddled on a bench, smoking furiously as though to keep warm. Her hair was as bright as mine was dark, an overbleached and frazzled crop. Statement hair. Two-fingers-in-the-air hair. I wondered if Mrs Ozzles had given her the hair-colour talk and this was her interpretation of a 'nice summery shade'.

'Hello. I'm Claire.'

She stubbed out her cigarette and stood up.

'This way.'

I had to run to keep up with her.

'Sorry. I didn't catch your name.'

'Never chucked it.'

I followed her through the arcade and into the entertainment centre. She switched on a bank of lights. Points of dust swirled upwards, carrying the smell of chips and lager through the echoing space. Taking a bunch of keys from the pocket of her tunic, she unlocked a cupboard. I helped her drag out the industrial-sized vacuum cleaner and a trolley of dusters, polish and antibacterial spray.

'Wipe the tables, hoover the carpet and sweep the dance floor. I'll be back in an hour.'

'Aren't you supposed to be showing me the ropes?'

'Are you stupid or something? It's cleaning, not brain surgery.' The door swung shut behind her.

I started at the back of the nightclub, wiping the rings of beer and dried blobs of ketchup from the tables, working my way around the semicircle until I reached the dance floor. Before I could vacuum, there were sweet wrappers, crisp packets and dirty napkins to bin, trodden-in chips and chewing gum to pick off the carpet. I stood up to plug in the lead and jumped back in surprise. The security guard from reception was sitting at a table near the entrance.

'How long have you been here?' I snapped.

'Long enough.' He lifted a hand, hard as a hammer, and crooked his index finger, slowly beckoning. 'Come 'ere,' he commanded, his voice soft with menace.

'I'm busy. I have to finish before… the other girl gets back. She should be here any minute.'

'I don't think so. She's gorn to the café for 'er breakfast.'

'She definitely said she was coming to check up on my work.' I turned away and switched on the vacuum cleaner.

From the corner of my eye I saw him stand up. *Please go, please go*, I whispered under my breath. I sped up, thrusting the machine forwards and back as though sawing through wood, always moving away from the dark presence behind me. The cable snagged round a table leg. I yanked it free. Suddenly silence. The security guard had pulled the socket from the wall.

Frozen like prospective roadkill, I searched for any quick and crushing words to throw in his direction. He sauntered forward, weaving around tables, shoving chairs out of the way. He bared his teeth, less a smile than a snarl, for his eyes were as cold as two glass marbles. *Keep calm. Don't look scared.*

He stopped in front of me, too close, legs apart, breathing hard. His arms hung away from his body to accommodate the heavy muscles under his jacket. I was alone in a sound-proofed nightclub with a steroid-pumping thug.

'You're a good little worker.' His teeth were as yellow and square as nicotine ingots. A silver stud bobbed on his tongue.

'I have to get on.'

'I won't keep you long,' he leered. 'Just want to get acquainted.'

'Nice to meet you. Now, if you'll excuse me…' I moved towards the socket as though to plug it back in, though I was planning to abandon the vacuum cleaner and run for the door. His hand shot out like a piston, and grabbed my arm as I pushed past.

'That's not very friendly.'

I pulled away. He didn't release his grip. His other hand flew up. For a moment I thought he was going to slap my face. His palm stopped a centimetre from my cheek, hovered, and then stroked downwards as though smearing something unpleasant on my skin. I leaned back as far as I could, the small of my back pressing against a table.

The double doors swung open with a bang. We turned to see my supervisor standing in the entrance, staring at the scene before her. She took a step back. The doors began to close in front of her expressionless face. My heart plummeted.

'Wait!' I cried.

The door opened again, slowly this time. I saw her small bleached head turn and look down the corridor outside.

'The witch is coming,' she hissed. 'She wants to check on the fresh meat.'

The security guard dropped my arm. He moved his hand away from my face and fingered a curl, giving it a sharp tug.

'See you later, 'gator.' He jogged across the dance floor, jumped up on the stage and disappeared behind the curtain. A door slammed in the distance.

I turned to my saviour.

'Scumbag!' she spat in his direction.

'I didn't want... I don't know what would have happened...'

'He likes to move in quick with the new girls 'cos they're less likely to complain.'

I sat down on a chair, my legs suddenly weak. She joined me and we sat together in silence.

'Boody.' She held out her hand.

'Claire.' I took hers and she gave it a sharp shake. 'Is that a nickname?'

'Short for Marianna. But don't ever call me that.'

A thought flashed to mind. I jumped up. 'Mrs Ozzles is coming!' I began pushing the disturbed chairs back under the tables.

'No she's not, you daft twinkie. I made it up.'

'Thanks. I really mean it.'

'He wouldn't have stopped for me, but he's scared of Mrs O. Remember that. He's bad, but she's worse.'

'Has he ever…?' The unfinished question hung in the air. We both knew what I was talking about. I pushed a lock of hair from my eyes with a shaking hand.

'What do *you* think?'

'He shouldn't be allowed to get away with harassing staff. We should make a complaint.'

Boody snorted.

'Chicken nuggets! It's your first day. Don't start the uprising yet. And there's no "we".' She gnawed a grubby thumbnail. 'There are ways to avoid him.'

'How?'

'He works nights on the door to stop the locals crashing the entertainment centre, and then on reception. He knocks off most mornings at 7.30, gets his breakfast in the café. He's usually gone home by nine. If I'm cleaning caravans early, I always lock the door when I'm inside, if you get my drift. Next time you're in here on your own, stick a chair under the door handle. There's no point locking the doors to any of the main buildings as he keeps the master keys. Sludger Trafford goes wherever he wants.'

'Sludger?'

'That's my private name for him. There's pond life. And then there's the sludge right at the bottom of the pond.'

'How can someone like him be working at a family holiday park? If Mr King knew, I'm sure he wouldn't stand for such behaviour.'

'Ooooo. "*Such behaviour!*" La-de-da. Listen to you. You've not been here on a Saturday night when the punters are on the lash. Trafford has his uses then, when people like you are safely tucked up in bed.'

I was about to say she didn't know anything about me or what time I might go to bed, but thought better of it. I needed a friend.

'I can't thank you enough.'

She shrugged her shoulders.

'Shut up. Just make sure you return the favour.'

'Of course. Absolutely.'

'*Absolutely!*' she parroted. 'Come on, Countess. Turn the bloomin' hoover on. We've still got the vans to clean.'

By the end of the shift I was exhausted.

'Strip the sheets and pillowcases and shove them in a white sack… towels too. If you stick them on the veranda, Sid'll come round in his van and collect them for the laundry. He puts clean sheets and towels in a clear plastic bag on the caravan steps on changeover days. We don't make up the beds. That's down to the punters.'

'They have to make their own beds?'

'Course! Who do you think we are, the Hilton?'

I lugged the bag of dirty bedding outside. Boody followed and pulled out a packet of cigarettes.

'Got a light?'

'Sorry. I don't smoke.'

She swore.

'Don't apologise for not smoking. Filthy habit!'

She rummaged in her tunic pocket and eventually pulled out a book of matches. She stepped out on the veranda. After lighting up, she took a lingering drag and exhaled on a smoky sigh.

'Next, the bog!' she shouted through the door. 'Squirt some bleach down the toilet, the shower and the sink. Leave it for five minutes, then go in hard with the antibacterial spray. All the surfaces, mind. The norovirus is a sneaky devil. Whatever you do, don't eat your lunch in the vans! I made that mistake once and chucked up non-stop for three days. You make a start. I'll follow once I've finished me fag.' She waved me away with an imperious hand, the cigarette glowing between her fingers.

I'd finished disinfecting the toilet and shower room by the time she returned.

'Now for the kitchen.' She pulled a roll of refuse sacks from the cleaning caddy and ripped one off. 'Black bags for rubbish. We're supposed to sort and separate the plastic, glass and cardboard, but it takes so-ooo long to lug them to the recycling boxes. Forget saving the planet. I'm saving me legs! Anyway, stick the black bags out front by the white sack of dirty bedding. Sid will come round with the honey wagon once he's done the laundry run.'

'What's the honey wagon?'

'The rubbish truck. He empties all the bins on site. In the summer, the flies and wasps follow him like he's a pot of honey. Oh, my days! You can smell him coming a mile off.'

While I cleaned out the fridge, Boody went through the kitchen cupboards. She found a jar of coffee, a box of stock cubes and a half-finished bottle of washing-up liquid. She unfolded a shopping bag from her tabard pocket and placed the items inside. She caught me watching.

'If the punters can't be bothered to take their stuff home, I will. It's only going in the bin. Waste not, want not. Today you're cleaning my vans. When you've got your own list of vans, you can keep anything that's left behind.' She rummaged through the half-empty packets and jars in the fridge. Although I tried to control my expression, she must have seen my disgust.

'You won't be so high and mighty when you gets your wages. They don't buy nuffing.' As if to demonstrate the point, she pushed her hand down the back of the settee that ran the length of the caravan and pulled out a pound coin in triumph. She pocketed it with a flourish.

While I washed the kitchen floor, she stretched out on the sofa which doubled up as an extra bed, and read a magazine left by the previous occupants.

'Make me a black coffee when you've finished, mother!' she called. 'There's a jar in me shopping bag.'

After I'd cleaned six vans to Boody's satisfaction, she went outside for another smoke, rushing back almost immediately.

'Shuttlecocks! Ozzy Osbourne really *is* coming!' She grabbed the broom from my hand.

Mrs Ozzles flung open the door.

'Afternoon, Mrs O,' Boody chirped. 'I was just showing Claire Bear how you have to get right into the corners.' She pushed the brush into the space between the cooker and the fridge.

'I see.' The housekeeper walked round the caravan, her eyes scanning for imperfections. After checking under the beds, she turned to us at last. 'I see you've made an effort, Boody.'

'Yes, Mrs O.'

'And how is Claire getting on?'

'She's learning.'

Mrs Ozzles turned to me.

'You've had an easy start. In the high season you'll be expected to clean twice as many vans as this every day, and on your own. Do you think you can do that?'

'I'll try.'

'I'm not interested in trying. Can you do it?'

'Yes.'

'Good.' Her mouth moved into a tight smile. I noticed a lipstick stain on her front teeth. It looked like a splash of blood. 'This week you can collect your wages from me at the end of each day, once I have checked your work is satisfactory. After that you'll be paid on Thursdays. One of the perks of working here is that on Thursday nights the cleaning staff are allowed a free pass into the entertainment centre, isn't that right, Boody?'

'Yes, Mrs O.'

'It's good for staff morale. And it will help you get to know our little family better and understand the ethos of Fun World. I suggest you go.'

'Yes, I will. Thank you, Mrs Ozzles.'

After the door shut behind her, I turned to Boody.

'Will you be going on Thursday?'

'I'll go to the bingo. I might stay for a drink. Thursday nights are the pits. They like the staff in the club so it don't look half-empty. After a week of hangovers, the punters are looking for an early night. Some will be packing up to leave on Friday morning. Friday, Saturday, Sunday and Monday are changeover days. That's when you and me is busiest. If you get bladdered on Thursday night, you'll regret it. Besides, it ain't much fun watching people puke on the carpet, knowing you're going to be the one cleaning it up the next day.'

I knocked on Mrs Ozzles' door on my way out to collect my wages. She counted £30 into my hand. £30! There wasn't much you could buy in the Greenacres gift shop for £30. I was used to spending more than that each week on styling products for my unruly hair.

My mind ran through my expenses. I was paying Mrs Bungay £25 a day and not even getting breakfast now I started work at 6.30. I couldn't see how I could live on £5 a day for food, toiletries, clothes and petrol. In my lunch break I'd spent more than that on gammon, egg and chips, a jam doughnut and a coffee in the campsite café.

I was glad of the stash of cash I concealed in the glove compartment of my car during the day, and hugged close under my duvet at night. I didn't know how long I'd be working at Fun World or how soon it would be before I could locate my real father. I resolved to economise in the meantime.

I parked my car in a quiet side street and napped for half an hour until it was time to return to the bed and breakfast at four. I was looking forward to a long, hot bath to ease my aching muscles. But five minutes after arriving back in my room, and before I had the chance to undress and slip across the corridor to the bathroom, Mrs Bungay knocked.

'Visitor for you downstairs,' she shouted through the door.

My heart leapt, first with excitement that Marcus or Paloma had tracked me down at last, then with fear. What would I say to them? How could I explain my behaviour? They would want to know why I hadn't spoken to them first before running away.

I looked down at my nylon tunic. I didn't want them to see how far I'd fallen so I tore it over my head and stuffed it in a drawer. The navy polo shirt and jogging bottoms didn't look too bad. I buttoned an oversized cardigan over the polo shirt to cover the Fun World logo, ran a hand quickly through my hair and hurried towards the stairs. I could hear my landlady in the kitchen, rattling plates and dishes in the sink. I turned on the half-landing. Zavier Marshall was standing in the hall below.

'What are you doing here?' I snapped.

'You missed your appointment. Ten o'clock Thursday, remember? You were going to return my file.'

'I forgot. How did you know I was here?'

'It's my job to know.'

The clattering in the kitchen stopped. Mrs Bungay was listening to our conversation.

'You'd better come up,' I said.

He mounted the stairs. The kitchen door opened with a bang and Mrs Bungay hurried into the hall, inhaling with a wheeze and exhaling on a loud huff.

'No visitors upstairs! No gentlemen visitors!'

'I'm not a gentleman, Brenda,' Zavier replied before I could answer.

'I know you're not!' She took a deep breath. 'You can speak to her in the sitting room.'

'This is private business,' he called down from the landing.

'I know all about your kind of private business. I'll be speaking to your father…' She struggled to catch her breath.

'We'll leave the door open,' he shouted back.

'Just you keep both your feet on the carpet!'

He laughed. A hot wave of embarrassment swept my cheeks as her meaning sunk in. He followed me into my room and deliberately shut the door.

'I thought we were keeping it open.'

'She won't know. I don't think she's going to make it up those stairs in a hurry.' He sat down on the end of my bed and bounced gently. 'Nice!'

'How did you find me?'

'I followed you here the first day we met. I've always known where you are. I like to keep my clients close, and their wallets even closer.'

I clucked with annoyance.

'You weren't at the swimming pool on Saturday afternoon, by any chance?' I asked.

He ignored my question.

'Looks like you couldn't bear to be too far away from yours truly.'

'What do you want?' I sank down onto the small stool by the dressing table.

'A cup of tea for starters. Then I want to know why you didn't bring my file back. Did it tell you what you wanted to know?'

'No.' I stood up and filled the small kettle with water from the sink.

'I didn't think it would. But it must have told you something, something you didn't want me to find out. Otherwise, why wouldn't you bring it back and discuss its contents with me?'

'I've been busy. There was nothing in the file. I chucked it away,' I lied. 'I've got to move on with my life, forget about the past. I'll be leaving Westhatch tomorrow. I won't be requiring your services any more.'

'I see.' He scratched his chin. 'So you don't want to know the current state of play with the investigation?'

'You've found something?' My voice was eager.

'I've been to Fun World today.'

I dropped the cup I was holding onto the plastic tray with a clatter.

'Yep,' he continued proudly. 'I had a meeting with the housekeeper this morning.'

'Did you tell her about me?' I turned my back and popped a teabag in the small metal pot so he couldn't see my anxious expression. I wondered if he'd blown my cover and whether we'd come close to bumping into each other earlier in the day.

'Some credit, please. I *am* a professional. I told her I worked for a probate company and was trying to trace any relatives of an ex-employee, now deceased. I said one of the ex-employee's cousins had died without a will and left quite a large estate. I wanted to know if anyone knew Sandra Hewitt and, if so, who her next of kin was. Whoever they were, they were due a ton of cash.'

'What did she say?'

'It looked as though she was going to be helpful, until I mentioned your mum's name. She backtracked then like crazy, tried to put me off by saying she couldn't discuss any member of staff, past or present, because of data protection. I said we didn't need any personal details. Then I asked if any of the current staff had worked at Fun World for more than twenty years and could she please give them a copy of my card so they could ring me if they had any information.'

'And?'

'Usually people want to help reconnect relatives with their inheritance. I suppose they hope one day it will be them. They get a kind of vicarious thrill being part of the investigation. It's unusual to meet someone so unhelpful. There's something more going on. I have a kind of instinct when people feel uncomfortable, when there's something they're not telling me. Like you, Claire. What are you not telling me?'

'Me? I'm not paying you to investigate *me*. I thought we were talking about Mrs Ozzles.'

'How did you know I was talking about Mrs Ozzles? I never mentioned her name. I just called her "the housekeeper".'

'Because… I remembered her name from the papers I found about my mother. She wrote a letter about the funeral –'

'But how did you know it was the same woman? There could have been several housekeepers since your mother's time.'

'I just assumed…'

'Mmmm.'

'Was it Mrs Ozzles?' I asked, unable to meet his eyes.

'You know it was.'

I passed him his tea and ladled sugar into my coffee.

'It'll make you fat.'

'Let me worry about that.'

He stretched his legs out on the counterpane, leaned his head against the buttoned velour headrest, and curled his fingers around the cup. I sat back down on the dressing-table stool.

'You're sweet enough already,' he winked.

'I don't think you're in any position to comment on my bad habits… or addictions.'

I sipped my tea, feeling his eyes upon me. 'I've been doing a little digging of my own,' I said, changing the subject. 'That's how I knew Mrs Ozzles was still at the holiday camp.'

'Amateurs!' he muttered. 'You've made her suspicious with your meddling. That's why she clammed up when I interviewed her.'

'No way. I never discussed my mother with her. All I did was establish that she still works there. *You* probably tipped her off with your cock-and-bull story about being a probate investigator.' I glared at his leather jacket and ripped jeans. 'You look as though you should be busking on the high street or queuing at the Job Centre.'

'I wore a suit. And I wasn't lying. I do actually carry out probate work for a company in London off and on. When they need to trace relatives around the Westhatch area, they give me a ring so I can get there quickly and sign them up before a rival firm contacts them. They have a network of people like me all round the country. It saves them sending someone out from London every time. Time is money. The important thing is that when I showed her my official Antler Star Probate identification, she didn't suspect a thing. She told me she'd worked at Fun World for more than twenty-five years. That's when I mentioned Sandra's name and the shutters came down. After that she went on about how many girls had worked there over the years. She couldn't be expected to remember everyone.'

'Where does that leave us? It's a dead end.'

'It means she's hiding something. She remembers, all right. People don't forget when a young woman dies in strange circumstances, particularly if you were their boss and the girl had run away because she'd got herself pregnant. We know she was at your mother's funeral. If you knew there was a large inheritance waiting for Sandra's next of kin, wouldn't you mention that she had a child?'

'Of course. Unless I was an evil, vindictive hag who was jealous of another's good fortune.'

I remembered the housekeeper's eyes, sharp as flint, and the slash of red lipstick on her teeth. But I also remembered she'd given me a job when she could have sent me packing. Sonya too. Boody said Mrs Ozzles stood up for the cleaners if there was a dispute with the Pink Jackets. And Trafford was frightened of her, so she couldn't be all bad. She might be a stickler, but she didn't always wield the stick.

Zavier interrupted my thoughts. 'I don't think it's that. She was wary. I asked if she could look up Sandra Hewitt on the computer records to see if it would jog a memory. She said they'd updated their computer systems a couple of years ago. Ex-staff prior to that wouldn't be on the system. Their old personnel files are now stored in the basement. She said she was too busy to go and look. She told me to leave her my card, which I did, but I'm not expecting her to be in touch any time soon.'

'So you came to tell me that you don't know anything more than you did before.'

'We know a lot more. We know there are personnel files in the basement. We know that current staff files are on her computer system. We know Mrs Ozzles knows more than she's letting on. It's a cover-up!'

Chapter 9

The next few days dragged endlessly. I walked around in a haze of bleach. Blisters stung my palms. My back ached from stripping beds and lugging laundry bags onto caravan steps. There weren't that many holidaymakers on site, but they made an awful a lot of mess. I knew things would only get worse.

'It'll be stuffed here next week,' Boody observed. 'Brace yourself, flower, the parasitic swarm's on its way. School holidays. Low season prices. Punters can't afford to fly somewhere sunny or come here in the high season. Instead, they come now, turn up the heating and bake like beans in a tin while it tips it down outside. They make as much mess as they can in the vans. That's how they know they're on holiday. They don't have to clean it up.'

'At least there's an indoor pool,' I observed. 'If they close their eyes they can imagine they're by the Mediterranean.'

Boody snorted.

'The smell of chlorine on the breeze. Urine on the changing room floors. Verrucas thrown in for free!'

Sonya was being shown the ropes by a Jamaican woman called Martisha. At six thirty every morning Sonya and Martisha cleaned the staff offices, corridors and reception area, while Boody and I cleaned the entertainment centre, club bar and arcade. Although the work was exhausting and boring, I was glad not to be on the team that cleaned the café and swimming pool, where the cleaning chemicals used could strip the skin from the back of your throat if you breathed too deeply. Boody joked that the chlorine mix in the pool was strong enough to split the atom.

I introduced myself to Sid Tulitt, maintenance manager, on my second day when he collected a couple of rubbish sacks I'd left outside a caravan door. He threw them onto the back of his van, turning when I greeted him.

'Mornin',' he echoed. The skin of his face was raw and flaking as though it had been scrubbed clean with a wire brush. Scales of eczema spread across his cheeks and forehead and up into his scalp, where it clung to his thinning hair in thick yellow crusts.

Trying not to stare, I told him I was new and asked how long he'd worked at Fun World.

'Nearly thirty years.' He scratched his head and a small avalanche of flakes drifted onto the shoulders of his blue overalls.

'You must have seen a lot of changes.' I arranged my lips into a smile, encouraging him to talk.

'There's not much I ain't seen. All the dirty washing and all the rubbish. There's not much goes on around here I don't know about.'

'You must have some good stories to tell. I'd like to know what it was like in the olden days. My Auntie Sandra used to work here a long time ago. Sandra Hewitt. Perhaps you knew her.'

'Sandra Hewitt.' He scratched a dry patch on his chin. 'How long ago would that be?'

'Nineteen… twenty years ago perhaps.' I kept my tone light and disinterested, but the possibility he could be my father crossed my mind.

'The name rings a bell, but I can't put a face to her. Half of Westhatch has worked here at one time or another, then they move on.'

'But not you.'

'No, not me.'

'You must like it here.'

'I never said that. No, I never said that. I could just never get away.' He opened the van door.

'I'll bring a photo of her to show you,' I called.

He started the engine and drove off, leaving me standing on the caravan veranda wondering whether he'd heard my parting shot.

The next day I carried a picture in my tabard pocket. It was the photo of Mum sitting alone on the beach in her white sundress. Several times I saw Sid's truck in the distance, but there never seemed to be an opportunity to speak to him. Boody became impatient.

'Fish and chipsticks! Stop looking out the window. What's the matter with you? Don't tell me you fancy the new bloke who's helping Sid. He's a proper ugly mug.'

'Course not! I'm keeping my eye out for Mrs O. You know how she likes to sneak up on us.'

'Then clean the caravan, slacker.'

By Thursday I was fed up sitting night after night in my bedroom at the B&B. I slipped on a pair of black leggings and the sequinned butterfly jumper from the charity shop and drove back to Fun World in the evening. Nights out in the past had consisted of scientific lectures or a Shakespeare play at the theatre (Theo's choice), a night at the opera or a meal in a quaint Italian restaurant (Paloma's favourite), or trips to the cinema with colleagues from the garden centre, Marcus included. I shivered with excitement at the thought of bingo and dancing. More importantly, I wanted to get a good look at Chucky Skittles. He'd also been a contemporary of my mother's. He was on my shortlist of potential fathers along with Maxwell King and Sid Tulitt.

On the way I picked up Sonya. We'd had lunched together a couple of times that week, chatting about our workload and her life back in Albania, buying hot dogs from a seafront snack bar to avoid paying the inflated prices at the holiday camp café. She didn't have a nest egg to fall back on like me, and was worried about the rent at the hostel in Eastbeach Street where she lived.

She was waiting on the pavement when I drew up, wearing the same clothes as the day of her interview: sensible shoes, long skirt and a headscarf over her hair.

'Jumping jumblesales!' Boody exclaimed when we slipped into the entertainment centre just after seven. 'Make an effort, girls, why don't you!' She was wearing a body-hugging acid-green minidress and stilettoes. Without the unflattering cleaning tunic, she was whippet-thin. 'Go on, get in the queue for the bingo tickets. They'll stop selling once the kids' show starts in ten minutes.'

'What is bingo tickets?' Sonya whispered.

'It's a game. You buy a card with numbers printed on it. Each ticket is different. A computer randomly selects the numbers and you cross them off on the ticket once they're called out. As soon as you've crossed off all your numbers, you shout "Bingo!" If you're the first, you win.'

'What is the win?'

'Last week a woman won eighty-four quid,' Boody said. 'It's not always that much. The size of the prize depends on how many people buy tickets. In high season you can win a couple of hundred.'

'Eighty-four quids?'

'That's pounds,' I explained.

'Is a lot of money. How much is ticket?'

'£2. I bought five,' Boody bragged.

We joined the queue and purchased a ticket each. At the bar, Sonya bought an orange juice. Boody persuaded me to go halves on a bottle of white wine. She weaved through the chairs and tables, holding the bottle high in one hand and the stems of the upside-down glasses in the other while we trailed behind; the edgy girl with her nerdy acolytes. I noticed a couple of men turned to watch as she swung past.

The children's show was about to start. Gavin Flynne leapt onto the stage wearing multicoloured Bermuda shorts, a pink jacket and shiny bow tie. A microphone headset curled across his cheek towards his mouth. From where we were sitting, it looked as though his skin had split between his lips and ear and congealed into a dark scar.

A blast of music erupted from the speakers. The disco ball sprayed the floor with points of spiralling light. His naked calves, surprisingly vulnerable beneath his baggy shorts, stepped neatly from side to side in time to the music. Performing a complicated hand jive, he began to sing.

Turn up the music, switch on the lights
We're eager for your pleasure.
Let down your hair, forget your cares
There's fun here without measure.

Welcome mums and welcome dads
Hello girls, high-five the lads
Follow the fun, join in the dances
There's competitions so take your chances
With Patty, Harry and the Pink Jacket crew
All on a mission to entertain you.

Turn up the music, this is the night
To discover Show Time treasure
Get off your seat, jump to your feet
Devote yourself to pleasure.

'Hands together now,' he shouted, holding his arms above his head, clapping.

The adults at the half-empty tables continued their conversations, shouting to each other to be heard over the music. A scattering of Pink Jackets joined in and a toddler in pyjamas, alone on the dance floor, jumped up and down. When the music finished, Gavin bowed with a flourish.

'Ladies and gentlemen, boys and girls, he's been here since the dawn of time. He's pulled himself out of the primeval slime... and evolved into the lovable slob he is today. I'm just busting to introduce the funniest, fattest trouper on site, weighing in at over twenty-eight stone, it's... drum roll please,' the audience banged their hands on the tables, 'the chuckle meister himself, MISTER CHUCKY SKITTLES!'

An enormous man in a shiny pink jacket and sparkly bow tie romped onto the stage, his signature tune blaring over the sound system.

'Good evening, children! Good evening, mums and dads! Good evening to all the other inmates! It's time for Chucky Skittles' silly songs and games. Come on, kids. Come down here onto the dance floor where I can see you.'

A couple of children wandered to the front and sat cross-legged on the floor.

'I know there's more of you than that. Come on. Don't tell me there's been another prison break. Out of the woodwork, my little slugs and slugettes. It's party time!'

A woman stood up and walked down to the dance floor pulling a small child by each hand.

'That's right, darling. Big girls can come too.'

A troupe of boys, just arrived, raced through the chairs and tables and dived onto the dance floor, sliding on their bottoms and stomachs until they reached the front.

'Here come the boys!' Chucky called. 'We love the hyperactive ones, don't we, mums and dads?' A spasm of sarcastic laughter rippled round the room. 'Right, while the rest of you kids make your way to the front, I think it's time to meet our park mascots. You know who they are. Boys and girls, mums and dads, let's see if we can coax them onto the stage. Music please, maestro.'

A cheeky tune roared from the enormous speakers on either side of the stage. A seven-foot pizza sidestepped into view. A pair of oversized gloved hands flapped like flippers from the front of the yellow-and-red plush costume. Sidling crablike to the centre of the stage, the pizza kicked out her legs in a grotesque can-can, skinny calves encased in pink tights, terminating in enormous fluffy slippers.

The music morphed to a rap anthem and a giant hot dog appeared from the other side of the stage, arms swinging in an exaggerated swagger. His legs were brawnier than those of the giant plastic statue at the entrance to the park, and he was out of time with the music.

'It's Patty Pizza and Harry Hot Dog!' Gavin screamed.

The boys and girls sitting on the dance floor jumped to their feet and rushed forward to the front of the stage, waving at the cartoon characters.

'Away from the stage, boys and girls, please,' Chucky ordered. 'Back behind the white line. That's right. Patty and Harry, everyone! Let's give them a cheer.'

'Who's inside the costumes?' I yelled to Boody over the fading music.

'Don't know. Probably new Pinkies. Everybody hates being Patty and Harry. I did Patty once when half the Pinkies were struck down with food poisoning. Festering armpits! I thought I was going to die. The gig gets rotated, but the newbies get landed with it until they squeak or collapse from heat exhaustion. By the size of the legs, I'd guess Harry is Jezza.'

'Who?'

'Jeremy. The fat Pinkie who started the same day as you two.'

I sipped my wine slowly. Boody had already poured herself another glass. Sonya held her untouched juice with an expression of wonder on her face as Patty and Harry bopped around the stage with Chucky Skittles between them.

'This is boring,' Boody yelled, 'but you have to get here early if you want a good table. After the kids' show it fills up pretty quickly with the bingo crowd. The sprogs get sent to bed or play in the arcade while we get down to the numbers.'

'What happens after the bingo?' I shouted in her ear.

'There'll be a cabaret or karaoke. Sometimes a stand-up comedian. Then dancing till one o'clock. It's all naff.'

'I not want to be late,' Sonya said. 'My shift start at half-six tomorrow.'

'Don't worry,' I reassured her. 'My landlady locks the door at eleven.'

Boody swore.

'Remind me not to party with you two good-time girls again, won't you?' She gulped down her second glass of wine and poured herself another. 'I can't hack the pace!' She pushed the bottle towards me. I put my hand over my glass.

'I'm driving.' She rolled her eyes.

After leading the children in a couple of party dances celebrating the jolliness of junk food, Patty and Harry left the stage, still waving but a little less bouncy after their frenetic routines.

'Poor slob,' Boody said. 'He doesn't stand a chance. Betcha it ends in tears before the weekend.'

'That hot dog is good person,' Sonya replied. 'He very kind to me when I lose my staff card. He let me through the door and helped me find it.'

'Perhaps he wants to get to know you better,' Boody smirked.

'He is just good person,' Sonya insisted.

'He won't last long. The Pink Jackets are piranhas. What a loser!'

Sonya didn't hear Boody's aside to me because she was watching the stage. Chucky had stepped into the spotlight holding a microphone, perspiration shining on his bald head. I watched him closely. Could he be the man with the unruly hair in the photo with my mother? With passing time and an increase in weight, it might be possible. He'd worked here long enough to remember Mum, in theory. I made a resolution to become one of Chucky's most attentive fans.

'I need a girl,' he cried. Someone wolf-whistled from the audience. 'Which one will I have?'

My stomach fluttered. Perhaps this was my chance to join him on the stage.

'I'm looking for one about five or six years old.'

Of course. How stupid. I was glad I hadn't waved or stood up. He peered down at the children cross-legged on the dance floor, urgent hands thrusting up and waving like spears of corn.

'Little girl in the pink,' he pointed. 'Come up here.'

A wispy child wearing a ballerina dress with a pink net skirt skipped up the steps. Her pale hair floated down her back in thin strands.

'What's your name, darling?' He bent and held the microphone to her mouth.

'Libby.'

'Libby Lipstick! And how old are you, Libby?

'Five.'

'And where do you come from?'

'I don't know.'

'This world? Or have you wafted down from paradise, my angel?'

She put her hand in front of her mouth and giggled, twisting her slim frame from side to side. Chucky put his hand in front of his own mouth and imitated her girlish sway. After the children had finished laughing, he thrust the microphone in front of her face again.

'England,' she gasped, before another fit of giggles. A patriotic cheer rose from the audience.

'And do you have a boyfriend?'

'Yes.'

Chucky stepped back dramatically.

'You've got a boyfriend?'

'Yes,' Libby giggled.

'And does your father know?'

'No. He doesn't live with Mummy and me any more.'

'And are you a Pizza or a Hot Dog?' Chucky asked, changing the subject.

'I don't know.'

'You don't know much, Libby Lipstick from England. If you're in a caravan with an odd number, you're a Pizza, and if you are in a caravan with an even number, you're on the Hot Dog team. Go and ask your mummy and come back and tell me!'

Libby ran down the steps to a table near the back of the entertainment centre. Chucky wiped a hand over his sweating forehead, plastering a damp strand of straying hair back in place, and turned to the children.

'Anyone else who doesn't know whether they are a Pizza or a Hot Dog, go and find out from your adults now.'

Half a dozen children leapt up and disappeared into the darkness surrounding the dance floor.

'Our head Pink Jacket, Gavin, is a Pizza and helps Patty's team. I'm chief trainer for the Hot Dogs. I'm a low-down hot diggidy dog!'

Libby returned to the stage.

'I'm a Pizza.'

'OK. Now put your hands up, kids, if you're a Hot Dog. I need someone to come up here and play a game against Libby to win points for Harry's team and,' he paused dramatically, 'to win one of our wonderful Fun World prizes.'

Another crop of hands waved from the floor. He chose a boy.

'What's your name?'

'Preston.'

'Is your surname Northend?'

'No.'

Chucky laughed at the child's puzzled face.

'And where are you from?'

'Basingstoke.'

A cheer rose up from a table near the bar.

'Basingstoke! Well you need a lucky break, mate. Give me a high-five.' They slapped hands.

'How old are you?

'Six.'

'And do you have a girlfriend, Preston?'

'No!'

'Sweet. I'd set you up with Libby here, but apparently she's already taken. Are you going to win for me and Harry?'

'Yes.'

'Good man.'

Chucky turned to the audience, did a funny little shuffle and shouted, 'It's Libby Lipstick for the Pizzas against Preston Northend for the Hot Dogs! You two run down and get one of your grown-ups on stage to help you.'

The children darted away and both returned dragging their mothers. While they were gone, Chucky announced there were twenty minutes left to buy a bingo ticket.

'The game is this. I'm going to ask you both a question. The one who gets it right, or is closest to the right answer, gets to go first. The question is... If you add my age to Gobby Gavin's age, what age would it be? When you think you know the answer, run to me and squeeze my hooter.' He pulled from behind his back a large horn with a long trumpet and red rubber bulb. 'In your own time, kids. When you think you've worked it out, Gavin's age plus my age. You can ask your mums for help.'

Preston's mum whispered in his ear and he ran and honked the hooter.

'Right, Preston, if you added Gavin's age and my age together, what would you get?'

'A hundred and eight.'

'A HUNDRED AND EIGHT! Remind me to have a word with your mother afterwards.'

Libby ran up to honk the horn. It emitted a small squeak.

'She's only gone and broke it!'

The child looked stricken.

'Never mind,' Chucky said. 'What's your answer, Miss Lipstick?'

'Fifty-three.'

'Fifty-three? You're both wrong. The answer is eighty-five, ladies and gentlemen. EIGHTY-FIVE. I'm twenty-nine and Gavin's fifty-six. Preston was the closest, but Libby gave me the answer I like the best.' He gave the thumbs up to her mother. 'Nice one, missus. Libby gets to go first!'

Preston looked at his mother, an expression of outrage on his face.

'The game is this,' Chucky continued. 'You have to throw a ball through the hoop. Every time you get one in, your mum has to put on a T-shirt. You've got thirty seconds, and each ball will earn your team twenty-five points.'

Gavin staggered onto the stage with a basketball hoop and a ball, followed by a glamorous Pink Jacket carrying a pile of multicoloured T-shirts. Chucky took the ball and bounced it hard against Gavin's forehead.

'Yep. Just as I thought. Hollow! Here you go, Libby Lipstick. Catch.' He softly threw the football at the little girl. Her arms encircled thin air as it bounced past. 'That's a good start. You catch like a girl, darling.'

Gavin set the hoop down at the back of the stage. Chucky yanked Libby's mother to the side so that she stood next to the pile of T-shirts. He placed Libby centre stage and stood behind her, a hand the size of a small ham on her shoulder. Her collarbones were as thin as a sparrow's. One pink strap had slipped over the top of her arm. She was dainty as a flower against his sweating bulk.

'When I honk my hooter, you start throwing the ball. Gavin will shout out the score.' He turned the child to face the hoop, her back to the audience. 'Each time you get a basket, I'm going to help your lovely mum put on a T-shirt.' Chucky sounded the horn, now miraculously recovered. A musical impression of a clock ticking down to zero boomed through the speakers.

Libby threw the ball, too short then too low. When Chucky's back was turned to pick up the first T-shirt on the pile, Gavin dropped the football into the net and yelled, 'One.' Chucky made a show of helping to pull a yellow T-shirt over the mother's chest. She laughed and squirmed away from his chubby hands, trying to smooth her dishevelled hair.

'Dirty old man!' Boody said.

'Two!' Gavin shouted. Chucky grabbed another T-shirt, but before Libby's mum had pulled it over her head, Gavin shouted, 'Three.'

'You cheated!' Chucky bellowed.

'Oh no I didn't,' Gavin cried.

'Oh yes you did,' the children at the front screamed.

'Cheat, cheat, cheat,' Chucky cried, gesturing to the audience to join in the anthem. At that moment, Libby managed to score her first basket unaided.

'Four!'

Chucky ran back across the stage and yanked a green T-shirt over the woman's head. The music reached a crescendo and there was the sound of a synthesised explosion followed by a ripple of applause.

'Your turn now, Preston. I want you to win. After all, you're up against a girl. But just enjoy yourself, keep smiling. It's the taking part that counts. Oh, one last thing. DO NOT LOSE. Do it for the Hot Dogs! Think of all the girlfriends you're going to get if you win.'

Chucky continued talking. The audience was laughing, but I no longer heard what was being said. Someone had sidled up to a table nearby, holding a pint in his hand, and wearing a black T-shirt with a skull on the front. Sludger Trafford. He sat down deliberately and returned my stare.

Chapter 10

'What's he doing here?' I whispered to Boody. 'I thought you said he didn't come on duty until eleven?'

'He doesn't usually bother coming in early,' she shrugged. 'He's not the bingo type. He'll be on the door later to stop any trouble.'

'Well, he's giving me the creeps. Is he still staring?'

Boody turned her head.

'Don't look!' I hissed.

'How can I tell if he's watching if I can't turn round, moron?'

'Just ignore him,' I said.

But it wasn't easy. While Preston threw the ball at the net, and Chucky eased stretchy cotton over another mother's chest, all I could think of was Trafford sitting close, staring at us with his black eyes. Not moving, except to bring his pint to his lips. Not blinking, like a snake.

When the music counted down to a second explosion, Preston's mother was wearing six T-shirts. Chucky fussed round her, pulling the hems down and adjusting the necklines while she made a giggly attempt to push him away.

'You look very nice. Very nice indeed, Mrs Northend. Now the bit I like best. I'm going to help these ladies take off their T-shirts so I can verify the scores.'

'Now, now, Chucky,' Gavin interjected. 'I'm sure our gorgeous Pink Jacket, Shannon, can help the ladies.'

'I *am* the adjudicator. Isn't that right, boys? It's my job to take them off.'

'Take them off, take them off,' chanted a chorus of male voices. Chucky turned back to the ladies, but they'd hurriedly ripped off the T-shirts and were disentangling their inside out piles. Chucky turned his attention to the children.

'You did absolutely brilliant, kids. Give each other a kiss.'

Libby crossed her arms across her narrow chest and stuck out her chin.

'Give each other a hug, then... shake hands?'

She shook her head. He clenched his fist in front of his face, a pantomime gesture of anger. But despite his cheeky grin, irritation at her defiance crackled from his body like static electricity.

'Give them a big round of applause, ladies and gentlemen. Go and get the prizes, Gazza.'

Gavin disappeared behind the stage curtain and reappeared almost immediately.

'Close your eyes, kids, and hold out your hands.'

They held their hands in front of their bodies, palms outstretched.

'Not so wide. What do you think this is? Butlins?'

He pushed their hands together so they touched. He took a small goody bag and placed it in Libby's palms. He positioned a slightly larger plastic bag in Preston's outstretched hands. They opened their eyes.

'You've both won a selection of Fun World special sweeties, and a child's free ticket for the go-kart track or the crazy golf.'

Gavin passed Chucky a white card with colourful lettering on the front.

'And here's your winner's certificate, Preston Northend from Basingstoke. Give them both a big round of applause, everybody.'

After the clapping stopped and the children returned to their seats, Chucky allocated 100 points to the Pizzas and 150 points to the Hog Dogs. He dished out certificates to other children who'd won contests during the day: the best portrait of Patty and Harry, families who'd managed to complete the cryptic treasure hunt, the winning ping-pong team. Each winner was asked if they were Pizzas or Hot Dogs, and were awarded 100 points for their team.

With a flourish, Patty Pizza and Harry Hot Dog were ushered back onto the stage. The screen on the back wall flashed up the previous day's accumulated team points. Patty was in the lead.

'Eyes on the screen, everyone,' Chucky roared into his microphone. 'We now have the final results for today, as verified by NASA. Our computer is adding tonight's points to the running total from the rest of the week. Have we got the score? Let's count down now, ladies and gentlemen, boys and girls.'

Large numbers flashed on the screen. Chucky led the audience in the countdown.

'Five... four... three... two... one.'

Lights flashed. A sound-effects explosion boomed. The final points fired onto the screen.

'Pizzas, 1,350 points. Hot Dogs, 1,475. The Hot Dogs are tonight's winners!'

Cheers and groans from the children were obliterated by Harry Hot Dog's rap theme tune, which blasted out at the volume of a jumbo jet preparing for take-off. Inside the costume, Jeremy made a half-hearted attempt at a victory dance.

'Pizzas, you were very, very good. Give them a round of applause... But Hot Dogs, you were better!'

Clapping, cheering and stamping of feet echoed round the room. The adults, several drinks inside them, were beginning to relax.

'Don't blame yourselves, Pizzas,' Chucky crowed. 'We only beat you by 125 points. It was *not* your fault. The responsibility lies with your team leader, Gobby Gavin. He's not been motivating his side or spending time with them like I have. I think we should punish him for letting the Pizzas down. Shannon, go and get him.'

She ducked behind the curtain and returned with her arm under Gavin's elbow. He'd removed his jacket and bow tie and pulled his Bermuda shorts up to his armpits.

'You look ridiculous,' Chuckie shouted. 'Pull your shorts down!' Gavin turned his back on the audience and obeyed, revealing a ludicrous pair of spotty underpants. The children screamed with laughter. Shouts and whistles from the adults echoed across the dance floor.

'Pull them up, you idiot!' Chucky smacked him on the bottom with his microphone. A loud acoustic 'woof' belched from the speakers. 'Gazza, it's time to face the music. Because you've let your team down, you're going to get a custard pie in the face. Do you think that's fair, kids?'

'YES!'

Gavin shook his head from side to side. Chucky put a plump arm around his shoulder and forced him to face the front. He was taller than Gavin. The Pink Jacket looked as slender as a girl in his embrace. Shannon and one of the new girls appeared behind them, carrying a large rectangular bowl, a bucket and a towel.

'You need to kneel down here, Gazza, and face the kids so they can see how sorry you are.'

Gavin knelt, bent his head and put his hands together in prayer.

'To keep the mess to a minimum I'm going to put this bowl in front of you to catch any drips.' Chucky reached back and took the bowl from Shannon and placed it on the floor in front of Gavin. 'For health and safety you have to wear this blindfold. It'll stop you getting custard in your eyes.'

He passed Gavin a pink satin face mask, the type women wear in bed to block out the light. Chucky flicked the elastic at the back and Gavin's head rocked back and forth. The children shrieked with excitement.

'I suggest you shut your eyes as well, mate, just in case.'

Chucky stood behind Gavin and took the bucket. He held his nose dramatically and wafted the air above it. He put his finger over his lips to quieten the children. Then, with unexpected speed and aggression he lifted his leg, pushed Gavin's head into the bowl with his foot and poured the contents of the bucket over his head.

'Waste not, want not! It's the leftovers from the restaurant. Mushy peas! Spaghetti! Baked beans! Custard! What a stink! You deserve this, for letting down the kids.'

His foot pressed Gavin's head firmly. The sticky mess covered his face. My breathing instinctively quickened at the thought he might not be able to breathe himself. Gavin grabbed Chucky's leg. Chucky staggered back and threw down the bucket. As Gavin lifted his head and began wiping the orange and green slop from his mouth, the head of entertainment grabbed him from behind and pushed his head back into the bowl.

'Do you think he's been punished enough yet, kids?' he bellowed.

'No! No! No!'

'Drown him!' shouted a male voice from the shadows around the bar.

A small figure leapt to her feet at the foot of the stage. Libby flew up the steps, her gauzy skirt fluttering as light as a moth around her legs. When she reached Chucky she thumped him on his back with her small fists, her face contorting, her mouth opening and shutting noiselessly as her screams were drowned out by the Chucky Skittles signature tune. After a moment, he noticed the tugging on his jacket and released Gavin, whose head shot out of the bowl. Coughing and spluttering, he wiped his mouth and nose with the sleeve of his shirt. Shannon passed him the towel and he staggered to his feet.

'What can I do for you, lovely?' Chucky asked Libby. 'Did you want to help punish Gavin for losing tonight's competition for your team?'

'I hate you!' she shouted into the microphone.

'Women! One minute they're taking your sweets, the next minute they hate you. Isn't that right, lads?'

Raucous laughter rose up from the darkness. Chucky smiled benevolently, bent down and pinched the little girl's cheek.

'We're just having a bit of fun, darling. Cheer up. It might never happen.' He straightened and turned to the audience, one arm outstretched. 'Ladies and gentlemen, please give a big round of applause for your head Pink Jacket and all-round good sport, Gavin Flynne, and his superhero girlfriend, Libby Lipstick… Sit back down with the other kids, darling, and stay behind the white line.' He straightened his bow tie. 'There's five minutes left to buy your bingo tickets, but that's all for our kids' entertainment tonight. What a blast! I'll see you back here same time, same place tomorrow for more silly games and dances. Now get on your feet for a last party dance. I'm Chucky Skittles and it's my job to bowl you over. Goodnight!'

The sound system switched to a disco anthem. The children jumped up. Several girls held hands with younger toddlers and swayed in time to the music. Boys played tag, racing in between clusters of kids who were jumping up and down or pretending to be superheroes. A few mums and dads drifted onto the dance floor to bop along with their children.

From the corner of my eye, I saw someone walk up to our table. An empty chair was dragged towards me and Trafford sat down without being asked, his knee knocking mine as he forced himself into our group. He stank of cigarettes and fried food. He put his drink on the table and stared menacingly at Boody.

'Payment time!'

Chapter 11

'You'll get your money,' Boody snarled. 'Now shove off, you're cramping our style.' Trafford looked at me, then Sonya, an insulting expression on his face. He laughed.

'What style's that? Pierre Cardigan? Frumpo Chanel?'

'Sling yer hook.'

'Not without my money.'

'I told you, you'll have it.'

'When?'

'Tomorrow.'

'It's tonight or you'll have to pay interest.'

He stuck out his pierced tongue and waggled it aggressively from side to side. Despite her heavy make-up and the coloured lights, Boody paled and finished her glass with an angry gulp. From her reaction, I guessed the interest being charged wasn't financial.

'You'll get it,' she spat. 'I haven't got it on me. I'll find you on the door later.'

'Don't think because I'll be working I won't collect your debt.' He pushed back his chair. 'Have a nice evening, *mingers.*' He lurched away, his gait wide to accommodate the thigh muscles that pushed tight against his trousers, his fists heavy at his sides.

'What are you two gawping at?' Boody shouted above the music.

'How much you owe?' Sonya asked, her eyes frightened.

'Keep your snozzie to yourself. It's none of your beeswax!'

'Have you got it?' I asked.

'I might. After the bingo.'

'And that's the plan, is it?' I asked, incredulous. 'You're betting everything on a win?'

'Why not?' she shrugged. 'I like to live dangerously.'

'No, you don't! I can see you're petrified. Why did you borrow from that gorilla?'

'I didn't borrow it exactly. He charges some of the girls on the campsite.'

'What for?'

'Security.'

'I don't understand. Are you saying he's charging you for doing his job?'

'Something like that,' she mumbled. 'I don't want to talk about it.'

'Will he charge me?' Sonya asked anxiously.

'No. You don't live on site. I share a staff caravan with Shannon.'

'I didn't know you lived here,' I said.

'Why should you? I don't know where you live, do I?'

'I didn't realise there *were* staff caravans.'

'They don't dish them out to everyone. It's because of the antisocial hours. They know we're on site if anything crops up. They get their extra pound of flesh,' she said bitterly.

'Are they better than hostel?' Sonya asked expectantly.

'How should I know? I've never been homeless. But don't start dreaming of gleaming kitchens, instant hot water and extra-wide living areas. They're the old caravans. Too rank to rent out to holidaymakers. Sid and his team dragged them behind that small wooded area at the top of the North Drive. It's fenced off so the punters don't see.'

'Why do you need security?' I asked.

'Because Trafford and his mates threaten all sorts could happen to us. We have to walk through that wood in the dark. Late at night, when the drunks are on the prowl. It's terrifying. He says nothing will happen to us if we pay up. One girl last year refused. You can guess what happened?' She pulled an ugly expression.

'Did the police get involved?'

'Of course. But the security team is in cahoots with the Westhatch coppers. After all, they're doing their job for them, keeping the thugs and druggies under control over here so they don't go down into the town. Silly girl,' Boody said softly. 'She should have paid up. Nothing was proved. I bet Trafford did it himself, to teach her a lesson. She'll never be able to have kids now.'

'What about your family? Can they lend you the money?'

Boody snorted.

'Ha! Dad did a bunk straight after he left school. Stepdad number three's a complete loser. He tries to scrounge money off of *me*, 'cos I'm the only earner in the family. Mum made sure she was proper qualified for a lifetime of benefits and daytime TV by having all us kids before she left school. I'm the success story here.' She grabbed her glass and gulped down the last mouthful, her mouth twisting into a small, bitter smile.

The music faded and the house lights went up. Shannon and a male Pink Jacket I'd not seen before walked onto the stage carrying a bingo machine.

'Tickets sales for the bingo have now closed,' Shannon announced. 'Please take your seats, ladies and gentlemen. Children should sit quietly if they wish to remain in the entertainment centre. Alternatively they can hang out in the arcade, or go with Gavin to the indoor play den where he's organising a musical statues tournament. A craft table has been set up for those who would like to make a novelty crown for tomorrow morning's Royal Pageant. Once again, I would ask you all to be quiet during play. The first game will be on the purple ticket, and will be for one line only.'

Boody unzipped her white plastic clutch bag and pulled out a marker pen and a sheaf of bingo tickets.

'Eyes down,' Shannon called, switching on the bingo machine.

The computer flashed up a red number.

'Legs eleven. Number eleven.'

Silence descended, heads were bowed, pens poised. The drunken chatter of a few minutes earlier gave way to an eerie hush. More numbers were called, but I couldn't concentrate. I was still thinking about what Boody had said. I glanced sideways to see the progress she was making. She only needed one number to complete her top line. Her jaw was taut. I could sense the excitement rolling from her like waves of static.

'BINGO!'

Boody threw her pen down in disgust as a large woman stood up and waved her ticket in the air.

The numbers were checked and verified and the next game began. After half an hour of tension, it was over. Boody screwed up her tickets and stuffed them in her empty glass, cursing bitterly.

'What are you going to do?' Sonya asked.

'Tell us how much you owe him,' I asked. 'We might be able to help.'

Boody sniffed and wiped her nose on the back of her hand. One bare leg was crossed over the other, her green dress pulled tight over her thighs. Her black stiletto shoe jerked up and down as her leg shook with uncontrolled adrenalin.

'Don't be stupid! You can't help me. Nobody can.'

'Tell us,' I insisted, grabbing her hand and pulling her forward so she had to face me across the table.

'It's nearly a hundred quid, OK? Happy now?'

'A hundred quids!' Sonya murmured in disbelief.

'Cut the echo, dumbo! I'll think of something, I always do. The lift doesn't travel to the top floor with Trafford, if you catch my drift. I've sidestepped him before.'

'I need to go to the toilet,' I said, standing up.

'Yeah, right. Go and powder your nose, darling. No hurry. Don't worry about anything. Take all the time you need, daisybell.' She looked away and swore under her breath. 'That's the way to empty a room in five seconds flat!'

'Wait here, both of you. We'll talk about it when I get back.'

I hurried away before either of them had the chance to join me. Instead of turning left to the toilets, I carried straight on into the amusement arcade. It was heaving with kids and teenagers holding plastic pots filled with coins. Bells rang, lights flashed, music blared, money rattled down metal funnels like silver rain. Computerised racing cars revved their engines. Machine guns fired at enemy helicopters. Excited children who should have been in bed an hour ago chattered and screamed as precariously balanced coins edged ever closer to the drop zone; twenty coins fed into the machines for every one that fell into the tiny, optimistic hands.

I worked my way to the exit and out into the icy night. The smell of chips, sausage fat and the sharp tang of vinegar flavoured the air. Holidaymakers were still making their way into the arcade and entertainment centre for the evening's main attraction – Freddie Baylard and the Bayettes. A tall security guard stood by the door checking tickets. He was a family friendly version of Trafford. Boody had made it clear that the heavy mob would be needed later when the big-screen football finished and the men drinking in the club bar spilled out to hunt down women in the Midnight Disco.

I weaved along the walkway towards the car park, glancing left and right for Trafford's squat, shaven head amid the throng. He was nowhere to be seen. I slipped through the darkness to my car and locked myself in. Opening the glove compartment and taking out the wad of cash from my beanie hat, I peeled off five £20 notes, rolled them up and posted them up my sleeve. After checking there was no one else in the car park, I scuttled back to the pulsating hub of the holiday park.

Freddy Baylard and the Bayettes were already on stage. The dance floor had thickened to a bubbling soup of swaying bodies. Boody and Sonya were watching, their faces grim. When I slid into my seat, Sonya turned to me.

'We go home soon?'

'OK,' I said.

'That's just brilliant!' Boody sniped.

I grabbed her hand across the table. She tried to pull away, but I used my free hand to pull the roll of cash from under my sleeve and force it into her palm. She looked down at the paper, flicked the end to count the number of notes and looked up sharply.

'Who are you? The Artful Dodger? Where did you get this?'

'It doesn't matter. It's yours now.'

'Shut the front door! And there's me thinking you're a hoity-toity, Miss Pure and Holy.' She smiled. 'You… are… baaaad… girl!'

'I owe you one, from the other day. Remember?'

'Yeah. I guess you did. But this is… just… bloomin' marvellous.'

'Did you steal?' Sonya asked.

'No… yes… sort of, I suppose. But don't worry. Nobody's going to miss it.'

'Thanks, Countess… Really. Can I use one of the twenties in the arcade to see if I can win me a little extra?'

'No! You go and find Trafford and pay him off *now*. Over the next few days we're going to put our heads together and think of a way to stop this racket he's got going. We need to catch him doing something he shouldn't.'

'What then? Grass him up? He's got a lot of friends,' Boody said.

'I don't care how many friends he's got. We're friends now. We're going to look out for each other and find other girls who also want to stop this harassment. We're clever enough to outwit that brain cell of his.'

'Too right!'

'I know this type of mens,' Sonya said. 'They have the power. Is not easy. I don't want troubles now I have this good job.'

'Don't worry,' I was exhilarated by my grand gesture. 'I'll make sure nothing bad is going to happen.'

Chapter 12

I drove Sonya to her hostel at half-past ten. As I weaved back through town to the B&B, a light on top of the dark expanse of the Downs caught my eye. It was the dome, lit like a beacon to guide weary travellers home. I ground my teeth in annoyance at the waste of electricity. So much for Greenacres' environmental credentials! What was Marcus thinking, leaving the lights to burn so late into the night? Theo would never authorise such extravagant behaviour.

Once again, I parked round the corner and walked briskly along the road, hugging the fat packet of cash under my jumper. As I neared the front door, I became aware of quick footsteps behind me. It was probably just a jogger, but the sound of feet slapping the pavement caused my heart to beat in time with the pounding rhythm. I sped up until I was running, hurtling up the steps to the B&B and pumping the doorbell. A dark figure loomed behind me. A frightened squeak leapt from my mouth.

'Shut up, stupid. It's only me.'

'Zavier!' I smacked him roughly away, my hands shaking. 'You idiot. You scared me half to death. What are you doing?'

'Waiting for you,' he gasped.

'Why?'

'Because I was worried. Where have you been?'

'Out.'

'I gathered that from when I called to see you earlier. I've been waiting for you to get back.'

The front door opened.

'What's with all the ringing?' Mrs Bungay complained. 'I heard you the first time.'

She raised a suspicious eyebrow when she saw Zavier panting behind me on the doorstep.

'You again!'

'Thank you, Mrs B,' I said, stepping inside.

Zavier also pushed past.

'You know the rules,' she cried.

'Don't worry. My feet are firmly on the ground.' He put his hand at the small of my back and pushed me up the stairs.

'What?!' I objected.

'You've got five minutes and then I'm coming up,' Mrs Bungay shouted to our retreating backs.

I turned to face him when we reached my bedroom door.

'You can't just – ' I objected, but he put his hand firmly over my mouth.

'Shhh. I've got something to tell you.' He pushed open the door and shut it behind us. 'Make us a cuppa. I've been freezing my socks off waiting for you to come home.'

'I never asked you to!'

'You're my valued client. I'm hoping that after tonight you might like to reassess our agreement and pay for a few more days of my time, seeing as how I've gone the extra mile and all that.'

'I told you I was dropping the case. I've given up trying to find my father.'

'You were giving me the brush-off.'

'Shame it didn't succeed,' I said switching on the kettle.

'Do you want to know why I'm here, or what?'

'OK. Why are you here?'

He sat down on the dressing table stool, his knees pushing awkwardly against the end of the bed. 'I've found out you're in a lot of trouble.'

'Trouble?' I picked up a small pink scatter cushion from the bed and plumped it vigorously.

'I'm not the only one who's been trying to track you down.'

'Oh, that!' Even I could hear the relief in my voice. Someone was looking for me after all.

Zavier raised an eyebrow.

'These are not the kind of people you want to be found by, believe me.' When I didn't comment, he continued. 'Why would a couple of paid heavies be asking about your whereabouts?'

'Heavies?' I echoed, a vision of Paloma's plump frame and Marcus' broad shoulders flitting before my eyes.

'Professionals. What have you done, Ava?' His voice was gentle. I remembered the stolen money and credit card. It wasn't until later I realised he'd used my real name.

'I haven't *done* anything! I've left home, that's all. I'm of age. My family's probably looking for me, that's all. They've hired someone to help. But I don't want to be found. Not yet, anyway.'

'Then why are you looking so guilty?'

'I took some money.'

'How much?'

'Several thousand.'

He looked surprised.

'They wouldn't be going to the trouble of hiring top private security for that amount of dosh. Anything else?'

'A company credit card. But I've already withdrawn the limit and cut it up.'

He stroked his chin and gazed out of the window.

'I think you'd better tell me the whole story.'

'No. I think you should tell me *your* story. I'm the one paying, remember. How did you find out about these men?'

'I thought you might be a runaway, so I've been checking the missing persons' websites. No one matching your description is on there.'

I must have fingered my hair subconsciously because he unexpectedly asked, 'Is that your natural colour?'

'I should have dyed it blonde,' I replied, ignoring his question.

'I like it,' he countered. 'I had a black poodle as a child. You remind me of her.' He laughed when he saw my irritated expression. 'She was grumpy too.'

'Can we get back to the point?'

'As nobody has reported you missing, I decided to do a little fishing among my colleagues in the Westhatch investigative community. I let it be known I was looking for a stroppy Goth.'

I threw the pink cushion at his head and he deftly caught it.

'One of my contacts in the police mentioned someone had been asking about a girl – small, slim build, long curls, eyes as green as emeralds, skin as smooth as full-fat cream – '

'Shut it!' I exclaimed, now grabbing a box of tissues from the bedside cabinet and throwing it at his head. He batted it away easily.

'I said it didn't sound like the girl I was looking for but,' suddenly his face was serious, 'they're offering a reward of £50,000 for information leading to your whereabouts.'

We stared at each other for a long moment. I couldn't speak. *£50,000!*

'They gave my mate a card for Excelsior Security. I've checked them out. These are the big boys. They're not like me, looking for stolen pets and spying on errant husbands. These are the type who carry guns. What are you mixed up in?'

'Nothing… nothing,' I said, desperately trying to make sense of what he'd told me. Why would Marcus and Paloma employ security specialists to track me down rather than report my disappearance to the police and the Missing Persons Bureau? It didn't make sense. And where would they get £50,000 from? Apart from a small reserve, all profits from Greenacres were ploughed back into the dome, Theo's experiments and the Golden Acres project in Africa, much to my exasperation.

'I'm worried about you.' His eyes watched me closely.

'You don't need to.'

Mentally comparing the £50,000 reward with the fee I'd paid Zavier, I stared at the carpet, not wanting him to guess the direction of my thoughts.

'If I can find you, they can find you.'

I darted a glance in his direction.

'Don't look at me like that. I'm not about to turn you over.'

'Why not? You look as though you need the money.'

'Client confidentiality, remember.' He smiled, but I was not reassured.

'I thought that only related to doctors and solicitors and… priests.'

'You can trust me. Tell me what's going on.'

He reached across and touched my arm. I realised I was trembling. His grey eyes were full of an emotion I couldn't place, the gold flecks at the centre radiating out as his pupils darkened.

With a rush, I began to talk. Once I started, I couldn't stop. All the words I'd bottled up came spilling out. My discovery that Theo Gage wasn't my biological father. The news my mother had worked at Fun World Holiday Camp, fallen pregnant and run away. He passed me the box of tissues and busied himself with the tea tray.

'Running away seems to run in the family,' he remarked. 'As a rule of thumb, I think it's always better to face difficulties head-on.'

'Well, I'm not *you*, Mr Creeping-about-in-the dark-and-hacking-into-other-people's-computers.'

'Point taken.'

I explained Mum had gone to work for Theo and married him shortly after my birth. He sat in silence as I recounted the facts about her death. I dug his father's file out from the bottom of the wardrobe where I'd hidden it. He raised an eyebrow, but didn't mention I'd lied when I said I'd thrown it away. He flicked through the pages as I told him of my journey to London and the lengths to which I had gone to cover my tracks.

'Clever,' he said, 'but they obviously think you're still here.'

I told him about my email account and how nobody seemed to have missed me. I didn't admit I'd used his home as a forwarding address for my mail. I also decided not to tell him about my job or my car. However sympathetic his expression, and whatever he said about his loyalty to clients, £50,000 was a big temptation for anyone. I didn't doubt his sincerity that night. When I looked into his eyes, I was sure he believed everything he was saying about trust and client confidentially, but I couldn't dismiss the suspicion that at some point he would give in to temptation, hand me over and claim the reward. After all, a drug habit was expensive and no respecter of promises. I would get as much advice and information from him as I could before packing my bags and changing my lodgings.

'You're as safe here as anywhere, as long as you lie low,' he said. 'I can keep an eye on things from across the road. And Brenda's not going to say anything to anyone. You're her first paying guest for months. You've only got to look at the state of her front garden to see why nobody else wants to stay here.'

I grimaced. He passed me a milky coffee with two sugars and I sat on the edge of the bed.

'Let me have another look at Dad's file. Something's been niggling in the back of my mind. We were trying to find your father, but perhaps we should have a think about how your mother died. Here it is.' He pulled out the autopsy report. 'Have you read it?'

'Not in detail. I didn't understand a lot of the medical jargon. In any case, it was talking about my mother's body. Not a pleasant read.'

He scanned through the pages while I finished my coffee, the hot sweet liquid calming the agitation I'd felt moments earlier.

'This is a bit strange. The pathologist noticed two small pricks to the back of her arm where the insulin was injected.'

'And?'

'Diabetics usually inject into their stomachs or thighs.'

'Why not the arm?'

'Because the stomach and thighs have a layer of fat just below the skin which helps to absorb the insulin, but not many nerves. It's more comfortable.'

'Perhaps Mum had a high pain threshold.'

'Think about it. It's not easy to inject yourself in the back of the arm. Doctors inject other people in the arm, but if you're injecting yourself surely you would choose an easier site. If Sandra had needle marks in the back of her arm, then someone else put them there.'

'So it wasn't suicide?'

'If it was, someone helped her.'

'It could have been murder!' I cried.

'Exactly.'

I put the empty cup on the bedside cabinet, pulled my legs up close to my chest and pressed my eye sockets into my knees. I felt the bed sink to one side as Zavier sat next to me.

'I feel sick.'

I could smell Zavier's aftershave. He put his arm round my shoulder.

'Sorry. I need to keep reminding myself that this is your mother we're talking about. It's easy to get caught up in the excitement of an investigation and forget there are real people involved. Perhaps this explains why the heavy mob have been asking about you at the local police station. Other than me, who else have you been talking to about your parents?'

'No one. Who would want her dead? And don't say Theo. He would never, ever do anything like that. He's the most loving, honest, gentle, honourable man in the whole world.'

'Then why did you run away?'

'Because I'm stupid, stupid, stupid! I was angry. I wanted to hurt him. But better to have him as my adopted father than all the biological dads in the world. You don't think my real dad did it, do you? Perhaps I'm a murderer's daughter... Oh, I can't bear it!'

'You don't know that. Let's look at this thing logically. Your mum was running away from something when she turned up at Greenacres. Was it because she was ashamed she'd fallen pregnant? Was it because she wanted to get away from your real father? Or was there was another reason?'

'What reason?'

'I don't know, but if you'd like to renew my contract I'll do my best to find out.'

Chapter 13

The previous evening had been a very expensive night out. As well as paying for half a bottle of wine and a bingo ticket, I'd given Boody £100 and Zavier another £175. This was to ensure I still warranted protection under his client confidentiality rule, and to convince him I still trusted him. If I was to make another sudden disappearance, I wanted to catch him off guard. Once again, I wondered if I'd been ripped off. He'd promised to contact his police buddy to ask for details about the investigation into my mother's death. He was also going to attempt to hack into the computerised personnel system at Fun World so we could draw up a list of current and ex-staff who might have known my mother. He promised to report back after a couple of days.

When I slammed the front door at ten-past six the next morning, I carried a plastic bag with bare essentials – toiletries, underwear, and my beanie hat stuffed with money. As usual, I wore my mother's jade necklace round my neck. I was still in two minds whether I would return that evening or whether I needed to do another runner.

Boody was quiet at work. She probably had a hangover. She didn't mention the money I'd given her, but I detected a softening in her attitude. Certainly there was less swearing than usual.

It was the Friday before half-term. By the evening, the campsite would be full. Boody and I divided the caravans between us to make them ready for check-in from three o'clock onwards. There was little opportunity to discuss Trafford and his threats, although I was keen to find out how he operated his little protection racket. I hated the injustice of it, the thought that someone like him – ignorant and brutal – was free to harass and steal from the female members of staff. I was determined to bring the matter to the attention of the management and involve the police if necessary, as long as I remained in the background. All I needed was proof, proof that wouldn't cause a problem for Boody or any of the other girls who were too frightened to report his behaviour.

There was no sign of Sonya at lunchtime. As usual, Boody disappeared for a cigarette. I grabbed a sandwich at the small supermarket on site and ate it as I wandered up the North Drive. I was curious to see the staff caravans where Boody lived and the wooded area where, according to her, drunken guests hung around at night unless moved on by the security staff.

It was a short walk to the outer perimeter, past concentration-camp rows of green and cream caravans. The drive ended in a T-junction, the left and right turnings leading back around the outside of the holiday park. Straight ahead I saw a wooden stile set within a tall laurel hedge. I crossed the road and climbed over.

It was like stepping through a portal into another world. Gone were the neatly clipped verges and landscaped borders. A tangle of brambles edged a rough track which ran uphill and disappeared into a shadowy copse. Stunted by the salty air and the rough winds that raced inland in winter, the cluster of trees lurched to one side, their naked branches streaming away from the direction of the sea like hair caught in a storm. I stepped under the skeletal canopy.

Immediately the temperature dropped. The air smelt dank, redolent with rotting leaves and flaking bark. The path was strewn with litter and cigarette butts, the soft mud indented with prints from the soles of trainers, boots and high heels. It was a well-travelled path. A twig snapped under my foot. I started as though a bullet had cracked through the silent air. A talon of fear squeezed my throat. I looked around but the track was deserted.

I hurried onwards. After a few minutes, the trail forked. One track was wider than the other and worn by many feet. I could see grey sky opening ahead, so I jogged along the main path until I escaped the gloom of the trees and found myself on the edge of what looked like a rubbish dump.

Squatting in the middle of a muddy field scattered with rusting cars, fly-tipped mattresses and rotting armchairs, were half a dozen mobile homes, smaller than the luxury models offered to Fun World's guests, dirty with mould and streaks of rust and silent as coffins. I stood under the shadow of a hawthorn bush and scrutinised the scene.

The two caravans nearest the copse were in a better state of repair. A string of coloured Christmas lights entwined the parapets of their small verandas, and hung from their roofs like garlands of tinsel. In daylight, the lustreless bulbs drooped like rotten fruit, but at night I imagined they would lend a cheerful gaudiness to the vans. An airer draped with stockings and knickers stood on the grass in front of the first of the caravans. A leopard-skin bra hung from the door handle, wired and padded, human content unnecessary to sustain its shape.

The caravans further away were a desolate collection of blank-eyed orphans, their windows dark, doors shut. As I watched, one swung open with a bang. A man in a stained singlet and jogging bottoms stood in the doorway oblivious to the wintry breeze, his naked arms grey with tattoos. He scratched his armpits like a silverback gorilla and spat onto the grass with a guttural cough. Trafford! It looked as though he'd just woken up. Although I was wearing my thick black jacket, I shivered under the trees, trembling because of the chill in the air and because I was looking at a man with a heart of ice.

I shrank back into the wood and began to run back along the path towards the laurel hedge. Twigs snapped beneath my feet and I heard the distant sound of a door slamming. What if he'd seen me and was coming after me? The story Boody had told the night before flashed to mind. I imagined the bruised and battered face of the girl who'd refused to pay protection money, and tasted her fear. When I reached the junction of the paths, I swung left and raced along the smaller path and into the centre of the wood. I hoped he would be too stupid to follow anything but the most obvious route.

The trees crowded closer. Brambles thickened and caught at my ankles. The trail twisted before me like an angry snake. My breath exploded from my mouth in short, vaporous gasps. I jumped over a fallen tree trunk that crossed the path and skirted a huge holly bush, suddenly finding myself in a clearing. I stopped in surprise, for here was another caravan in an even worse condition than the ones in the field.

It was a touring caravan, ancient, diminutive, its flaking grey paint disappearing into the undergrowth. Its rectangular frame was rounded at the corners, its roof curved and stained with mildew. There was only room for a front door and a small window on the side facing me. I looked at the ground by the step, searching for signs of habitation. There were no footprints that I could see, only a layer of decaying leaves from the previous year. I crept closer and gently tried the handle. It was locked. The window was too grimy to see inside, but I knew instinctively it had been abandoned some time ago.

I stood and caught my breath, listening for the sound of approaching footsteps. The silence was suffocating. My lunch break was nearly over. Boody would be looking for me. We still had half a dozen vans to prepare between us before the holidaymakers began to arrive. I'd overreacted. The slamming door was probably the sound of Trafford retreating inside for a late breakfast.

I retraced my steps along the path until I reached the original trail, then headed towards the laurel hedge, listening for footsteps all the while. Clambering over the stile, I slipped unnoticed onto the North Drive and hurried towards the reception area where I'd agreed to meet Boody. She would give me the key to my next van.

Sid Tulitt and his team had spent the morning stringing bunting along the fascias of all the communal buildings and planting real pansies and primulas in pots. Their soft petals and bright faces reminded me of Greenacres. I couldn't resist deadheading a couple on my way through the central square, their silky petals soft between my fingers.

A stab of nostalgia sliced my chest. I had a sudden vision of lush foliage and rainbows dancing in the fountain at the centre of the dome, Paloma calling my name as I played hide-and-seek along the hot aisles, the sharp sound of a spade cleaving the soil, the smell of Theo's soap and the rough texture of his wool jacket as I snuggled onto his lap as a child.

Homesickness dogged me the rest of the afternoon. What was I doing breaking my back cleaning toilets and fridges, when I could be monitoring seedlings in the Greenacres lab? I'd never felt scared or threatened at the dome. I never had to worry about money. I'd been respected and admired, cossetted and loved. But however many happy childhood memories I conjured, I still couldn't dispel the bitter taste of betrayal or the shame of my petulant response.

I thought of my mother cleaning caravans, her hands raw, her nose tingling with the sharp smell of bleach. For her it hadn't been an interlude to be endured, a means of discovering the truth. It had been a mindless, heartless, soulless regime of drudgery and indignity. I hoped my father had been kind. I hoped he'd been a bright splash of colour in a monochrome world, not a dark shadow that threatened and then succeeded in destroying her life. Had she been happy at Greenacres with Theo? Had she married him out of love or to avoid the stigma of an illegitimate child? Or was she giving me the best father she could find and the best life I could have?

If I were ever to return to the dome, I needed to know who my real father was first and the nature of his relationship with my mother. I wanted to speak to him face-to-face. I hoped he would love me, unconditionally. Perhaps if I knew I'd been conceived in love, I would be able to forgive Theo, Marcus,

Paloma and Uncle Colin and move on with my life. I needed a lead. The names of some of my mother's friends and colleagues would be a start.

By the time I'd finished the final caravan, I was physically and emotionally exhausted. I returned the last key to Boody and wandered over to Mrs Ozzles' office to collect my pay. Her filing cabinet was against the wall behind her desk. The first drawer was labelled 'Housekeeping Staff'. I watched closely as she took a small key from the metal cupboard hanging on her office wall. She opened her desk drawer and unlocked the petty-cash box inside. While she counted out my money, I strained my eyes to read the coloured fobs dangling from the hooks in the key cupboard. There were several large bunches which I recognised as master keys to the caravans. Boody carried a similar set so we could access the communal rooms and caravans on our list. She had to sign them out each day like all the other cleaners. Once I'd passed my induction I would be allocated my own set of keys.

Underneath the bunches was a row of single keys labelled 'Laundry Store', 'Cleaning Equipment', 'Hazardous Materials Cupboard', 'Filing Cabinet', 'Basement Store Room'. My heart quickened as I read the last two labels.

Mrs Ozzles returned the key to the petty-cash box to its hook and pushed the key cupboard closed. She didn't secure it, but left the key in the lock. I imagined she locked it at night and passed the key to the security staff along with her office key. A couple of times I'd arrived early for work and seen Trafford opening up the offices, entertainment centre and arcade in preparation for cleaning. As Boody had suggested on my first day, I always waited round the corner, out of sight, until I knew he was occupied and it was safe to start work.

It would be difficult to take the keys once they were behind the reception desk at night, but it would be almost impossible to break into Mrs Ozzles' filing cupboard and the basement store room during the day. I needed to grab the keys in daylight and return later when it was dark, hoping nobody would miss the keys in the interim or discover me poking around the holiday camp at night.

'Don't spend it all at once,' Mrs Ozzles said, a brief smile deepening the fissures in her cheeks as she handed me the money. 'Did you enjoy yourself last night?'

'Yes. Thank you.'

'I hope you didn't lose too much.' I must have looked surprised because she added, 'At the bingo.'

I remembered the money I'd given to Boody and worked to keep my expression neutral. I recalled the way she'd inspected my hands at our first meeting, as though reading my soul's journey in their palms. I wondered how much she saw today. Did she suspect I was an imposter planning a burglary, a spy intent on reading her confidential files?

'No. I only bought one ticket.'

A shadow of disappointment flickered across her face.

'And Sonya? Did she go with you?'

'Yes. We both went with Boody.'

'Good.'

I was mystified by her interest, but her tone suggested I was being dismissed.

As I pulled the door closed behind me, I glanced again at the key cupboard on the wall. At another time and in another place I'd plotted to steal a different set of keys to enter another forbidden kingdom. It would not be as easy to trick Mrs Ozzles as it had been to dupe Marcus, but I was determined to see inside the filing cabinet in her office and to search the archived files in the basement. Somewhere there was a clue to my father's identity, I was sure. Possibly the identity of my mother's killer too.

I walked across the central square to my car just before three o'clock. Weak February sunshine filtered through banks of purple cloud, infusing the chilly air with a sense of expectation. Banners fluttered. The newly swept pathways awaited the footsteps of gleeful children. Patty Pizza and Harry Hot Dog were roaming along the main drive as the first few cars began to arrive, laden with suitcases, bicycles and bags of supermarket food. I turned into the dingy staff car park behind the laundry.

I planned to phone Zavier to see if he'd managed to breach Fun World's online security. Having paid him another £175, I wanted to make sure he was getting on with the job. I was in two minds whether or not to return to Mrs Bungay's that night. I longed for a hot shower and something to eat. More than anything I needed a good night's sleep. Just the thought of having to find new digs and face questions from the proprietor of another bed and breakfast drained what little energy I had left. Perhaps after speaking to Zavier I'd have a better idea of whether he was planning to turn me over for the reward or not. I was usually pretty good at spotting whether someone was lying to me, I told myself. Then I remembered the deception Theo, Paloma and Uncle Colin had woven around me. My whole life, past and present, was one huge lie and I'd never suspected.

I was parked in the first parking space behind the laundry, having arrived before the catering staff and Pink Jackets. At first I thought someone had dropped a beer glass on the tarmac. A scattering of semi-opaque crystals glinted like crushed ice on the ground by my front tyre. Then I noticed the jagged hole in the driver's side window. The glass crunched under my feet as I wrenched the door. The glove compartment was open. I knelt on the driver's seat and leaned across, pulling out the owner's manual and the service record, a couple of pens and half a packet of digestive biscuits. The beanie hat with the money inside had gone.

I sat in the driver's seat and pulled the door closed, shaking from shock and from the wicked breeze blowing through the window. Why would anyone bother to break into this heap of junk unless they knew it contained something valuable? Was it a coincidence that only the previous night I'd retrieved £100 from the glove compartment for Boody? Perhaps someone had seen me sneak out to the car. Trafford? Or perhaps Boody herself had guessed where I kept my cash. My first thought was to contact the police. But then my cover would be blown and I

163

would have to explain how I came to be storing such a large amont of stolen money in the glove compartment. Plus the car was uninsured.

I couldn't report the theft to Trafford or any of his nasty-looking mates on security in case they were involved. I glanced around the car park. There was no CCTV, so nothing could be proved. All I had to my name was the £30 I had just been paid and about £25 in my back-pocket wallet.

Chapter 14

I think that was the first time I really understood I was on the down escalator of life. I'd stepped on it the moment I'd left Greenacres, but hadn't noticed because I'd been jogging upwards as the escalator went down. But however fast I'd been running up the steps, I'd been standing still at best. Now I was winded, unable to move. The escalator continued its inexorable descent and I was a helpless passenger.

All my life, progression and success had occurred without much effort on my part. I'd been on the up escalator. In my arrogance, I thought it was my due. In reality, everything I owned and all the opportunities I'd been offered had come from Theo. Then in a childish fit of defiance, I'd cut myself off from everything and everyone I'd known, throwing away my name and identity, my career and my home. I was an unqualified skivvy on less than minimum wage. My only friends were a foul-mouthed cleaner, an illegal immigrant, and a money-grabbing, drug-taking private investigator.

I sat with face in my hands and sobbed. That money had been my safety net. Now I was in free fall, with nothing or nobody to catch me. I thought of Boody and her bravado in the face of Trafford's threats, drinking, smoking, and gambling her last few quid on the random selection of computer-generated bingo numbers. I never dreamt I would have to live on the edge like that, grubbing around for loose change in my purse to pay for my next meal. I'd be surviving on £30 a day in future. Or not! The reality of my situation hit home. How could I afford to live?

I'd been thinking of leaving Mrs Bungay's establishment, but surely her rivals would be more expensive, particularly in the school holidays. How soon before I had to make the choice between eating and keeping a roof over my head? I could return to Greenacres with my tail between my legs, but I couldn't assume I was welcome there. The resounding silence following my disappearance spoke for itself. This wasn't a game any more, some kind of elaborate role-playing computerised fantasy. Nobody had rushed to find me. I was on my own.

I didn't have the funds to have my car window repaired. If I covered the hole with cardboard as a temporary measure, I wouldn't be able to see out to drive. But if I left it uncovered, vandals and the weather would do their worst. But what was the point in having a car if I couldn't afford to fill it with petrol?

A figure walked across the car park. I wiped my nose on my sleeve and batted away the tears. He stopped when he saw the glass on the ground, then sidled up to my broken window and poked his finger through.

'If you're trying to break out of the car, you could always use the handle.'

'Very funny, Sid!'

'They take much?'

'Enough.' If I told him I'd lost all my money, I might start to cry again.

'Scumbags! There's a garage on Clifton Rise.'

'I can't afford it.'

'Insurance?'

I grimaced. 'Are you one of the cash-in-hand lasses?'

I nodded. He leaned closer, his face millimetres from the broken glass between us.

'Best get away from here, girlie.'

'I haven't got anywhere else to go.'

'There's always another place. Fun World isn't good for someone like you.'

'Someone like what?'

'Someone who wants to belong, someone who's desperate.'

'I'm not looking for anything,' I snapped. 'I need a job to pay the rent.' I softened my tone, not wanting to alienate him. 'How am I going to drive like this?'

He ran his fingers carefully round the jagged edge, pulling some loosened glass away and dropping it on the ground.

'I've probably got something in the shed that'll hold it. Wait here.'

I could tell he liked having a problem to solve. I let out a breath, relieved that the panic threatening to engulf me had been temporarily stayed.

Five minutes later Sid returned with a hammer, a large sheet of thick transparent plastic and a roll of duct tape. I climbed out of the car. Standing beside him I noticed again the avalanche of dandruff on the collar of his overalls.

'I had one of them plastic greenhouses for seedlings a year or so back. It didn't last long,' he explained. 'A storm blew it halfway along the West Drive. Good thing I didn't chuck the panes away. You never know when things might come in handy.'

'Do you like gardening, Sid?'

'I've not got green fingers. Wish I did. Don't know how people get their pots to bloom. I use artificial flowers mixed in with the real thing now. It boosts the colour. Mr King likes lots of colour. And plastic last forever. The punters don't notice.'

'I noticed.'

He opened the door and knocked out the rest of the broken glass with the hammer.

'Do you water and fertilise your plants?' I continued.

'Yep. Doesn't work. The sea air here is too harsh.'

'Bone meal's good. Then you need to rake the soil over. The earth needs to be turned if you want your plants to bloom.'

'How do you know so much about it?'

'I knew a gardener once.'

Sid stretched the plastic across the window and secured it with duct tape.

'That should last you a few days until you get it mended,' He tapped the plastic window. 'Don't leave anything valuable in the car.'

'I haven't got anything valuable.'

'Yes, you have. You've got yourself. Look after *you*.' He held my gaze a little too long, and I looked away embarrassed. 'Think about what I said. This isn't a good place.'

'Maybe when the season's over I'll move on.'

He frowned. I tried to change the subject.

'*You've* been here a long time. *You* must like it.'

'That's different. Nobody bothers me. I'm not pretty enough.'

'What are you saying?'

'I'm just saying things are not always what they seem. This is fantasy land. People want to escape their lives, forget their worries. For one week they eat everythink they want, drink theirselves stupid. Stay up all night, sleep all day. Suddenly they're all stroppy teenagers, the little kids as well as the mums and dads. They do things they wouldn't dream of doing at home. They're in a kind of bubble, kidding themselves that the things that happen here won't affect their everyday lives.'

'Isn't that the point of a holiday?'

'Maybe. But you're not on holiday. Someone's got to pay for everyone else's fun.'

I held up my blistered hands.

'I *am* paying.'

'And the price is too high. Look what's happened to your car. This place has gone to the dogs. Not like the good old days. I knew as soon as I saw you that you're not the type of girl who should be here. Why would you come to a place like this?'

What could I say? That I'd run away and was living under an assumed name with no National Insurance number or fixed address? That I was looking for my real dad, and hadn't ruled Sid himself out yet? The light was beginning to fade. Dark clouds with golden bellies rolled overhead, pushed inland by an unfriendly breeze that stung my cheeks and reddened Sid's ears and nose.

'Thanks for mending my window, Sid. Perhaps you could tell me more about the good old days sometime. I've always been interested in local history.' I suddenly remembered my mother's photograph and pulled it out of my coat pocket. 'Look, here's that picture of my Auntie Sandra I was telling you about. She used to work here about twenty years ago. Do you remember her?'

He scratched his head and a few white flakes fell onto the photograph.

'You're like her,' he said after a long pause.

'You remember!' I exclaimed.

He grunted.

'She had a look about her as though she was searching for another life.'

'Searching for what?'

'For love… for the truth.'

'And did she find them?'

'Sometimes it's best to leave things alone. Don't go raking things up.' He waved his hammer at me. 'That's what I told her and that's what I'm telling you now. Get yourself home and in the warm. I've got jobs to do.'

He turned and walked away.

I parked in my usual spot around the corner from the B&B, with the mended window facing the road. Hopefully pedestrians wouldn't see the damaged window. Now I'd lost my money, I had no choice but to return to my room at Mrs Bungay's, unless I wanted to sleep in the car. On my way over I resolved to call in on Zavier and pull him from the case once and for all. I needed my money back. It would be a difficult conversation, particularly if he'd clocked up any hours during the day.

His basement office was in darkness, but a light glowed behind the curtains of the ground-floor bay window. I ran up the steps and rang the doorbell. I waited a couple of minutes and pressed again. In case the bell wasn't working, I raised the handle of the brass knocker and rapped three times. The door opened a crack. A long arm stretched through the gap, grabbed me, and pulled me through. The door slammed shut. The hall was in darkness apart from the light spilling through the doorway from the front room.

'What are you doing here?' Zavier hissed. 'You shouldn't have come.'

I couldn't read his expression but I could hear the fear in his voice.

'I wanted to talk to you. There's a problem,' I said.

'You bet there's a problem! Wait here.' He darted through the door and switched off the light in the living room. I heard a brief swoosh, as though the curtains had been pulled aside a few inches.

'What's going on?' I called.

'I'm checking to see if anyone's watching the house.'

'Are they?'

'Not that I can see.' I heard the curtains close. Zavier switched on the light.

'You can come in now.'

I walked into a large, untidy room. Zavier threw himself down into a leather armchair. I was shocked at his appearance. His face was misshapen, his lip split and scabbing over. His left eye was a narrow crack embedded in a cushion of swollen flesh, a parody of a grotesque and lascivious wink. His undamaged eye was dark with fear.

'I had a couple of visitors this morning. They were looking for you.'

I sank down on the settee, my eyes never leaving his face.

'I didn't tell them anything, don't worry. Someone must have told them I was asking about a runaway.'

'How do you know they were looking for me and not for someone else?'

'They asked if I'd heard of Theodore Gage or Sandra Hewitt. I pretended ignorance, of course. I can be pretty good at that when I want to.'

I bit back a sarcastic retort.

'It's Friday the 13th,' he observed. 'I should have guessed something would go wrong today.'

'I don't believe in that superstitious nonsense. The brutes who did this to you are to blame, not a date on the calendar.'

He touched his lip gingerly.

'Does it hurt?' I asked.

'Not too bad. No kissing for a few days.'

'If you'd just done what I paid you to do, find out about my father rather than trying to find out about me, this would never have happened.' My fear was turning to anger.

'But where's the fun in that?'

'You're sure you convinced them that you know nothing?'

'Yes. They turned over the office, trashed all Dad's files. Thankfully you've got the file on your mother so there was nothing to find. I'd jotted down a few notes on the back of an envelope at our first meeting but they didn't spot it among the junk mail. Sometimes it pays to be disorganised.'

'Does your dad know?'

'He's away working on an important case. I'll tidy it all up before he gets back.'

'If you did such a good job convincing them you know nothing, why do you think they might be watching the house?'

'Paranoia. And the fact that they're professionals. I wasn't expecting to see you here tonight. I probably overreacted. I don't want them to connect us. It's not safe for you. I was going to phone you tomorrow from a payphone and arrange to meet somewhere neutral, once I'd made sure no one was following me. From now on, we'll have to be very careful. I won't visit you at Mrs Bungay's and you shouldn't visit me here.'

'There's no "from now on". That's what I came to tell you. It's over. I want to stop the investigation. I'm serious this time.'

'What! You can't do that. Not now we have definite evidence that something's seriously wrong. Don't you want to know who's after you? This isn't a concerned parent trying to trace their missing stepdaughter.' He moved from the chair and sat next to me on the sofa. 'Are you sure you don't know what this is about?'

'I've no idea what's going on. It must be to do with the fact that Theo's not my real father. Maybe my biological dad doesn't want to be found and he's behind it. Perhaps my mother *was* murdered and the killer thinks I might be trying to rake up the past.'

'What if Theo's behind it? Have you thought of that?'

'I told you before. He would never do anything like this.' I gestured to Zavier's face. 'Theo has dedicated his life to helping people, making the world a better place, rescuing the lost. He's in Africa now setting up an agricultural project.'

'And this guy, Marcus. You mentioned him the other day.'

'He might be irritating, but I've never known him do anything bad or dishonest. He sometimes gets angry, but it's always directed against those who exploit the weak.'

'He sounds a barrel of laughs.'

'Actually he does have a sense of humour. Sometimes he gets a bit above himself, but underneath I think he's a good bloke. It's just that he always makes me feel as though I'm missing the point, as though the things I want for my life are second best, or not enough. We used to get on when I was younger. I think I outgrew him.'

'OK. So, we're ruling out Theo and Marcus for now. Apart from me, have you spoken to anyone else about your real parents?'

'No…' I remembered my conversation with Sid only an hour ago.

'Ava?'

'Yes… no… yes. I did tell someone I had an aunt called Sandra Hewitt who used to work at Fun World.'

'What!' he exploded. 'What's the point of employing me if you're going to go and interfere with my investigation? Who is this person?'

'Just a handyman at Fun World. I showed him a photograph of Mum and asked if he remembered her.'

'And did he?'

'Yes, but he was very vague. I didn't find out anything. And I only spoke to him this afternoon so it can't be him if you were beaten up this morning.'

'What were you doing at Fun World? Honestly, Ava, why employ a dog if you're going to bark yourself?'

I looked down at my hands and blinked back a rush of tears.

'OK, OK. Let me think… The only way those thugs could have found me is through the police. Someone at the station's taken a backhander and told them I've been asking around.'

'This is horrible. I hate it. I hate the fact that you've been hurt because of me.'

'Don't worry about it. I think I convinced them that I'm looking for a woman who left her husband and ran off with a toy boy. I told them you were fat and ugly.'

'Thanks!'

He leaned closer. 'They said you're a red-head.' He tucked a stray lock behind my ear. 'I'd like to see that.'

I tried to swallow but my mouth was suddenly dry. He pushed a clump of hair away from my scalp.

'What are you doing?' I said, pulling away.

'Trying to find the light under the black cloud. Yes, there it is. A glint of gold. You'll need to retouch your roots soon, Ava.'

I stood up, my throat tight, blood hammering in my ears. I couldn't think straight. The blow of losing my money followed by the shock of seeing Zavier's injured face had left me dizzy with anxiety. Now I was feeling jittery for another reason entirely.

'However much you try to cover up your roots, I see who you really are. The tough image, the big boots, they don't fool me. You're a nice middle-class girl from a good home. I know what bad parenting does, and it hasn't happened to you.'

'I have to go. You must stop the investigation. It's too dangerous.' I couldn't bring myself to ask for my money back after all he had been through.

'I'll walk you home. After all, it's Valentine's Day tomorrow.'

'Is it? No... I'll be fine, really.' I darted for the door and reached the hall before he'd heaved himself from the sofa.

'Goodbye,' I called, wrenching open the front door and running down the steps into the shadowy street.

I heard him call my name but didn't look back. With my last remnant of energy, I raced along the street to the questionable safety of Mrs Bungay's guest house.

Chapter 15

Although it was only half-past five, I fell asleep the moment I flopped onto the bed. I awoke at three in the morning after a turbulent dream.

Trafford had been chasing me through a dark forest, wielding a hammer and muttering 'Look after *you*. I'm going to look after *you*.' When I reached the road where I'd parked my car, Zavier was sitting in the driving seat. He started the engine and edged forwards. I bent to open the passenger door but it was locked. He leaned towards me, winked through a gaping hole in the window and floored the accelerator. I was left standing on the empty road, watching his tail lights disappear over the crest of a hill.

I lay sweating and trembling under the duvet, the words 'I'm going to look after *you*' resounding in my head as though Trafford had been lying next to me, whispering in my ear.

I was ravenously hungry. Shocked at losing my contingency fund, I'd forgotten to pick up a sandwich on my way back from work. I switched on the small bedside lamp and filled the kettle from the sink with a shaking hand. While it boiled, I crept across the landing to the bathroom.

My heart rate gradually steadied, but the dread remained. Trafford really was a threat to be avoided. Zavier had become an expensive liability. I couldn't risk being discovered by the thugs who'd beaten him up. What if they returned and managed to prise my whereabouts out of him? What if they *had* been watching his house and followed me back to the B&B? Worse still, what if Zavier weakened, pocketed the reward and abandoned me to the darkness of an unlit road?

Back in my room, I stood behind the curtains and opened the crack where the material met in the middle. It must have rained while I slept. The street outside was deserted, the tarmac wet and greasy under the glow from the street lamps. Cars lined the pavements on either side. It was too dark to see whether someone was sitting inside any of them. My breath left a patch of mist on the glass. I shivered and reached for my baggy black jumper.

I sipped my tea in bed and considered my next move. I could no longer afford the familiar inhospitality of Mrs Bungay's guest house. I hadn't told Zavier I was working at Fun World so if I changed my accommodation I could continue working as a cleaner as long as I kept a low profile. I would need to step up my investigation and access those personnel files as quickly as possible.

I hadn't spoken to Chucky Skittles yet, nor Maxwell King – though he appeared to be unapproachable for an employee like me. Ever since the induction session, he'd been visiting his other business ventures along the south coast. Sonya cleaned his office every morning and mentioned his bin was always empty. I resolved to orchestrate a conversation with Chucky that evening, before the kids' show if possible. We needed to be on speaking terms at least if I was to extract any information from him. I could also try to ask Sid some more questions.

I finished my tea and began to gather up my belongings. I was too restless to sleep. My alarm would be ringing in a couple of hours in any case. I dressed for work then emptied the wardrobe, stuffing as much as I could into my backpack. I folded the extra clothes I'd bought in the charity shop into carrier bags, along with garments I'd washed and left to dry on the radiator. By 5.30 I was ready to leave. Checking again that the road outside was clear, I shrugged into my coat and staggered onto the landing with the rucksack on my back and a carrier bag in either hand. Shutting my bedroom door silently behind me, I stood and listened for Mrs Bungay's snores. Once I was sure she was still asleep, I crept downstairs and let myself out of the house.

As usual, Boody and I started work in the entertainment centre at half-past six. It must have been busy the previous night, for the tables were stickier than ever, the floors bestrewn with sweet wrappers and crumpled bingo tickets. She spent ten minutes telling me that Harry Hot Dog had jumped in the swimming pool the previous afternoon and fished out a struggling swimmer.

'Saved the kid's life. No doubt about it. How he swam in that costume, I'll never know. Waterlogged, it must have weighed more than Maxwell King's ego.'

I grunted in reply.

'What, no questions?' Boody asked twenty minutes later when we were bleaching the urinals in the men's toilets.

'Sorry?'

'You're usually giving me the third degree about something by now. What's Chucky like? Is he married? Has he got kids? When's Mr King going to be back at Fun World? Is Mrs O the reincarnation of Lady Macbeth?' she parroted. 'Cat got your tongue?'

'Having a bad day, that's all.'

I hadn't realised my questioning had been quite so obvious. The last few days I'd been pumping Boody hard. I'd discovered Chucky Skittles was a lech and ruthless bully, hated by everyone (including an ex-wife), except for the guests and their children. Sid Tulitt didn't join in with any of the staff social activities. He'd never married and had no children as far as anybody knew. Mrs Ozzles had started out as a Pink Jacket, but when Maxwell King bought out the previous owners, he found other uses for her particular skills.

'She never had the face for the stage,' Boody explained. 'She terrified the kids. She used to do an Olivia Newton-John tribute act. "Ozzilia Newton-John" she called herself. Can you imagine that body in black lycra? Who'd want that ugly mug under the spotlight? That's why she hates the Pink Jackets. They think they're better than us, and she knows they're right. It's all about the pecking order here.'

'She must have been very hurt. I'm surprised she stayed.'

'Maxwell House must have made it worth her while. She has other talents.'

'Such as?'

'She knows how to squeeze every drop out of blood out of the losers who work for her.'

'If you hate it so much, why don't you leave?'

'You can't leave Fun World. Didn't you know that? I only came for a season. I was saving to go to beauty college but I'm still here five years later.' She swore under her breath. 'I'm snookered. If I leave, I've got nowhere to live. Where else am I going to find digs at £40 a week? You think they're doing you a favour letting you live on site. It's a trap. Mrs O's like a giant spider. She pulls everyone into her web. Better watch yourself, Countess. She's got her eye on you… and Sonya.' Boody glanced at me from the corner of her eye. She wasn't stupid. She knew something was seriously wrong. 'On the lash last night, were you?'

'Didn't get much sleep. Someone broke into my car yesterday afternoon. The window's smashed. I can't afford to mend it.' I watched her closely to see whether there was a flicker of guilt, any indication *she* might have been the one searching for extra cash after it became obvious I wasn't as hard up as I looked.

'Bummer. That's how it starts.'

'How what starts?

'The curse of the Lucksucker. Once you're on the downward slope, the Lucksucker won't let you pick yourself up and climb back up. Oh no! It's like one of those black holes. You're going to get sucked in. It's some kind of law. You're down on your luck, you deserve a break, but that's abso-bloomin-lutely out of the question. Good things only happen to those who've already got it made. The rich get richer. The poor get poorer. The Lucksucker will kick you when you're down every time. It's so hungry it's going to eat your whole world. You're a bit short of cash in the middle of the month so you ask the boss for a pay-day loan at a gazillion per cent interest. You can't pay it back. You end up living in some grotty caravan, working all hours day and night. You wake up and all your dreams are gone… pouf… like that.'

'And I've parted company with my landlady.'

'What did I say? It's the Lucksucker. She evict you?'

'Something like that. I don't suppose I could sleep on your floor for a couple of nights? I would have slept in my car but it'll be freezing.'

'Aw, don't make me feel bad,' she whined. 'I know you lent me the money an' all, but Shannon's a pain in the posterior when it comes to overnight guests. I once let a bloke stay the night. She went ballistic. Reported me to Mrs O'Blisters for breaching the rental agreement. Shannon's your genuine troll. Also, she's thick with Trafford. Never pays to get on the wrong side of her.'

'OK. I understand.'

'Don't look like that. You're killing me. I know you helped me, but – '

'Honestly, Boody, don't worry about it. I'll find somewhere.'

I rubbed the washbasin taps with disinfectant. Silence descended, as thick and unpleasant as the smell of ammonia.

'I might know somewhere you can crash… if you're not too fussy.'

'Anything. I'd be grateful for anything.'

'You'd have to keep quiet about it. Or we'd both get in trouble.'

'Quiet as the grave,' I replied.

'It's empty but I can get the key. No one goes there any more. If you're careful, you could stay there for a few days until you get back on your feet.'

'That sounds great. Where is it?'

'I'll show you, but we have to be quick.'

We left the cleaning trolley outside the toilets and hurried through the fire exit at the back, weaving our way between the silent caravans and avoiding the main driveways. It was still dark, but fingers of icy light had begun to claw above the eastern horizon. All but the most enthusiastic campers were sleeping off the previous night's revelries. A baby cried, not caring that its mother was on holiday and shouldn't be woken at quarter-past seven in the morning. A middle-aged man jogged up the North Drive. We followed him in the shadows until he turned left to run around the perimeter road. Reaching the laurel hedge, we climbed over the stile.

'This is the way to the staff caravans,' Boody said.

I didn't let on I'd been there the previous day.

'I thought I couldn't stay with you.'

'You can't.'

We stumbled along the muddy path and into the trees. I understood why the girls were frightened of walking through the copse at night and why they were willing to pay Trafford and his mates to warn away those who might consider them easy targets. Twigs entangled our hair and scratched our faces as we hurried along the invisible trail. A bramble caught my feet; I tripped and crashed into Boody just ahead.

'Dirty dusters, Claire!' she hissed. 'We're supposed to be inconspicuous.'

'Sorry.'

When we arrived at the junction, Boody turned off the main track. The darkness deepened as we hurried further into the wood. By now I knew we were headed for the derelict caravan.

'Here we are,' she puffed, stopping in the clearing.

The sky, grey as smoke, opened up above our heads. Darkness was retreating, hiding among the slimy tree trunks that encircled us. It was just possible to make out the outline of the caravan. Boody walked towards it, then bent and searched around the base of the steps among a pile of stones and broken plant pots.

'A couple of Romanian lads lived here last year. They worked in the laundry. Don't know what happened. One day they were here, the next they just disappeared. Probably homesick. Anywhere's got to be better than working in the laundry and living in this dump. Here it is!' She stood up and inserted a key in the door.

After a couple of hard pushes, it creaked open.

'There used to be quite a few caravans out here in the trees,' she continued. 'Years ago holidaymakers liked all that nature bunkum, peace and quiet and boring the pants off their kids. Now they want to be living on top of the café and arcade. Never mind the noise. It'll save their chubby legs a few precious steps.'

I followed her in. The entire space was smaller than my en-suite bathroom back at Greenacres. The dim air smelt of mould and cigarettes and something else which was hard to define. Despair, perhaps?

Boody picked up something from the floor and fiddled with it for a moment before it clicked awake, illuminating her face with a ghostly white glow.

'Camping lamp. Batteries still work, but you should buy more. There were some old candles here last time I looked. Here. You can have my lighter. I've got another one.'

I caught the pink plastic lighter and put it in my tabard pocket.

'Thanks.'

She waved the lamp around the interior, revealing a padded bench running along the far wall. The stained material was torn at one end. Yellow foam spilled out like crumbled cheese. In front of the seat was a narrow Formica table, scratched and littered with dirty mugs, cigarette packets and mould-covered lumps – the unidentifiable remains of half-eaten food.

Boody turned on the tap in the small kitchenette. A stream of dirty water spurted into the crockery-filled sink.

'You'll need some bottled water, too. I wouldn't bother trying to fill up the water tank, not unless you have a death wish. The hot plate's broken ... but look! That's a bit of luck.

Someone's left a camping stove.' She picked up the small single burner. 'I think there's some gas left. You'll be able to make a cup of tea.'

I opened the fridge. The stench of rotting vegetables and the sour odour of curdled milk punched me in the gut. I slammed the door shut.

'All it needs is a good clean,' Boody said.

'What with? A blowtorch?'

She opened a door and peered inside. I assumed it was a cupboard.

'You may not want to use the loo. Pee in the woods.'

I stood in the middle of the room and gazed despondently at the squalor.

'I can sneak a duvet and pillow from the store.'

'Thanks.'

'Keep this to yourself.' She looked at me anxiously. 'You need to keep quiet or you'll get us both in trouble. If you draw the curtains, nobody will see the light from the main path. If you're careful, Sludger and Mrs O will never find out.'

'We'd better be getting back,' I said. 'Thanks, Boody.'

'Don't get mushy on me. It ain't the Ritz.'

I blinked away my misery and smiled through the tears.

'I'm just grateful, that's all.'

After a gruelling shift, and three £10 notes from Mrs Ozzles, I sneaked a bottle of cleaning fluid into a carrier bag together with bleach, washing-up liquid, polish, a packet of dish clothes, a duster and a roll of black sacks. I borrowed a dustpan and brush from the cleaning cupboard. After storing these in the boot of my car, I popped to the Fun World minimart for basic supplies. Water, milk, teabags, sugar, bread, margarine, a block of cheese, a box of cereal, some tinned fruit and a packet of batteries. I now had just over £70 left in my wallet.

I drove up the North Drive, and turned onto the perimeter road, parking the car behind a small electricity substation. Checking there was no one nearby, I sauntered along the laurel hedge looking for another opening. I wanted to avoid the stile, if possible. The last thing I needed was to bump into someone walking along the path in the opposite direction.

I found a gap in the hedge where the branches thinned. Perhaps the overlapping laurel leaves had been pushed aside by foxes commuting down to the campsite refuse bins. I checked the road. It was deserted. The caravans opposite the hedge had their backs to me with only the opaque bathrooms windows facing the hedge. I crawled through the gap, scratching my hands on the branches as I tore the glossy leaves. Once I'd made a proper opening, I hurried back for the bags of food and cleaning materials.

On the other side of the hedge, the temperature dropped and the shadows thickened. The distant sound of children playing was smothered by a thick, unnerving silence. Pushing past a dense cluster of brambles and a large holly bush, I stumbled between leggy saplings and rotting tree trunks, forging my own trail until I eventually reached the clearing. I emerged behind the caravan and circled to the front. It looked even worse than I remembered.

I unlocked the door. Despite the chill of the afternoon I left it open to release the smell, which leapt at my throat like an uncaged animal. I dumped my bags and opened the windows to scour the filthy air. Donning a pair of rubber gloves and pulling a black sack from the roll, I began to clear the rubbish from the table. Next I tackled the kitchenette. Sorting through the dirty crockery and cutlery in the sink, I salvaged what I could – bleaching and rinsing a small saucepan, a couple of plates and cups, a knife, fork and spoon - and throwing the rest in the black sack. After scrubbing the table and kitchen surfaces, sweeping the floor and the cobwebs from the ceiling, I returned to the car to collect my backpack and clothes.

Although it was only half-past four, the night was drawing in. I retraced my steps to the hedge, anxious not to lose my way. By the time I reached the road, the street lights were on and the caravans glowed and hummed with life. Though a window, I saw a woman at the sink, children squabbling in the background, the television flickering in the corner. A man walked into sight, shouted and changed the television channel. Normal family life with chores and arguments. I thought of Theo and Paloma and the childhood they'd given me, secure and loving despite the absence of a mother or siblings.

My mountain bike was still in the back of the car. I wrenched the light off the front and used it as a torch to light my way back through the hole in the hedge. When I reached the caravan, Boody was standing outside, a black sack on the ground by her feet and a sealed packet of clean linen in her arms. She jumped when I emerged from behind the van.

'Shuttlecocks! You scared me. I've brought you the duvet.'

'Thanks.' I lifted the carrier bags in my hands. 'Supplies! I can make you a cup of tea to christen my new home.'

'I'll carry you over the threshold if you don't hurry up and open the door.'

I'd left the window ajar. The sour and smoky odour was overlaid now with the stench of ammonia and the cold woodiness of trees at night. Boody shivered at the table while I boiled a saucepan of water on the camping stove for a cup of tea.

'Were you born in a barn? Shut the window, frostyknickers.'

'But the smell – '

'Rats to the smell. You'll die of hypothermia.'

I closed the window while she tried to kick-start the calor gas radiator.

'It doesn't work,' I said. 'Neither does the hot water, the cooker or the fridge.'

'You won't need to worry about the fridge. You're living in one!' She pulled a packet of cigarettes out of her pocket and lit up.

'Do you mind?' I protested.

'Seriously! You're worried about passive smoking! You're sleeping in Chernobyl, remember. Think of this as air freshener.'

'You're right. Give me one of those.'

I pulled a cigarette out of the box and thrust it between my lips. She flicked her lighter a couple of times and held the flame before my face. I dipped my head towards its wavering brightness and tentatively inhaled.

'Novice!' she laughed as I choked on the smoky fingers that stroked my airways.

We lit a couple of candles and puffed in silence, Boody blowing a thin column of white from the corner of her mouth while I spent a disproportionate amount of time tapping ash onto a cracked saucer and pretending I wasn't nauseous.

The water took twenty minutes to boil and the tea tasted faintly of bleach. After one sip, Boody cupped the mug between her hands for warmth but didn't attempt to drink any more. I could tell she wanted to leave. I didn't blame her. If I had somewhere else to go, I would have left too.

'I'm off.'

I stood up briskly.

'Of course.' I rubbed the seat of my trousers. 'Is your bottom damp?'

We felt the bench we'd been sitting on, trying to work out if the cushion on the top was moist or merely cold.

'So much for the bed!'

'It's a water bed,' Boody joked. 'Sexy!'

'Could be the seabed,' I replied weakly.

'Or a riverbed. Cut open this plastic sack and lay it out on the cushion. That should stop the sheets getting wet... You gonna be all right?'

'I'll survive,' I replied, more to convince myself than her.

'Shannon eats before the kids' show. If I don't get back to my van soon she'll nick my sausages.'

'Thanks again,' I muttered.

'No probs. Catch you tomorrow. Sleep tight. Don't let the bedbugs bite.'

'Bedbugs!'

'Keep your pants on. It's a rhyme. My mum used to say it. Bugs can't survive sub-zero temperatures. Don't you know nothin'?'

'Night, Boody.'

'Night, Countess.'

After she left I made myself a cheese sandwich. I hadn't looked in any of the cupboards or drawers, arguing that if they were tightly shut whatever was in them wasn't getting out. It wasn't just spiders and mice I was worried about. Alone again, with darkness falling, I had an irrational feeling that I might find something deeply disturbing in their depths, blood-stained clothing or a severed finger, perhaps. I would keep my belongings in my rucksack and carrier bags, uncontaminated and ready to evacuate at a moment's notice.

I was exhausted after my bad night's sleep, but I'd vowed I would speak to Chucky Skittles that day, break the ice at least so I could follow up with a more in-depth conversation later. There was nothing else to do in the caravan except sleep, but if I crashed too early there was the possibility I'd wake in the middle of the night again. If I'd been frightened by a dream at Mrs Bungay's house, what would it be like lying awake, freezing and alone, in the middle of a dark wood?

Deciding not to change out of my warm cleaning uniform into something deep-frozen, I pulled on a jacket and locked the door. This time I would stick to the track and hope no one would see me. I switched on the bicycle light and edged along the trail until I approached the junction where it joined the main path to the staff caravans. Switching off the light, I paused and listened for approaching footsteps. After a moment, I turned left and hurried towards the stile.

Crossing onto the other side of the hedge was like leaving the silence of a tomb. I remember having my ears syringed as a child, and the startling pop when something shifted deep within my head. Eyes watering from the warm fluid forcing its way against my eardrum, I realised with surprise that the world was a louder, more demanding place than I'd thought. I recalled

Paloma's harsh Italian vowels firing at the doctor like an artillery round. He wiped my neck with a towel and dropped the syringe into a metal bowl with a sharp clatter. Curious, I peered inside the basin. A brown bullet of wax was floating in an inch of water, circling the surface like a dead bee. Wandering dizzily from the surgery, I'd flinched at the roar of a passing lorry.

'Has it always been this noisy?' I'd asked Paloma.

She laughed.

'The world is a noisy place. It shouts loudly. But we do not have to listen to its rackets if we don't want to.'

I'd put my hands over my sensitive ears. She pressed my chest.

'There is always a quiet place here if you look for it.'

That day I was glad to escape the frightening hush of the wood and hear the thump, thump, thump of the music that greeted me as I jumped over the stile. Lights glowed from caravan windows and from the street lamps lining the North Drive. In the distance, the garish neon signs of the campsite shops and takeaways cast a haze of red and green into the night, an artificial aurora borealis drawing holidaymakers to the pulsing hub of the holiday park. The nocturnal monster was stirring, hungry for prey.

Young girls in party dresses and high heels skipped towards the music. Sullen boys in baseball caps kicked at stones. Parents, overweight and underdressed, shivered and swaggered their way to Nirvana with their babies in tow. They were pilgrims on route to the cathedral of pleasure. Consumers ready to consume and be consumed. Empty stomachs. Vacant hearts. Whirlpools of desire and wishful thinking. I joined the swelling crowd, shrugging off my jacket and slipping past the security guard on the door, invisible in my cleaner's uniform.

In half an hour it would be the kids' show. I strolled as confidently as I could through the 'Staff Only' backstage door into a corridor filled with broken scenery and spare lighting equipment. I picked up a broom that was leaning against the wall. A flight of stairs led to the basement and the Pink Jackets' dressing rooms. I hurried down the steps.

I was faced with a windowless, dimly lit corridor. The walls were painted grey. Doors lined one side of the passage like cells in a prison. On the other side, a rack of colourful costumes and a giant cardboard cut-out of Chucky Skittles dressed as a pantomime dame pouted at the parade of closed doors opposite. I edged past the first, labelled 'Girls Dressing Room', the concrete floor resounding with each footstep. I swept as I went, glancing nervously behind me as I passed the boys' dressing room.

Music from the entertainment centre above throbbed and vibrated through the ceiling. An icy sweat beaded my top lip. I was trapped inside the belly of a huge beast, hearing the blood pump and echo through the valves of a vast and primitive heart. Or was that my own heart beating? I reached a door painted blue with yellow spots. The sign read, 'Mr Skittles, Head of Entertainment.' Next to it was the basement store. I tried that handle first in the hope I could slip inside, locate the personnel records and perhaps find the answers to my questions without bothering Chucky. It was locked. The final door, furthest from the stairs, led to the toilets.

I turned at the sound of footsteps running down the stairs behind me. Gavin Flynne jumped the bottom two steps and skipped along the corridor.

'Swish swish,' he called. 'Keep brushing, Mrs Mop.' He blew a kiss in my direction and darted into the girls' dressing room.

I stepped towards Chucky's door, hands shaking, I knocked and turned the handle. It opened easily. I pushed and peered inside.

Before I could process the contents of the room, a soft and rubbery missile hit me directly in the face, exploding in a shower of freezing water.

'Shove off!' a voice yelled as I gasped and wiped the liquid from my eyes. Water dripped from my hair onto the floor. The broken skin of a yellow balloon lay at my feet.

'Who are you?' Chucky shouted from his dressing table.

'I'm the cleaner. What did you do that for?' Icy droplets were trickling down the back of my neck.

'Because I don't want to be interrupted, stupid!'

I swallowed an angry retort.

'I just wondered if you wanted your bin emptying, Mr Skittles?'

'My bin! MY BIN? It's twenty minutes to show time and you want to empty my bin? Don't stand there dripping on my floor. Shove off!'

'Sorry.' I tried to smile, even though I was fuming at the rudeness of his behaviour. 'I'd better wipe up the puddle. Health and safety. You might slip and hurt yourself.'

He swore loudly, but turned back to the mirror and smoothed a thin strand of hair across his forehead. He was wearing pink trousers and an unbuttoned white shirt. His stomach folded over the top of his waistband and across his lap like an enormous lump of hairy dough.

'I also wanted to say I'm a big fan.' I swept the water towards the skirting board and looked around the room for something to soak it up. Spotting a half-used toilet roll on the dressing table, I stepped forward. 'I've always wanted to be a Pink Jacket.'

He grunted and began to do up his buttons. I slipped the toilet roll off the top of the dressing table, stepped back and pulled off a long strip of paper. I wiped my face and pulled off another half a dozen sheets. Wadding them into a ball, I crouched and dabbed at the floor.

'The kids really love you.' I forced my voice into a girlish murmur.

'They're the reason I do the job, darlin'.'

I stood up, a wet ball of disintegrating toilet paper in my hand, and glanced in his direction. He was staring at me through the reflection in the mirror, his eyes sharp and assessing.

'How old are you?'

'Twenty-one.'

'You look younger. You could be fifteen.'

'I'm small-boned.' I spotted a bin in the corner and walked towards it, throwing in the toilet paper. 'As I've already interrupted you, can I empty your bin?'

'You can do anything you like, sugar.'

I picked up the broken skin, all that was left of the water balloon, and dropped it in the waste-paper basket. Gripping the bin tightly to my chest, I cleared a crisp packet and a couple of empty lager tins from the coffee table in the corner, aware all the while that the eyes in the mirror were watching.

'If you ever need another Pink Jacket, I'd be happy to step in,' I gabbled. 'I'm just a temporary cleaner. I've always wanted to be on the stage. My auntie used to work here as a Pink Jacket years ago. Sandra Hewitt. Perhaps you remember her?'

'I remember everyone… all the Pinkies I ever worked with. It's my special gift.' He turned and looked at me directly. 'You're lying.'

'What? No… What do you mean?' I stuttered. 'I *do* want to be a Pink Jacket.'

'Not about that. She were a cleaner, your auntie. Not a Pink Jacket.'

'Oh! I thought – '

'You thought wrong.'

'You knew her quite well, then?'

'I knew her. That's all.'

He turned back to his reflection and pulled a slither of pink material from the top of the mirror where it had hung like a sequinned snake. He held an end in each hand and snapped the length tight before lifting his collar and draping it around his neck. His fat fingers were surprisingly adept. Within seconds he'd knotted and tweaked the tie into a perfect bow.

'She died before I had a chance to know her. What was she like?' I asked, aware that I was going too fast but unable to stop.

'She was like you. Sugar and spice. Always wanting to clean up, get rid of the mess. Sweep out the dark corners.'

'Was she popular? Did she have lots of friends? Boyfriends?'

'If you go looking for dirt, honeybun, that's what you'll find.'

'Oh! I'm not looking for anything. I just wondered – '

'Perhaps you'd like to come back after the show. I could give you an audition. See if you're cut out for show business.'

'I'm not sure about tonight… my shift – '

He raised an eyebrow.

'The Great and Marvellous Oz is working her minions extra hard, I see. I've never had my room cleaned this time of night before – '

'It's half-term,' I interrupted. 'We're short-staffed. I stepped in. It's an extra shift.'

He stood up. I backed towards the door.

'Did Delia send you? Are you my Valentine's Day present?'

'Sorry about the interruption.' I reached for the handle, the wicker bin hugged to my chest.

'Yeah. You owe me for that.' He darted forward, surprisingly fast for a heavy man and grabbed my wrist. 'You can pay me with a kiss, sweetheart.'

I wrenched open the door with my free hand and we both jumped back. Standing in the open doorway and filling the entire space was Harry Hot Dog, his hand raised as though he was just about to knock. I pressed myself against his plush costume and squeezed past. Chucky swore, stepped back into his dressing room and slammed the door in Harry's face.

'You're a life-saver, Jeremy.'

He didn't speak and I darted up the stairs. When I reached the top I was still clutching Chucky's bin.

Chapter 16

Hurrying over the stile in the hedge, I missed the turn-off in the dark and I found myself at the edge of the coppice, staring down at the staff caravans in the field below. The Christmas lights on the first two caravans had been switched on. The curtains were drawn and the red material shed an angry glow into the night. Someone was playing reggae music. I heard laughter, shouting, a door banging. The clatter of plates echoed into the darkness. Shadows flitted between the caravans like demons in an icy underworld.

Turning to retrace my steps, I heard a rustle of foliage. A man swore. I switched off my bicycle light and shrank behind the trunk of a tree, its bark rough and slimy against my hands. Footsteps. Stifled laughter. Lights growing closer and the sound of gruff voices. Suddenly half a dozen men lurched out of the wood and stumbled onto the tufted grass. They cheered as they saw the caravans.

Stumbling forward, with boxes of beer swinging by their sides, they chanted, ''Ere we go, 'ere we go, 'ere we go.'

The door of the first caravan opened before they reached it, framing a woman I didn't recognise. She was wearing a short silk robe, her dark hair loose around her shoulders. Cheers and wolf-whistles greeted her appearance. The men quickened their pace. The door to the second caravan opened. Shannon stood in the doorway dressed in a lacy bra and panties, holding a red heart-shaped helium balloon. Even from where I was hiding, I could see she was shivering. The men broke into two groups, jogging in their haste to reach the vans.

I turned away, sickened. It didn't take much imagination to know what was going on. Male guests were visiting girls in the caravans after dark. So much for love and romance. I was surprised Shannon had got herself entangled in the sordid business. She was a Pink Jacket, earning twice as much as me. Perhaps she'd fallen foul of Trafford and his protection racket and decided to earn a little extra cash on her night off. I prayed Boody was locked safely in her room. No wonder she didn't invite me to sleep on her floor!

I turned back towards my own caravan, desperate to get off the path and conceal myself somewhere warm and secure. Unfortunately the caravan was neither. I bolted the door from the inside, aware that one sharp kick would be all that was needed to break through the rotting wood. I didn't dare switch on the light, terrified in case other guests were stumbling through the trees in search of a party and found my hideaway instead. I wriggled out of my uniform by the light of the torch and dressed in as many layers as I could before diving under the duvet, teeth chattering from the cold and the dread of discovery.

I will never forget my first night in that caravan. The bitter cold. The lumps in my makeshift bed. The smell that burned my eyes and seeped into the back of my throat until I could actually taste the roll-ups smoked by the Romanians long ago. The scream of a fox that chilled my heart and tortured my imagination. Worst of all, the fear I would be discovered and the terror that I would never be found.

In the darkness, I imagined I was a small animal – a rabbit or mouse, perhaps – tucked away, unseen in a warm burrow. It was a fantasy I'd used to lull myself to sleep as a child. I pulled my legs up under my chin, making myself as small as possible, hugging my body in the absence of anyone else to hug.

Paloma used to chuckle at my independent streak. She liked to remind me of the occasion when, as a very young child, I refused to hold her hand to cross the road.

'I can hold my own hand!' I'd argued.

'You were such a... how do you say it? ... an incorrigible one. All those red rings of hair. Stamping your foots at me and holding your hands tight together. It is good to accept help from others, Ava. We are not meant to face the danger of this life alone.'

I shook the memory away and concentrated on conjuring my mind to a place of safety, but it was impossible. How could I have left my loving, comfortable home for this squalor? How I wished I could take Paloma's hand now, or that Theo would open the door a crack to check I was asleep, lay his hand upon my cheek and whisper a blessing.

I slept fitfully towards dawn, always aware of the cold and the sound of the trees creaking in the wind. As the light turned from black to grey, I dreamed of Greenacres, the lavish warmth of the dome, its shady green leaves and vibrant flowers. The central pond tumbled with open mouths and fins and scales, its surface ruffled by droplets as clear as crystals falling from the fountain above. Butterflies as large as birds swooped through the air, feeding from lilies and irises before rising to kiss the protective glass of the vaulted ceiling. Silhouetted against the translucent blue they looked like angels ascending to heaven.

A loud scrabbling woke me with a start. Someone was on the roof, moving from one end to the other. I gazed anxiously up at the ceiling. The scratching continued. I sat up, wrapping the duvet around my body, terror sucking at my heart. I listened for several minutes, craning my neck towards the window to see if I could catch a glimpse of the trespasser.

There it was again. I leapt from the bed, frantically opening cupboards and drawers in the kitchenette in search of a knife or anything sharp. Old newspapers, mouse droppings, a saucepan with no handle. Rummaging through a drawer filled with empty cigarette packets, I pulled out a disposable lighter and stubby pencil. I spotted a hypodermic needle at the back and withdrew my hand quickly but not before grabbing a pair of rusting scissors. Gripping them tightly I moved towards the door.

The noise was still coming from the roof, too harsh and random to be the scraping of a branch. I unlocked the door and peered out, pointing the scissors ahead and ready to stab any hand that might grab me from above. Nothing. I jumped down the steps, turning mid-air to land on my feet. Crouching and with the scissor blades thrust out in front, I faced the caravan. Standing on the roof was a massive crow.

'Shoo!' I cried in relief.

I picked up a broken branch, threw it at the bird and missed. It flapped its greasy wings like a dark flag, but didn't fly away. Instead it glared down, its eye upon me like a curse, black as night and shining with anger.

Breathing deeply to quieten my galloping heart, I retreated to the caravan and locked the door. I heard the crow strut back along the roof, its hooked claws scratching the surface, setting my teeth on edge. I switched on the camping stove and huddled under the duvet waiting for the saucepan of water to boil. Every part of my body ached: head, back, neck, heart. I hungrily gulped the hot, sweet caffeine that my body craved, but it couldn't wash the taste of ashes from my mouth.

'Galloping ghosts! I didn't think anybody could be that white without being dead,' Boody exclaimed when I arrived at work. She was sweeping the arcade.

'I *am* dead.'

I've got something that'll make you feel better.'

'I don't think anything will make me feel better.'

She rummaged in her tunic pocket and pulled out a packet.

'No, thanks. I don't do drugs.'

'It's not drugs. Not hard ones, anyways. It'll take the edge off.'

'I'll stick with the edge.'

I must have looked really bad because she persisted.

'What about a hot shower?'

'What about it?'

She lowered her voice. 'I've got a key to Mr King's executive toilet! It's got a shower and everything. I use it sometimes after hours 'cos the shower in our caravan's rubbish. They'll never know. He's never there. You need to take your own towels and soap and clear up after. What's the harm?'

'You've got a key to Maxwell King's office? How did you get your hands on that?'

'I came across Trafford one night. He'd been on a bender. The big ape was gone. Solid gone. He had a bunch of master keys in his jacket pocket. I borrowed it for a couple of hours. A friend of mine runs one of those shoe-mending places. He cuts keys too. He owed me a favour. He cut a copy of all Trafford's keys. I returned his bunch before the slacker even knew what'd happened.'

'You've got copies of all the master keys?'

'That's what I said. Are you listening, cloth-ears, or what?'

'And you would lend me the keys so I can go and take a shower?'

'Duh! What do you think, stupid?'

'That would be great... wonderful!' I could hardly contain my excitement. This could be my chance to get inside the offices and look through the personnel files.

'If you're thinking of nicking anything,' she said, 'forget it. All the desks and cupboards are locked.'

'I'm guessing you've already tried.'

'Why not? I reckoned I was owed a little extra, the hours I work. Didn't get me nowhere, though.'

'All I want is a shower. I feel disgusting.' I looked at my watch. It was nearly 7.30. 'It's too late now. The office staff will start arriving for work soon. Can I borrow the keys tonight?'

'I'll let you have them at the end of the shift. Just don't get caught.'

My body felt as though it had been kicked every shade of blue, but my spirits had lifted. I had a plan. Weak sunshine filtered through the February clouds. Half-term holidaymakers in plastic raincoats and coloured fleeces sauntered down to the café and shop in search of breakfast. Bunting flapped in the breeze; the plastic flowers in hanging baskets bobbed and shivered as though alive. Children shrieked in the play park. A boy climbing the wrong way up the slide laughed at his friend at the top of the ladder, refusing to let him pass. A little girl carrying a Patty Pizza character doll skipped down to the arcade with a pot of coins and began to feed the slot machines. Televisions blared from the caravans as we wheeled the cleaning trolley along the drive.

Although it was Sunday, we'd been asked to deep-clean a caravan on the East Drive where a family of four had been staying. The children had suffered sickness and diarrhoea as soon as they arrived on Friday night and the parents had left yesterday, cutting their holiday short in case they became infected and were too ill to drive home later in the week.

We'd also been asked to deliver clean sheets to another caravan.

'There's always one,' Boody complained. 'Filthy brats. They should keep them in nappies if they can't hold their bladders.'

'Accidents happen,' I replied, remembering my own childhood. Although annoyed, Boody smiled and joked with the mother when she collected the dirty sheets.

'Going soft?' I asked.

'I'm thinking of my tip at the end of the week,' she explained.

I ran into Sid on my lunch break. He was sitting on a bollard behind the laundry having a smoke.

'All right?' he asked as I approached.

'Surviving. You?'

'Same as always. How's your car?'

'Still broken. At least the sun's out. Hopefully the guests will have a good week of weather for the school holidays.'

'Rain's coming later,' he said. He blew out a stream of smoke. 'Don't get caught in the storm.'

I had the feeling he wasn't talking about the weather any more.

'What did you mean the other day when you said this wasn't the place for me?'

He sucked on the cigarette and thought for a moment.

'Fun World will wear you down, like the sea battering a cliff. You have to be made of hard stuff not to get eroded.' He brushed a microscopic speck of ash off the leg of his overalls. 'Anything soft gets washed away. The hard ones survive. Ones like Boody.' He stared until I looked away, pulling self-consciously at my hair. 'It's wearing you down already.'

'I didn't sleep well last night.'

I remembered the men who'd visited the staff caravans the previous night. A picture of Shannon standing at the open door, waiting for her visitors.

'You've been here a long time, Sid. What about you? Has it worn you down?'

'I watch it happen. It doesn't happen to me.'

'Why not?'

'Because I'm not looking for anything, and nobody's looking to get anything from me. That's the secret. If they know you want something, they'll use it. That's when they get you.'

I thought about this for a moment.

'And my aunt, Sandra Hewitt? What did she want?'

'What everybody wants. Belonging. Love. She were a poor little orphan girl. She didn't stand a chance.'

My pulse quickened.

'And did she find it?'

'What?'

'Love.'

'Maybe. Maybe not. I don't know. What is love, anyway? All I know is she were one of the ones that got washed away.'

'She was soft-hearted?'

'She gave people the benefit of the doubt. She trusted.'

'Sid, if you knew something was going on at Fun World that shouldn't be, you'd report it, wouldn't you?'

'I just do my job.' He sucked hungrily at the minute stub in his mouth, then flicked the remains of the cigarette on the ground.

'For evil to flourish, all it needs is for good men to do nothing,' I said. 'That's the saying, isn't it?'

'Perhaps I'm not good.' He stood up and squashed the fag end under his boot. The conversation was over.

When I collected my money from Mrs Ozzles at the end of my shift, she also commented on my appearance.

'This is a holiday camp, not a concentration camp. Sort your hair out. Put some make-up on. I expect to see more of an effort. This is your final warning, Claire. You won't like the consequences if I have to speak to you again.'

It wasn't an empty threat. I believed her.

That evening, I once again followed the holidaymakers down to the entertainment centre and arcade. They were enticed by the lights and the music and the smell of hot dogs and onions. I was lured there by the possibility of a breakthrough in the search for my father, and the overwhelming desire to wash myself clean. I hadn't come this far, endured the drudgery and the misery of the last few days, not to find answers to my questions. I couldn't go back to Greenacres without knowing who I was, if I could go back at all. The only way was forward. Homeless and penniless now, my biological father was my only hope of a way out of the hole I'd dug myself.

I carried a bag of laundry – my own soiled clothes and a couple of filthy cushion covers from the caravan. I wore my cleaner's uniform in order to blend into the background, but if anyone asked why I was still on site on a Sunday night, long after my shift concluded, I would tell them I was waiting for my wash cycle to finish in the campsite launderette.

Except for the swimming towel I'd bought, I threw the contents of the bag into the machine and set it for a forty-degree wash. Chucky's show time had already started. I hovered in the darkness outside the entertainment centre, waiting for a moment when I could slip past the evening receptionist.

A couple of guests wandered into the foyer. I managed to sneak behind them while the receptionist hunted through the lost property box for a pair of flip-flops left in the indoor pool. I darted through the door I'd entered on the day of my interview with Mrs Ozzles and hurried to the end of the corridor. My first port of call was the housekeeper's office. I fumbled through the bunch Boody had lent me until I found a key that fitted. I entered Mrs Ozzles' office and switched on my small torch.

The desk was completely clear. The trays of papers and pen pot I'd seen at my interview had gone. I flashed the light into every corner. It was an empty room, swept clean, devoid of personality. Apart from a desk, a chair on either side and a filing cabinet, the only item that gave any indication of the temperament of the occupant was the noticeboard on the wall. The staff rota for the month was pinned in the middle. A 'Psychic Moods' calendar hung to the right of the rota declaring February to be the month of Crystal Meditation. On the left was a postcard from Ibiza and a placard which read 'A tidy desk = a tidy mind'. If that was true, Mrs Ozzles' brain was a complete blank.

Leaving the bag with my beach towel by the door, I tried opening the key cupboard, the filing cabinet and the desk drawers. All locked. None of the keys on the bunch were small enough to fit. There was nowhere obvious that keys could be hidden, no plant pot or vase in which to be concealed. I kicked the filing cabinet in frustration. I froze as the sound reverberated round the room.

After waiting a moment I opened the door an inch to check the corridor was clear. I relocked the office and hurried past 'Sales' and 'Finance', making my way round the corner to the door marked 'Chief Executive'. I let myself in.

The room was large, with a glossy table and six chairs at one end and a matching mahogany desk at the other. A black leather sofa stretched out under the window. Again, all the surfaces were clear. The bland blue-and-beige speckled carpet laid throughout the Fun World public spaces had been replaced with an expensive hardwood floor. I tiptoed quietly across, shining my torch along the walls, the darkness shrinking as I approached.

A 'Businessman of the Year' certificate awarded by the Westhatch Chamber of Commerce hung on the wall, together with several photographs of Maxwell King shaking hands with local dignitaries – a Member of Parliament, the Westhatch-on-Sea mayor, Miss Great Britain. In each picture he looked relaxed, his hair swept off his broad forehead, his smile impossibly white.

I gazed at his features, looking for a similarity to my own. Given the choice of Sid, Chucky or Maxwell King, Mr King was by far the most palatable option for a father. Perhaps I'd inherited my determination and head for business from him. It was highly unlikely there would be anything in his desk to connect him with my mother, too much time had passed, but I rattled the handles of the drawers nevertheless. No joy. A dark wood filing cabinet and matching credenza were also locked. I checked through Boody's bunch of keys. Again, none of them were small enough to fit the cabinets. Another dead end.

I opened a door at the back of the office. As suspected, it led to a luxurious shower room with toilet, sink and bidet in white marble. There were no windows. I locked the door and switched on the light. An extractor fan whirred into life.

Ultra-modern stainless steel fittings gleamed under the recessed spotlights. Fresh white towels hung from a heated towel rail. I began to undress, desperate to wash away my night in the caravan and the galloping ache in my temples.

For a moment I stood naked in front of the mirror. I'd lost weight in the last few days. My ribs pushed against my white skin like limbs under a sheet. My cheeks were hollow, my eyes dull and deeply shadowed. The anger and fear I'd kept caged in my heart since leaving Greenacres had roamed free, scratching worry lines on my forehead and tearing the bloom from my skin.

I lifted the dark fringe away from my forehead to reveal a line of natural red at the roots – embers glowing through the coal. As Zavier pointed out, the colour would need to be touched up. Either that or a complete change, perhaps bleaching it blonde as Mrs Ozzles had suggested.

I'd been wearing my mother's jade necklace every day under my uniform, not wanting to leave it at Mrs Bungay's house nor, thankfully, trusting it to the car. It glinted against my white throat, echoing the colour of my eyes. So far, it hadn't brought me love or money as predicted by Mrs Ozzles, but perhaps it would keep me safe tonight. I undid the clasp and laid it carefully on the sink.

Stepping under the hot spray, I lathered my body with the small bar of soap I'd concealed in my tunic pocket. I massaged my hair with conditioner from a promotional sachet, knowing from experience that shampoo would only worsen the frizz.

Afterwards, I put the toilet lid down and sat wrapped in the beach towel, enjoying the steamy warmth while I combed through my curls. I was in no hurry. The best time to break into the basement storage cupboard would be later, when Chucky Skittles and the Pink Jackets had finished their show and were no longer backstage or hanging about in the dressing rooms. I'd checked the evening programme. From 10.30 to midnight an ABBA tribute band would be playing, followed by dancing until one in the morning. Better to wait here than out in the cold.

I heard a muffled bang. The office door had slammed. Someone entered Maxwell King's domain. Flicking off the light, I launched a silent prayer they wouldn't hear the drone of the extractor fan through the door or the frenzied beating of my heart. I fumbled in the pocket of my discarded tunic for the bike light, a sensation of claustrophobia taking hold now that my exit from the warm shower room was blocked.

Reassured by the light of the torch, I crept to the door to check the lock was securely bolted. I pressed my burning cheek to the cold wood and listened. Footsteps paced across the wooden floor. I heard the low tone of a male voice. From the rhythm of the conversation – the pauses, the rise and fall in volume and the lack of another voice – I assumed the man must be speaking on a mobile phone.

The extractor fan switched off. I held my breath, scrunching my face and squeezing my eyes shut. Surely the subtle change in background noise would alert him to my presence. But talking and listening appeared to have deafened the speaker to the faint whirr emanating from the toilet, followed by the sudden, unexplained silence. The conversation showed no sign of stopping. I sank to the floor and huddled against the door.

An unexpected beep. It took a moment to realise it was my own mobile. A text! I launched myself across the washroom and fumbled in the pile of clothes for my phone, switching it to silent mode with a trembling hand. I looked at the screen. There was a message from Zavier. I'd been ignoring his messages all day.

'Stop ignoring me. Where R U?' I made a split second-decision and texted back.

'In trouble. Fun World Holiday Camp. Can you come?' I pressed Send.

Almost immediately, I regretted my action. It was a stupid thing to do. I'd vowed to cut the tie and continue the search for my father on my own. Unidentified thugs had connected me with Zavier. He was a liability. But I was scared and had no one else to turn to. He probably wouldn't want to help, I rationalised. And if he did, what could he do? I'd got myself into this mess and would have to think my way out.

I pulled the beach towel tight under my arms. The first thing to do would be to get dressed. Perhaps I could invent some cock-and-bull story about doing overtime, cleaning the toilets with headphones on and not hearing Mr King's arrival. My phone vibrated. Another text.

'On my way.'

I texted back instructing him not to ring because I couldn't talk.

'Hiding in chief executive's private toilet. Can U distract so I can slip out? Go to reception and through door marked 'Staff Only'. CEO's office at end of corridor.'

I eased into my clothes, silently mopped up the puddles on the floor and waited. The voice grew louder. A drawer dragged open and shut with a bang. Whoever it was had a key. He must be sitting at the desk, close to the toilet door.

'Forget the Romanians. They were a mistake. I need another supplier.' I recognised the voice of Maxwell King. This was bad, very bad. 'Trafford hasn't got the brains… OK… that sounds good. I can work with that. As long as it's a quality product… Shipment on 19th February? Tell Mr Bones I'll meet him myself at midday at the funfair. Yes. On the train. Got it!'

Discussion concluded, I waited for the dreadful moment when he would attempt to open the toilet door. Whatever he was talking about, it didn't sound good. Not the sort of conversation you would want someone else to overhear.

An eternity passed with no sound from outside. I perched on the toilet, my bottom numb from the cold seat. I stood up and stretched. I wiped the evidence I'd recently used the shower off the mirror and prayed the condensation wouldn't return.

'Hi. It's Max… Yeah… Sorted… New supply coming in two weeks… Here, the clubs, the hotel, anywhere the punters are. Make sure security is tight this time, and our friend in the police knows what he's got to do.' His voice became indistinct. He must have walked away from the desk, pacing at the far end of the office by the conference table.

I pressed my ear against the door. Banging. Voices. A disturbance of some kind. I silently slid back the bolt and pushed the door open a crack. Mr King was standing at the entrance to his office with his back to me. Zavier was in the corridor, smiling and pumping Maxwell's hand.

'… buy you a drink…'

'That's very kind,' Maxwell replied. 'Glad you're having a good holiday. Why don't you get yourself back to the club bar and enjoy the rest of the night?'

I caught Zavier's eye. There was a flash of recognition before he staggered against the doorframe.

'I'm not as thunk as you drink I am,' he mumbled.

Maxwell put his arm round his shoulder. 'Steady. Let's get you back to the party.' He turned Zavier away from his office and they disappeared into the corridor. This was my chance.

Grabbing my towel I darted from the toilet and out of the chief executive's office. If I followed them towards reception, there was every likelihood Mr King would usher Zavier through the staff door, turn around and bump into me on the way back to his office. I dashed to the right and dipped into the ladies' toilets. Another washroom. Once again I stood behind a toilet door, my breath coming in anxious gasps, waiting.

Footsteps. A door slammed. I peered out. All clear. I ran as fast as I could to the end of the corridor and gently pushed the door that led back into the reception.

Zavier was talking to the receptionist.

'I'm afraid Mr King is very busy tonight,' she parroted. 'But he's always pleased to receive positive customer feedback.'

'Can I buy you a drink, darling?' he slurred.

'That's very kind, but I'm on duty. Let me give you one of these feedback forms. That's the best way to express your appreciation.'

She passed Zavier a form. He fumbled as he took it and it floated to the floor behind her desk. She bent to retrieve it. He turned, saw me peeping through the narrow opening and frantically beckoned me through. I ran across the reception area and out of the glass entrance door. Zavier followed immediately, shielding my body from sight so that when the receptionist straightened up all she could see was his retreating back.

'Your form!' she cried.

The door swung shut behind us. Instantly, the drunken idiot disappeared. Zavier grabbed me by the hand and we raced round the corner and along the West Drive, skimming the edge of the road, staying as much as possible in the shadows. When we reached the adventure playground at the outskirts of the caravan park, we sank onto a wooden log to catch our breath.

'Nice outfit,' he said, looking at my polyester cleaning tabard.

'It's this year's look.'

He raised an eyebrow. 'Tell me everything.'

The log was hard and uncomfortable and I squirmed under his scrutiny. Although we were a long way from the nearest lamppost, the moon was bright and full, the sky sprinkled with stars. It was as though we'd fallen into an old black-and-white movie, a mad-cap crime caper perhaps, or a clichéd romance.

'I was in the chief executive's office. He came in and I was trapped in the toilet. That's it.'

He sighed. 'What exactly are you up to, Ava?'

'You know what I'm looking for. I'm trying to find my real dad. I thought there might be some records in his office.'

'And were there?'

'I don't know. Everything was locked.'

'This is stupid,' he exclaimed. 'I was happy to take your money and go off on some wild-goose chase, but this is getting out of hand. It's dangerous. It has to stop.'

'But – '

'No buts. And why is your hair wet?'

'I took a shower.'

'You took a shower! You were about to be arrested for breaking and entering and you took a shower!'

'I didn't break anything. I had a key.'

'You're mad. You should leave this stuff to the professionals.'

'I don't know any professionals,' I replied tartly.

'What about the one who just saved your bacon?'

'Yeah… well… thanks.'

'Think what could have happened if I hadn't come to the rescue.'

'I would have had time to pluck my eyebrows, file my nails, curl my eyelashes. I wasn't in any real danger,' I pouted.

'So why ask for my help?'

'It would have been embarrassing if I'd been caught snooping. And if you're worried about those thugs, they're never going to find me. No one knows where I'm living at the moment, not even you.'

'So Brenda tells me,' he scowled. 'But I'm not just thinking about them. What if you'd been caught tonight? The police might have been called. We know there's someone down at the local station who's happy to pass on information to whoever is trying to find you.'

'I hadn't thought of that.'

'I don't want you getting hurt.'

'I'm not going to get hurt.'

'Put your chin back in, titch. I'm not just talking about physical hurt. You're setting yourself up for a massive disappointment. You're never going to find your dad. He's one sardine in the sea. If by some miracle you do find him, what are the chances you're going to like what you find? He hasn't made any effort to look for you over the years. Face it, Ava, he doesn't want you.'

'You don't know that! He might not even know about me,' but I could no longer trust my voice.

He put his arm around my shoulder.

'It's time to leave the pity party you've been throwing. You're not the only one in the world who doesn't know who their dad is. Shall I tell you the definition of confusion? Father's Day in Westhatch. Get over it and move on.'

'It doesn't matter if he doesn't love me,' I sobbed. 'I just need to know the truth. I need to know what's real.'

'Everything you've told me about Greenacres and your life back there, that's what's real. That's where you belong. Go home. Go back to the people who love you, the ones who've stuck by you in the past. Stop chasing a fantasy father and accept the one you have.'

'But they didn't stick with me, did they? Theo, Paloma, Marcus. Where are they now?'

'You turned your back on them, remember. *You* left. Greenacres is still where it's always been.'

'I can't go back. It's too late. I've burned my bridges. I feel too ashamed to face them.' I shook his arm away and straightened up. 'The only way is forward. I'm going to continue my search with or without you.'

'You dumped me, Ava. Just like you dumped your family. Why did you move out of Mrs Bungay's place without even saying goodbye? Why can't you trust me?'

I sniffed and shrugged.

'Thanks for coming, Zavier. I won't take up any more of your time.' I stood up.

He grabbed my arm.

'Where are you going?' He was standing so close I had to throw my head back to look up into his face.

'I've got things to do.'

'I'm coming with you.'

'No you're not! I can't afford to pay you any more.' I attempted to shake myself free.

'Forget about the money. It's not about the money -'

'What *is* it about then?'

'It's about this.' His head dipped and he kissed me softly on the lips.

Chapter 17

I pushed him away. We were both breathless. There was an awkward silence.

'Why did you do that?'

'Because you were giving me the brush-off. I thought you ought to know what you're missing before you take me off the case.'

'You arrogant...' I clenched my fists and shook my head, trying to find the right words.

'I should have guessed you wouldn't sit around on your skinny backside waiting for me to come up with the answers.'

My head shot up at his uncomplimentary remark.

'That determined chin and flashing green eyes. You had trouble written all over you from the start. But you need me, Ava. Tonight has proved you can't do this alone.'

'You're a luxury I can no longer afford,' I replied stiffly.

'Don't be stupid. I don't want your money. You can't afford *not* to let me help. I wouldn't be able to sleep at night knowing you've got yourself caught up in something serious, and I was the one who tipped off the bad guys that you're in the area.'

'Exactly! Put it like that and I think you owe *me*!'

'You're right. I owe you my support, a shoulder to cry on, perhaps. And I owe you for pulling me out of the rut I'd been in lately, giving me a reason to get up in the morning instead of slobbing my days away.' He stroked a lock of hair away from my forehead, pulled it straight and let the curl ping back. 'So what's the plan, Sherlock?'

I wasn't sure whether I liked him touching me or not. Everything was happening too fast. But I still had one more place to visit and this time I wouldn't be alone.

'I've managed to get hold of a set of master keys for tonight only. I've checked out the housekeeper's office and Maxwell King's pad. All the filing cabinets are locked. I was going to try the basement storage area next. It's probably my last chance at finding my mother's records.'

'Resourceful as well as beautiful! Let's go.'

'You don't have to come.' I wanted to be sure.

'It's Sunday night. What else would I be doing? With my track record, this counts as a hot date. Oh, by the way, I bought you this.' He rummaged in his pocket and pulled out a small package.

'What is it?' I unwrapped the pink paper to find a small box of pink soaps shaped like miniature hearts.

'Happy Valentine's Day.'

Heat surged to my cheeks. I was glad of the darkness.

'It was yesterday.'

'I know. But you'd gone missing.'

'Thank you.'

'Sure.' He looked down, shuffling from foot to foot. After an awkward silence he grabbed my hand. 'Come on. Let's do this.'

I was glad he changed the subject. I stuffed the soaps in the pocket of my tabard.

'It's not going to be easy. There's always a bouncer on the door. You can't get into the entertainment centre unless you have a guest pass. They'll let me in if I say there's been a spillage and I've been called to clear it up. Are you any good at climbing through windows?'

'I've had some experience. Better not to ask,' he replied.

'The gents' toilets back on to the staff car park.'

'You seem to have a particular fascination with men's toilets. What's that about?'

I tried to ignore the long fingers stroking my hand.

'I clean them every morning. I can get a yellow "Closed for Cleaning" cone from the cupboard and stick it by the door. I'll open the fanlight window. You'll have to do the rest.'

'Then?'

'Then we make our way backstage, sneak past the dressing rooms and into the storage room. Once inside, we can lock the door. I've got a torch... well, a bicycle lamp, really. If you don't mind, we can lay your jacket down by the bottom of the door to block out the light.'

'I don't mind laying my jacket down for a lady.'

He pulled me closer but I slapped his hands away, feeling shy and out of my depth.

'Concentrate, Zavier! If there's no window, which I don't imagine there will be in the basement, we can switch the lights on. If we're quiet we can probably stay there all night.'

'I'm liking the sound of this plan.'

'Come on.'

I hurried across the grass, stumbling a little on the uneven ground. He caught up with me easily and we made our way through the trees to the road and down towards the throbbing music.

As before, breaking in proved the easy part. Trafford was on the door, but he grunted and let me through when I told him someone had been sick in the men's toilet. As I walked past, he took a thick roll of cash out of his pocket and deliberately flicked through it, a cruel smirk splitting his face. The mystery of who had stolen my money was solved.

Zavier was surprisingly agile, wriggling his lanky frame through the small window and landing on the bank of sinks. Once in the entertainment centre we blended into the dark swirl of hot bodies crowding around the bar and dance floor. Everywhere people were shouting, laughing and drinking, their bodies broken into disjointed pieces by the disco lights flashing red, purple and green.

The music was deafening, the bass reverberating in my chest like a second heartbeat. I stood on tiptoe and shouted in his ear, aware of his cheek rough against mine. I told him I would check the basement first to see if the coast was clear. He nodded and bopped at the edge of the dance floor, watching the backstage door.

I slipped through. It was a quarter-past ten. The ABBA tribute act was setting up behind the stage curtains. Chucky Skittles and the Pink Jackets had gone off stage for the evening and were presumably in their dressing rooms or making their way home. I crept downstairs.

Harry Hot Dog was standing by a rack of costumes, struggling to unzip his head. He looked up as I reached the bottom step. At first I thought he hadn't seen me from inside the costume, but he waved in my direction.

'Hello, Jeremy. Good show?'

He gave a thumbs-up.

'I'm on a late shift,' I lied. 'Need to check the cleaning supplies in the storage room. Please don't tell anyone I'm here. I'm trying to avoid Trafford.'

He nodded. Trafford's unpleasant reputation was known even to a newcomer like him.

Hurrying to the door, I pulled out the keys. Aware of Jeremy hovering behind me, I raced through the bunch. From the size of the keyhole, I was looking for a large mortice rather than a Yale key. After several blunders, I found the right one and opened the door. Waving dismissively to Harry, I turned on the light and locked the door behind me. I texted Zavier.

'I'm in. Corridor not clear. Stay put for now.'

I surveyed the large rectangle, more a room than a cupboard. There were no windows. One side was cluttered with old furniture – a desk, several swivel chairs and a flipchart stand. On the other, a row of six filing cabinets. Boxes of brochures and promotional flyers were stacked against the far wall. I tried opening the filing cabinet drawers. All locked.

One of cabinets was labelled 'Personnel'. I was so frustrated I could have thrown the flipchart stand against it and bashed my way through the grey metal. To be so close and yet not be able to see the contents! If only I could pick the mechanism somehow and open the drawers.

In books and films, locks are easily opened with hairpins and credit cards. I checked the pockets of my tabard for a useful implement to no avail. I walked over to the battered desk and opened the top drawer in search of a paperclip or letter opener. To my utter surprise, there was a cluster of small silver keys. Whoever was responsible for the storage room was more laid back about security than Mrs Ozzles and Maxwell King.

Grabbing the keys in excitement, I fumbled through the bunch until I found the one that fitted the personnel cabinet. My mobile bleeped.

'What's happening? R U OK?'

'All OK. Reading files,' I replied.

There were two drawers of staff files arranged in alphabetical order. I went straight for the letter H and pulled out a slim brown file marked 'Hewitt, Sandra'. I flicked quickly through the pages. Holiday slips, sickness records, a note from her doctor signing her off for a week in 1983 citing nausea and fatigue. I did a quick mental calculation. She would have been about two months' pregnant. Moving further back in the file I found a character reference from the head teacher of Westhatch-on-Sea comprehensive. The last document at the back was my mother's application form, filled out in blue ink in a round, childish hand. She'd been just seventeen.

I was startled by a soft knock on the door.

'Ava!'

It was Zavier. I darted across the room and turned the key in the lock. He slipped inside.

'I told you to wait!'

'I was worried.'

'Did anyone see you?'

'No. The corridor was empty. Did you find anything?'

'Just this. My mother's file.'

He took it from me and turned the pages.

'There's nothing here.'

'I know. We might as well go.' My voice was flat with disappointment.

'Not so fast. Let's have a look at the other files. Make a note of the names and addresses of those people who worked here at the same time as your mother. If they haven't moved we might be able to contact some of them, find out what they know. I could do my probate investigator routine again.'

We began to work systematically through the files. Zavier had a pen in his jacket pocket and he wrote down a list of names and addresses on the inside cover of my mother's file. As well as housing the records of ex-staff, there were also several bulging files relating to current staff. I pulled out 'King, Maxwell', 'Ozzles, Delia', 'Skittles, Charles', and 'Tulitt, Sidney' while Zavier continued to cross-reference the employment dates in the other files.

The paperwork in the old files was all dated before the year 2000. New files must have been opened for staff after the Millennium. Again, most of the material related to holiday and sickness records. I was interested to see the progress Maxwell King had made through the organisation, starting as a Pink Jacket and working his way up to head of entertainment two years later. His file came to an abrupt end the year he bought out the old management. Presumably, the chief executive didn't need a staff file after that.

A new appraisal system had been instigated sometime after my mother's departure. Mrs Ozzles had consistently been rated as 'outstanding' when interviewed by Mr King. Chucky Skittles had one reprimand on record relating to an undisclosed incident with an eleven-year-old girl. Her family had been given a rebate on their holiday and the matter had been taken no further. My stomach heaved at the thought of what might have occurred.

Sid Tulitt's file was thinner than the others. His appraisals were marked 'Good' or 'Satisfactory'. He never took his full holiday entitlement and over the years had very little sick leave. My eye was caught by a carbon copy of a petty-cash slip. It was a small piece of paper which I could easily have overlooked, but the date jumped off the page because it was the week before my mother left the holiday park. The letters were ornately looped, the carbon smudged, but I recognised the handwriting as belonging to Mrs Ozzles. My heart froze as my mind assimilated what I was reading. '£1,000 for SH Termination'. It was countersigned by Maxwell King.

SH… My mother's initials…Termination! The word sent a shiver through my soul. A week after the money had been paid, my mum had run away from Fun World and found refuge at Greenacres. Fifteen months later she was dead in her car.

'Ava?' Zavier was shaking my shoulders. 'What's the matter?'

'Look.' I pointed to the petty-cash slip. 'The maintenance manager was paid £1,000 the week before my mother left Fun World. These are her initials. It's a contract. Maxwell King and Mrs Ozzles put a contract out on my mother's life and – '

'Hold on, hold on. Not so fast. Why on earth would anyone here want your mother dead?'

'She must have seen something. There are things going on here, Zavier, you wouldn't believe. There are men visiting the Pink Jackets at night and I found a hypodermic needle and I think I overheard Mr King organising a drug shipment while I was stuck in the toilet this evening.' I was shaking so hard, I could hardly speak through my chattering teeth.

'Shhh. Calm down. Let me think.' He flicked through Sid Tulitt's file and then through those belonging to Maxwell King, Mrs Ozzles and Chucky.

'There's no evidence of criminal behaviour here, except for Mr Skittles and the child. That might be of interest to the police,' he whispered.

'But my mother's initials!'

'That could be anything.' He thought for a moment. 'Screwdriver handles, for instance.'

'Why would you terminate screwdriver handles?'

'I don't know. I was just guessing. And that's what you're doing. We should get out of here, take these files and read them thoroughly somewhere safe. I've been through both drawers and got all the names and addresses of possible contacts.'

'Perhaps we should look at the financial records too. See if there's anything suspicious. You know, drugs money.'

'We're not the police, Ava. That's none of our business. We're just trying to find your dad, remember? We shouldn't poke our noses where they're not wanted.'

'I suppose so.' I remembered my conversation with Sid earlier in the day. 'But all it takes for evil to flourish is for good men to do nothing.'

'It's not our fight. Let's go.' Zavier gathered up my mother's file and the files for Maxwell King, Mrs Ozzles, Chucky and Sid. I unlocked the door and looked down the corridor.

To my horror, I caught a glimpse of thick legs in black trousers and heavy boots descending the stairs. I yanked the door closed before the face came into view. Thankfully the music from above drowned out the slight click. I knew who was coming. Trafford!

'What is it?' Zavier asked.

I put my finger to my mouth, slowly turned the key and switched off the light.

'Security guard!' I whispered.

A thin line of light shone beneath the door. Zavier gently lowered the files on the floor and stood behind me, his arms around my waist. I was too frightened of being discovered by Trafford to object.

'Don't worry. You're safe with me,' he murmured. A dark shadow crossed the line of light. Someone had walked past the door to the toilets. I heard voices. Trafford was talking, perhaps to Chucky or Jeremy, I couldn't tell. Then he was swearing. A door slammed shut. Again a shadow passed the door, then another. This time the second shadow paused. The handle turned. My hand flew to my mouth. Zavier tightened his grip around my waist.

Unable to open the door, the person outside moved away. We stood locked together for what seemed an age, my heart beating so hard I thought I would collapse if Zavier let me go.

'I think they've gone,' he said at last.

'Let's wait a little longer.'

'I need to get home. I've got the jitters.'

'Me too. But it's better to be safe.'

'I've really got the jitters,' he said slowly. 'I need a dose.'

'Oh!' I jerked away as though his touch had contaminated me. He needed another hit – a smack of horse or a bang of Charlie, whatever they called it.

'You'll just have to wait!' I hissed. I couldn't believe I'd forgotten about his habit and allowed him to ambush my emotions so easily.

'I can't wait.' He staggered against a filing cabinet in the darkness. I heard him slump to the floor. Reluctantly I switched on my torch. His face was pale and beaded with sweat. His breaths were coming in short deep gasps.

'What's the matter?'

'Have you got anything to eat? A sweet or a chocolate bar?' My hands automatically dipped into my tunic pockets, but I already knew the answer.

'Soap?'

'I need my medication,' he groaned.

'Get up,' I whispered. I tried to pull him, but his body was limp.

'I can't. Go and find a vending machine. Get me a cola or a packet of sweets. Quick.'

I could hear the panic in his voice. I'd never seen the effects of drug addiction before, but I'd heard of cold turkey. Perhaps Zavier was suffering from severe withdrawal. Whatever the cause of his ailment, I needed to get him out of the storage cupboard before he lost consciousness completely.

I unlocked the door and checked the corridor. It was empty. I locked the door behind me and walked briskly along the corridor. Once at the bottom of the steps, I slowed down and crept up until I was behind the stage. Trafford was standing in the wings watching the tribute band as they performed 'Dancing Queen', arms folded across his powerful chest. I froze.

What was he doing here? He was supposed to be on the door or patrolling the club to prevent any trouble before taking over at reception for the rest of the night, not blocking my exit. I stepped back and bumped into something large and fluffy. I jumped and turned, falling into the arms of Harry Hot Dog.

He steadied me, his hands at my elbow. I stood on tiptoe to reach the small viewing hole in the costume at Harry's neck.

'Trafford's hanging about backstage,' I shouted above the music. 'I don't want him to see me. He gives me the creeps.'

Harry nodded. I couldn't see his expression, but caught the gleam of his eyes in the dim light. He moved me firmly to his right side and placed his hand at the small of my back. He pushed me forward. I understood immediately. We would walk past Trafford together. If the security guard looked in our direction, I would be shielded from view by Harry's enormous costume. We walked quickly and were past the danger zone and through the backstage door in a matter of seconds.

The club was heaving and we struggled to push our way past the dancing couples and crowded tables to the entrance. Women in low-cut tops grabbed at Harry as he lumbered past, taking selfies with him on their mobiles. Their sweating partners jeered and punched him on the chest. The heavy doors swung shut behind us. We were out in the vestibule by the toilets. A vending machine of drinks, chocolates and crisps gleamed in the corner.

I toyed with the idea of asking for help. With Jeremy on board I could slip back past Trafford with the can of cola and sweets, and we could lug Zavier up the stairs together. But what would he think if I told him there was a semi-conscious intruder in the basement? I didn't know him very well. He always seemed anxious to please, but he didn't look the type who'd be comfortable breaking the rules. If he suspected something illegal was taking place, he was likely to report the matter. I decided it was too much of a risk to confide in him.

Thanking him for rescuing me from Trafford's unwanted advances, I told him not to wait as I would be cleaning the ladies' toilets for the next half hour. For the third time that evening, I hid in the toilets.

After five minutes, I ducked out and shoved a handful of coins in the vending machine. A can of cola thumped into the drawer below, followed by a packet of fruit pastilles. I stuffed them in my tunic pocket and pushed open the door to the entertainment centre. Skirting round the room, invisible among the throng of drunken holidaymakers, I kept my eye on the backstage door, scanning the crowd for any sign of Trafford.

There he was, muscling his way towards an argument at the bar. I dipped into the shadows and pushed through the dancing, sweating, swearing horde. Once through the backstage door I raced down the stairs and along the corridor, unlocking the door of the storage room with trembling hands.

Chapter 18

Zavier was where I'd left him, lying on the floor, deathly pale. I locked the door behind me.

'I've got you a drink. And some sweets.'

His eyes fluttered open. I pulled the tab on the can. The frothy liquid erupted out of the hole and spilled over my hand after its bumpy journey down the corridor.

'Here, drink.'

I raised his head and held the can to his mouth. He sipped, closing his eyes as he swallowed the cold liquid.

'Better?'

He nodded.

'Give me a few minutes,' he croaked.

He held his hand out for a sweet. I unwrapped the top of the packet and popped one in his mouth. He chewed and swallowed.

'Another.'

After finishing half the packet, he held up his hand to stop me unwrapping any more. He sat up slowly and swigged the rest of the cola. I was glad to see the colour returning to his cheeks and his breathing slow to a steady rhythm.

'Do you think you can walk?'

He shook his head.

'Not yet. Give it another half an hour.'

'I thought you needed to get home to get your stuff.'

'This is my stuff.' He gestured to the empty tin and half-finished sweet packet. 'I needed the sugar.'

'You said sugar was poison.'

'It is. But I skipped dinner to come and help you. I suffer from hypoglycaemia.'

'Hypo-what?'

'It's diabetes.'

'You're diabetic!'

Suddenly the picture of him with an empty syringe in his hand flashed to mind. His snide comments about my sugar intake also now made sense, and the way he'd spotted the anomaly of the needle mark in the back of my mother's arm.

'I'm sorry,' I stuttered. 'I didn't know.'

'Forget it.'

'Why didn't you tell me when I found you with the syringe? Why did you let me think you were using drugs?'

'It's not cool to be diabetic. I learned that at school. I didn't want you to think I was some kind of defective. When I first met you I thought you looked the kind of person who would be more impressed by drug use than insulin dependency.'

'That shows how much you know me!'

The music upstairs suddenly stopped. A roar of applause filtered down through the ceiling.

'The band's finished.'

'I'm not deaf.'

I swallowed a sharp retort, deciding now wasn't the time or place for a squabble.

'We've got about another hour before everyone goes back to their caravans. The club's doors will be locked and the alarm switched on. We don't want to get stuck here all night,'

We waited another thirty minutes. Zavier didn't want to talk so I flicked through the staff files again and thought about my conversation with Sid Tulitt earlier: 'Don't get caught in the storm,' he'd said. Perhaps he'd had a premonition.

I picked up a blonde wig from the costume rack on our way back along the corridor, and slipped a purple-sequinned shawl around my shoulders to hide my cleaning tabard and the files. We crept through the backstage door and into the club with Zavier leaning on my arm like a drunken raver. There was no sign of Trafford. Big Ron, one of the other bouncers, was on the door chatting up a couple of giggling twenty-year-olds. He wasn't interested in the holidaymakers drifting back to their caravans. His job was to check the people going in, not those leaving. We followed a group of scantily clad ladies across the grass. They screeched like exotic parrots, their men shouting drunkenly to each other across the park. I sat Zavier down behind a wheelie bin in the staff car park.

'How did you get here?'

'On my bike.'

'Cycle or motor?'

'Motor.'

'Where is it?'

'I parked it on the Promenade and sneaked in on foot. I didn't want to run into the goon who guards the barrier to the car park.'

'You're in no fit state to drive home, let alone walk to the seafront. You can collect it tomorrow. I'll get my car. Stay here.'

I jogged down the North Drive to where I'd hidden my battered estate, holding the wig on my head with one hand and the shawl round my shoulder with another. Someone wolf-whistled in the dark. I was glad when I reached the car. I locked myself in and started the ignition.

I swung by the laundrette and collected my washing before making my way back to the staff car park. Zavier swore when he saw the state of the bodywork and the broken window.

'When you said you had a car… This is not a car! It's a pile of – '

'Stop it!' I wasn't in the mood for a lecture on its faults. 'It will get us where we're going.'

'Are you sure?'

I didn't reply but watched as he slumped into the passenger seat and leaned forward with his head in his hands.

'Seat belt!'

'OK, OK,' he groaned. 'Keep your wig on.'

After the tension of the evening, I couldn't stop myself from smiling in the dark. He was obviously feeling better. The car park security guard had gone home for the night and the barrier opened automatically as we drew near.

'How did you do that?' Zavier mumbled. 'This place is like Fort Knox. I was given the third degree when I came to pump Mrs Ozzles about your mother.'

'Getting out's no problem. Getting in is a different matter. If there's no one on duty you have to have a guest pass or a staff card to swipe yourself in.'

'How did you do it?' He sat up a little straighter.

'That's for me to know – '

'… and me to find out,' he interrupted. 'Do you know someone on the inside?'

'Maybe.' I thought about what he'd just said. 'Do you think the security is a bit over the top for a caravan site?'

'It had crossed my mind.'

'Has there been trouble here in the past?'

'Not that I know of. Maxwell King's always in the local newspaper spouting off about how he cooperates with the local council and police to keep Westhatch-on-Sea the family friendly resort it's always been. The locals love Fun World. It's one of the main contributors to the local economy. It brings in the tourists, provides jobs.'

'Maybe that's how he does it.'

'Does what?'

'Keeps trouble away. Keeps the tourists coming back. Keeps the money flooding in.'

'By making it difficult to get in the car park? I'm not following.'

'By ruling Fun World with an iron fist.'

Out of habit, I parked around the corner from Mrs Bungay's bed and breakfast. I opened the passenger door and helped Zavier climb out.

'Are you going to be all right? Is there anyone at home? Your parents?'

'It's just me and dad. He's away a lot on business. I'm on my own tonight. You're welcome to stay and look after me.'

I scowled at his unsteady grin, but was pleased to see him more animated. The thought of fighting through the undergrowth in the middle of the night to sleep in a derelict caravan filled me with dread. Could I trust him to let me sleep undisturbed on his sofa?

'We've got a spare room.'

We turned the corner into Seacombe Road. Zavier suddenly grabbed my arm and yanked me back behind a parked saloon car.

'What?'

'Shhh,' he hissed. 'There's someone sitting in an SUV opposite my house. I saw the spark of his cigarette.'

'Are you sure?'

'Take a look if you don't believe me. No one's going to recognise you in that wig.'

I shuffled to the corner and gazed at Zavier's house, then at the cars parked across the street. I squinted in the darkness. He was right. I could make out the faint glow of a cigarette end and a couple of shadows sitting in the front of a large 4x4. They were silhouetted by the light of the street lamp.

'Do you think it's them?' I asked, returning to Zavier who was standing next to my car.

'I don't know, but I don't want to take the chance. Where are you staying? Can I bunk with you?'

'Get back in the car,' I ordered. 'I know where to go.'

Ten minutes later we were outside Westhatch Hospital's Accident and Emergency Department.

'What are we doing here?'

'Someone ought to check you over.'

'I thought you were going to do that.'

'In your nightmares, maybe!' I parked in an ambulance bay. 'Come on. It'll be warm. No one will find us.'

224

I pulled him through the automatic doors and sat him down on a chair in the waiting area. I gave his name and address to the receptionist, telling her he was a diabetic whose blood-sugar levels were out of control.

'I'll go and park the car properly,' I told him after I'd finished speaking with the receptionist.

He nodded. I hurried outside before he could say anything else. I had no intention of returning to the waiting room, or making my way back to Fun World. Even though my car window was patched with plastic sheeting, I felt safer in the car than anywhere else. I just needed somewhere to park, unobserved, so I could curl up on the back seat under the shawl I'd borrowed and sleep until first light.

I manoeuvred onto a grass verge and parked under the shadow of a hawthorn tree. Pulling on the handbrake, my fingers brushed a ball of stiff crumpled paper resting in the console tray between the front seats. I absent-mindedly smoothed it out. It was the photograph I'd thrown out of the car window and which had been returned to me by the trolley guy in the supermarket car park. I looked at the picture for a long time, stroking the faces of Theo, Paloma and Marcus until a tear splashed onto its creased surface. I wiped the droplet away and carefully placed the photo back in my wallet.

I gazed up the road at the bright dome ahead. The glowing glass dimmed the stars and plunged the surrounding landscape into greater darkness. Why was the dome lit up like a giant cat's eye at two o'clock in the morning? A spurt of anger at the wastefulness temporarily drowned the whispered yearnings of my heart. Was Theo home? If not, what was Marcus thinking? The lights were always switched off at 6.30 in the evening, except for the security floodlights in the car park. This was the second time to my knowledge that the correct procedures had not been followed. *Cat's away, mice at play*, I thought. I climbed out of the car and walked up the dark road, a moth enchanted by the artificial incandescence of a giant light bulb.

I passed the gravel drive which led to Marcus' cottage and the farmhouse beyond. Both were in darkness, except for a light glowing in my bedroom window. Was there someone there, or had nobody bothered to turn off my bedside lamp since I'd left? How I longed to slip inside and lay my head on my pillow and sleep, but I'd defiantly left my house keys on the kitchen table the night I'd left and there was no way in.

I turned from temptation and stepped into the empty car park, my arms crossed around my waist for warmth. I stepped into the circle of silver light spilling across the tarmac and looked up at the vast structure. The delicate arches were as beautiful to me as the strands of a cobweb glistening with morning dew. I peered inside the vast dome. The greens of the foliage were more vivid than I remembered – jade and emerald, olive and lime, tender, spiky, lustrous, moist. A river of blooms cascaded from a wooden pergola by the entrance. Purple bougainvillea and palest clematis entwined around an ornamental trellis. White camellia blossoms glimmered like pearls amid the dark gloss of evergreen leaves. I stood and gazed upon my past life as a starving vagrant might watch diners through the window of a restaurant, and dream of the life that others possessed.

A wave of memories flooded my consciousness: the redolent smell of the earth, the warmth of the air, the sweet smell of wet leaves after the irrigation system had completed its cycle. Theo and I would sometimes walk through the dome in the cool of the night with only the moon to guide our footsteps. Soft fronds would stroke my arms and face. The fragrance of jasmine and roses and the sharp tang of rosemary and mint would consecrate our conversations. Usually I would chatter away and Theo would listen in that way he had, his head on one side, always giving his complete attention to my concerns as though they were the most important matters in the world.

I turned to look back down the hill the way I'd come. The blank space of the Downs. The black expanse of the ocean. The velvet sheen of the night sky, and Westhatch glimmering like an oasis in a desert of darkness. The street lamps were a string of pearls following the contour of the seafront. The Promenade and funfair were pinpricks of coloured light. Fun World Holiday Camp with its tawdry entertainments and casual corruption was a grid of white dots. Someone there knew the identity of my father, I was sure. Probably the same person who'd wanted my mother dead.

I spun on my heel and pressed my hands against the cool glass, as if by touching it I could pass through the transparent boundary and enter the protective warmth inside. Greenacres. My paradise lost. I'd lived there with my adopted family in a bubble of happy ignorance. How could I return to that life now I knew the truth? How could I be accepted back into the fold when I carried with me the stigma of illegitimacy and rebellion? Maybe they hadn't searched for me because they were relieved I'd disappeared. Perhaps I'd been an unwanted package all along, deposited by my mother nineteen years ago and now conveniently delivered somewhere else at no cost to themselves.

I thought I saw the faces of Theo, Marcus, Paloma, even Harmony, in the glass, but I was fooling myself. It was just the reflection of a girl, tired and alone, needing forgiveness and love but too proud to ask for fear of a rebuff. I walked sadly back to the car. By letting me go, they'd already rejected me. I wouldn't give them a second chance.

Curling up on the back seat, I allowed the adrenalin of the last few hours to dissipate along with the warmth from the car heater. I couldn't go back to Greenacres. There was nothing for me there. But I couldn't bear the thought of returning to Fun World either. The contrast with my former home was too great. The derelict caravan, the domestic drudgery, Trafford, Chucky, Mrs Ozzles, Maxwell King. Apart from the longing to find my father, what was there to keep me in Westhatch? Boody? Sonya? Zavier?

I remembered the way Zavier had pulled me into his arms. I tried to recall the feel of his lips on mine, the scratch of his jaw against my cheek. At the time, the unexpected shock of his embrace had scattered my thoughts like sand upon the wind. Had I enjoyed his touch? If so, why had I pushed him away? Then I thought of his face, pale and sweaty as he lay on the basement floor, struggling to breathe. I'd been scared then, more scared than I'd ever been in my life. More scared than I was of Trafford or when I'd been trapped in Maxwell King's washroom.

There had to be another place for me, another kind of life. There was a father out there who didn't know his daughter, a shadowy presence sketched in hope but surrounded with fear. I needed to know who he was, but I was terrified it might be a man who turned a blind eye to evil, or a clown with wandering hands, or a businessman with the whitest smile and the murkiest deals.

Surely there was someone who could help me unearth the secrets of my past, rescue me from the trap I'd so stupidly walked into and help untangle the emotional muddle I was in. Not a missing father, nor an adopted father. Another kind of father altogether. As a tsunami of exhaustion crashed over me, a last thought flickered before I plunged under the black waters of sleep. My godfather. Colin Hildreth.

Chapter 19

I was awoken at first light by a car driving up the hill to Greenacres. The crunch of tyres and the beam from the headlamps jolted me upright. It was probably a member of staff starting the early morning shift. Hopefully they wouldn't have noticed my car in the shadow of the hawthorn tree. I climbed through to the driver's seat. My back was aching. I had a crick in my neck, but there was no time to stretch my legs. I needed to get away before anyone recognised me. Jamming the blonde wig back on my head I executed a hasty turn and sped down the winding country lanes to the seafront.

My shift would be starting in forty minutes. I'd slept in my housekeeping uniform. There was no time to change into fresh underwear and a clean polo shirt. I munched a stale biscuit from the glove compartment as I thought about everything that had happened the previous night. I wondered whether Zavier was at home or still at the hospital. I was tempted to text him, but resisted. The personnel files we'd stolen were in the footwell of the front passenger seat. I was anxious to begin following up the names of ex-staff members to see if any of them remembered my mother. I considered bunking off work for the day and spending it in the library, perhaps going for a swim and shower at the Leisure Centre first, but knew that until I found another way to sustain myself, I needed the money.

After considering all my options, I drove back down the hill to Westhatch, but instead of travelling along the Promenade to Fun World I parked on an impulse at the Leisure Centre and phoned Uncle Colin.

'Yes,' he barked down the line, not recognising my new number.

'Uncle Colin. It's me. Ava.'

'Ava. My dear, dear child. Where are you? Are you safe? I've been so worried. Whatever were you thinking?'

'I wasn't really thinking… Sorry to disturb you so early. Did I wake you?'

'Never mind that! Where are you?'

'Westhatch, but I – '

'Right. Stay where you are. I'm coming for you now. Give me your exact location.'

'I'm in a car park in town at the moment. I've been staying nearby. I can't talk long. I've got to go into work.'

'Get all your things packed up. I can be down there by… let me see… with traffic it will probably be between two and a half… three hours. Shall we meet at Greenacres?'

'No! No, I can't go back there. Not yet. I need to speak to you first.'

'OK, poppet. Where can I find you?'

'My job – '

'Call in sick. If they sack you, you can come and work for me.' He was telling me what I wanted to hear. I capitulated immediately.

'OK. I'll be in the Leisure Centre in town. There's free parking and I'll wait in the café until you arrive.'

'Make sure you pack up all your things. If you don't want to go back home, you can come and stay with me in London until we figure this whole thing out.'

'OK.'

'I'm so glad you called, Ava. I've been beside myself. I would have contacted the police, but Marcus said he had everything in hand.'

I'm sure he did, I thought, clenching my teeth in case I said something I shouldn't. It could wait until we were face-to-face.

'Ava? Are you still there?'

'Yes. I'll see you later.'

I texted Boody I was sick, then drove back to Fun World hoping to sneak in and out without anyone seeing me. My shift had started fifteen minutes ago. I certainly didn't want Boody or Mrs Ozzles seeing me out and about. Boody would be hopping mad at having to clean the entertainment centre and arcade all on her own.

Parking by the electricity substation at the top of North Drive, I squeezed through the hole in the hedge. Sharp twigs scratched my hands and yanked at my hair. When I reached the caravan and saw my reflection in the dirty window, I finally understood the phrase 'dragged through a hedge backwards'. I couldn't bear the thought of my godfather seeing me like this. Despite the cold, I stripped off my crumpled uniform and washed in the icy water from a plastic bottle. Shivering, I dragged on a clean pair of jeans and a thick jumper which had begun to smell of mildew. I sprayed myself with the air freshener I'd nicked from the stock cupboard. Eau de Lemon Fresh! After combing the sticks and leaves out of my hair, I started to pack. Most of my stuff was still in my backpack or carrier bags, including the brown envelope with my birth certificate and the photos of Mum inside. I abandoned the duvet and linen. Boody could collect it before the fortnightly stocktake.

Locking up, I popped the key back under the pot by the front door. I debated whether or not to leave a note, but decided I could text my goodbyes to Boody and Sonya if everything worked out with Uncle Colin. Loath to make more than one trip, I slung my rucksack on my back and picked up a carrier bag of clothes in either hand. It would be too difficult to crawl back through the hedge with my heavy load, I reasoned. Quicker to risk taking the path down to the stile.

It was mid-morning. The cleaners would be busy at work. Depending on their shifts, the Pink Jackets would either be organising games and competitions for the children, or relaxing before the evening entertainment. The night security would be asleep. Having made the rough calculation that I was unlikely to meet anyone on the way to or from the staff caravans, I hurried along the path, slowing down and listening as I approached the junction.

Drat! Hearing a murmur of voices, I jerked back behind a mossy tree trunk, squeezing myself as thin as I could, hoping no one would hear the rustle of plastic bags as I shoved them behind a bank of brambles.

'Stop snivelling. You got your fifty quid didn't you?' It was a female voice with a pronounced Irish accent. Shannon! 'And there's more where that came from. Play your cards right an' you won't need to clean the bogs ever again.'

'I am good... cleaner.' It was Sonya. Her voice broke and rose on a sob.

'Look on the bright side. You can be a good something else now.'

'I be cleaner.'

'Not any more. You're no longer needed in housekeeping. There's a couple of new girls starting this week. Girls with National Insurance numbers. But don't you worry. Mrs Ozzles will look after you, if you do as you're told. An' if you don't do as you're told, you'll be having a word with Trafford.'

I waited for five minutes after they passed, sickened by what I'd overheard. I vowed to tell Uncle Colin. He would know what to do. Shady work practices, drugs, intimidation, the sudden disappearance of the Romanians squatting in my caravan. And now it sounded as though Sonya was being dragged into prostitution. Colin Hildreth was a man of influence. A man people listened to. We could go to the police together and if they didn't believe us we would go to the press. I would not abandon Boody and Sonya to this place.

It was much too early to meet my godfather. I thought about texting goodbye to Zavier, but decided I didn't want to hear his reply. I hoped he would have better sense than to return to Seacombe Road until he was sure whoever was watching his home had gone. Perhaps that was another mess Uncle Colin could help sort out. I couldn't walk away from Westhatch knowing the investigation into my parentage had placed Zavier in danger.

I flung the bags onto the passenger seat of the car. Impatient to be gone, I revved the engine, swung the car round and accelerated down the North Drive, praying I wouldn't be spotted by Boody… or Mrs Ozzles… or Trafford. My eyes darted left and right, searching the caravan verandas for any sign of a minute, peroxide-blonde cleaner on a fag break. I was so busy trying to escape unnoticed that I missed the small crowd of children clustered ahead. In horror, I suddenly registered Harry Hot Dog stepping onto a zebra crossing, trailing a band of excited youngsters behind him. My foot automatically stamped on the brake. I jolted forward against the seat belt. The wheels screeched. The tyres locked but continued to slide on the slippery road towards the children.

I remember the fear on their faces. Eyes and mouths open wide. Harry, hearing the squeal of the brakes, turned slowly to face me in his bulky costume. Why didn't he jump aside like the children? Couldn't he see me coming through the peep holes in his sausage body? Would the car stop in time?

Split seconds… An eternity of helplessness… I watched the drama unfold before me, unable to prevent the forward motion of the vehicle or react quickly enough to punch the horn. He froze, then unbelievably raised an arm and held up his hand like a policeman directing traffic, his cartoon fingers in their thick plush gloves strangely authoritative. I hurtled the final few feet towards him, the smell of hot rubber in my nostrils, and came to a standstill a few inches from his body.

I slumped forward across the wheel, my hands still gripping the cold plastic. Visions of what could have happened flashed to mind, bodies flying like skittles before me, screams, blood, the ominous silence of an unmoving costumed figure.

A muffled knock sounded on the plastic panel that Sid had stuck on to replaced my broken window. Harry's unruffled, grinning face was looking down on me through the cloudy sheet. Shaking uncontrollably I opened the door, expecting a sharp rebuke.

'Are you all right?' Jeremy asked, his voice muted by the material over his face.

'Yes... I'm so sorry. I could have killed you... the children... I can't believe I stopped in time. Are *you* all right?'

'Yes.' He turned his head awkwardly towards the children. 'All right, gang? Let's hear your Harry cheer!'

'Hooray for Harry!' they shouted, jumping in the air, arms outstretched. He turned back to me. I caught a glimpse of his eyes through the small viewing hole. There was no anger there. Was I mistaken, or was there warmth in their brown depth? His gaze flicked to my bags on the passenger seat.

'Going somewhere?'

'No... yes... I hope so. I hope I'm going home. Or somewhere much like it.'

'Drive safely.'

'Yes, of course. I'm so sorry about that. I wasn't thinking.' He stepped away from the car.

'Goodbye,' he said, waving.

'Goodbye,' the children chorused, waving too and running beside the car as I slowly pulled away.

Rattled, I drove to the Leisure Centre and bought myself a coffee. I would wait to be rescued, however long it took. I put the near miss on the drive out of my mind and thought of the meeting ahead. I was too nervous to eat anything. I nibbled my fingernails instead, heart thumping with adrenalin as I rehearsed what I would say. An apology would be required, of course. I would explain my shock at the discovery of the adoption. I could suggest the psychological trauma had affected my reasoning powers. Now was not the time to accuse Colin of complicity in the lie that had been woven around me. I didn't know all the circumstances and couldn't afford to burn any more bridges. I wiped my sweating palms on a paper napkin and smoothed my hair. What was taking him so long?

After an hour and a quarter, his stocky frame hurried through the glass doors. He scanned the tables, his eyes passing over me without recognition. I stood up, trembling, and took a step towards him.

'Uncle Colin.'

'Ava!' He strode towards me and took me in me in his arms. His woollen coat was cold and smelled of cigars. I buried my face in his grey beard and allowed myself to be enveloped. Sobs racked my body. An overwhelming sense of relief flooded my eyes with salty tears. I was no longer lost. I'd been found by someone who loved me and who would help me rebuild my life.

'I didn't recognise you… Your hair… and there's nothing of you.'

Laughing shakily, I wiped my face with the palm of my hand.

'Bad decision.' I tugged at a black curl. 'Chalk it up to teenage rebellion.'

'I need a strong coffee. You look as though you could do with some food.' Still standing, he picked up the menu on the table and frowned. 'Come on, let's get something to eat and you can tell me all about it.'

We grabbed a couple of trays and queued at the counter. I glanced at him as he ordered a burger and chips for himself and a cheese and tomato Panini for me. It was a far cry from the discreet and expensive restaurants he frequented in London.

He didn't look cross. We sat in silence, picking at our food, as I struggled to decide how to start.

'I can explain everything,' he unexpectedly announced.

'No, no. You don't have to explain anything, Uncle Colin. I don't blame you. Really I don't. Not now that I've had time to cool down. I've been very stupid.'

He looked confused.

'You're going to have to tell me everything, Ava.'

As we ate, I told him what had happened that morning after he phoned me on the day Theo flew to Africa. I described the way I'd tricked the keys from Marcus and worked out the code to the safe.

'I should never have got you involved with my problem,' he groaned as I explained about the brown envelope and its contents. 'Nobody would have wanted you to learn about the past that way. I'm so sorry you had to go through this alone.'

'It's OK. I should have trusted Dad – I mean, Theo – or Paloma or you with my questions. I was hurt and angry.'

'Anything could have happened. I can't bear to think… I'm so glad you're safe. Where have you been?'

'Here. In Westhatch. Losing Theo as a dad has made me determined to find my real father. I need to know who I am and where I come from. You do understand, don't you?'

'Of course I do.' He squeezed my hand. 'And did you find anything?'

'Not anything I wanted to know. I hired a private investigator, but nothing came of it. Did Mum ever say anything to you, Uncle Colin?' I twisted a paper napkin in my hands.

'We can talk about the past later. At the moment I'm more interested in the present. Where have you been staying? What's all this about a job?'

I didn't want to admit how far I'd fallen so I was deliberately vague in answering.

'It's just casual. Tourism stuff at Fun World.'

'So you know Maxwell King?'

'Not personally.'

'He's a very astute businessman. I met him some years ago. He persuaded me to invest in the holiday camp during his management buyout. I've never regretted it. Business must be booming down there. I get a fat dividend every year.'

I didn't comment, planning to enlighten him about Maxwell King's business practices once more pressing questions about my parentage and my future had been discussed. He continued.

'But it's not the place for you. Let's get you back to Greenacres where you belong. There's a proper job waiting for you there.'

I tore the corner of my paper napkin into small white pieces and dropped them on my plate.

'How did Theo react when he found out I'd run away?'

'I haven't been able to reach him. He's still somewhere in rural Africa. There's no network coverage of course, no computers either. Marcus and Paloma couldn't tell me anything. I didn't know if they knew where you were or even whether you were safe or not. All I knew was that I couldn't reach you. Why wouldn't you return my text messages?'

'I chucked my phone in a bin the day after I ran away. I never got them.'

Something he had said was niggling like an angry mosquito bite. I scrunched up the remainder of the paper napkin and jammed it into my empty coffee cup.

'If you haven't been able to reach Theo, does he even know I've been missing?'

'I suspect not.'

'What on earth are Marcus and Paloma playing at? Why haven't they been looking for me?' I described how I'd checked my emails at the library and scoured the local paper. 'They did nothing. They let me drop off the face of the earth.'

Colin took a large bite of his burger and chewed thoughtfully.

'Perhaps Marcus never wanted to find me,' I continued bitterly. 'That would probably suit him just fine. If I'm out of the way, he's the heir apparent.'

He stroked his beard. 'You may be right. As you know, I've had my reservations about that young man for a while.'

'But what about Paloma? She's looked after me since I was a baby. Why wouldn't she do something?'

'She listens to Marcus. That's why. With Theo out of the country, Marcus is the one giving the orders.'

'Do you think she misses me?' I asked in a small voice.

'I'm sure she does.'

I blinked away the heat behind my eyes. The Panini stuck in my throat. I pushed the remainder away and took a long swig of cola.

'I'm not ready to go back to Greenacres. Can I come to London and stay with you?'

'Have you got your things?' He glanced under the table, obviously searching for a suitcase or bag.

'There're in my car.'

'You have a car?'

'Yes. I took some of Theo's money from the safe. I'll pay it back. I shouldn't really be driving it. I'm not insured.' I decided it would be better to come clean about everything while he was too relieved to see me to be really cross.

'Ava! I'm surprised at you.'

I hung my head.

'Never mind about that now.' He patted my hand. 'We can sort this muddle out now that you're back. Are you parked here?'

'Yes.'

'Let's go and get your stuff. We can leave your car for the moment. I'll drive us to London.' He pushed back his chair.

'We can leave it here for good as far as I'm concerned. I don't care if it gets clamped or towed. The driver's window is all smashed in and it will probably cost more to put right than it's worth.'

'You'll get a hefty fine if we do that. The bad guys always catch up with you.'

He shrugged into his double-breasted overcoat. He didn't know the car was registered to someone else's address or that the council would never be able to connect Claire Hewitt of 23 Seacombe Road with Ava Gage from Greenacres. With a pang I realised I would probably never see Zavier again. It was a rotten leaving present, landing him with the hassle of denying a parking violation.

'Don't worry. I'll have someone take care of it,' my godfather promised when he saw my expression.

Suddenly I felt like a child again. I remembered all the reasons I'd run away. It wasn't just about finding my father. I needed to be respected as an independent woman. I wanted my opinions to matter. I wanted the freedom to live life on my own terms. I swallowed down my frustration and thanked him meekly.

We walked through the foyer. I smiled at the girl behind the desk, who recognised me and looked surprised I was with such a smart gentleman. Out in the cold, Uncle Colin took my arm and steered me to the car park. We were heading in the direction of my car.

'I'm just over there,' I pointed.

'I know.' He tightened his grip and pulled me along until I saw my battered Ford. Next to it was a dark SUV.

'That's funny. You're parked alongside me!' I laughed. But from the look on his face he wasn't amused. Two men climbed out of the SUV as we approached. That's when I noticed the plastic sheet taped to the driver's window had been pulled away.

'Have you been in my car?'

'Nothing there, boss,' the larger man grunted. 'We've been through everything. Just this.' He handed over the brown envelope. Uncle Colin pulled out the papers and gave them a cursory glance.

'What are you doing?' I demanded.

'Where is it, Ava?'

'Where's what?'

'The file. The green file. It's important, Ava. We can mend your car. You shouldn't have left the file somewhere insecure.'

My mind went blank. I couldn't remember where I'd seen it last.

'Tell me,' Uncle Colin insisted, holding the top of my arms firmly.

'You're hurting me,' I protested. 'I must have left it at the bed and breakfast – '

'I told you to bring everything.'

'I didn't realise... I must have left it behind when I moved lodgings.'

I remembered the papers stuffed at the bottom of Mrs Bungay's wardrobe. I'd only ever been interested in the brown envelope. Perhaps the dossier relating to the ionised water project was still in the cupboard. My heart turned in my chest.

'Your meeting with the Ministry! I'm so sorry, Uncle Colin. How did it go?'

'I cancelled it, for obvious reasons.'

'I feel terrible – '

'We need to take this off-piste, boss,' one of the men said scanning the car park.

'Right. Let's go,' Uncle Colin replied. 'Saunders!'

The large man opened the back door of the SUV. He grabbed my waist from behind. Uncle Colin dropped his hold on my arms. I screamed and kicked out at the man pushing me towards the car, but he had the element of surprise. Another man wearing a leather jacket and black leather gloves was already in the back seat. He grabbed my wrists and hauled me in.

Uncle Colin climbed in the front passenger seat next to the driver who slammed his door and started the ignition. The heavy-set man who'd pushed me onto the back seat and whom my godfather called Saunders, jammed himself next to me. The driver activated the central locking. The back seat windows were tinted black. No one would be able to see I was being held against my will between two grim-faced thugs.

The thin man in leather stretched over and pulled the seat belt across my chest, his jacket and gloves creaking as he strapped me in. I slapped his hands away.

'Uncle Colin!'

'Gently, Skink. I told you the girl's special. She's very precious. I don't want a hair on her head to be damaged.'

'Who on earth are you getting involved with?' I protested.

'I'm sorry, Ava. This is for our own protection. There are some very unsavoury characters out there who are interested in the ionised water research. These gentlemen are from the security department of my organisation. Ex-army. No finesse, I'm afraid, but we don't want to attract attention to ourselves. It's absolutely imperative we get the file under lock and key, for everyone's sake. If you want to go some way to rebuilding bridges with Theo, you'll do everything you can to help.'

My mind was spiralling with fear and anger. Did large corporations really employ these sorts of hoodlums to do their dirty work for them? My godfather turned his head and smiled at me.

'I know this is frightening. Once we have the file, we can go to London. You can come and stay with me until Theo gets back and we can straighten out this mess.'

I muttered Mrs Bungay's address. The driver programmed the satnav and pulled slowly out of the car park. Within minutes we were cruising along the seafront. Murky waves pounded the shingle, stirred up by the east wind. The surface of the sea – an unhealthy, jaundiced colour, tainted by dirt and sandy particles sucked up from the deep – gazed blindly up at the leaden sky like a giant cataract.

The car turned into Seacombe Road and I directed them to the shabby B&B. We all climbed out of the car, Colin holding my elbow and steering me up the path, while his men leaned against the SUV and lit cigarettes.

'Oh. It's you!' my former landlady exclaimed on opening the door.

'Hello Mrs Bungay – '

'No vacancies!' she declared, despite the blue neon sign in the downstairs window claiming the opposite. 'You and your male visitors!'

'Good afternoon, madam. I'm the young lady's godfather.' Colin Hildreth held out a manicured hand. 'I wanted to thank you personally for looking after my goddaughter.'

She wiped her grubby fingers on her apron and gingerly touched his hand, her expression changing as she took in his expensive wool coat.

'I suppose that's different. I've got a very nice room at the front. Claire can have the box room – '

'We're not staying,' I interrupted. 'I think I left some papers in my room when I checked out. Could I just pop up and see?'

Mrs Bungay stood blocking the door, arms akimbo.

'Checked out! That's a joke. Did a bunk, you mean.'

Uncle Colin took a wallet out of his breast pocket and began unfolding several large bills.

'Perhaps you'd let me recompense you for any outstanding amounts. I'll be happy to offer a little extra for the inconvenience you've experienced.'

Mrs Bungay reached for the notes, but he subtly drew them back. The meaning was clear: no papers, no money.

'I haven't found anything. But then again I haven't had the chance to clean the room properly since Claire left. Save my legs and run up, dear. See if you can find anything.'

I darted away.

The file was exactly where I'd left it, at the bottom of the wardrobe. I stood and flicked through the pages. Spreadsheets, graphs, diagrams, jotted notes in the margins. All the annotations were in Theo's handwriting. The spreadsheets documented the growth rates of seedlings in the experimental greenhouse, those watered with ionised water and those in the control group which were irrigated with water from the mains. There were no drawings of water pumps and nothing in Uncle Colin's handwriting.

The penny didn't just drop. It exploded like a nuclear bomb. This file did *not* belong to Colin Hildreth. It belonged to Theo! No wonder he was so anxious to get his hands on it. He was stealing years of precious research, discoveries that would no doubt translate into valuable patents and contracts. There never was a meeting with the government. It had all been a ruse.

What could I do? Downstairs the murmur of polite conversation highlighted my predicament. There was no way to descend the stairs without being seen from the open front door. Even if I could climb down a drainpipe into the back garden, I'd have to negotiate my way over multiple garden fences before I reached the end of the row of terraced houses to escape onto the road.

Think, think! I needed to stop him stealing Theo's life work. It was the least I could do, bearing in mind it had been me who'd believed Colin's lies in the first place, me who'd opened the safe and absconded with the data. I rifled once more through the pages of the file, taking in at a glance the rigorous testing and retesting that had taken place. Right at the back of the file, on a crumpled sheet torn from a lined notepad, was a series of equations. This was the first piece of paper to be placed in the file. The other pages, mostly computer printouts, had been secured on top of it in date order, with the latest piece of data being the first sheet to be perused on opening the file. Of course! This scrap of paper at the back of the file was Theo's initial idea, the formula that had inspired all the experiments that followed.

I ripped the scrap from the back of the file and folded it into a small wad before stuffing it inside my boot.

'Found it,' I cried as I ran down the stairs with the file in my hand.

'Good girl.' He placed the money in Mrs Bungay's palm.

'Pleasure to meet you. If ever we come this way again, we shall certainly consider staying in your delightful establishment.'

He took the file, and pulled me back down the path. The door slammed behind us.

The hired help ground their fag ends underfoot and opened the back door for me to climb inside.

'Actually, Uncle Colin, could you drop me back at the Leisure Centre so I can collect my car? It's got all my stuff inside. I think I can drive myself to your place.'

'I'd much prefer it if you stayed with me. I've been so worried I can hardly bear to let you out of my sight. You look absolutely exhausted. I'm not sure you'd be safe driving on the motorway. What you need is a hot bath and a good, long sleep. I'll arrange for someone to collect your car tomorrow. I can send my secretary out for anything you might need tonight. London is the city that never sleeps. There's always a shop open somewhere if you know where to look.'

I shuddered inwardly as his hand rested on the small of my back and guided me into the SUV. The car edged away from the pavement, and began to accelerate. Almost immediately we passed Zavier's house. He was running down the front steps, wearing his leather jacket and carrying his motorbike helmet. I was relieved to see him looking better than the previous night when I'd dumped him at the hospital. He must be OK if he'd been discharged.

As we passed the concrete hard-standing that posed as his front garden, I leaned forward slightly and caught his eye. I was sure he'd seen me, but he looked away and jammed the helmet on his head. Then I remembered the tinted windows and my heart sank. He hadn't seen me at all.

Instead of taking the exit to the dual carriageway out of Westhatch, the driver chose the longer, more circuitous route along the lanes. This was the road I'd coasted down on my bicycle only a fortnight ago, speeded by defiance and righteous anger. It was also the route I'd taken the previous night, when I'd crawled back up the hill, frightened, cold and exhausted, with nowhere to sleep but a broken car under the shadow of a hawthorn bush, with the distant glow of the glasshouse to comfort me.

'This isn't the way to London,' I said.

'I forgot to tell you. We're making a slight diversion first. There are one or two details to be sorted out with Marcus. I know you don't feel up to returning to Greenacres, but I'm a great believer in facing one's fears, not letting them fester. Marcus is a reasonable man. We'll explain everything together. Then you can choose whether to stay with me in London or return home.'

Chapter 20

Relief flooded my body. We were going to the dome. Perhaps Colin really did believe bridges could be mended and things could go back to the way they were. But did he think he could get away with stealing Theo's research? And was Marcus helping him? Was that why they needed to meet? Or perhaps I'd misjudged my godfather after all, and his only concern was the security of the file in Theo's absence and the meeting with the government ministers.

I'd keep quiet. I would apologise to Marcus and Paloma for all the worry I'd caused. I would conceal my dismay at their indifference to my midnight flit. I would keep my own counsel and wait for Theo to return. Then I would tell him everything about Uncle Colin and the green file. I would give him the folded equation sheet hidden inside my boot. He might not be my father, but I knew enough about his character to know he was the one person I could trust implicitly.

The afternoon was closing in. Soon the winding road ahead would be dark. The driver switched the headlights on. He glanced in his rear-view mirror several times. Just before the crest in the hill, we pulled off the road and parked by a five-bar gate.

'We'll wait until Greenacres has closed for business. This needs to be a private visit,' my godfather said.

I nodded. Saunders took a packet of chewing gum from his pocket and relaxed back into his seat. Night rolled over the Downs, extinguishing the last bands of light clinging to the horizon. A headlight cut through the grey shadows and a motorbike buzzed past. I caught the driver's eye watching me closely in the rear-view mirror. I closed my eyes, ignoring him. The car heater breathed out warm, soporific air. I'd only managed a couple of hours of fitful sleep on the back seat of my car the previous night. Wedged between two perspiring hulks, I slipped into a hazy cocoon, far from my present difficulties and the squelch of gum being chewed by my bodyguard.

I awoke with a jolt of fear and a rush of cold air, slumping sideways onto the seat as the warm wall I'd been leaning against vanished. The creaking man on my other side slipped from his seat. I sat up, dazed and blinking, just in time to see the door close behind him. Uncle Colin activated the central locking system with a soft *thunk*. I was alone on the back seat. I heard a shout in the darkness, followed by several grunts and the sound of feet scuffling on the tarmac. Someone called my name. Then silence. The boot opened behind me. Something large was thrown into the back. The locks clicked open and my guards squeezed in beside me, breathless, rubbing their knuckles and smoothing their hair.

'He's out for the count.'

'Good.'

'Who? Who's out?'

'Your little friend. The one who's been helping you with your enquiries. The one who followed us here and has been skulking in the undergrowth for the last hour. You've made quite an impression there, poppet. I always knew you'd break hearts one day.'

'Is he hurt? You have to let him go!'

'I'm afraid I can't do that. He's begun to make a nuisance of himself.'

The driver turned the ignition and the SUV purred into life. We edged away from the gate and cruised silently towards the dome. I couldn't help remembering the sight of Zavier the previous night, white and breathless, lying on the floor of the basement storage area while I frantically plied him with sweets.

Now he was hurt again because of me. There was no sound from the boot. For all I knew, he could be dead.

The car park was empty. Yet again, the lights in the dome were blazing long after the garden centre had closed for the day. Uncle Colin climbed out of the car. I was yanked from the back seat by Saunders. I stumbled, shocked by the vicious chill of the evening air. My godfather steadied me.

'You're trembling. There's nothing to worry about. The prodigal daughter returns.'

'But Zavier – '

'He can come too.'

He jerked his head towards the man in leather.

'Get him.'

Skink sidled to the back of the car, his leather coat squeaking in the night air. He opened the boot. To my relief I heard a stifled groan. He pulled Zavier into an upright position and half-dragged him towards us, imprisoning his arms behind his back. He staggered against his captor as he tried to regain his balance. Even in the darkness I could see a trickle of blood on his lower lip and chin.

'Get the gear,' Colin ordered. 'The boy can carry the bags.'

'Can't you see he's hurt?' I protested. I stepped towards him but Uncle Colin pulled me back to his side.

The driver buried his head in the boot and emerged with two black sports bags.

He threw them down on the ground by Zavier's feet.

'Pick them up.'

'Let him go, Uncle Colin. Please don't hurt him. He knows nothing about any of this. He doesn't know who you are, who I am, even. You don't have to worry about him. You won't say anything, will you, Zavier? This is just family stuff. There's no need to involve anyone else.'

Skink let go of Zavier's arms. Saunders stepped forward until he was flanked on either side. Muttering several pithy expletives, Zavier picked up the bags. They frogmarched him round the outside edge of the dome. Uncle Colin and I followed. When we reached the private entrance situated near the farmhouse drive, my godfather pulled a cluster of jangling metal from his pocket.

'You have our keys!'

'Of course. Without my own copy, how would my men have broken into Greenacres in search of the file? Too bad you already had it. You could have saved everyone a lot of trouble if you'd just done as you were told.'

'But how did you get the keys?'

He tapped the side of his nose.

He pushed open the door. It was then that I noticed that Zavier and I were the only ones not wearing gloves. He limped after me, weighed down by the weight of the bags and followed by his bodyguards as we were marched through the glasshouse.

I breathed in the air like an alcoholic tasting the first drink of the day – the deep pungency of the turned soil, the sharp tang of leaves uncurling, and the sweetness of buds breaking into flower. It was the aroma of life, warm and moist. The smell of my childhood and my home. I hadn't realised how much I'd missed living among the plants, watching them change and grow, blossom and fruit. In comparison, the days spent in Fun World were tinted black and grey; I'd just walked into a technicolour paradise.

We skirted the central pond, still as a mirror now that the fountain had been switched off, and hurried past the entrance to the cafeteria.

'An Americano for me, thanks,' Zavier muttered.

He was rewarded with a slap to the back of his head.

We descended to the underground laboratory. The door was already damaged. It was pulled shut but looked as though it had been kicked in and the lock broken. I wondered why Marcus hadn't arranged for the repair.

'The inner sanctum!' Colin Hildreth declared, pushing the door.

Everywhere there was evidence of the break-in that had taken place the night I'd run away. Phials and test tubes were smashed, papers scattered. The filing cabinet had been jemmied open. Zavier put the bags down at his feet and looked at the mess, his brow wrinkled as though trying to solve a puzzle.

'Tut tut! A little housekeeping would be in order. Marcus must have been waiting for his master's return.' Colin turned to me. 'I've arranged to meet Marcus here to discuss the research but we've obviously got here first.' He spoke to his associates. 'There's no need to wait. You know what to do?'

'Yes, sir.'

Zavier was unexpectedly pushed across the glass-strewn floor. Skink pulled a small pistol from his leather jacket and aimed it at Zavier's head.

'What are you doing?' I cried.

'Everything will be all right as long as we all keep calm. Trust me, poppet.'

The other two men opened the sports bags. Inside each were two large plastic canisters. They took off the lids and began splashing liquid over the worktops, the papers and my father's stool. The sharp smell of petrol stung my nostrils.

Uncle Colin must have seen my horrified expression. He gave an apologetic shrug.

'Once I had the file in my hands, it was always going to be necessary to destroy the experiments and the prototype irrigation system here at the dome. Theo's too trusting. He always thinks the best of people. He hasn't patented the technology yet. There must be no evidence that it existed. I thought you'd rumbled me when we texted on the day of your disappearance. When you said you knew everything, I assumed you'd found the file and realised it wasn't mine. It didn't occur to me you'd discovered your birth certificate.

'Last time I visited Greenacres to talk to Theo I took measurements and photos when he stepped out of the room to deal with a staff query. I've all the information I need to build a replica ioniser and patent the formula myself. Your stepfather's discovery is too valuable to be left in the hands of a well-meaning eccentric, I'm afraid. In this life, Ava, the end sometimes justifies the means. Thanks to this young man's surprise appearance, the fire can now be blamed on the delinquent boyfriend of the boss' daughter. His fingerprints are all over the bags, which we will leave behind for the police to find.'

'Are you going to shoot him?'

'Of course not. But once we've finished here, I'd advise him to leave Westhatch immediately and for good. Forensics will place him at the scene. If he tries to incriminate me, he'll regret it.'

'Who do you think you are? Don Corleone?' Zavier snarled.

'I'll tell Theo what happened!' I said.

'And who's he going to believe? An illegitimate runaway looking for revenge, or his oldest friend? You've already demonstrated your disloyalty. Perhaps the police will think you're implicated with the break-in and the fire. You have a motive. You have an accomplice.' He nodded at Zavier. 'Don't make this more difficult than it needs to be. When you've had a chance to calm down, you'll understand that my corporation will be able to save more lives with this technology than Theo ever could. The world doesn't need do-gooders. It needs leaders – people who are not afraid to take difficult decisions.'

A torrent of filthy words streamed from my mouth. I called him every insulting name I could conjure from my breaking heart.

'It doesn't have to be like this, my dear,' he spoke as though I hadn't just cursed him to oblivion. 'You and I have always got on well in the past, haven't we? Open your eyes. You've broken free, become your own person. There are no rules out here in the big wide world. No right. No wrong. Just market forces. You understand that. I know you do. I'm going to offer Marcus a job and – '

'He'd never work for someone like you.'

'We'll see. If he tries to claim he contributed to this research, I'll make sure he never works in the scientific community again. He'll be sensible. Most people are.'

'We didn't deactivate the burglar alarm after opening the outside door,' I enunciated with cold fury, desperately trying to interrupt his plan. 'As we speak, alarms are screaming down at the police station. In about five minutes this place will be crawling with officers. If you leave now, you have time to get away.'

Saunders and the driver looked at each other in panic. Skink laughed.

'There was no alarm the last time we came. We were here for at least two hours in the middle of the night. That dozy manager didn't even realise he'd had a break-in until the next morning. You're wasting our time. Don't make me waste his life.'

I watched in horror as he struck a match and flicked it onto the floor. With a whoosh, the petrol ignited. A bright flash shot upwards to the ceiling. The counters were a mass of leaping flames. Theo's sticky notes flickered like candles on the walls. A test tube shattered with a sharp crack, spraying liquid across the floor where it bubbled and evaporated into nothing. The fire alarm suddenly screamed, loud and shrill, like an animal in pain.

Skink was still pointing the gun at Zavier. The driver took him by the arm and dragged him through the door and up the stairs. The rest of us hurried after them, followed by choking black smoke.

'I'm taking Ava to the SUV,' Colin yelled over the sound of the alarm. 'You take the boy with you and do what's needed. When you've finished, leave him outside and meet me back at the car. The fire brigade should be here soon. If you've any sense,' he shouted to Zavier, 'you'll get as far from here as possible. If you're picked up by the authorities, I'll make sure you get the blame.'

'Why can't I stay with him?'

'Because you're my goddaughter. You might not believe it, but I care very much about your future.'

My arms were flailing, trying to hit out at Colin and reach Zavier at the same time.

'Ava', Zavier mouthed, throwing me a scrap of a smile as he was marched into the green heart of the dome. Despite his attempt at bravado, his cocky mask had slipped. Next to these ruthless men, I saw he was little more than a boy. His gangly frame needed to fill out with muscle. His character was waiting to broaden with the delights and sorrows of experience. He was a sapling reaching towards the light, easy to snap or stunt. A sick sensation turned my stomach.

I kicked back and felt the heel of my boot connect with my godfather's shin. He huffed in pain but continued to pull me by the wrist around the perimeter of the biosphere towards the door we'd entered through about fifteen minutes earlier.

'Are you mad? Let me go! You can't do this... You can't make me – '

Just as we were about to reach the exit, a fur ball flew from beneath a large japonica and landed on Uncle Colin's thigh. He dropped my arm and jumped back, swatting at Ruby the Greenacres cat who was clinging to his leg, claws digging into his skin. I turned and dodged down an aisle to my left, doubling back almost immediately behind a tall trellis to put him off my trail.

The screaming alarm covered the sound of my footsteps as I ran round the circumference, peering into the heart of the glasshouse, looking for Zavier. Smoke billowed up to the vaulted glass ceiling from the furthermost side of the dome. The fire couldn't have spread that fast or that far, not without help anyway.

Suddenly the alarm stopped. The lights went out. The fire had damaged the dome's electrical systems. Plunged into silent darkness, I breathed deeply to still the gasps that were exploding out of my mouth, and listened for my pursuer. Footsteps and shouts echoed round the glasshouse. My ears were still ringing from the alarm and I couldn't be sure of the direction of the sounds. Grateful for the darkness, I crouched low and crawled behind the plant displays, plotting an oblique course through the greenhouse. The smell of burning became stronger every second. Behind me a wavering glow from the other side of the dome expanded like the sun rising through misty clouds.

I turned a corner. The moon sailed from behind a cloud and silver light filtered through the glass roof, painting bands of grey across the inky darkness. And there, slumped against an ornamental cherry tree, was Zavier.

At first I thought he was dead. His hands were tied round the back of the trunk.

'Zavier,' I whispered, tapping the side of his face. There was no response so I slapped his cheek harder.

'Keep your hair on, frizz,' he muttered.

'They're setting fire to the dome.'

'You better get out, then.' He opened his eyes and looked at me. 'Don't make me tell you twice.'

I felt round the back of the tree. The knot was convoluted and impossible to untie in the darkness.

'I won't,' I answered before sprinting away.

I knew what I was looking for. A pair of garden shears or cutters to sever the rope. The garden tools were displayed on the outside edge on the dome's east side, near the access door to the stairs to the roof. A man was standing in front of the door, grasping the handle. He turned as I skidded to a halt in front of a display of secateurs. It was Marcus. Angry words erupted from my mouth.

'You treacherous, ungrateful weasel! How could you betray Theo and agree to meet up with that thieving sleazebag? I'll never forgive you.'

In my rage, my voice travelled further than I expected.

'She's over there,' someone yelled.

I pushed a rack of seed packets over. Marcus jumped back as it crashed to his feet. Dodging back along the aisle towards the gardening equipment, I glanced back. Marcus watched me in silence, his eyes unreadable. I grabbed a pair of secateurs and plunged back into the biosphere.

As I ran, I ripped off the packaging. Zavier opened his eyes when he felt the tug of the rope around his wrists.

'I thought I told you – '

'I give the orders round here, remember.' I cut the rope. He pulled his arms stiffly to his sides.

'OK, boss. Anything you say.'

'I thought they were going to let you go.'

'That was said for your benefit. Better if the so-called arsonist ends up cremating himself. Open-and-shut case.'

'It's a good job your hands weren't chained.'

'The ropes were intentional. They would have burned away, leaving no evidence that I'd been restrained. They know what they're doing.'

'How could he?' I said, clenching my teeth.

'Let's worry about that later. We've got to get out of here.'

We crawled our way towards the entrance hall and rattled the glass door. It was locked. The automatic override on the keypad wouldn't work because the power was out.

'We'll have to go back through the dome and out through the staff entrance on the other side,' I whispered in Zavier's ear. 'I'm sure Colin didn't lock it behind him.'

The moon dipped behind a cloud and we tiptoed back across the dark foyer, stumbling into a line of trolleys. I froze in fear, but Zavier pushed me onwards into the glasshouse. We zigzagged through the interconnecting aisles that circled or dissected the biosphere, distancing ourselves from the noise we'd made. Catching our breath behind a large banana plant, a warm body pressed against my ankle and I stifled a scream. It was Ruby. I scooped her up and stroked her silky fur, whispering my thanks for her help.

'Where do you think they are?' His breath tickled my cheek.

'I don't know.'

'Let's cut straight through the middle. It'll be quicker.'

'But we could get trapped by the flames.'

'We're already trapped. They must have left themselves a way out. Can we do a shortcut and get out first?'

Without another word we ran along an aisle towards the centre of the glasshouse. We kept low, checking at each intersection before running across, Zavier clutching his side and wheezing in pain with each small sprint. I held a wriggling Ruby tight to my chest, refusing to leave her behind. The smell of burning pallets was overpowering. I smothered a cough in the neck of my jumper as we reached the pond.

Two shadows emerged from the darkness.

'Ahhh, there you are,' Colin Hildreth drawled.

Skink stepped forward and pulled his pistol from the dark folds of his jacket.

'Sit there where I can see you both.'

'And keep hold of that animal,' Colin added, nodding at Ruby.

We sat next to each other on the low wall surrounding the pond, unable to argue with the authority of the gun.

'Love's young dream. It's so touching you went back to rescue him, Ava. But so pointless.' Shadows distorted Colin's face into a grotesque mask. His eyes were deep sockets, his beard a dark stain on his skin. With the orange glow of the fire deepening behind him he looked like a demon about to take possession of our souls. 'If you two would just do as we say, no one's going to get hurt.'

'And that's why your thugs tied Zavier to a tree while setting fire to Greenacres, is it?' I spat.

'Just keeping him out of harm's way while they got on with the job in hand. They would have come back for him.'

Zavier snorted.

'Believe it or not, I'm trying to protect you, my dear. You're making this very difficult.'

A distant sound caught my attention.

'Listen!' I cried. 'Sirens. The police and fire engines are on their way.'

But there was something else. A voice calling from above.

'Ava!'

My godfather looked up.

'At last,' he breathed. Then, without a moment's hesitation, 'Kill him, Skink.'

'Ava!' Marcus called again, his voice echoing around the dome.

The anguish in his voice was unexpected. It ripped through my heart like a bullet and for a moment I wondered if Skink had pulled the trigger. Although my brain hadn't registered the sound of a shot, the pain in my chest was undeniable. I blinked at the glass roof, half-expecting a circle of light, or angels, or a tunnel leading to heaven, anything to speed me away from the crackle of the fire, the smell of brimstone and the agony in my heart.

Skink followed my gaze and cocked his pistol. Simultaneously Zavier yanked my hand. I half fell off the wall as he hauled me down the nearest aisle. A loud bang echoed in the darkness.

We ran, zigzagging then crouching behind a thick clematis, breathless with terror. The stink of petrol caught at the back of our throats. After a moment's silence, Zavier cautiously peered through the leaves.

'There's someone up in the roof.'

'It's Marcus.'

I edged forward. The golden glow had increased to a frantic pattern of flame and shadow. Flickering tongues were leaping upwards as if to lick the stars that glimmered through the glass. Silhouetted against the night sky, Marcus ran round the metal walkway, his footsteps clanging as he made his way towards the control panel for the irrigation system.

'Stop,' yelled a rough voice I recognised as belonging to Saunders.

He was heaving himself up the ladder, followed by another shadow. My godfather's driver.

Marcus reached the irrigation controls and pounded on the outer casing of the electronic panel. The men lumbered onto the walkway and ran in opposite directions around the circumference of the dome in a coordinated pincer movement.

Another shot rang out.

'They're not after us. Skink's firing at Marcus!' I shrugged away Zavier's arm which had been resting along my shoulders and jumped up, intending to run back in the direction we'd come to try to stop the shooting.

Zavier grabbed me round the waist.

'Are you mad? We have to get out of here.' He dragged me towards the staff door.

The sirens were closer, but so too were other more ominous sounds – the crackle of fire, the splinter of exploding window panes. Shrubs hissed and popped, emitting shrill whistles of pain as flames consumed their sappy flesh. A palm tree flared like a giant roman candle. There was no way past. We darted along another aisle, only to slide to a halt before a wall of fire.

Ahead was a sight more terrifying than the one we'd just escaped. An image from the halls of hell. Doused with petrol, the plants and pallets were a mass of leaping flames. Ceramic pots shattered with a crack. Bags of fertiliser spewed plumes of thick, acrid smoke. The hot breath of the monster scorched our cheeks, its crackling roar filling my ears with the certainty of death.

'We're surrounded,' Zavier cried in despair.

I looked up again at the crystal ceiling. The men had reached Marcus. The dark outline of several struggling arms and legs was impossible to decipher.

'Leave him,' Colin Hildreth shouted. 'We've got to get out. Now!'

The shape separated into distinct forms, one of them dangling from the railing. Saunders gave a last vicious kick to the flailing body before the men ran back towards the ladder. Marcus was hanging twenty metres above the flames. One hand slipped. A shriek escaped my lips. He was going to fall. He would plunge into the fire. We were all going to die, consumed by one man's burning ambition and ruthless determination... and my own stupidity.

Zavier was on his knees, trying to breathe the fresher air near the floor. Choking from the fumes and with Ruby still in my arms, I ducked down to inhale what would surely be my last smoky breath. I would never see Theo again, never have the opportunity to apologise and beg his forgiveness, never be enveloped by his arms, or fussed over by Paloma.

My eyes were stinging and watering so much it was almost impossible to focus through the smoke, but I could just about see Marcus above. He dangled by one arm for what seemed an eternity, his body still and calm. In reality it was probably seconds. I held my breath, willing his free hand to make a final grab for a metal strut so he could pull himself back to the safety of the walkway. He nodded towards me, a final salute perhaps, though my imagination might be playing tricks with my memory. Then his hand released its grip on the railing. He dropped like a sack into the mouth of the furnace. In that instant the pipe running round the roof spurted miraculous fountains of cool, ionised rain.

Chapter 21

I've laid the black letters on the white paper, the darkness on the light, and inched my way to the deadly heart of my story. Even now the horror of that night makes my soul sicken with dread. I hear the hunger of the inferno and smell the stench of its destruction, taste the twisting smoke and feel the terror snaking in my stomach. I've dredged every detail from my memory, examined every facet. Whichever way I look at it, I can't understand what happened. The electricity had been cut by the blaze. The alarm was silent and the lights were out. How had Marcus been able to activate the irrigation system?

Droplets fell onto our heads and ran down our cheeks. Rivurlets gushed down the back of my neck and upon the hands that gripped Ruby as though I was drowning in a sea of sorrow. My own tears were trifling compared with the cascade from above which washed away the heat and the sparks and the black ashes spiralling through the air.

Marcus had gone. Greenacres destroyed. One of its own had fallen, his body now enveloped by flame. I buried my face in Zavier's chest.

'There's nothing we can do for him.' He raised my head and cupped my wet face in his hands. 'Ava, please. We have to go.'

Furious flames hissed and spat, retreating from the jets of water and extinguishing in a haze of steam. A crash, heavy footsteps, voices shouting commands. The fire brigade had arrived.

Numb, I allowed Zavier to pull me through the smouldering foliage, out of the back door and into the freezing night. After a few steps, we turned and looked back. Smoke was pouring from a broken window on one side of the dome, a white pennant against the darkness. An acrid smell drifted on the wind. There was no sign of Colin or his henchman.

The emergency services were parked at the front. Although out of our line of sight, their flashing lights created a blinking halo around the dome, an urgent aureole in the sky.

'We need to speak to the police... Tell them what happened... Marcus... Uncle Colin – '

'No! Don't you understand? The scumbags who did this are above the law. Your godfather has connections. We already know he has a mole in the police station. What do you think will happen if we talk? We'll never be safe. And why would they believe us? You're a runaway. I've not exactly got a great record. Expelled from school, shoplifting when I was younger. My fingerprints all over the place. They'll pin it on me. Even if somebody did believe us, we'll never get to testify in court. They know where I live. There'll be some unexpected accident as we're about to give evidence. I've been in this business long enough to know the score.'

'Your father? Can't he help us?'

'No.' He must have seen my expression for he added, 'I'll explain later.'

'What then?'

'I don't know. But I do know we need to get out of here. We need to find somewhere safe to think through what's happened. Come on.'

I dropped Ruby onto the ground and she sprinted away into the night. I knew she would return in the morning and be rescued by one of the Greenacres staff. We stumbled down the path leading to the farmhouse, past Marcus' cottage and onto the lane, Zavier limping and cringing in pain. From the crest of the hill, more flashing lights could be seen in the distance, snaking up the dual carriageway towards the dome. After about five minutes, Zavier stopped and groped about in a thicket of bushes.

'What are you doing?'

'My bike… Here it is!'

He yanked his motorcycle from where he'd hidden it before being captured by Colin's security team. He handed me the helmet and clambered astride, wincing as he did. The engine awoke with a roar.

'Quick,' he shouted. 'Before anyone hears us.'

I scrambled on the back, holding his battered body as tightly as I dared as the machine lurched forward and we hurtled back down the winding hill to Westhatch-on-Sea.

'What are we doing here?' I asked as we stopped outside Zavier's house. 'They know where you live. It isn't safe.'

'I doubt anything will happen tonight. Besides, we need to find out whether they escaped or not. For all we know, they might all be burned to a crisp. Let's wait for a news bulletin. As long as we keep our heads down, the whole thing might blow over.'

I followed him up the front steps and into the hall, leaving my wet boots to dry on the mat and waiting until the door was closed before releasing a furious response.

'Blow over! Blow over! Is that how you see it? An innocent man has died putting out that fire. He died saving our lives. My father's work has been totally destroyed, his secrets stolen by someone he should have counted a friend, and all because of *me*. Don't you understand? None of this would have happened if I hadn't opened that safe in the first place. And I said some terrible things to Marcus before – '

'You can't blame yourself. How were you to know what would happen? That murderous villain… what's his name? Colin? He's responsible for tonight.' He raised his hand to stroke my arm.

I shrugged him away.

'Look, you're upset,' he continued. 'Now's not the time for a postmortem. We're both soaked and exhausted. We need a hot shower and clean clothes. I think we should get rid of what we're wearing so there's nothing linking us to the fire.'

He walked into the kitchen at the back of the house and pulled down the blind before switching on the light. He stripped off his jacket and shirt and stuffed them in a plastic sack. The black eye the men had given him on Friday 13th had faded to yellow, but his lip was badly split. Dark bruises bloomed along his ribcage where he'd been punched and kicked by the two thugs. He grimaced as he examined himself, flushing when he caught my eye. He hobbled up the stairs, returning a few minutes later in a towelling dressing gown with a tracksuit, T-shirt and hoodie in his hand.

'How did you manage to find me?' I asked. 'You couldn't have seen me in the back of the car when we passed your house. The windows were tinted.'

'Questions later. Put your clothes in this sack. I'll have to think what to do with them… After your shower you'll have to wear my clothes for a bit.'

I blindly obeyed, exhausted by fear and grief, glad of the hot cascade that warmed my shuddering body and stripped the ash from my hair. I stood under the spray until the black water spiralling around the plughole ran clear. But it couldn't clean my wretched, guilty heart. Marcus had died trying to save me. It should have been me. Ultimately this was my fault. In my usual pig-headed style, I'd run away on a surge of anger, self-pity and bruised pride without a word to anyone and brought disaster upon all our heads.

By the time I arrived back downstairs, Zavier was wolfing down a plate of beans on toast.

'How can you eat?' I asked, sickened.

'I have to. Or I'll get the shakes.'

I nodded, ashamed.

He filled the kettle with water and plugged it in.

'So… What were we saying?'

'How did you find me? Don't tell me you just happened to be driving up the lane to Greenacres, saw a car parked in the darkness and knew I was being held against my will.' I leaned against the fridge door.

'I'm a borderline genius detective, remember.'

'It all seems a little too convenient.'

'I wish you would trust me. I'm on your side... though to be honest, I *am* hacked off that you dumped me at the hospital.'

'I was thinking of your welfare.'

'Ha! So I've spent a horrible night in A&E followed by a long, cold walk to collect my motorbike from the Promenade where I'd parked it yesterday before rescuing *you* from some geezer's toilet. When I get back here, I see a group of goons hanging outside Brenda's B&B, the same toerags who'd roughed me up once already because of you. They bundle you into the car. I follow, get caught, punched, thrown in the boot, tied to a tree, shot at and framed for arson. Please, Ava, stop looking out for my welfare.'

'I'm sorry,' I mumbled, 'and thank you for coming after me.'

He made us both a cup of coffee and slotted two more slices of toast in the toaster. 'Perhaps you'd like to tell me your side of the story.'

I sat down at the table, opposite his dirty crockery.

'I'd arranged to meet my godfather. He was coming down from London to fetch me. I was fed up with running away but I didn't want to go back to Greenacres. Uncle Colin was a third option, a safe haven where I could regroup and have some of my questions about the past answered.'

'Some haven! So what's with him? Why the pyrotechnics?'

'It's a long story.'

'I'm a good listener.'

I took a deep breath.

'Theo and Marcus have been developing an ionised water system to improve plant growth. It's a big deal, apparently. Ionising water kills any bugs and makes crops grow better. I've not taken much interest in it, to be honest. The day I ran away, Theo had unexpectedly left for Africa to trial the project. I rang Uncle Colin to have a bit of a whinge. I was fed up that Marcus

263

had been left in charge and that he was taking me out of the gift shop and making me work in the laboratory with him for a few months.'

Zavier switched on a gas burner and stirred the remains of the tin of beans left over from his meal.

'Colin hadn't heard about Theo's trip to Africa. He was fed up about it too. He told me he'd left a file at the Institute for Theo to peer review, but he needed it back urgently. I said I'd get it for him. I knew I shouldn't have gone into Dad's study on my own, let alone open the safe. But I did. I wish I hadn't now because that's when I found my birth certificate. I grabbed Colin's file along with the brown envelope of documents about Mum's death and my adoption. I was going to take the file to him, except that when I'd had a chance to read all the papers in the envelope, I realised he'd known all along that Theo isn't my real dad. I was angry with him for being part of the secret. He owed me the truth, don't you think? Then with everything that's been going on, I completely forgot about the file. I left it at Mrs Bungay's by mistake.'

'That still doesn't answer my question. Why set fire to the dome? Your godfather was rambling on about prototypes and patents, but I was more worried about the thugs with the gun and the petrol cans... and the news that I was going to get the blame.'

'When we went to collect the file from Mrs B's, I flicked through it and realised it wasn't Uncle Colin's file at all. Everything was in Dad's handwriting. Basically, he's stolen all Dad's research and destroyed the laboratory and the prototype irrigation system. I don't know whether he's going to claim the discovery as his own, or sell the technology to the highest bidder. You can bet your life it's worth a lot of money if he's willing to lose his relationship with his oldest friend and with his goddaughter. I hope he thinks it's worth it.'

'So the reward on offer was probably for finding the file, not for returning you to the bosom of your family?'

'I guess so,' I said in a small voice.

The toaster popped.

'Come on. Don't start crying.'

I sniffed and wiped my eyes with the sleeve of his hoodie. He buttered the toast and poured the beans on top. He placed the plate in front of me, with a knife and fork.

'Thanks.'

Even though the thought of eating made me nauseous, I knew I needed an injection of energy to cope with the next few hours. I pulled the overlong sleeves of his hoodie up to my elbows and picked up the cutlery.

We sat in miserable silence until I'd finished eating. I didn't want to think about it any more. I couldn't get the thought of Marcus out of my head. The ghastly smell of the flames. His body falling into the inferno.

When he told me he'd been left in charge of Greenacres, I'd wanted to bring him down a peg or two and prove I knew as much if not more than he did about running Greenacres. I wanted him to jump when I whistled and be worried when I ran away. Like a typical teenage drama queen, I'd placed myself centre stage. The mistreated heroine stirring up a witch's brew of trouble: desire for revenge, a plea for sympathy, a demand for attention, the need for control. But most of all, I acknowledged sadly to myself, I'd wanted him to come after me, like a knight on a white charger, and prove he cared more for me than for anyone else.

With a shuddering realisation I recognised the pain that had pierced my heart when I heard him call my name from the roof of the dome. Deep had called to deep. His anguish had been for me, not for himself. He'd been distracting Skink, drawing his fire. Bitter longing swept through my heart. Marcus had cared more for me than I could have imagined. But now he would never find me, never bring me home. I had to face the truth. My fit of petulance had cost a man I loved his life.

'Do you have any money?' Zavier asked, startling me from my train of thought.

'No. Do you?' I wiped my damp face.

'Unfortunately not.'

'What about your dad? Why can't we ask him to help?' I asked, not wanting Zavier to probe into my state of mind.

'It's a long story. When my mum walked out on us a few years back he went a bit...' he tapped the side of his head, 'you know... cuckoo. He already had a drink problem. Hazard of the job. All those late-night stakeouts and rummaging around in other people's mess. You need something to cheer you up. At first it was just the booze. Then he got addicted to prescription meds. He had a complete breakdown about six months ago. He's been sectioned. He's in a psychiatric hospital at the moment.'

'Why didn't you tell me?'

'Because you're a client. How likely were you to employ my services if you thought I was limping along on my own? Hardly inspires confidence, does it? You needed my dad's records. I needed your money. I don't have a licence to practise as a private investigator, or the legal authority to run the agency without him. I have to pretend that Dad's somewhere in the background overseeing everything. I've picked up some odd bits of work here and there. I'm trying to pay the bills, hang on to the house so that he has somewhere to come home to when he's released, hopefully in a couple of months' time.'

'I want a refund!' I mumbled.

'No chance, honey. I'm all funded out.'

'What are we going to do?'

'We need to find somewhere we can hide out for a few days until we know exactly what happened tonight. Whether the police – or anybody else, for that matter – are looking for us.'

'We can't let them get away with it.'

'I understand. I really do. But our fingerprints are all over the scene of the crime. With possible corruption in the Westhatch police force we have to tread carefully, buy ourselves some time to decide what to do. Go to the newspapers, perhaps. Contact our MP. Try to get in touch with Theo to tell him what's happened. In the meantime, I think it would be safer if we disappear for a few days.'

'Do you have any friends who could help?'

'Not ones I'd want to explain your presence to.'

'Charming! Don't worry about me,' I declared. 'I can look after myself.'

He ruffled my damp hair as though I were a small child.

'Keep your curls on, sparky. Where would you go? Not back to Brenda Bungay's, I hope.

'As if!' I pictured the derelict caravan. 'I've got a bolt-hole.'

'Where is it?'

'Not far from here.'

'Will anybody be able to trace you there?'

'I don't think so.'

'Good. Then I'm coming too.'

We stuffed our smoky clothes in the washing machine and put them on a hot wash. A strange sense of unreality had settled over us. Perhaps we were in shock; I was certainly exhausted. After packing a sleeping bag, radio, torch and change of clothes, and emptying the contents of his fridge into a backpack, we climbed wearily onto his motorbike and drove to the Leisure Centre. I clung to his waist, leaning forward to counterbalance the weight of his rucksack on my back, aware of his lean shoulders. My car sat alone in the empty car park. He threw his belongings onto the back seat, on top of my own bags. He locked his bike in the area reserved for motorbikes and climbed into the front seat. On the way, I explained about my cleaning job and Boody and the caravan.

'It's got to be better than the car, right?' he asked.

'Maybe. Maybe not.'

'Great!'

We drove through the gates of the holiday park at half-past eleven. The revelries were still in full swing down at the entertainment centre. Distorted pop music echoed along the deserted drive as we approached the security kiosk. Although I had my staff card, Big Ron lifted the barrier and waved me through when he recognised my battered car. He didn't see Zavier, huddled and groaning in the passenger seat footwell.

We parked in my usual spot behind the substation and pushed through the hole in the hedge. Hoisting my own rucksack across my shoulders, I carried Zavier's sleeping bag while he carried his backpack and the bag of food. Despite the torch, we made unsteady progress through the trees.

The key was exactly where I'd left it. Nothing had been touched. It didn't look as though Boody had visited in my absence, which surprised me. I'd texted her I was sick that morning. Surely a concerned friend would have checked I was OK.

'Crikey!' Zavier exclaimed as I opened the door. 'I think I'll sleep in your car.'

'You can if you want,' I replied tartly. 'By the way, the loo doesn't work. You'll have to pee in the bushes.'

'Is that what you do?'

'I have the bladder of a camel.'

'You mean you've got the hump of a camel.'

'Yeah… that too.'

We dumped the bags. I rummaged in the recess under the bench in search of another mattress. I hadn't investigated inside previously for fear of what I might find. I sent up a silent prayer for some cushions at least and that we wouldn't have to share the couch. I pulled out a thin mattress, one end badly chewed by a mouse and the other covered in droppings and mould.

'You're the tough guy,' I said, passing it to him as he grimaced. 'The world-weary investigator who's seen everything.'

'Nothing like this! Can I bunk with you?'

'No. In any case, my mattress is no better. It's just the long cushion for the bench and it's damp. That's why it's covered with a plastic bag.'

'Wet it, did you? I thought you had the bladder of a camel.'

'Moron!'

He gingerly brushed off the droppings and shoved the cushions in the corner. He pulled out his sleeping bag and climbed inside. Sitting like a caterpillar with his back to the wall, he fiddled with the radio. I wrapped myself in my duvet and lay on the bench.

It seemed impossible to believe Marcus was dead, despite the fact I'd witnessed it with my own eyes only a couple of hours earlier. Perhaps I was in a nightmare where everything was the opposite of real life: senseless, upside down, turned over.

'A good gardener has to turn the soil,' Theo said to me once. 'Plants need the good stuff – water and fertiliser – but they also need a little of the bad stuff if you want them to bloom. Earth needs to be stirred up, just like people. Trials and tribulations are opportunities for growth, not despair. Sometimes a little disruption can loosen things that have become hard and impacted, things that prevent love and joy from blooming. Don't be scared when life bowls you a googly.'

But he'd been talking about difficulties at school. The sniggering when I entered a classroom, the girls who blanked me in the corridor. How trivial it all seemed now!

Zavier listened to pop music and adverts for twenty minutes, waiting for the local news, while I considered the wasteland that was my life. On the hour, a broadcaster announced a traffic accident in Westhatch, the arrival of quadruplets at the hospital and some local sporting fixtures. There was nothing about the dome.

'Must be too early,' Zavier said. 'There'll be a report in the morning. Best try to get some sleep.'

I curled up into a tight ball and let the events from the evening wash over me. Colin Hildreth was a liar and a thief, an arsonist and a murderer. I hated him! Even with my eyes closed I could still see the silhouette of Marcus falling, a dark shape against the rich orange of the flames, as though I'd been looking into the sun too long and the image had been branded to the inside of my eyelids. I wanted to cry, but the horror lay on my heart like an immovable stone, sealing me up, crushing me down.

'Ava,' Zavier whispered in the darkness. 'Are you all right?' When I didn't reply, he asked again.

'No,' I muttered, to shut him up.

'Don't cry,'

'I'm not.'

'There was nothing we could do.'

'I know.'

'Do you want to talk about it?'

'No.'

'Do you want a cuddle?'

I swore at him.

'I didn't mean it like that. Just a hug.'

'Go to sleep. We can talk in the morning.'

I lay awake until Zavier's soft snores told me he'd eventually fallen into oblivion. I would have sworn I had no sleep at all that night. Certainly the darkness and the cold and the anguish stretched endlessly, a desert with no oasis, an ocean with no island to rest upon. There was no way back to my previous life. It would be as impossible to return as putting back together the shattered glass of the dome or bringing back to life the incinerated plants. The home that had sometimes felt like a gilded cage had gone, the windows blown out. I was wheeling through a great emptiness, not free but dragging with me memories and regrets that would weigh me down for a lifetime. Just as the birds began to sing and I'd put thoughts of sleep behind me, I was startled awake by a loud banging on the caravan door.

'Get your skinny backside out of bed, Claire. No one gets more than one sickie a year at Fun World.'

I rolled off the bench, duvet wrapped tight around me, and shuffled to the door. Zavier grunted when I stepped on him.

'Sorry, Boody,' I said, opening the door an inch. 'I can't come in today.'

'Yes you can, slacker. I'm not clearing up yesterday's swillage on my own.'

Zavier groaned and rolled over in his sleeping bag.

'What's that? Is there someone with you?' Boody pushed the door roughly and I stumbled backwards.

'Sick, are you? Who's this, then? The love doctor?'

'It's not what it looks like – '

'Get dressed! We've got five minutes till our shift starts. You're gonna give me a nervy B, Claire. Honest to goodness, I'm telling you if you don't come now, I'll come back with Godzilla herself. I've covered for you once. I won't do it again.'

'You better go,' Zavier mumbled. 'Low profile, remember.'

I turned in despair and shuffled towards my backpack. Boody followed me into the caravan, stepping dismissively over Zavier. He gave her a lopsided smile.

'You can keep a secret, can't you? I'll be no trouble.'

'Men are always trouble!'

I pulled some clothes out of the bag. Under cover of the duvet, I wriggled into a pair of jeans and a jumper.

'Where's your uniform?' Boody asked.

'In the car. I'll pick up my tabard on the way out.'

Hopefully nobody would notice I wouldn't be wearing the Fun World polo shirt underneath. I splashed my face with cold, bottled water and combed my hair with my fingers.

'I'll be back around half-two,' I told Zavier.

'OK. We'll talk then.'

'We'll talk when you get back,' Boody mimicked scathingly, as we hurried down the path. 'How romantic! Not just a one-night stand, then? He wants to *talk*! Wowsers, Claire! He must be a keeper.' Her voice dripped with sarcasm.

'It's not like that. We didn't – '

'Save it! I don't want to know. I did you a favour getting you that caravan. I wasn't expecting you to turn it into the honeymoon suite. Who is he, anyway?'

'Just someone I met. He's helping me – '

'I bet he is!'

'– with family stuff. It's complicated.' She stared at me hard. I must have looked terrible, for her voice softened.

'Families always are. Better off without 'em. That's what I think.'

Although exhausted from lack of sleep and the shock of the events the previous day, spending the morning sweeping and scrubbing was probably the best thing for me. Boody's constant caustic remarks prevented me from thinking too deeply about Marcus, or worrying about how Theo, Paloma and the Greenacres staff would react to the news. It was too unbearable to think about their pain when I couldn't process my own. I worked like a zombie, distracted by mundane tasks that usually bored me to exasperation. I saw Sonya in the distance, following Mrs Ozzles into the hair and beauty salon. She looked as pale and miserable as me.

'Back to the love shack, is it?' Boody said at twenty to three as I closed the cleaning cupboard door.

'Boody. Please... Don't say anything.'

'OK, Countess. I won't. Maybe I'm jealous. He's quite a spice.'

I snorted in reply.

Zavier was dressed but dishevelled when I returned. A pale shadow of blond stubble lined his jaw. His hair was sticking out in all directions. I slumped down on the plastic-covered bench. The sleeping bag and duvet were neatly folded at one end. Without asking, he filled the saucepan with water and placed it on the camping stove to boil and poured me a bowl of cereal.

'What's the news?' I asked, dreading his reply.

'Arsonists have struck Greenacres. One body discovered, male, as yet unidentified. Motive unknown. The police are not looking for anyone else in connection with the crime. They're trying to contact the owner who's overseas.'

'Is that all?'

'Yep.'

'They're going to get away with it, aren't they? Once they discover it's Marcus' body, do you think he'll get the blame?'

'I wouldn't be surprised. Those toe-rags seem to have the police in their pocket. It would be logical to point the finger at Marcus now. More difficult to blame the fire on us because we've escaped. Your godfather – '

'Don't call him that!'

'*Colin,* then. He must be spitting tacks that I've escaped. It will be difficult to implicate me without implicating himself. There might be a drop of my blood in the boot of his car, for instance, something to verify my account if he drags me into it. If he's got any sense, he'll just let me slip out of the picture.'

'Us? You mean "us", don't you?'

'Whatever he's done, he made it pretty obvious he cares about you and doesn't want you to come to any harm. He doesn't give a toss about me.'

'Then the longer you can keep out of his way, the better… You've obviously given this a lot of thought.'

'I've had nothing else to do all morning.'

'I don't want to think about it. It's too… awful. I can't stand it!'

He passed me a cup of coffee and sat down by my side, his arm slipping round my shoulder.

'I'm sorry, Ava. It's terrible. I can't imagine what you're going through. But you have to be strong. We can't lose our heads. There are some very dangerous men out there. We have to decide what to do next. We have no money. I can't go home. Neither can you.'

'I don't have a home. I can't ask Theo to take me back now. His beautiful dome has been destroyed because of me. His partner and probable successor is dead. I'm the one who walked away, remember?'

'So what are you going to do?'

I sipped my coffee, but my hand was unsteady. I put the cup down on the floor to stop myself from spilling the hot liquid.

'I wish I could unwind the clock and start again. I had everything and didn't realise it. I don't know why I couldn't be satisfied. What's the point of looking for my real father now?

He won't match up to Theo. It's going to be someone ghastly like that sleazebag Maxwell King, or even worse that disgusting lump, Chucky Skittles. It would be better not to know. Better to have no father at all. From now on I'm going it alone. It's just me against the world. I've got to stop living life as if I'm the female lead in a fairy tale. I've learned that much from Boody. I've lost everything and everyone I ever loved,' I hiccupped on a sob, 'and I don't want to love anyone ever again.'

'Are we talking about Marcus?' Zavier asked, pulling his arm away from me and standing up, ostensibly to pass me a toilet roll so I could dry my eyes. He knocked over my coffee and swore.

'Of course I loved him! What was not to love? He was kind, generous, funny – '

'I thought you didn't like him.' He ripped off a wad of tissue and bent down to mop up the puddle of coffee, his expression unreadable.

'That was just… I don't know, me protecting myself. I didn't like the fact that everyone loved him… and he loved everyone back. There wasn't a bad bone in his body. And now he's dead and all because of me… and *that* man… and I can't do anything to make it better.'

'Ava… '

'No, don't! Don't touch me. I can't do anything about Marcus or the dome. I'll never be able to make amends for what happened, but I *can* get some kind of revenge. If Colin Hildreth thinks he can destroy my world without suffering the consequences, he's badly mistaken. If I can't get him for what happened last night without dragging you into it, I'm going to get him for what's going on at Fun World.'

'I don't understand.'

'He's a friend of Maxwell King. An investor in the holiday park. He gets a fat dividend every year.'

Zavier shook his head.

'Don't try to stop me.'

'Grief can make people do the craziest things. It pushed my dad over the edge. Don't do anything rash.'

'I'm not mad, you know. I'm being perfectly rational. It's not just retaliation for what happened at Greenacres. Colin Hildreth is an investor in Fun World. Maxwell King is using the holiday park as a front for drugs and prostitution, possibly even people-trafficking and enforced slavery. We owe it to the people who are being exploited to stop him. He has a string of holiday resorts and clubs. This thing could be huge. Marcus would never stand by and watch people suffer. It would be my way of honouring his memory. "Speaking truth to power" he called it. And if Colin Hildreth is an investor, some of the mud has got to stick.'

'Can you prove any of this?' Zavier asked doubtfully.

'Not yet. But I will. When I was trapped in Maxwell King's washroom I heard him on the phone. He was talking about a drugs drop at the funfair. Something about a man called Mr Bones and a train. What's the date today? The seventeenth? Then it's in two days' time at noon. The nineteenth. Yesterday you mentioned getting the press involved. Do you know any journalists?'

'Only someone on the local newspaper. An old school friend.'

'That will do. What we need is evidence Maxwell King is a drug dealer and Colin Hildreth is profiting from that sick trade. I'm going to destroy his world just as he destroyed mine.'

Chapter 22

The next day was the most miserable of my life. The weight of guilt and grief pressed down so hard it was a physical struggle to hold myself upright, let alone conduct a conversation. I was going through the motions, cleaning mechanically, hardly listening to Boody's innuendos about Zavier.

'What's the problem, Countess? He's proper fit, isn't he? You should be chuffed as chocolate biscuits.'

Fed up of my monosyllabic replies, we eventually worked in awkward silence.

'Someone's obviously not getting enough sleep,' she sniped.

I kept my head down when collecting my wages from Mrs Ozzles. I didn't want my cheerless appearance to get me the sack. My money was paying for our meals – fish and chips, burgers and cheese sandwiches smuggled down to the caravan from the onsite concessions – and the toffees I kept on me in case Zavier's sugar levels suddenly dropped. I tried to coincide my visits to Mrs Ozzles' office with Sonya, who if anything looked worse than me, although my Albanian friend seemed to be in the housekeeper's good books. On one occasion she even stroked her newly highlighted hair.

'I think it would look pretty up in a knot. I will speak to Chantelle in the beauty salon. I'm sure if I have a word with her she would show you how to do it. No charge.'

Sonya nodded, staring at the floor.

'Are you OK?' I whispered as we walked out of the office.

'I will live in caravan now. Very nice.' She glanced nervously behind her.

I looked back. Mrs Ozzles was standing by the door, listening to our conversation.

'Shall we grab a cup of coffee? You can tell me all about it.'

'I busy now. I still packing.'

'Would you like some help?' I offered, hoping to warn her to flee Fun World immediately, but knowing with a sick dread it was probably too late.

'Shannon is helping. Thank you very kindly.' She hurried away.

I heard Mrs Ozzles' door click shut. She had heard what she wanted to hear.

I spent a wretched afternoon and evening in the caravan, trying to keep warm, huddled by the radio listening to the local station for any further news about the investigation into the fire. Marcus' body still hadn't been formally identified. Dental records were being sought. Just the thought of it made my stomach churn.

Zavier was out for a large part of the day. He had visited his father in hospital in the morning, hoping to glean some advice on the best way to record conversations of people who were under surveillance. He didn't tell me how the visit had gone but from his gloomy expression things were still bad. He also sneaked back home to fetch his video camera and laptop. As far as he could tell, no one was watching the house and nothing had been disturbed inside. He'd spent a couple of hours using the broadband connection in his basement office trying to hack into Maxwell King's private email account. He'd been surprised by the sophistication of the security system installed to protect Fun World's internal computer network, bearing in mind it was primarily used for holiday bookings, accounts and employee records.

That night, the night before the drug drop was scheduled to take place, we drove to the seafront and parked as near to the funfair as we could. Despite the cold, the half-term holidaymakers poured through the gates, bundled up in coats and scarves, tipsy with excitement.

The coloured lights on the big dipper and Ferris wheel reminded me of Christmas, not two months past. So much had happened since then it seemed like another life, another me. Memories of the dome drowned out the icy shush of the waves on the shingle. It had been a wonderland of sparkling decorations and pine needles. Banks of scarlet poinsettias, cyclamen and Christmas anemones had lined the aisles leading to the pond like carnival-goers cheering a parade. Home-made ginger thins, crisp and spicy, curled in cellophane bags tied up with red ribbon. Marzipans and sugared nuts, dried fruits dipped in chocolate, cinnamon cookies and jars of Paloma's redcurrant jelly were piled in pyramids in the gift shop.

In the dome, amaryllis bulbs slept in presentation boxes. Hyacinths and miniature daffodils nestled in hand-painted pots, pushing their green spikes through the crumbly compost. Outside, a forest of Christmas trees clustered the slopes – a mini-Switzerland with a crystal mountain at its peak.

I'd organised a programme of free Christmas crafts for the school holidays. I was keen to entice the busy mums up the hill during the cold, fraught days of December, anything to charm the shoppers into making last-minute, impulse purchases. Christmas crowns from silver paper. Angels made from lace. Stars from golden wires. I'd cut out paper circles in red, green and white tissue, leaving them by the Christmas grotto so children could write their wishes down and pin them to the tree. The first few were covered in childish scrawls asking for dolls and bicycles and mobile phones, but slowly there were other requests, some in neater script. 'Please make Daddy better.' 'Look after Grandma in heaven.' 'Let there be enough.' 'Make it stop.'

As usual, Theo had donned the white beard and red costume of Father Christmas. He'd listened to the children's dreams and blessed them with a smile and a candied orange. I could almost hear the soft sound of Christmas bells floating from the overhead speakers.

Zavier pushed me across the road through a gap between the cars driving along the Promenade, jerking me from my daydream. In comparison, the funfair was loud and gaudy. The Wurlitzer flashed to an aggressive hip-hop rhythm, words distorted by the loudness of the music and the biting sea breeze. A smell of hot dogs and onions greased the air. We pushed through the crowds and made our way along a row of booths: lucky ducks, a shooting gallery, hoopla and crazy darts. Crudely made stuffed toys and startled goldfish hung from the roofs in plastic bags, their baleful eyes as black and empty as the horizon.

'The Ghost Train.' Zavier pointed to a wooden building at the bottom of the path.

Tell Mr Bones I'll meet him myself at midday at the funfair, Maxwell had said. This was the only train at the funfair, unless you counted the big dipper which was modelled in the shape of a snake.

We joined the queue. Each metal carriage was big enough for two. Each one set off on its journey alone with a clang and thump, pushing against the double doors that opened into darkness. We watched as the doors swung back with a menacing groan. The screams of the passengers could be heard from where we were standing, feverish, shrill, fading to silence until the swing-doors opposite the entrance banged open and they arrived back at the start, their faces flushed with laughter. I timed the journey; the entire circuit took less than three minutes.

We paid for our ticket and shuffled our bottoms across the cold metal seat. A swarthy man, thin to emaciation, thrust the thick safety bar across our laps and locked it fast.

'Keep your eyes open,' Zavier whispered in my ear, his breath warm and comforting. 'We're looking for anything that looks like bones or any way Maxwell King could drop off cash and pick up drugs during the ride.'

I nodded. He gripped my hand as we shunted forward and thumped into the spring-loaded doors. They closed behind us and we were plunged into darkness.

279

Immediately something soft and stringy brushed my face. Although I knew it would be a web of cotton threads, I ducked instinctively and swatted them away from my skin, shuddering at the thought of spiders and dead desiccated flies.

'Keep looking,' Zavier hissed at my bowed head.

I forced myself to sit up just as a fluorescent purple bat swooped in front of us. I screamed and clasped Zavier's arm. He chuckled and patted my hand. With a judder we turned a corner.

An eerie green light illuminated a dungeon scene. Groans of pain and shrieks of despair blasted over the sound system. Papier-mâché models of prisoners hung from the slimy walls, their writhing bodies ensnared in chains, or encased in mechanisms of torture. Frightful eyes stared accusingly at us as an animatronic rat scuttled across the floor.

The carriage began to climb, pushing through another swing-door then dropping suddenly with a rush of wind. A white sheet flew over us, its corners flapping at our cheeks. A stench of rotten flesh blew in our faces.

Another sharp turn. We entered a dim chamber. Flickering images of vampires and werewolves, monsters and ghouls flashed on the tunnel walls as we shuddered along the track. More cobwebs stroked our hair, sudden cackles of laughter blasted from above. I jumped as we unexpectedly banged through another door.

Plunged back into darkness as thick as velvet, I remember thinking we must be near the end of our journey. It hadn't been as scary as I thought. It was easy to see through the artifice of the cheap props and costumes and rationalise the images projected onto the screens. I squeezed Zavier's hand.

The carriage shuddered through a rubber curtain. The carriage jolted to a stop, throwing our bodies against the safety bar. With a blood-curdling yell, a shape lunged out of the blackness. My heart leapt to my throat, strangling my scream.

An unearthly face thrust itself to within three inches of my own. A skull as pale as death. Two black holes for eyes, a gaping mouth leering to reveal a cemetery of crooked teeth. The skeleton cavorted before us as only a living thing can. It took a moment for my brain to register that the creature must be a man in an invisible black bodysuit, his bones picked out in luminous paint. As quickly as he arrived, he disappeared and we whooshed through the final door and out into the neon hubbub of the funfair.

'Mr Bones!' I breathed.

After the ride we sat on a bench, hunched over cups of steaming coffee from a nearby kiosk.

'It's not going to be easy to plant a video recording device in there,' Zavier remarked. 'We were barely in that last section for twenty seconds. Mr Bones was there the whole time. He would see if I tried to rig anything up.'

'But that must be where Maxwell King is going to do the swap. Money for drugs. It's completely private. He could go in with a bag of cash and come out with an identical bag of drugs. Who would know?'

'We're going to have to go round again,' Zavier said. 'See if we can get a better picture of the surroundings. How wide apart are the walls? How high is the ceiling? Are there any ledges or beams we could attach the camera to?'

'But it was so dark.'

'That's where these come in.' He pulled a small case out of his pocket and opened it to reveal a pair of heavy-rimmed glasses. 'Night vision!'

'I hope you've not been using those in the caravan,' I exclaimed, remembering how we undressed each night in darkness.

'What do you take me for?'

'You don't want to know!'

I borrowed Zavier's woolly hat to cover my distinctive hair and paid for another ticket each. We didn't want the man on the gate to recognise us as previous customers. With surprise as its main fascination, the Ghost Train was not the kind of ride worth paying for twice.

Although I knew what was coming, my body still jumped at the cobwebs and the bat. I braced myself as we pushed through the rubber curtain, knowing the carriage would judder to a halt and not wanting to fall forward across the bar. This time I saw the skeleton pull back a sliding door and step into the chamber. He lunged towards me, arms outstretched, an unearthly shriek accompanying his arrival. As planned, I screamed as loudly as I could and flapped my hands against his body to distract him from Zavier who was calmly scanning the walls and ceilings. Within seconds, Mr Bones stepped back into his secret cupboard and slid the door closed.

'What do you think?' I asked as we walked away.

'It might be possible. There's a metal strut running along the wall on my side. There's nothing on your side because that's where Mr Bones opens the door. If I rig the camera up on some kind of clamp, I might just be able to attach it to the strut. I'll have to stick something over the little light that comes on when it's recording.'

'How will you switch it on?'

'I can do it remotely when we see Maxwell King get into the carriage. There's only about thirty minutes of recording time on it. I don't want to waste any of it on the other punters. We'll have to come back tomorrow and take another ride to fix it on, then go round again after the drop to retrieve it.'

'The ticket man's going to recognise us. Mr Bones probably got a pretty good look at us too.'

'Can't be helped. When we come back tomorrow night we'll have to make sure we're wearing something completely different.'

'I've got that blonde wig,' I said, remembering the one still in the back of my car I'd borrowed from the rack of costumes backstage at the entertainment centre.

'How could I forget?' he winked.

After reconnoitring the funfair, we drove back to Fun World, Zavier curled down low on the front seat. The security guard gave me a cursory nod as I swiped my staff card to raise the barrier.

I parked in front of an empty caravan near the launderette. Both of us were low on clean clothes. We'd planned 'Operation Laundry' with military precision that afternoon, throwing the black sack of dirty clothes into the back of my car before we left for the seafront. I knew which caravans were uninhabited from the cleaning roster, and had chosen one with an overhanging tree at the front which plunged the gravel parking space into the deepest gloom. Trafford knew my car by sight and I didn't want any awkward questions as to why I was skulking around the holiday camp when I'd finished work hours ago.

The laundrette was deserted. It was karaoke night down at the entertainment centre, and a big football match was being screened live on the wide-screen TV in the club bar. I jammed the pile of smelly clothes in the machine, not bothering to sort them into lights and darks, and fed the slot with pound coins.

We sat next to each other on hard plastic chairs, glad of the steamy warmth and the competing fragrances of fabric conditioner and soap.

'Do you think you'll be able to do it?' I asked.

'Of course.'

'And your journalist friend... he's going to be there?'

'He'll be milling about with his camera trying to look like a tourist. Even if we don't get a clear recording of the drop-off, we'll hopefully get some other evidence we can use. I've found encrypted files in the computer directories of Maxwell King and Mrs Ozzles. I haven't been able to access them yet, but the level of security is pretty suspicious for a holiday camp.' He took hold of my hand. 'What are you going to do when this is over?'

'I don't know. Look for another job, I suppose. There won't be work here for a cash-in-hand girl who grasses up the big boss to the police. My old job at the dome is gone. I don't think Theo would want to give me a second chance after everything that's happened. Would you?'

'I'm not a father...'

'Neither's he.'

'... but I'm pretty sure he would want to know you're safe.'

'I'll let him know. When I'm settled. I can't face him yet.'

'You could always come and stay with me for a while, if you like. There's plenty of room.' His thumb gently massaged the hand he was holding.

'I don't know if that's a good idea.' A little bubble of panic – or was it excitement – fizzed in my tummy.

'You know I like you, Ava. I'm guessing you probably don't feel the same. I think you could disappear at any moment without saying goodbye.'

I shook my head, but he was right. I'd already made one attempt to walk away when I'd telephoned Colin Hildreth for help. My cheeks were warm, and not just because of the heat radiating from the washing machine.

'It's not that I don't like you, Zavier. It's just – '

He cut me off, not wanting to hear more.

'You've been through a lot. I know that. There's no rush. I'm willing to wait.'

'I don't want to think about the future right now. A man has lost his life because of me. Marcus always stood up for the weak and the poor. I owe it to him to help Sonya and Boody and the other girls. And the way Chucky Skittles treats Gavin and the other Pink Jackets. It's not right. I'm sure that creep's involved in something despicable. There's a can of worms here, and I want to lift the lid and let the magpies peck through the mess.'

'As long as you're sure. We're dealing with dangerous people. I don't want you to get hurt.'

'I'm already hurt, more than you know, and I did it to myself. Maxwell King isn't capable of inflicting the kind of hurt I'm feeling right now. You don't have to come if you don't want to. Give me the surveillance camera and I'll fix it up myself.'

'Don't be silly. Of course I'll come. It's my job. You're my client, remember, and I think I'm falling in – '

'All I know is Marcus would never sit by while bad things happened to other people,' I interrupted.

I thought of Sid Tulitt working unobtrusively for years around the campsite, seeing more than he would tell, his blistered skin a hint perhaps of the fears and furies buried deep beneath the surface. I was sure he knew of the bullying and abuse of power, the illegal working practices, the drugs and corruption at the heart of the holiday camp, but he'd kept his mouth shut. I didn't think he was a criminal, but he was culpable nevertheless. I'd been led astray and done things that had terrible consequences. But it would be worse to know of a powerful evil and refuse to take action, doing nothing when there was something to be done.

Chapter 23

It was my first day off since starting work at Fun World. The previous two mornings I'd dragged myself into work, blotting out the horror as best I could. On the third morning, I lay shivering under the duvet at ten-past six, longing to fall into the oblivion of sleep but fearing the dreams that would haunt me: dreams of lush foliage crumbling to ash. Visions of butterflies soaring to a glass ceiling, trailing smoke, their wings alight, their screams slicing my heart like a knife.

This was the day I would make amends as best I could. The past could not be altered, the future was a desolate expanse of emptiness, but today I would do something to change a small corner of England for the better. I would speak truth to power. I would send a message that the likes of Maxwell King, Delia Ozzles and Chucky Skittles could no longer crush the weak in order to feed the appetites of the strong. It was what Marcus would have wanted. Hopefully Colin Hildreth would be toppled when the house of cards came tumbling down. Although Theo would probably never find out, it was my way of apologising and thanking him for all the love he'd shown me in the past.

Zavier was snoring. I let him sleep, remembering the words he'd spoken in the laundrette. *What are you going to do when this is over?* I could stay with him for a while and try to find another job. But would that be fair? I would be grieving for Marcus for the rest of my life. I didn't know if I'd ever be able to have feelings for anyone else. I hardly knew Zavier. We'd somehow skipped the 'getting to know you' stage of the relationship. After everything we'd been through, I couldn't imagine going out on a date to the cinema or a restaurant, worrying about what I should wear, the nervous anticipation of his kiss. He'd seen me first thing in the morning with no make-up, my eyes swollen with tears, wearing his old tracksuit. There were no illusions. We'd faced death together. We were bound by dark secrets. How to return to the innocence of a first romance?

In any case, how could I continue to live in Westhatch when the crumbling carcass of the dome stared accusingly at me every time I gazed at the Downs? Perhaps my future lay in the direction of the sea. I could travel, as many my age did. Escape to another country. Adopt a different language that had no words to express the beautiful life I had lost.

Zavier rolled over and opened his eyes. Two clear, silver disks met mine.

'Second thoughts?'

'I'll put the water on to boil,' I replied.

We ate a meagre breakfast of stale bread and coffee. He pricked his thumb to check his blood-sugar levels before injecting insulin into his arm.

'I thought you said it was difficult to inject in the arm.'

'It is. But I don't have enough fat on my stomach or thighs to ease the sting. Look! Washboard or what?' He lifted his sweatshirt and displayed an impressively tight stomach. 'I rotate injection sites to give my skin a break. Are you blushing? No need to be embarrassed. I know I'm hot!' he teased.

'I'm not embarrassed. I'm a red-head, remember. Blushing is an occupational hazard. I blush at an undressed salad.'

We shrugged into our clothes with our backs to each other and in silence. I stuffed my wayward curls under the blonde wig and applied a dusting of powder and a smudge of lipstick. Mrs Ozzles would be proud of me, I thought, as I examined my face in my compact mirror.

Impatient to leave the campsite before too many campers were up and about, we scrambled through the hedge and back to the car, Zavier carrying with him a small bag of gadgets. We'd agreed to meet his old school friend on the Promenade at 10.30. We were much too early.

Adrenalin crackled and fizzed through my veins. I couldn't sit in the car and wait. Jumping out, I ran down to the beach and hobbled across the larger stones, my ankles turning in my black boots until I reached the damp shingle near the surf. I flung a pebble into the heaving water and watched the ripples circling outwards, competing with the onward rush of the waves. I picked up a flat grey stone and swung my arm to the side and back, before flicking my wrist forward and propelling the missile towards the sea, hoping it would defy gravity and bounce on the water. But there was no skipping on the surface of life any more. I was no longer a gravity-defying pebble, eluding the deep waters. My charmed life was over. The stone sank to the bottom, leaving behind a ripple of reckless circles on the dark expanse.

I sat on the shingle with my back against a windbreak, while Zavier went to meet his friend. We decided it would be better if I kept a low profile. We weren't sure whether he would have heard the story of a runaway daughter. Journalists have a nose for a scoop and I didn't want him to recognise me.

The sea breeze scoured my face and whipped back my yellow nylon hair. I reached into my jacket pocket and pulled out my woolly scarf. I draped it over the wig and tied it under my chin to stop it blowing away.

'You look like my gran,' Zavier said when he returned. 'And I mean that in the nicest possible way.'

'I feel old enough.'

'Or perhaps like a little girl dressing up in her mother's clothes.'

'I would have liked to have done that.'

'Sorry. I forgot.' He sat down beside me.

'As a child I had this idea of my mother. She was never a real person, just a gap into which I threw all my longings and all my mistakes. If only she'd been there for me, I would have survived school. She would have shown me how to tame my hair. She would have placed a sticking plaster on my pain, smoothed my edges. I was the poor little girl with no mum. Old ladies would give me sweets and sigh and pat me on the head. It excused my hotheadedness. I could get away with things that other girls couldn't because people felt sorry for me.'

Zavier squeezed my hand. I didn't pull away.

'I put on this mask. A victim, I suppose. Someone with a chip on their shoulder. Someone who deserved more. I missed my mother's love more than I enjoyed the love I had. Her love was unknown and therefore unmeasurable. It could be as vast and as perfect as my imagination could make it. She would have loved me because she'd given birth to me and because I carried her genes. But Theo loved me for no other reason than that he chose to and carried on choosing to. Hopefully today I'll get the chance to do something for him and Marcus. Get some kind of justice. Do something to help those people at Fun World who really *are* victims.'

'I forgot to say,' Zavier cut in, 'when I was rummaging round the holiday camp intranet yesterday, I discovered Colin Hildreth is actually a non-executive director of Fun World. If we can disgrace him, he'll lose a lot of his friends and influence down here, and perhaps it will have repercussions for his work in London. If enough mud sticks, we could even think about telling the police he was responsible for the fire at Greenacres.'

'Fingers crossed.'

He rummaged in his pocket. 'I bought this for you.' He held in his palm a large yellow smiley face badge.

'Really, you shouldn't,' I said drily.

'I thought girls liked jewellery.'

'They do. So what's this?'

'A little token. It made me think of you. You make me smile. You brighten up my day. You're a little ray of sunshine.'

'Per-lease!' I retorted, rolling my eyes to cover the blush that burned my cheeks. But I couldn't conceal the shy smile that hovered at the corner of my mouth.

'Wear it for me, Ava.'

Before I could object he grabbed my lapel and stuck the pin through the thick material of my coat.

'Thanks.' I stroked the little badge with shaking fingers, intensely aware that he was sitting too close, but unable to move away.

A distant throb of music rose up from the direction of the funfair.

'Listen. It's open now,' I said, changing the subject. 'Tickets are half price from eleven until four. It will be fairly quiet. Most people prefer to come at night when the lights are on.'

'When the dirt and tat is hidden.' He stood and pulled me up, not letting go of my hand.

'They don't see it like that. They think its dreamland. Why else would they keep coming?'

When we arrived at the fairground, Zavier pointed out the journalist, a young fresh-faced junior who looked like he should be editing the school magazine. He mooched about among the tourists, eating a hot dog and trying to look inconspicuous. Zavier said the reporter knew what Maxwell King looked like and was on the alert to take photographs of everyone he talked to from the minute he arrived.

I was relieved to see that the man selling tickets for the Ghost Train was not the emaciated operative of the previous day. Looking geeky in his infrared glasses, Zavier hid the surveillance camera under my scarf which was folded on his lap, as the ticket man locked us into the carriage. The minute device was mounted on a spring-loaded clip, ready to be attached to the wooden strut in the split second before the skeleton appeared. To buy more time, I would need to keep Mr Bones' attention firmly fixed on me and away from Zavier's nimble fingers, encased in black gloves to blend with the darkness of the chamber. He'd covered the camera's small green on-light with a blob of chewing gum.

We knew the route by heart. Cobwebs, bats, prisoners, rats, monsters, skeleton. I was shaking so hard by the time we thumped through the heavy curtain that it was no effort at all to release a blood-curdling screech as soon as Mr Bones jumped out of the cupboard. The strength of my reaction was a surprise to me, and seemed to startle the skeleton himself for he hesitated before reaching towards us with his bony fingers. In seconds it was over and we were thrust back into the grey light of a February morning. I laughed, hysterical with relief, as we clambered out of the carriage.

'Did you do it?' I whispered.

'Yes.' He slung his arm around my shoulders and gave me a squeeze. 'I'll activate it remotely once we see your boss.'

I nodded. Then I spotted them. Arm-in-arm and lingering by the shooting gallery, a bronzed man with steel-grey hair and teeth that outperformed his face, and a squat woman bundled up in a camel-coloured coat, suede boots and an enormous furry hat. Mrs Ozzles looked like a cross between a butterscotch toffee and the Russian mafia. I nudged Zavier.

'Look!'

They were too early. The deal was scheduled for midday. And why had Maxwell King brought the Fun World housekeeper with him? I watched from the shadow of the Ferris wheel as they spoke to the employee at the shooting range. It appeared they knew him well.

Zavier signalled to his friend and gestured in their direction. The journalist immediately raised his camera and snapped a photograph.

After several minutes they shook hands with the ticket man and sauntered over to a fortune-telling booth. *I know your future,* I thought angrily. *A tall dark stranger is going to handcuff you and lock you away for a very long time… I hope!*

'What do we do? I can't let Mrs Ozzles see me.'

'She won't recognise you in that wig.'

'But she might recognise you as the probate man.'

'That's true.' He pulled me behind a group of Chinese tourists eating candyfloss. 'It looks as though they're pretty well-known around here.'

'Why has he brought her? You don't think they're an item, do you?'

'Not if physical appearances are anything to go by.'

Maxwell King threw back his head and laughed with the fortune-teller, before waving his hand and moving on like royalty working a crowd. He steered Mrs Ozzles towards the Ghost Train.

'This is it.'

From the corner of my eye, Zavier's friend moved too, casually traipsing past the fortune-teller and snapping the couple as they squeezed into a carriage.

'You've got to be joking!' I muttered. 'Talk about cosying up to the boss!' Then I realised. 'They don't have a bag! How are they going to swap cash for drugs if they don't have identical bags to switch?'

'They may have a different system. Maybe they've already paid. Maybe this is just a pick-up.' He reached into his pocket, pulled out a remote control and pressed the switch. 'Activated! Now we just have to wait and see.'

In a matter of minutes they were through the ride and out the other side. They clambered out of the seat, Maxwell helping Mrs Ozzles up by the arm and escorting her to the coffee concession, followed by the journalist.

'There's no bag!' I cried. 'Why did they go on the ride if not to pick up the gear?'

'You stay here, Ava. I can retrieve the camera on my own. I can probably grab it before Mr Bones bounces out of his cupboard. You made such a big impression on him with your scream earlier that he might get suspicious if he sees you again. I don't think he even noticed me.'

Unexpectedly, he grabbed me by the collar of my coat and pulled me towards him, kissing me swiftly on the cheek before darting away.

There were only a couple of teenagers ahead of Zavier in the queue. He shifted from foot to foot, rubbing his hands together to keep warm. He climbed on the ride and disappeared through the swing-doors. I looked down at the yellow badge and stroked the shiny surface. Like a miniature sun, its cheeky grin spread a glow of warmth throughout my body. I smiled too.

I checked my watch. One minute. Two minutes. Three minutes. A mother and her young son climbed into an empty carriage, waiting until Zavier's car came crashing through the doors behind them to begin their ghostly journey. The doors opened and swung shut with a bang. Zavier's carriage was empty.

Chapter 24

I didn't know what to do. Should I wait? Should I ask the ticket man what happened? Should I go on the ride? But then I might disappear myself. Had Zavier done something stupid, or had Mr King and Mrs Ozzles somehow become aware of our plan? Impossible! We'd told no one else except the journalist, and Zavier only told him to take pictures of Maxwell King, promising there was a potential scoop that would be explained later. Nothing was said about drugs, the Ghost Train or Mr Bones.

I walked round to the back of ride. It was a prefabricated shed with only one door at the rear marked 'Private. Strictly No Admittance'. In desperation I pulled out my phone and sent Zavier a text.

'Where are you?'

No reply.

I hurried back to the front of the ride. Everything appeared normal. Nervous and excited children were going through the swing-doors, flushed and giggling children clattered out the other side. I peeped round the corner to the coffee kiosk. There was no sign of the journalist. Feeling sick, I sank down on a bench. I would give Zavier five more minutes. After that I would take another ride on the Ghost Train myself.

As twilight fell, I knew it was hopeless. I'd spent the afternoon searching every inch of the funfair, even trespassing in the men's toilets and the kitchens at the burger joint. I'd ridden the Ghost

Train until I'd used up all my money, convinced Zavier was hidden in a dark recess somewhere inside.

The crowds swelled as the sun sank below the horizon, nocturnal hunters stalking cheap thrills and fish and chips. Desperate to find Zavier's tousled head and cool grey eyes, I scanned the heaving mass. Disembodied faces reflected the red, green and blue of the neon lights that flashed with the riotous music. Exhausted and hungry, dizzy with the shouts and laughter all around me, I pushed through throngs of jostling bodies, sometimes catching a glimpse of a familiar expression or voice, only to be disappointed. The ghosts of my past were haunting me that evening. A tall man with a coat like Theo's. A bearded figure disappearing round a corner, only to materialise into a stranger when I ran to catch up. I've learned since this is a symptom of grief: the visions, echoes and scents of those who have died or are lost to us linger long after they're gone, appearing in unexpected places.

Then the doubts came, slippery as serpents. Had he abandoned me, crept away with his journalist friend to laugh at the gullible fantasist who believed the town's most respected citizen was a drug dealer? Had we been on a wild-goose chase all along? I dragged my frozen feet along the Promenade. There was nowhere to go except back to the derelict caravan. Maybe Zavier was there, wrapped up in his sleeping bag and listening to the radio.

Looking both ways before crossing the road to the car, I noticed a white van exiting the fair's trade entrance. It turned right, the direction I would be taking once back in my own vehicle. The logo on the back of the van was familiar, and so too was the face of the driver. Trafford!

I raced across the road to my wreck of a car. What had he been doing? What were the chances he would be at the fairground on the same day as Maxwell King and Mrs Ozzles, Zavier and myself? Surely it couldn't be a coincidence.

The engine protested as I floored the accelerator and sped along the seafront back to Fun World. A light blinked on the dashboard; a smell of hot metal permeated the interior. The van was several cars ahead when it turned into the holiday resort. I slowed down to let Trafford swipe his card, and watched as the barrier lifted. Waiting impatiently until he turned left into the staff car park, I edged my protesting vehicle to the barrier and inserted my staff card. Nothing. I swiped it again, glancing anxiously at the guard in the kiosk.

'It doesn't seem to be working. I've had it next to my mobile phone. Could that have damaged the magnetic strip?'

I didn't think for one minute the card was faulty. Someone had discovered I knew more than I should about Maxwell King's business deals. My card had been cancelled. I'd been expelled from the Fun World family. I prayed the news hadn't yet been communicated to the rest of the staff, banking on the unthinking indolence of the man on car park duty,

The security guard opened the window and leaned out.

'Caravan number?'

'I'm not a guest. I work here. You remember me, don't you? It's Claire.' It was then I realised I was still wearing the blonde wig.

'Bit late, isn't it?'

'I've been called in to clean up a mess in the swimming pool changing rooms. A kid's been sick everywhere.'

He grunted and raised the barrier.

I cringed as the car rattled up North Drive, turning the heads of holidaymakers strolling down to the entertainment centre. So much for being inconspicuous! I dumped it as soon as I could in front of the empty caravan near the launderette and sprinted round to the staff car park. The van was parked in a dark corner, near to the door to the security and administration offices. Although terrified of coming face-to-face with Trafford, I had to check whether Zavier was in the back of the van.

Stomach flipping like a fish in a net, I crept closer, tripping a motion sensor to the security lamp and flooding the car park with harsh white light. I ducked behind an industrial-sized rubbish bin, panting with anxiety. A wide expanse of concrete stretched from the bin to the van. I dithered in the shadows like a mouse about to plunge across an open field, fearing the hawk yet desperate to reach the bale of straw. A vision of Zavier lying unconscious flashed before my eyes.

A quick dash and I crouched beside a back tyre. Creeping closer I checked the front seats were empty before gently trying the doors. As expected, they were locked. I tapped on the side of the van hoping to hear movement, a grunt, perhaps Zavier's voice. The silence was as loud as my beating heart. I jumped up to squint through the small windows at the rear. The tinted glass was impenetrable, but as I landed I noticed a dark splash on the silver bumper. I touched it warily; the wet mark stained my finger red. Blood! I scanned the ground and noticed a trail of small splashes leading to the 'Staff Only' door.

I'd come this far. If it was Zavier's blood, I couldn't abandon him to Trafford's ignorant brutality. I remembered the Romanians who'd suddenly disappeared, leaving their clothes and half-eaten food in the caravan as if expecting to return. I'd lost everything already. No family, no home, no job, no money. Zavier was my only friend. I turned the knob and pushed open the door.

I recognised the corridor. It ran between reception and Maxwell King's office. The office staff had gone home half an hour ago, and a heavy silence had descended upon the windowless passage. There was no sign of blood on the carpet. I pulled back my shoulders and strode towards the chief executive's office, reasoning I was less likely to be challenged if I looked as though I had every right to be there. I hesitated at the door, leaning towards the polished wood, alert for every sound.

Muffled voices, one low, the other higher-pitched, were conversing on the other side. Surmising they belonged to Maxwell King and Mrs Ozzles, I strained to catch their words or the presence of another voice which might belong to Zavier, but it was impossible to hear what they were saying. I didn't have a plan, but I knew it would be madness to enter and madness to continue standing outside, exposed and defenceless.

A hefty hand grabbed my shoulder and swung me round. Trafford's massive face was thrust in mine, his breath stinking of cigarettes and garlic. A frightened squeak slipped from my mouth as he turned the handle and shoved me through the chief executive's door. I stumbled forward.

'Caught this little girlie listening at your door.' Trafford held my arms fast from behind, his breath hot on my neck.

Mr King was sitting at his desk with Mrs Ozzles standing by his side. Seated on the black leather settee was Colin Hildreth.

'Miss Hewitt! We've been expecting you. We haven't been formally introduced. I'm Maxwell King. This is one of our directors, Dr Hildreth. Mrs Ozzles you know.'

The politeness of his words belied their grim delivery. Anger simmered behind his smile like a lid rattling on a boiling saucepan. I glanced at my godfather, who didn't seem to want to acknowledge our relationship. I couldn't think of anything to say, so I said nothing.

'I'm very disappointed, Claire. I gave you an opportunity, and this is how you repay me.'

'I'm sorry, Mrs Ozzles.'

'I warned you about poking your nose in other people's business, didn't I?'

'Yes, but… I don't know anything,' I gabbled.

'Why are you here?' Mr King barked. 'You're not really a cleaner. Are you with the police?'

'No, no… of course not.'

'One of my competitors, then? A journalist?'

'No!'

'Why were you listening at the door just now?'

'I was looking for my friend. I thought he might be here.'

'Stop this nonsense now!' Mrs Ozzles ordered. 'We know you've been spying on us.'

She reached past her boss and opened the top drawer of his desk.

'Mr King found this in his executive washroom.' She held up my mother's jade necklace. 'Of course, I recognised it as belonging to you straight away. I believe you were listening to Mr King's telephone calls.'

The chief executive stood up and walked round to my side of the desk.

'I deferred the meeting with my suppliers until tomorrow,' he enunciated deliberately. 'At... great... personal... inconvenience.'

Unable to meet his stony glare, I looked down at the floor.

'But I was curious to find out why one of my cleaning staff was interested in my private business. Delia kindly agreed to accompany me today. After all, I didn't have a clue who you were or what you looked like.'

'I didn't recognise you at first.' Mrs Ozzles gestured to my wig. 'But I was right about going blonde. It suits you. You had such potential. It's a pity no one else is going to appreciate your new look.'

I ignored the veiled threat, and pulled against Trafford's grip. 'Where's Zavier?'

Mrs Ozzles clicked her tongue.

'I think you should be worrying about yourself, Claire, not some yob from the seedier side of town. If I'd known you had an appetite for young men, I'd have taken you off cleaning duties days ago and given you something more financially rewarding to be getting along with.'

'You're disgusting. This whole place is a pack of lies. So much for the perfect family holiday. It's all a front for your criminal activities. I have evidence,' I bluffed. 'If you don't let us go, this place will be crawling with police.'

'Is this what you're talking about?' Mr King took a small device out of his jacket pocket. I recognised the spring-loaded clamp. 'Your friend made rather a hash of retrieving it, I'm afraid.' He dropped it on the floor and crushed it under a gleaming black shoe. 'Tell me who you're working for.'

'I'm not working for anyone.' I lifted my chin in a gesture of defiance. 'I wanted to find a relative who used to be an employee. I thought perhaps someone here might remember them.'

'If that's all, why not ask?' Mrs Ozzles paced across the office. 'I think I'm beginning to understand. I thought I recognised your friend tonight. He was wearing a suit. His hair was slicked down.' She turned to her boss. 'A few weeks ago I had a visit from a probate investigator. He was trying to find relatives of an ex-employee. I should have seen the link. Hewitt. It's a common name. He wanted to find relatives of a Sandra Hewitt. She used to work here about eighteen years ago.'

'Why didn't you tell me this?' Maxwell snapped.

'It was a routine personnel issue.'

'Twenty,' I corrected. 'She worked here twenty years ago.'

'She was a cleaner. Got herself knocked up. One day she just upped and left,' Mrs Ozzles said.

'Was she one of your special girls?'

'I had my eye on her. She didn't have any family. That's why I gave her a cleaning job in the first place, but she told me she had a boyfriend. I was waiting for her heart to get broken. In time, perhaps she would have blossomed. When she fell pregnant we offered her money for a termination. She told me where to stick it and the next day she was gone. It happened years ago. A few months later she died. I went to the funeral, not because I cared particularly, but because in the meantime she'd married Theodore Gage.'

'The Greenacres guy?' Mr King asked.

'Yes. I'm not sure how a nobody like her ended up marrying such an influential man. I certainly underestimated her. I wanted to check she hadn't been a security risk, but Mr Gage didn't seem to know anything about her life at Fun World. The matter was closed. Until now.'

They both looked at me.

'She was my mother. I wanted to find out about her. She died when I was a few months old. I was hoping if I worked here as a cleaner – like her – I would feel closer to her.'

'You'll be feeling very close to her in a minute,' Maxwell King threatened.

'Perhaps I might say something at this point,' Colin drawled.

'I'm sorry you've had to see this... what shall we call it? Staff appraisal?' Maxwell said. 'I know you don't like getting involved with the nitty-gritty of the business.'

'I think I should declare a conflict of interest, Max.' Colin turned to me. 'I've been worrying about you, poppet. I'm glad to see you're all right. So this is the little job in tourism you mentioned.'

'You know each other?' Mrs Ozzles snapped.

'I'm her godfather. Her real name is Ava-Claire Gage.'

'Of course,' Maxwell murmured. 'I knew you had some kind of association with Theo Gage. You went to university together, right?'

'Yes. We used to come down here during the university holidays. He wanted to study the wildlife. Coastal flora and fauna, that sort of tosh.' He fixed his eyes on my face and addressed me directly. 'I worked at Fun World as a Pink Jacket. I fancied myself as something of a magician in those days. Sleight of hand, smoke and mirrors. You know the kind of thing. Of course, that was well before your mother's time, but it's when I met Max here, another Pink Jacket. Very ambitious. I knew straight away he was the kind of chap I could do business with. After graduation I landed myself a pretty plum job and decided to invest in an enterprising young man.'

The two men nodded at each other.

'He's a scumbag!'

'He's an entrepreneur. He knows what people want and is willing to get it for them. You can be sure he recognises an opportunity when he sees it. I like to foster talent. In that way, I'm not so different from Theo.'

'You're nothing like Theo,' I spat. 'Do you know what he's up to? Drugs, prostitution... who knows what else!'

'The day-to-day business is Max's affair. I gave him the leg-up he needed. He took over an old-fashioned, loss-making, kiss-me-quick holiday camp and turned it into a real money-spinner for himself... and for me. I spotted your mother when I came down for a Board meeting. Pretty little thing, even in her cleaner's uniform. She always wanted to be a Pink Jacket... shame, really. It's when you want something too much that you make bad decisions. You running away, for instance. I've been searching for you ever since you disappeared – '

'I wanted to find my real father,' I interrupted.

'– but I didn't come here tonight to look for you in the first instance. Max wanted us to meet up because he had a problem with an important deal. A member of staff was snooping about. He told me he'd found an item of jewellery in his executive washroom. That's when I put two and two together. He was referring to you. You see, I gave that particular necklace to your mother twenty years ago.'

There was a long silence. He gave a rueful shrug.

'*You're* my father!'

'Ker-ching.'

'But... but... '

'Why didn't I say anything? Let's say I was happy to remain in the background. I didn't have the time or inclination to babysit. I knew Theo would be a good parent. I have to admit I enjoyed watching you grow up more than I thought I would, knowing Theo was lavishing his love and money on *my* child, knowing my genes and not his would one day inherit the fruit of his labours. It's ironic, isn't it? You've been off on some wild-goose chase in search for your father, and I was right under your nose all the time.'

I remembered the photo of Mum at the funfair. The white of her dress and the blue of the sky. The Ferris wheel in the background and the clean-shaven man at her side. If his dark hair had thinned and turned to grey, and if he had grown a beard and removed his sunglasses, could it be Colin Hildreth? I knew with a lurch of my heart that it was. 'Does Theo know?'

'I don't think anyone really knows what he's thinking or what he knows. As far as he's concerned, he became your father the moment he saw you on the ultrasound. You were what he wanted,' an edge crept into his usually smooth voice, 'and what Theo wants is all that matters.'

'But you and my mother –'

'Aahh, yes. The delectable Sandy. After we graduated, I probably would have lost touch with Theo. But Sandy was my favourite seaside attraction. A puff of pink candyfloss. I became a regular weekend visitor to Westhatch, keeping an eye on my investments here and watching as Theo built up a pretty impressive business of his own. She found out she was pregnant at about the same time she found out about… How shall I say it? … the less salubrious side of my business interests. She bolted before I had a chance to smooth things over.'

'You should have told me you were involved with one of my girls,' Mrs Ozzles complained.

'You would have charged me,' he joked.

'Yes, she would,' Max said, 'if she'd caught you dipping your hand in the honey jar.'

'Did you love her?' I demanded, holding my breath, not wanting to hear the answer but pushing on anyway.

'In my own way. She had scruples. I liked that. It was so much fun thinking of ways to overcome them.'

'I wish I was an orphan!' I spat.

'Don't be like that.' He spoke in an even tone as though I hadn't just wished him dead. 'We're so much alike, and we have so much to catch up on.'

'What are we going to do with her?' Mrs Ozzles asked.

'She's my problem. You can leave the matter with me,' Colin replied. 'I've been planning on leaving the country for a long holiday, in any case. I'll take Ava-Claire with me. I'll make sure there are no repercussions.'

'I'm not going anywhere with you. I hate you!'

'You won't have a choice, I'm afraid. If you'll excuse me, Max, I have to make the necessary arrangements. I have a private jet standing by already, but if you could babysit Ava for a couple of hours, I'd be most grateful... Listen to me! I've only been a father for five minutes and I'm already arranging child care.' He took his mobile out of his breast pocket, chuckling at his joke and scrolling through his contacts as he left the room.

Maxwell King waved a dismissive hand in my direction. 'Take her down to the basement, Trafford. Make sure you confiscate her phone.'

The security guard thrust his hand into my pocket and pulled out my mobile. I slapped at his face, catching him under the jaw. He twisted my arm viciously behind my back and shoved me towards the door. I screamed as a jolting pain shot from my shoulder to my elbow. Unable to catch my breath let alone struggle because of the agony of my arm, I whimpered as he half-pushed, half-dragged me out of the office. As I was leaving, I caught the final words whispered between the chief executive and the housekeeper.

'Jumper's Mount... properly weighed down... Deep-clean the van afterwards.'

Stars danced before my eyes. I fought against the darkness that threatened to smother me, hardly registering where I was being taken. Pounding music echoed the pounding in my arm, a whirl of coloured lights flashed behind my closed eyelids. I heard Chucky Skittles laughing into his microphone.

'And that's why the elephant touched his toes. Bah boom!'

Suddenly the air cooled. We were backstage. Holding my good arm, Trafford propelled me down the stairs to the basement. My right arm hung at my side, sickeningly limp. He unlocked the store room and threw me in.

'If you make a noise, I'll hear you and give you a slapping!' He slammed and locked the door.

Enveloped in darkness as black as tar, I groped for the light switch on the wall, stumbling against a stack of boxes. I flicked the button and blinked. Zavier lay on his side, his arms and legs

304

tied together, a strip of duct tape across his mouth. I knelt with difficulty and touched his cheek. His eyes flickered open.

'Are you all right?' I whispered.

He grunted. I ripped the tape from his mouth.

'Ouch!'

I put a finger to my lips.

'That hurt,' he mumbled.

'You've obviously never had your legs waxed. Now be quiet.'

'My hands,' he gasped, rolling onto his stomach so I could untie them.

I grappled with the knot for some minutes. My right arm was useless. The throbbing pain had worsened and it was unable to bear any pressure.

'Déjà vu or what? We've been here before,' I said drily. 'You on the ground. Me trying to get you to stand up.'

'Somehow I can't help feeling our roles should be reversed. Whatever happened to the hero rescuing the heroine?'

'He read an equal opportunities manual.'

'Nope. Doesn't sound like me.'

'Anyway, I'm no heroine. No one can rescue me now. I'm too lost.'

'Ditch the self-pity and hurry up! If you're going to save me you need to get a move on.'

'I'm trying.' I knelt with my face close to the floor and anchored one end of the nylon rope with my teeth.

'What *are* you doing?' he complained.

'I think my arm's broken.'

He was silent for a moment before growling, 'I'm going to kill the person responsible!'

'No, you're not. There. It's loose.'

He shook himself free and sat up, rubbing his arms and hands.

'Pins and needles.' He untied his feet, then knelt next to me and took my arm gently in his hands.

'Does this hurt?'

'Don't!' Nausea rolled through my body in a dizzying wave.

'Sorry.'

'Just don't touch it. I might be sick.' I cradled my arm across my chest. 'Tell me what happened in the Ghost Train.'

We sat down against the far wall.

'Mr Bones jumped on me before I had a chance to retrieve the camera. I must have been on the ride too many times. A big bloke tied me up and shoved me in some kind of storage space under the ride. After a while a security guard threw me in a van. I can't remember much more. I've been a bit out of it. How did they get you?'

'I saw Trafford – that's the knucklehead of a security guard – driving out of the fairground in a Fun World van. It seemed a bit of a coincidence. I followed him back here. There was blood on his bumper.'

Zavier touched the back of his head gingerly.

'He caught me eavesdropping outside Maxwell King's office. I was trying to find out where you were.'

'They took my phone.'

'Mine too. They were expecting us at the Ghost Train today.'

'*What?* Stop shushing me, woman. They won't hear us over the music.'

The reverberating beat of Harry Hot Dog's signature party dance throbbed through the building. Whether Trafford was outside or not, no one was going to hear our cries for help.

'But we didn't tell anyone.'

I couldn't stop the blush that surged to my cheeks.

'I accidentally left my necklace in Mr King's toilet the night I overheard him planning the drugs pick-up. Mrs Ozzles recognised it. They knew I'd been listening. They were looking for me today, but didn't recognise me in this wig. Mr Bones would have been on the alert for anything suspicious. I guess that's how he rumbled you. It's all my fault.'

'What about the transaction?'

'They'd already cancelled it. It's going ahead tomorrow.'

He swore under his breath.

'That means there was nothing on the camera anyway. It was all a waste of time.'

'They found the camera. It's smashed. I'm sorry for getting you involved, Zavier.'

He shrugged. 'I had a choice. You didn't force me.'

'Why, oh why, did you get involved?' I sobbed. He put his arm gently around my shoulder. 'I'm just trouble, from beginning to end.'

'Why? Well, firstly, you're the best paying customer I've had this year. Secondly, working for you has been much more exciting than finding lost cats and teddy bears. Thirdly, you've given me a reason to stop slobbing around and get out of bed in the morning. Fourthly, you do an excellent job of scraping me off the floor, and last but not least, you have the prettiest green eyes –'

I bumped my side gently against his in a mock rebuff. Even such a small movement jarred my arm. I swallowed back the pain, not wanting him to notice and pull away. Despite the circumstances, I felt safe in his arms.

'Give over, curlytops! I've collected enough bruises these last few weeks to last a lifetime. Speaking of which, I wonder what they're going to do with us.'

I kept my tone level and matter-of-fact.

'When the holidaymakers are safely tucked up in their caravans, they're going to drive you to Jumper's Mount and push you off.'

'Are they indeed! And what about you?'

'I'm going on holiday with Colin Hildreth. It turns out he's my biological father.'

'I'm not sure which is worse.'

Despite his flippant tone, Zavier was very pale. I wondered when he'd last eaten.

'Are you all right?' I rummaged in my money belt and pulled out a toffee.

'I don't think that's going to solve anything. As it stands, it might be a relief to lapse into a diabetic coma.'

I put my hand back in my money belt, a smile slowly spreading across my face.

'What about this, then?'

I pulled out a small bunch of keys. It was Boody's duplicate set lent to me so I could take a shower in Mr King's washroom, and which I'd forgotten to return.

Zavier grabbed my face between his two hands and kissed me firmly on the lips.

'I don't know why you need me around, Ava-Claire Gage. You have all the right cards up your sleeve – '

' – and all the right keys on my person. I forgot I still had them. Do you think it's safe to go now?'

Zavier stood up and pressed his ear against the door.

'I think someone's coming!'

He sat down immediately and put his arms behind his back as though they were still tied up. I shoved the bunch of keys into his hand where they wouldn't be seen and kicked the ropes and duct tape behind a pile of boxes. Before I had the chance to sit down next to Zavier, Colin Hildreth walked in followed by Skink, who locked the door behind them and stood in front of it, arms folded across his black leather coat.

'Let us out, Uncle Colin. Please. They're going to hurt Zavier.'

'The boy's not my concern.'

'They're going to throw him off Jumper's Mount.'

'What happened to your arm?'

'I think it's broken. Trafford – '

'I gave strict instructions that you should not be harmed.' Colin turned to Skink. 'When we're finished here, I'd like you to teach that idiot a lesson in obedience.' His eyes were as cold as flint.

'If you care about me so much, please stop them hurting my friend. I'm your daughter.'

'Yes. And you seem to be as fickle as your mother. A moment ago you hated me. Now you want something from me, it's a different story.'

'What did you expect? You've stolen Theo's research and destroyed Greenacres. You're in cahoots with a bunch of criminals. You treated my mother badly. You never told me you're my father. But if you let us go, perhaps we can start again…'

'I didn't treat your mother badly. I was busy building my career in London, only able to visit Fun World every couple of weeks. I sent her money. I would have looked after you both. But she upped and left. Theo had just finished constructing the dome with the profits from his early scientific discoveries. He was probably looking for a new project. An unmarried mother would have been irresistible. He's always looking for a lost cause.' He paced back and forth across the small space, hands behind his back.

'It was some time before I discovered where she was. I used to look in on Theo on my way down to Fun World for Board meetings. You can imagine the shock when I turned up one day to discover the new Mrs Gage was Sandy. By then you'd arrived on the scene. It must have been a whirlwind romance. Not very flattering, really. I must admit, I was a little hurt. But she was as desperate as I was that Theo shouldn't find out.'

'Then why are you my godfather?'

'I insisted. It was the price of my silence. Sandy didn't like it, but what could she do?'

'I'm surprised Theo allowed it.'

'Why not? I was his oldest friend. One of the few people he could talk to about his research.'

'Tapping his brain for any new and brilliant idea that might further your own career,' I snapped.

'So young, and yet so cynical. A chip off the old block.'

I clamped my mouth shut, too angry to speak, overwhelmed by the amount of new information I had to process.

'Unfortunately for the boy, I don't like loose ends. Keeping things ship-shape is one of my special gifts. Mess from the past catches up with us, Ava. It always does. It happened to your mother. She thought she'd been given a new start. Then I turn up like a bad penny. At first she believed, like me, that it was in neither of our interests for her new husband to know I was your father. But a few months at Greenacres stiffened her backbone. She telephoned to say she was going to tell Theo everything, including my business activities. It was with some sadness I had to let her go.'

'Let her go?'

'Yes. But I can assure you it was quite painless. She agreed to see me secretly at the farmhouse. I told her I was going to resign as a director of Fun World. I think she thought she could rehabilitate me, somehow sort out the whole debacle and get back to her fairy-tale ending. Some sleeping tablets in her coffee. Her own diabetic medication. A little prick and the note she left me when she ran away. And *voila*! Another kind of ending entirely.'

'No, no, no!' I cried, ignoring my throbbing arm and lurching towards him, pummelling his chest with my right fist.

He grabbed my bad elbow and I screamed in pain.

'Don't hurt her!' Zavier yelled.

I shook my head to stop him leaping to my defence and giving away the fact that his hands were free. Skink would be too strong for him. We needed to pick our moment. He understood my signal, though Colin and Skink probably thought I was grimacing in pain.

'She's your flesh and blood. What kind of a man are you?'

'I'm a man who wants everything this life has to offer, and Ava has something I want above everything else right now.'

A flicker of hope. I thought of the small scrap of paper in my boot. Maybe he'd noticed the formula was missing from the file. Perhaps I had a bargaining chip that would alter the balance of power after all.

'What?' I asked.

'Your heart.'

'As if I could ever love you again. Or even stand to see the sight of you –'

'You misunderstand me, my dear. I want your heart… Literally.' He let go of my arm and stood before me with his hand over his chest. 'I'm sure you'll be concerned to learn that I have a congenital heart defect. My doctor tells me the only possible treatment now is a transplant. I've been waiting for the right donor, someone young and healthy who'll be a good tissue match… and I've found her!

'You might remember the small accident we had with the garden shears when I visited Theo before he left for Africa. I dabbed the scratch on your hand with my handkerchief. I've been assured by my specialist that we're perfectly suited. I already have a buyer for Theo's research. My lawyer is in the process of registering the patent. Once we've received confirmation that the paperwork has been completed, the money will be transferred to my bank account, probably by tomorrow. It will pay for our private jet to Dubai and the Russian surgeon who's standing by to prep us both for the op.'

I stared at him, open-mouthed. I couldn't believe what I was hearing.

'I assure you it will hurt me more than it will hurt you.'

'What sort of twisted, parasitic psychopath would do that to their own daughter?' Zavier hissed.

'I gave Ava the gift of life, and now she's returning the favour. Families should pull together in a crisis, don't you think? You've ruined your life in any case, poppet. What do you have to live for now?'

'You're stark raving mad. You can't possibly think you can pull it off!' I cried.

'I think you'll find I can. My contacts in the local police will be happy to say they've discovered your dental remains in the laboratory fire. They're still sifting through the basement ashes for forensics. After all, you won't need your teeth any more after today. I'll send them down with Skink tomorrow. The beauty of you running away is that so many birds have been killed with the one stone. I've obtained the technology to pay for my

311

transplant. That sanctimonious prude up at Greenacres will have his heart broken... and mine will be replaced. Sorted!'

A string of expletives spilled from my mouth.

'Language, Ava. You weren't brought up to be so unladylike. Skink!'

'Sir!'

'I think it's time you took this young man outside to get some fresh air. The van will be less conspicuous now while there's still traffic on the road. It will be dark enough up on the cliffs.'

'Please let him go,' I pleaded. 'Whatever you're going to do to me, he doesn't deserve to die.'

'Unfortunately I can't do that. He's going for a brisk walk on the cliffs followed by a skinny-dip in the sea. Skink assures me there's some kind of rip current that will pull him under and wedge him under the rocks. No evidence.'

'Nice! Sounds like he's done it before.' Despite his flippant tone, Zavier's eyes were as hard as flint.

'I have,' Skink grunted. He took a mobile from his pocket. 'No signal. I'd better check Trafford has got the van parked right next to the fire exit. You all right in here on your own for a couple of minutes, boss?'

'What can a girl with a broken arm and a boy who's tied up do? But lock us in just in case.' He patted his coat pocket. 'I have a firearm.'

He was facing the door as Skink closed and locked it. Behind him, Zavier instantly leapt to his feet. His arm coiled round Colin's neck, yanking his head backwards with a sharp tug. With his other arm, he grappled with the hand that was reaching for the gun.

'Get the keys, Ava!'

They were on the floor where Zavier had been sitting. I fumbled through the bunch. searching for the one that would open the storeroom door. Behind me, grunts and scuffles competed with the constant beat of the music upstairs.

'Hurry up!' Zavier panted.

At any moment I expected to hear the shot of a gun. The seconds it took to find the key were an eternity of clumsiness.

'Got it!'

I shoved the metal in the keyhole and turned to face the struggling men. Colin's face was red, his lips blue. He was gasping for breath, one hand clutching his chest.

'Stop it, Zavier! You're killing him.'

Zavier loosened his headlock and my godfather slumped forward, pulling at his tie. I opened the door a fraction. The dim hall was empty.

'Let's go.'

We darted through the door and I locked it behind us.

'Do you think he's having a heart attack?'

'I'm not hanging around to find out,' Zavier panted. 'Come on. There are still holidaymakers upstairs. They can't touch us in the nightclub where there are witnesses. We need to borrow someone's phone. Call for help.'

We hurried as best we could down the corridor. Zavier took the stairs two at a time, while I staggered after him, holding my arm firmly under the elbow to stop it moving too much. The music was louder than ever. We pushed through the swing-door at the top of the steps and found ourselves backstage. We huddled between some old scenery and the folds of the heavy stage curtains to catch our breath, shielded by darkness and the pounding beat of the music. From the wings, I caught a glimpse of Chucky on the stage; Patty Pizza and Harry Hot Dog, either side of him, were swinging their arms and kicking their legs in time with the music.

'Who should we call?' I whispered 'I don't trust the police. Do you think they're more likely to believe us, or the chief executive of the town's largest employer – one who's happy to give a backhander to keep them quiet? We don't have any evidence, remember. And you've just attacked a member of the Board.'

'What about this?' He tapped the yellow badge on my jacket.

'What about it?'

'I was worried about you. Put it down to an overactive imagination. It's a GPS tracker with a small video recorder inside. I gave it to you in case we became separated.'

My heart sank a little. He hadn't chosen it especially for me. There was no significance to the smiley face. It was just another piece of spy kit!

'The lens is hidden in the eye. I activated it when I went into the Ghost Train, in case you disappeared by the time I came out.'

I remembered how he'd pulled me close by the lapels and kissed me on the cheek.

'You were the one who disappeared,' I sniped.

'Yes. I should have put a GPS tracker on me. Anyway, the video recorder's voice-activated. Did Maxwell King or any of the others say anything incriminating to you?'

'Yes!'

'If the police won't act, then we have something to show a lawyer or the press. They can't hush this up forever. Let's go.'

We crept into the entertainment centre, reassuringly packed with sweating campers following the dance routines on stage. Music thundered through the strobing darkness. The dance floor fizzed with overexcited, overtired children. The tables around the edge were filling with evening-ready women, clutching bingo cards, smoothing down shiny blouses and brushing invisible fluff from their too-tight skirts. I checked my watch. In about ten minutes' time the lights would be up and all eyes would be down for bingo.

I spotted Maxwell King standing by the bar. Mrs Ozzles was perched incongruously on a tall stool next to him sipping a cocktail. Horrified, I nudged Zavier.

'Look!'

He grimaced then nodded towards the exit. I followed the direction of his eyes. Trafford was leaning against the door, arms folded across his chest, eyes staring blankly at the stage. Instinctively, we both stepped back into the shadows.

'What are we going to do?' I whispered in his ear.

'Is there a fire exit?'

'Over there.' I gestured to the wall opposite. To reach it we would have to cross the dance floor or navigate around the entire room.

'We haven't got much time,' I cried. 'The lights will be switched on for bingo in a minute.'

'Maybe that's a good thing. What can they do with everyone watching?'

'We'll be escorted off the premises. It happens all the time. If we struggle they'll just say we're drunk and disorderly, or that we've been pickpocketing or something. Wearing this wig doesn't help our case.' I decided not to mention his battered face and bloodstained hair.

'All right, Countess?' shouted a familiar voice. 'Having a bad hair day?'

I turned to find Boody by my side carrying a half-pint of lager. Of course! It was Thursday. Staff night out.

'Got your bingo ticket?'

I shook my head.

'What's the matter with lover boy?' She jerked her head in Zavier's direction.

'We've had a run-in with Trafford. We're trying to get out of here, but the thick brick is on the door.'

Her features instantly puckered in anxiety.

'Did he find out about the caravan? Fudge nuggets! You won't tell him I showed it to you, will you?'

'Course not. Don't worry.' I glanced at Zavier, wondering how much to tell her. 'We found out Trafford's involved in drugs. We've got proof. But we need to get out of here before he gets his hands on it.'

'Can you stitch him up?'

'Good and proper,' Zavier shouted in her ear. 'But we need to get the evidence to the police.'

'Do you want me to distract him?'

'Could you?'

'Did Adam eat the apple? Hold this.'

She thrust her half-pint glass towards me. Letting go of my damaged arm to take it, I winced as a dart of pain shot through my elbow. The glass fell and smashed to the floor, spraying brown liquid on the occupants of a nearby table. A curvaceous woman with impossibly backcombed hair and brilliant white trousers leapt to her feet, swearing loudly.

'I'm so sorry,' I gabbled.

Zavier stooped to pick up the broken glass. The other women at the table patted the woman's legs with paper napkins.

'That's done it!' Boody exclaimed.

I looked across the room. Despite the darkness, the flashing lights and the mingling bodies, the disturbance had been spotted. Trafford was standing stiff and straight as an effigy, his stony eyes boring into mine. He reached for the radio on his belt. Without taking his eyes off the kerfuffle around us, he spoke into the handset.

I pulled Zavier up from the floor.

'We've got to go... Now!'

He shoved a handful of shattered glass on the table. The group of women screeched and gesticulated at him as we retreated to the corner by the stage door, their words lost in the beat of the music.

If we went back down the stairs we'd be trapped in the basement. The dance floor was blocked by hordes of children jumping up and down to a hip-hop rhythm as Harry Hot Dog shuffled onto the stage. My eyes darted desperately around the nightclub. Trafford had been joined by Big Ron. After a brief discussion, Ron hurried over to Mr King, and pointed in our direction.

'Fishsticks! The big boss is here. What have you two done?' Boody cried.

More dark uniforms appeared at the exit. Suddenly security staff were everywhere. Ron was moving towards the fire exit.

'It's no use,' I sobbed to Zavier. 'There's no way out.'

He squeezed my hand. I turned to Boody.

'You better disappear. There's no point you getting mixed up in this.'

'I am mixed up in this. We're mates. We can't keep letting that knucklehead get away with this kind of stuff. There's not a girl on the staff he hasn't pestered or pushed around – look, if you've got the evidence, let's fix him now.'

'Do you mean that? Will you take a risk for us? I ripped the badge from my jacket. Take this. It's a video recorder.'

She took it in her hand and turned it over. Zavier reached across and pulled the yellow smiley face apart. It separated into two half-moons, a USB stick inside.

'Just put this in a computer port to view the footage.'

She nodded.

'Be careful who you show this to. Make sure you make a copy and put it somewhere safe. As insurance,' he added.

She pressed her lips together. 'I know exactly what to do with this.' She turned swiftly and weaved through the tables towards the bar.

'Can we trust her?' Zavier asked.

'I don't know. I hope so. Let's get out of this corner. I don't want to be locked back down in the storeroom.' I grabbed his hand and pulled him onto the dance floor.

Among the children we stood out like tall weeds in a newly dug border.

'Dance!' I commanded, swaying as best I could to the music, as Patty led the kids in an aerobic disco routine.

'They're coming,' Zavier shouted.

About half a dozen security guards were fanning out and moving to the edge of the dance floor. It was only a matter of time. The music stopped. Chucky Skittles stepped forward.

'Bingo tickets are no longer being sold, mums and dads. But never mind that! It's time for today's results. Our mega computer has totted up the scores and added them to our accumulated totals for the week. Will the Pizzas or the Hot Dogs be ahead?'

The children screamed around us.

'Pizzas!'

'Hot Dogs!'

'Have we got the final results, Gavin? Let's count down now. Ladies and gentlemen. Boys and girls.' Large numbers flashed onto the screen. 'Five... four... three... two... one.'

In that moment, it seemed as though the holidaymakers were counting down my spiralling descent of the previous few weeks. Stealing the keys from Marcus. Discovering the brown envelope. Running away. Watching the dome burn. Finding my biological father.

Trafford stepped towards us onto the dance floor. Lights flashed. A sound-effect explosion boomed and reverberated around the club like a death knell.

'Miss Hewitt! We've been expecting you. We haven't been formally introduced. I'm Maxwell King. This is one of our directors, Dr Hildreth. Mrs Ozzles you know.'

Instead of the team scores, a grainy image of Mr King's office flashed onto the screen.

'I'm very disappointed, Claire. I gave you an opportunity, and this is how you repay me.'

'I'm sorry, Mrs Ozzles.'

Chucky Skittles stared at the screen in bemusement. A few of the holidaymakers jeered and whistled, laughing at the technical hitch.

'Just waiting for the scores, boys and girls. Pull your finger out, Gavin.' Chucky huffed into his microphone.

'Why are you here? You're not really a cleaner. Are you with the police?'

Chucky frantically drew his hand across his throat, signalling for the feed to be cut. I looked up at the small balcony where the projectionist sat. Boody was standing next to Gavin. She gave me a thumbs-up.

'I deferred the meeting with my suppliers until tomorrow. At... great... personal... inconvenience.'

Trafford changed direction and lumbered through the children towards the stairs to the balcony.

318

'You had such potential. It's a pity no one else is going to appreciate your new look.'

'Where's Zavier?'

'I think you should be worrying about yourself, Claire, not some yob from the seedier side of town. If I'd known you had an appetite for young men, I'd have taken you off cleaning duties days ago and given you something more financially rewarding to be getting along with.'

A hush fell over the crowded tables.

'You're disgusting. This whole place is a pack of lies. So much for the perfect family holiday. It's all a front for your criminal activities. I have evidence. If you don't let us go, this place will be crawling with police.'

Trafford was climbing towards the projectionist's desk. Gavin flapped his arms in panic and threw a Fun World mug at the security guard's head. Boody leaned over the parapet and screamed to the onlookers below.

'I've shared it on Facebook, everyone. Don't let this ignorant bully touch us. He's nothing but a pimp and druggie. You're my witnesses. I'm speaking up for the downtrodden nobodies at Fun World. The ones who work here for a pittance and get all the flack. We're not going to take it any more, Mr sleaze-well King. The police are on their way. You're going *down*, mate.' She imitated one of Harry Hot Dog's rap moves. 'The great and mighty Oz too. We're cleaning this place up. Ain't that the truth, Claire? We're the deep-clean dream-team.'

Grim-faced, Mr King pulled his mobile from his jacket pocket and strode from the nightclub. Mrs Ozzles tottered after him, her careful façade of lipstick and powder crumbling into an expression of terror.

Chapter 25

'A right funny onion you turned out to be,' Gavin said as he sat with me and Zavier in the back of an ambulance.

Trafford hadn't been able to resist one last punch before being dragged away by two policemen.

'I'll be buzzed if my nose is broken. I've always dreamed of cosmetic surgery. What do you think? Should I ask for a Brad Pitt or a George Clooney?'

Zavier and I smiled at each other.

'Brad Pitt,' I answered, resting my head on Zavier's shoulder. 'Who would have thought Boody would be the one to stand up and be counted? I always had her down as a pragmatist, a survivor, someone who kept their head down.'

'That's the Harry Hot Dog effect,' Gavin explained. 'He's all, like, "Life can be different, campers." "There's always a choice."'

'Quite the revolutionary,' I observed. It was difficult to imagine the plump boy from the day of my interview inspiring anyone. 'And a nice boy too,' I continued, remembering how he'd helped me in the past, and how reasonable he had been when I nearly ran him over on the zebra crossing.

'A fizzing fantastic bloke,' Gavin corrected. 'Proper zesty. Anyone who can survive Chucky's bullying and share a caravan with Trafford has to be a solid geezer.'

My arm wasn't broken, just badly sprained. A nurse put it in a sling and gave me some pain-killers. I was told to keep the sling on for a couple of days. If it was no better after a week, I should go to my GP and ask for a course of physiotherapy.

Zavier's cuts and bruises were quickly cleaned up. Thankfully there was no sign of concussion from the bump on his head.

'Come back to my place,' he said. 'We both need a good night's *rest*,' he emphasised when I raised an eyebrow. 'We've got to be at the police station at ten tomorrow morning, remember, to give a full statement.'

'What about Colin and Skink? They're still out there.'

When the police arrived, Zavier had directed them downstairs to the storage room, warning that a collapsed man with a gun was inside. The door had been swinging open and the store was empty. Skink must have returned and released his boss. They were nowhere to be found on site.

'What can they do now? As a member of the Board, Colin's bound to be implicated in the drug and prostitution ring, plus we have his confession at the end of the smiley badge recording that he murdered your mother and was conspiring to kill us both. No doubt he's on that private jet as we speak. I think it's safe to go home. I don't know about you, but I'm shattered.'

'I'll have to pick up my car first. It's got all my stuff inside. Much as I appreciated wearing your clothes last time, I think I'd like my own pyjamas tonight.'

'We'll take a taxi to the holiday camp. Then I'll drive your car back to mine. You can't drive with that sling.'

On the way we passed the funfair where police lights mingled with the flashing colours of the Wurlitzer and big wheel, no doubt searching for Mr Bones. Back at Fun World, the security barriers were open but there was no one on duty in the kiosk. Police cars were parked in front of reception. Although it was after four o'clock in the morning, several curious holidaymakers were huddled in a small group nearby, swigging back cans of lager and sounding off about the events of the evening. They ignored our taxi as it turned towards the far end of the camp where my car was parked. Thankfully I had enough money in my belt to pay the driver and give him a generous tip. I was too tired to care about how I was going to manage financially in the days ahead.

'While we're here, I might as well get my stuff from the caravan,' Zavier said. 'It's a good-quality sleeping bag and I don't want anyone to nick my radio. You stay in the car. There's no point you stumbling through the wood with that arm.'

Numb with exhaustion, I switched on the ignition and waited for the engine to warm up before turning the heater to its highest setting. I couldn't see beyond tomorrow and the police interview. Sometime in the future there was bound to be a court case, or maybe several: one relating to the illegal goings-on at Fun World and another for the destruction of the dome and the murders of Marcus and my mother. It was crazy to think that Zavier and I had been fleeing for our lives twice in as many weeks, firstly from Colin Hildreth and secondly from Maxwell King.

The ramifications of the last few days stretched endlessly into the future, cold and dark as the outer reaches of space where starlight plunges into oblivion. The police, the press, the notoriety. I couldn't see a way forward, or imagine that anyone would want to employ me after the mess I'd got myself into. And where would I live long-term? Although my feelings towards Zavier were softening, he could never fill the void left by Marcus.

Then there was my parentage to come to terms with. How to forge an identity now I knew my genetic inheritance? I was the daughter of a dangerous sociopath. Would the tainted blood pumping through my body one day turn me into a monster? I knew my heart was self-centred and impatient. How to prevent it blackening into something worse?

It was time to swallow my pride and beg Theo's forgiveness. I didn't deserve it. His life's work was in ruins. The man he looked upon as a son was dead. The rest of my life would be blighted by the fact that Marcus had died instead of me, a good man in the place of a petulant, self-centred idiot. I couldn't imagine Paloma's distress when she learned how low I'd fallen, after all the tenderness she'd lavished upon me. Perhaps I'd be allowed to become a cleaner if they rebuilt the dome. At least I had experience in that area. It would be more than I deserved.

A tall shadow loped along the drive. I recognised the tubular outline. Harry Hot Dog was making his way to the staff caravans. I opened the car door, tumbling out in my haste.

'Jeremy! Jeremy!' I called, jogging as best I could after his retreating back.

He turned as I reached him.

'I just wanted to thank you.' Breathless, I clutched my side. 'If it wasn't for you, Boody and Gavin wouldn't have had the courage to help expose what Mr King and others had been up to.'

'Alfie.' My nickname floated on the night air like the fragrance of home.

'How did you know – ?'

'Because I've always known who you are. Don't you know me, Ava?'

He lifted his arms and pulled the top off the plush costume as though taking the lid off a biro.

'Marcus!'

He dropped Harry's smiling head on the ground and laughed.

'Yes. It's me.'

'But... but you fell into the flames. I saw you. They found a body.'

'That was a man called Saunders, trapped by the snare of his own making.'

'But how did you survive?'

'I landed on a pile of compost sacks.' He rubbed his side. 'Three cracked ribs and some smoke inhalation. I spent a couple of nights in hospital but it's all fine now.'

'But the fire?'

'The irrigation system extinguished the flames fairly quickly.'

The moon cruised from behind a cloud. I saw him clearly for the first time.

'Your face!' I reached up and touched the blisters that ran across his forehead and trailed over a newly shaven head.

'My hair caught fire. It's healing. The ionised water cooled and sterilised the burns. There'll be scars but no lasting damage.' He removed the cartoon gloves from his hands and took my good hand in both of his. I felt the scrape of scabs and the soft bubble of blisters on his palms. 'Come home, Ava.'

'How can you want me back after what I've done? What will Theo say when he finds out?'

'He knows everything. He sent me to find you. I've been watching over you the whole time.'

I shook my head slowly from side to side.

'But Jeremy…'

'He only lasted a day. Chucky has no patience with other people's sensitivities. Despite your attempt to hide your identity, Sid recognised you under that black mop. He's an occasional visitor to the dome, picking up summer bedding plants and compost for the holiday camp. We've talked a couple of times. He was worried about you. He phoned to tell me where you were.'

'Why didn't he tell me? Why didn't *you* tell me?'

'Because you didn't want to be found.'

'I thought nobody wanted me,' I sobbed.

'The lights were always on at the dome, calling you home.'

'I thought you were glad to be rid of me. I thought Sid had been paid to kill Mum.'

'Mrs Ozzles asked him to offer your mum money for an abortion. She refused, of course. He gave the money back. He's been ashamed ever since that he allowed himself to be used as a messenger boy just because he and your mother were friends.'

'I wish Mum had gone ahead with it! I wish I'd never been born. I'm not Theo's daughter. I'm nobody.'

'You're the most precious thing in the world. Theo's heart is breaking. He loves you more than you can ever know. Come home, Ava. We all miss you like crazy.'

'I can't face him.'

'I'll come with you. There's no need to be frightened.'

I looked into his intense brown eyes. He'd worn a humiliating costume for me. He'd put up with the heat inside the plush material and the frenetic party dances. He'd survived Chucky's bullying. He'd dossed in a staff caravan with Trafford as a roommate. He'd watched over me and rescued me from the flames that would have killed me. What further evidence did I need that I could trust him? He was right. I was ashamed, but there was nothing to fear.

'Ava?'

It was Zavier. He walked towards us, carrying a backpack and a rolled-up sleeping bag.

'It's all right. This is Marcus. Look! He's alive! I still can't believe it. The unidentified body at the dome was Saunders. Marcus is going to take me home.'

Zavier stopped in his tracks.

'Is that what you want?'

'Of course. I need to apologise to Theo and Paloma. I can't go forward until I've gone back. I know things can never be the way they were. I've done too much damage. The dome... everybody's jobs... the irrigation system ruined. Oh!' I turned to Marcus. 'Colin has the green file. All the research into the ionised water! I stole it from the safe. I thought it was his. I didn't know.' I hung my head, despair vibrating through every fibre of my being. Then I remembered. I tore at the laces of my boot, frustrated by my sling.

'Help me get this off, Zavier.'

He dumped his bags on the ground and trudged to my side, purposely ignoring Marcus. He knelt down and yanked the boot free.

'Look inside,' I commanded. He put his hand in and felt down to the toes, pulling out a small wad of paper.

'Open it! It's the formula for ionising water. I took it from the file and hid it so Colin wouldn't get it.'

Zavier gingerly unfolded the wad but it fell apart in his hands.

'No, no! Be careful with it.' I grabbed at the crumpled fragments. They were rubbed clear of any handwriting. Only blue smudges remained. My heart sank. I had nothing to give after all.

Marcus smiled. 'The knowledge written on that paper hasn't been destroyed. There's a new dome being built in Africa — Golden Acres. Theo took a copy of the plans with him. Ionising pumps are being developed out there even as we speak. The research was patented before Theo flew to Africa. Whatever Colin has stolen, it's valueless. Theo wants to tell you all about it. He flew home yesterday and he's waiting at the farmhouse now.'

I couldn't speak. Tears rolled down my cheeks. I leaned on Zavier as I pushed my foot back inside my boot.

'Goodbye, Cinderella,' he whispered.

'How will we get there?' I croaked. 'I can't drive like this.'

'Zavier's going to drive us in your car, if he's willing.'

Zavier's head snapped back.

'Theo very much wants to meet you. And thank you, too. You've been a good friend to Ava. I know you're tired. There's breakfast and a bed if you want it. Paloma's been cooking and filling the freezer for days. Yesterday's behind us. It's already tomorrow. Tonight, after you've had a chance to catch up on your sleep, we're throwing a welcome-home party. Everyone's invited.'

As we drove up the hill, the dawn danced on the horizon, pushing back the darkness and swallowing the stars in a halo of light. When we climbed out of the car, Marcus stepped between us, placing his arms on our shoulders.

'It'll be all right.'

I allowed myself to be ushered up the track, each step heavy with guilt and exhaustion. As we passed Marcus' cottage, the door to the farmhouse further up the lane flew open and Theo stepped into the pale light.

'Ava!' he cried, running down the path towards the garden gate as fast as his tall frame would allow.

His white hair was aglow with the warmth of the rising sun. I couldn't see the expression on his face. He was outlined against the sky, surrounded with light as new and fresh as the day itself.

My heart was full of shame and regret. How could I put into words how sorry I was for running away and for the unholy mess that had spewed out as a result? The destruction of his beautiful dome... the scars on Marcus' hands and face. I kept my eyes on my stumbling feet.

'My treasure,' he said. 'Home at last.'

I looked up at his eyes, blue as the sky. His arms were outstretched. I'd never seen his arms stretch out in such a wide embrace, wide enough to encompass me and Zavier and the Downs that stretched all the way to Westhatch and the sea beyond.

'I'm sorry,' I mumbled, 'I don't know if I can ever... But I'll do everything I can to try to repay you for the damage...' I choked on the words. 'I can work as a cleaner. I don't mind. I'll do anything.'

His eyes were bright with love and tears. 'You're home. That's all that matters.'

He pulled me towards him. I rested my face on his chest. I was a little child again. I'd been frightened and alone, but now, miraculously, everything was all right. A crescendo of emotion swelled through my body and spilled from my mouth.

'Daddy!' I sobbed. 'Daddy.'

He hugged me tight. 'I'll always be your dad, Ava. I chose you when you were just a wriggling lump in your mother's tummy. I can't put into words how much it means to me that you've now chosen me to be your father. I'll love you for the whole of this life and into the beyond. Just promise me you'll come to me in future if anything's troubling you.'

'I will.'

One of his arms loosened. 'I'm Theo and I'm very pleased to meet you, young man. I hope we can be friends.'

I turned in his arms to see him shaking Zavier firmly by the hand.

'I hope so, too, Mr Gage.'

'Call me Theo.'

Still keeping one arm around my shoulders, he punched Marcus lightly on the chest.

'Good job. I knew I could depend on you to bring her back. Thank you.' He sniffed the air. 'Can you smell that? Paloma's been baking her special Italian bread. And coffee's on. I hope you've both got good appetites. It's a new day. Let's start it as we mean to go on, with full stomachs and satisfied hearts.'

Chapter 26

Ten years have passed since the events of this story. I've written them all down, just as they happened, because I want to have an accurate record to warn my own daughter of the dangers of disobedience. She has my red curls and impetuous nature, so of course she'll have to learn the hard way. Sometimes we can only find the right by getting things wrong. Plans fall apart. Pieces slot into place. It's two sides of the same coin.

Zavier and I were married six years ago, my mother's jade necklace clasped around my neck. You might be surprised. I was too. But once reunited with my father's love, I found I had some love to spare. Love is like that. It multiplies. Marcus will always have my heart – Zavier understands that he's like a brother to me – but the love I share with my husband is one of imperfect equals, born out of trouble and confusion, a love that needs to be wrestled with every day, an act of will and service, passion and romance.

Theo and Marcus are both out in Africa continuing the work at the agricultural centre. A broadband connection has been established and we talk to each other regularly by email and Skype. The Golden Acres dome is even more impressive than the first one, a huge structure harnessing energy from the sun as well as soaking the parched earth with ionised water. Sand becomes soil. Thorns become wheat. Orange and lemon trees blossom in the desert.

When it's finished, Marcus will come and get us. Then, Zavier and I and our little girl, Marianna Boody Marshall, will have a new home and a new life, a future of fulfilment under the glittering glass. In the meantime, Zavier, the baby and I live in the farmhouse that was my childhood home.

A few weeks after the events described in this account, a bloated body was retrieved from the sea. It was badly battered, all identifying features eroded by the salty deep and the creatures which had fed on its swollen flesh. The local lifeboat crew testified that its position among the rocks suggested a fall from Jumper's Mount.

Dental records confirmed it to be the body of Colin Hildreth. DNA tests, however, said the body was not related to me. For a while I worried about the contradiction. Did the body belong to Colin Hildreth, or had he managed to switch dental records with someone else and disappear? Or perhaps Colin hadn't been my biological father after all – despite his belief that he was – and my mother had taken the secret of my paternity to the grave.

I realise now it doesn't matter. I know who my father is. I've stopped jumping at shadows, or worrying about a plot to steal my heart. Instead I rest in the protection and love of Theo, Marcus, Paloma… and Zavier.

The Greenacres dome couldn't be rebuilt; the damage was too great. I have a new project now. Ironically, my godfather left me everything in his will, including a major shareholding in Fun World Holiday Camp. He'd drawn it up when I was a toddler and never bothered to change it, presumably thinking at the end I would die before him. I've renamed the holiday park 'Greenacres' and turned it into a not-for-profit organisation specialising in holidays for people living with disabilities or mental health issues and those who would not otherwise be able to afford a break. Nurturing people is not so very different from looking after plants: water the thirsty, support the wilting, prune back the dead wood and protect the tender from the frost.

Maxwell King, Delia Ozzles and Trafford are all serving long-prison sentences. The other Fun World staff members have been released from the soul-destroying sentence of working for them. I appointed Boody as the new housekeeper.

She runs an unexpectedly tight ship. She's Marianna Boody's godmother. We chose her as a namesake when we discovered 'Boody' was a skewed form of 'Beauty'. Somewhere along the line her family found her beautiful, even if the origin of the tag later became lost in a haze of parental drunkenness.

Chucky Skittles stood trial for numerous inappropriate incidents involving children stretching back years. It seems the scandal we uncovered emboldened several families to complain about his behaviour. He won't be released for another decade at least.

Gavin was fizzed to have been promoted to head of entertainment. Sid continues as maintenance manager, his skin much improved. Ted's been appointed campus groundsman and there's not a plastic flower in sight. Veronica and Harmony manage the gift shop, and Walt Marshall has a part-time job as a security guard, manning the night-time reception with kindness and care.

Paloma helps with the baby as well as overseeing the catering at the camp, revamping the menus to contain a more healthy selection of dishes alongside the usual favourites of fish and chips, pizzas and hot dogs. She's a great comfort to me while Theo and Marcus are abroad. Everyone agrees her lemon polenta cake is the best they've ever tasted.

Zavier is in charge of security and information systems. He manages to control the more uninhibited holidaymakers with a combination of wit and gentle persuasion. He's beginning to remind me of Marcus. His gangly frame has filled out. He's quite a spice, as Boody would say.

Sonya was taken ill shortly after Marcus' miraculous return from the dead. Years of poverty and worry had weakened her system. Unable to legalise her immigration status, Theo pulled a few strings and took her with him to Golden Acres. I hear she's developed quite a talent for horticulture.

Sometimes our work at the holiday camp is difficult and unrewarding; the soil is hard, the seeds refuse to grow, weeds and pests impede our progress. At other times our visitors leave

Greenacres with a little more joy in their hearts and a spring in their step, their petals opening towards the light. I remind myself that a plant is not an end in itself. It's there to bear fruit for others.

I am all grown-up but, as Theo says, 'There's plenty of growing still to be done.' I'm learning to be a gardener. I dig. I prune. I water. My own roots are stronger now that adversity has pushed them deep. I'm learning how to be a parent. It's harder than it looks. My own mother would be forty-nine now if she'd lived. I sometimes wish, 'If only... ' but am comforted by the presence of Paloma, who inspires me to be a mother as loving and joyful as herself. I understand Theo so much better now that I have a little one of my own to care for. I want to protect her from harm, build a wall around her, but I know it's more important to build her character so she can make good choices for herself once she grows up.

I wonder what it will be like when I have to start saying 'No' to our baby. Paloma tells me not to worry about that. The problems will start when Marianna starts saying 'No' to me! She tells me Marianna will probably need to go through 'No' before getting to 'Yes'. That's the nature of free will. It's born in rebellion and redeemed by grace. 'If you love someone, set them free' might be a cliché but perhaps that's because it's true. Children need the freedom to leave in order to have the freedom to return.

I cannot earn my father's love. I cannot lose it either. Nothing I do will make him love me more; nothing I do will make him love me less. I could choose to live outside the circle of his affection, but that's another matter altogether. I've tried it and it ended in disaster. Now I accept his love as a gift freely given, showing my gratitude by doing the best I can in my own little patch of soil. My muscles sometimes ache, and there are blisters on my hands. There's soil under my fingernails too. But what else would you expect? I'm the girl who was lost and the girl who was found again; the girl who rebelled and the girl who repented. I'm a child restored, who *was* loved, and *is* loved, and *will be* loved forever.

I am the Gardener's daughter.

Epilogue

A man sits in a wheelchair at the top of a track with a view of the South Downs. Grassy undulations roll towards cliffs as sheer and deadly as a fall from grace. He knew a man once who fell from the cliffs into the cold cruel sea and died, leaving his identity behind for someone else to use.

Trevor Skink squints at the horizon with bloodshot eyes, dazzled by the brilliance of the low winter light. A dual carriageway slithers past the ruins of an enormous glasshouse down to Westhatch-on-Sea and the caravan site peppering the fields at the far end of town.

The pain in his heart is worse since the attack. Weakening tissues strain with each pulse of blood. His driver waits by the car, irritated by his master's obsession and impatient to return to the great metropolis.

His team of hackers regularly attacks the Greenacres' computer system, but they've been unable to do any lasting damage. A couple of times he's planted a spy in the camp, to identify disgruntled members of staff and stir up dissent. Both times the infiltrator has chosen to quit and become a genuine member of the Greenacres' team.

He's hung on this long, far exceeding the doctors' estimate of life expectancy, kept alive by regular transfusions of hate and intravenous doses of wrath. He knows he can no longer hurt the ones he detests the most. They're bound too close by the power of their love.

Love makes them strong, but love also makes them vulnerable. There's a younger, fresher heartbeat now, throbbing

334

with childish desires, doted on by her family. He comforts himself with the thought that his blood runs through her veins. Children can deal the cruellest of blows to a parent. Although he won't be there to see it, he nurses a malevolent hope that *she* will be his revenge.

K A Hitchins studied English, Religious Studies and Philosophy at Lancaster University, graduating with a BA (Hons) First Class in English, later obtaining a Masters in Postmodern Literatures in English from Birkbeck College, London. Her first two

novels, *The Girl at the End of the Road* and *The Key of All Unknown*, were both shortlisted for the *Woman Alive* Readers' Choice Award 2017, with *The Key of All Unknown* reaching the final three. She is married with two children.

Stay in touch with the author via her website: www.kahitchins.co.uk

Follow her on Twitter @KathrynHitchins

or connect via her Facebook page: Kathryn Hitchins, author

Kathryn would love to receive honest feedback about this book. Please consider leaving a review on Amazon or Goodreads.